P9-CRD-553

AU

0

MAYWOOD PUBLIC LIBRARY
121 S. 5th AVE.
MAYWOOD, IL 60153

All Manner
of Riches

All Manner of Riches

BY

Mary Elmblad

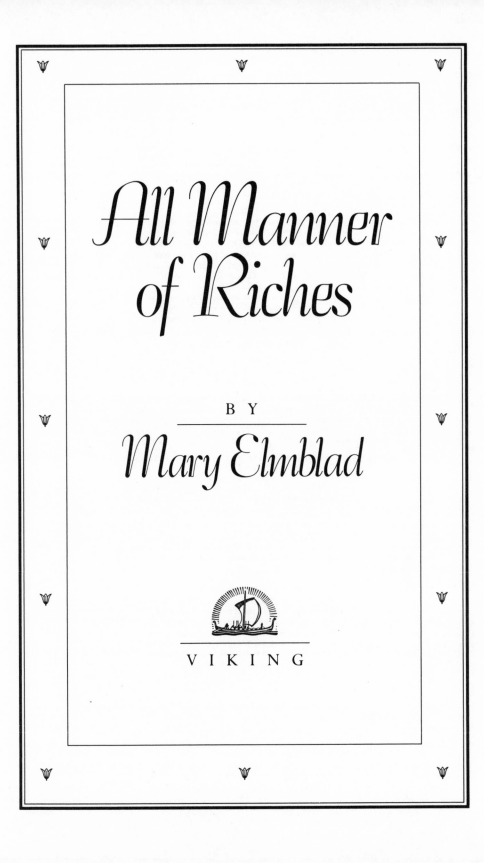

VIKING

VIKING
Viking Penguin Inc., 40 West 23rd Street,
New York, New York 10010, U.S.A.
Penguin Books Ltd, 27 Wrights Lane, London W8 5TZ
(Publishing & Editorial) and Harmondsworth,
Middlesex, England (Distribution & Warehouse)
Penguin Books Australia Ltd, Ringwood,
Victoria, Australia
Penguin Books Canada Limited, 2801 John Street,
Markham, Ontario, Canada L3R 1B4
Penguin Books (N.Z.) Ltd, 182–190 Wairau Road,
Auckland 10, New Zealand

Copyright © Mary Elmblad, 1987
All rights reserved

First published in 1987 by Viking Penguin Inc.
Published simultaneously in Canada

Grateful acknowledgment is made for permission to reprint excerpts from
"The Waste Land," "The Love Song of J. Alfred Prufrock," and "The Hollow Men"
from *Collected Poems 1909–1962* by T. S. Eliot. Copyright 1936 by Harcourt Brace
Jovanovich, Inc. Copyright © 1963, 1964 by T. S. Eliot. Reprinted by
permission of Harcourt Brace Jovanovich, Inc., and Faber and Faber Limited.

LIBRARY OF CONGRESS CATALOGING IN PUBLICATION DATA
Elmblad, Mary.
All manner of riches.
I. Title.
PS3555.L629A45   1987   813'.54   86-40494
ISBN 0-670-81274-9

Printed in the United States of America by
The Book Press, Brattleboro, Vermont
Set in Perpetua
Designed by Amy Hill

Without limiting the rights under
copyright reserved above, no part of this publication
may be reproduced, stored in or introduced into a
retrieval system, or transmitted, in any form or by
any means (electronic, mechanical, photocopying,
recording or otherwise), without the prior written
permission of both the copyright owner and the
above publisher of this book.

Acknowledgments

The author would like to express her gratitude to all those who have helped her along the way, notably the late Helen and Frank McManus and Alice and Bob Mathis, the author's parents and grandparents, who were part of the history; Emilie Jacobson, agent and friend, and Dawn Seferian, a perceptive and enthusiastic editor, for bringing it all together; Frances Rosser Brown, Virginia and Bennett Guthrie, John McManus, and the late Malcolm Morrison, for information about Eastern Oklahoma; Alice McManus Spaulding and Inez M. Elmblad, for memories of Dallas; Jean Elmblad Blue and Randi Mezzy-Steeves, for leading the way through the maze of the law.

Any errors of interpretion are the responsibility of the author.

To Jean, John, Susan, and Victoria,
with love

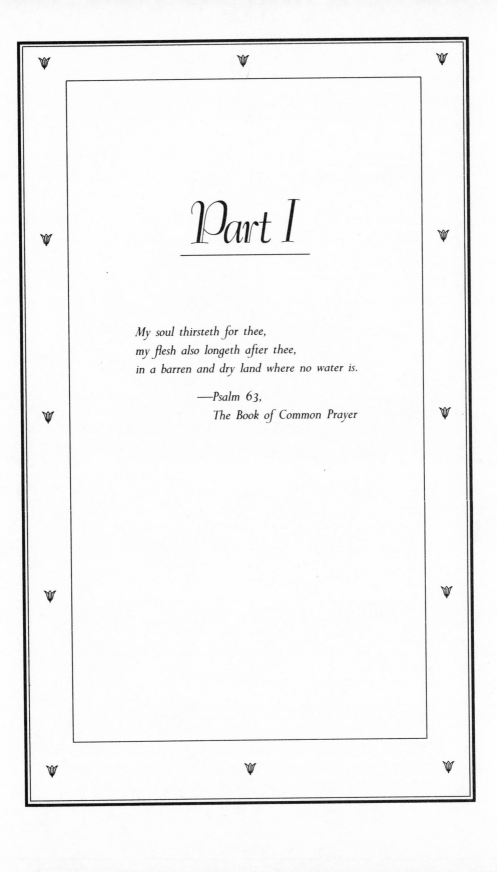

Part I

My soul thirsteth for thee,
my flesh also longeth after thee,
in a barren and dry land where no water is.

—*Psalm 63,*
The Book of Common Prayer

Chapter 1

THE CLEARING in the scrub oak woods lay silent in the sullen noonday heat. The sun beat down on the rusty corrugated iron roof of a tenant house, a shack built of rough-sawn pine planks grayed to splintered silver by the cold wet winters and burning summers of Eastern Oklahoma.

There was not much to the place: the shack, a rough tool shed and a privy that leaned to the east. Down the hill from the house a garden patch withered in the August sun.

A tall post oak cast a puddle of shade on the packed red earth of the dooryard, and in the shadow a little girl sat surrounded by a scatter of objects: a cardboard box with a torn feed sack trailing out of it, a cracked enameled pan and the metal head gasket from a Model A Ford. She hugged a rag doll with a crooked, penciled smile and laid it in the box.

The raucous cry of a crow broke the silence, and as if on cue the girl began to sing in a thin, tuneless voice.

> *"Hush little baby, don't say a word,*
> *Papa's gonna buy you a mockingbird."*

Cassie Taylor was five years old that August of 1930, a thin hungry-looking child with lank blond hair and a heart-shaped face. Her nose was sprinkled with freckles, and her large eyes were a deep smoky blue set behind thick dark eyelashes. She patted her doll, and then with a child's sudden change of mood she picked it up and shook it.

"Francine! What you caterwaulin' about? You want your mama to whup you? You want Misteel to come and carry you off?"

She caught her lower lip with her teeth and glanced over her shoulder warily. She had said it, "Misteel," right out loud. She did not know what it meant or who it meant, but she had heard her grandmother say it in a voice thin with anger: "And what do you think Mist' Steele's goin' to say to that, Howard?" Her father had answered with a tremor of fear that made Cassie want to run and hide. "How the hell do I know, woman? Don't care, nohow. Mist' Steele, he ain't God!"

Cassie hugged the doll as much to reassure herself as Francine.

"It's all right, baby. Granny ain't goin' to let Misteel bother us none." She laid the doll in the box. "Now, you rest yourself while Mama fixes you some supper, hear?" She poured red dust into the saucepan and stirred it with a stick. "I'll make you some nice mush." As she held the stick to the doll's penciled mouth, she looked up, and what she saw made her rise slowly to her knees.

A cloud of dust was coming toward her from the blacktop highway to the east, coming fast, like a big red-gray caterpillar scooting its head along the ground while its body swelled and dissipated in the wind of its passing. Cassie ran for the porch.

"Granny, somethin's comin'! Granny!"

A thin woman in a faded housedress appeared in the doorway. Her hair was gray, pulled back to a bun, and there were deep wrinkles around her firm mouth and her pale blue eyes. She gripped a broom worn lopsided by use. "What is it, child? One of them stray dogs? I'll get shut of him before you can say——" She stopped, looking past the child.

"Granny, it's a car! There's a car comin'! Can I fetch Papa?"

The woman pushed at her glasses, steel-rimmed spectacles mended at the bridge with adhesive tape. "He's comin' yonder. I reckon he saw the dust, too."

Howard Taylor was thirty-five that summer, a wiry man with a tanned, weathered face. He waded through the dry weeds, raising puffs of dust with each step, and stopped in the dooryard to tug at the crotch of his faded overalls and settle his stained felt hat more firmly on his head.

"You reckon it's Mist' Steele, Howard?" Granny said.

"Don't rightly know." There was a look of fear around his thin lips. He looked back. "You, Bo! I told you to mind that mule!"

Cassie's half brother was crouched in the weeds at the edge of the dooryard. Bo was ten, a swarthy boy with coarse black hair that fell down over his low forehead, so that he looked out from behind it like a fox looking out through a fringe of brush.

"It's his car," Howard said. "What's Mr. James High-and-Mighty Steele doin' out here?"

A dark blue 1929 Buick sedan labored up the rocky track and pulled to a stop on the hard bare ground of the dooryard. A tall man in his early forties got out of the car, took off his Panama hat and wiped his forehead with a white linen handkerchief, a heavy man with broad shoulders which he carried high and slightly forward. He jammed his handkerchief into his hip pocket and nodded to Granny.

Cassie slipped behind her grandmother's skirt and peeked at him. She had never seen a man in a starched white shirt and a necktie, not to mention blue serge pants and polished shoes. His face was broad and smooth-shaven and his eyebrows were black, like his hair. His eyes were dark and were, she realized, looking directly at her.

When he frowned his heavy eyebrows almost met at the bridge of his long thin nose. "And who is this child?"

Cassie buried her face in her grandmother's skirts, but Granny pushed her toward the man.

"This here's my little granddaughter," she said. "Leona's girl."

Cassie peeked from under her eyelashes, but the man was no longer watching her. He and her grandmother were looking at each other steadily, as if they were talking with their eyes instead of their voices.

Granny said, "Her name's Cassandra, but we call her Cassie."

"I remember now. Cassandra. A big name for such a little girl."

"She's named for my mother." Granny nudged Cassie. "Missy, you mind your manners. Say hello now, like I taught you."

"How old are you, child?"

She was afraid to look at the man. "Five," she whispered.

He laughed. "What's the matter? Cat got your tongue?"

Granny tugged at her arm. "Speak up!"

"I'm five!" Frightened or not, Cassie felt that she had to say more. "I can read my letters!"

"You know the alphabet?" Mr. Steele raised his heavy chin. "Did you learn it from a spelling book?"

"Ain't got no books save Granny's Bible, but I can read me the letters on the newspapers."

Steele frowned. "You take the paper, Taylor? That's expensive."

"No, sir, Mr. Steele! I got them old newspapers tacked up to keep out the cold. Her granny taught her from them old papers on the wall."

Steele looked past him at the gaping holes between the vertical gray boards of the cabin. His face darkened, but he turned back to Cassie's grandmother. "And how have you been, Mrs. Hendricks?"

"Doin' about as well as any, I reckon, considerin' the heat."

He shook his head. "The *Farmer's Almanac* promised us a cool damp summer for 1930, didn't it?"

Howard Taylor laughed nervously. "Just shows to go you, don't it? I mind a time back in '27, when it said——"

"I want to talk to you, Taylor," Steele said abruptly.

Color rose in Howard's cheeks. "Yes, sir, Mr. Steele. I'll be mighty proud to——"

"Inside, man." Steele scowled at Howard and then turned to Granny. "That is, if you don't mind, Mrs. Hendricks?"

Granny stepped aside, pulling Cassie with her.

"Granny," Cassie whispered, "is that man——"

"Hush!" Granny gave her a shove. "Get back out there to your play place, go on now."

"But I want to——"

"I don't care what you want, missy, you get yourself out there."

From her place under the post oak tree, Cassie could hear the voices in the house, Mr. Steele's angry one and her father's voice, softer, almost a whine. Finally the big man came out, nodded stiffly to Granny and went to his car. The way her father looked when he stepped down from the porch reminded Cassie of the stray dogs Granny chased off with her broom.   At his car Mr. Steele stopped and looked back.

"You got that straight, Taylor? If I hear any more about your drinking up money you owe me, I warn you, I'm going to—"

"Yes, sir," Howard said hastily. "You ain't got no cause to worry about me, no cause at all."

Steele slammed his hand down on the hood of his car with a crash that made Cassie jump. "By God, that better be right!" He jerked open the door of the car, climbed in and drove off as suddenly as he had come.

"I knew it!" Granny said. "I told you, Howard Taylor, I—"

"Shut up! You hear me, woman? Just shut up!"

"You ain't goin' to shut me up that easy. I knew all the time what you was doin' down there in town, hangin' around that DX station."

They wrangled on, taking out their anger and fear on each other, but Cassie paid no attention to them. She watched the car and the cloud of dust that trailed behind as it sped down the dirt road toward the highway. When it was out of sight she squatted in the shade of the post oak tree and picked up her doll.

"Francine, you got to eat your dinner now. If you don't eat it all up, Misteel's goin' to get—" She looked over her shoulder at the place where the man himself had stood. Mr. Steele was real to her now and a person too frightening to be used to frighten.

In sudden remorse, Cassie hugged her doll to her thin chest. "Mama didn't mean it! Mama ain't never goin' to let Misteel get her baby!"

UNTIL OKLAHOMA achieved statehood in 1907, the eastern part was officially designated as the Indian Territory. It was the homeland the federal government had chosen for the Indians uprooted from their ancestral lands to the south and east. The Five Civilized Tribes were settled into the Territory: Cherokee, Seminole, Chickasaw, Choctaw and Creek. Unofficially, Eastern Oklahoma was called Lapland, because it was said that the state of Arkansas lapped over into Oklahoma on the Ozark Plateau, where the Boston Mountains eased down into rolling hills. To the west those hills spread out into plains, into the Great American Desert that reached to the Rocky Mountains.

The Territory was a rich and beautiful land. The hills were forested with pines and oaks, cedars and hickories, and the foothills were thick with game. Springs trickled from the limestone cliffs to become creeks and flow down over rocky beds to the rivers in the valleys, the Illinois River, the Arkansas, the Kiamichi.

The Tribes were not the only settlers. Mountain people drifted west from Arkansas as they had previously drifted to the Ozarks from the highlands of Virginia and the Carolinas. Farmers came from Tennessee and from the Deep South, Alabama and Mississippi, people who had lost everything during what they called the War Between the States or during the Reconstruction that followed it. They bought land and planted the crops they knew, corn and cotton, but as the crops depleted the soil and the harvests became smaller, they had to borrow against their crops or against the land itself just to get by. Another kind of settler began to thrive, the banker or lawyer or businessman who took the land and hired its former owners as tenant farmers: sharecroppers.

The shock waves of the Crash of '29 spread out across the country and hard times came to America. They were desperate times for the Southwest, where a string of dry summers had evolved into full-scale drought. By August of 1930 some of the sharecroppers had begun to leave Eastern Oklahoma, heading west as their fathers had done before them, west to make a new start. There was talk of a land of milk and honey where there was work for everyone, and food, and oranges to be picked right off the tree. They packed their hungry kids and their few belongings into old trucks and took off for California.

There were those of the poor who refused to accept poverty. Instead of migrating west they turned outlaw and hid out in the Cookson Hills, where their neighbors fed them and protected them from the law. When they needed cash they went to the places where cash could be found. Pretty Boy Floyd and Clyde Barrow took so much money out of country banks that Oklahoma's bank insurance rate was soon the highest in the United States.

Most of the tenant farmers stayed on the land, either because they had the strength to fight drought and Depression or because they did not have the strength to pack up and leave. They stayed on, hoping and praying that times would get better, that the rains would come.

There was no rain. The once verdant fields and hills of Eastern Oklahoma dried in the sun and the hot winds lifted the topsoil and carried it away.

Lapland became an area where the Dust Bowl lapped over onto the Ozark Plateau.

THE TOWN OF BALLARD was the county seat of Clifton County. West of Ballard there were prairies and large-scale wheat farms and ranches. To the east State Highway 12 narrowed to a blacktop highway that climbed gradually through stands of fire-dry oaks and pines and cedars, then coasted down into the valley and swung south through the scatter of houses and stores that was the village of San Bois, which was pro-nounced "San-boys" in spite of the French origin of its name. The highway wandered on like a lazy blacksnake, through fields where cot-ton plants curled and withered in the heat and brown brittle cornstalks stood in the still air like tattered flags. Three miles south of San Bois was a red dirt road bordered by ditch weeds, wild oats and Johnson grass and cockleburs, and by tangles of blackberries with swooping dust-covered canes entwined in sagging barbed-wire fences.

A mile west of Highway 12 a rocky track climbed a hill to end in the hard-packed dirt dooryard of the cabin where Howard Taylor lived with Bo, his son by his first wife, who had died young. Leona, How-ard's second wife and Cassie's mother, had died young, too, died in the birthing of a stillborn son. Her mother, Mrs. Martha Hendricks, was a widow of fifty-six when Leona died and stayed on to care for Cassie, who was three.

The two rooms of the shack were papered with layers of newspa-pers tacked to the flimsy plank walls. The family cooked and ate in the front room. There was a wood cookstove, black iron, with a chrome handle on the oven door and a rusty carriage bolt to take the place of the missing handle of the firebox door. A rough wood table was covered with green-patterned oilcloth that had long since worn through to the fabric. There were a rocking chair with a torn cane seat, three straight chairs and a low narrow bedstead with a limp mattress on woven rope springs, where Howard slept. In the corner was a bedroll for Bo. Open shelves on the wall held bags of flour and cornmeal and dried beans along with a few cracked plates, a handful of forks and spoons and a butcher knife with a split wooden handle wrapped in baling wire.

Like the front room, the back one had two windows with four-paned sashes that were pushed up and braced with chunks of firewood. The family's few extra clothes were hung on nails driven into the plank walls, and on the wall that separated the back room and the front, there was a 1928 calendar with a garishly colored picture of a buxom young woman pointing a coy knee toward a large black tractor tire. There was only enough floor space in the back room for an iron double bed with no sheets, just two limp ticking-covered pillows and a few cotton quilts.

ON A HOT SEPTEMBER day three weeks after Mr. James Steele had come to the house, Cassie Taylor rocked Francine and sang to her.

> *"And if that diamond ring is brass,*
> *Papa's goin' to buy you a looking-glass."*

As she sang, a hazy memory came to her of the summer when Granny made Francine for her. Cassie's mother was alive then.

"You come on outside now, missy," Granny said, "and let your mama get her some rest. I'm fixin' to make you a play-pretty."

Granny drew the shape on a clean feed sack and cut around it: legs, body, arms, head. She sewed it together with small, careful stitches. "Now we'll stuff your dolly with these here clean rags."

Cassie thought it was magic when the flat cloth took on form and meaning and became the body of a doll-child. Her grandmother used a crochet hook to pull tufts of brown yarn through the fabric of the head, and then picked up a stub of indelible pencil and licked the point.

"Eyes, now. And a nose." She drew an *L* and then put two dots below it. "I wish I had me a red pencil for the mouth, but I reckon this will have to do." She licked the pencil point again and drew a flat crooked smile that made the doll come alive.

Cassie took a deep breath as if she were breathing not only for herself but also for the new creature that had come into her life. "Francine," she said.

"Now, where in tarnation did you get a name like that?"

Cassie shook her head. She did not know. "Francine," she said again. "Her name's Francine."

The bad time was after that. Cassie was only three then but she remembered when Mama could still get up from her bed. She sometimes held Cassie on her lap and sang to her but the time always came when she had to go in and lie down. Mama got fat, so fat that Cassie could not reach around her even with both of her arms stretched out as far as they could go. And then a night came when the house was filled with screaming. Granny sent Bo and Cassie out to the front porch, but Cassie could still hear it. She heard the screaming and she heard Papa telling Granny that the doctor could not get there in time. She heard the screaming and Granny crying and then she heard the silence, the end of screaming.

Cassie sat in the shade of the post oak and hugged her doll close, but suddenly she held the doll out at arm's-length and shook it, taking out her anger on the doll.

"You eat your mush, Francine! You eat it all up or Misteel—I mean, the boogey man, he's goin' to get you! That boogey man, he's going to get you for sure!"

THE RAINS were sparse in Eastern Oklahoma that year and the next, but the spring of 1932 brought new hope. Creeks ran fresh and dogwood trees filled the woods with lacy white blossoms.

On a warm morning in late March, Mrs. Martha Hendricks sat in the rocking chair on the front porch of the Taylor cabin with her granddaughter gripped firmly between her knees. Her thin mouth softened when she looked down at the child. Two weeks before her seventh birthday, Cassandra Taylor was as leggy as a colt. The baby fat had melted from her face and revealed high, prominent cheekbones and the beginnings of a strong jaw.

Cassie fingered the pattern in the dress that covered her grandmother's knees, tracing the paisley shapes on the faded blue background. She leaned forward and the comb caught in her hair. "Granny, that hurts!"

"How'm I to comb you with you bouncin' around that way?"

"I just wanted to pick up Francine."

"Well, you got her, so stand still. I can't sit here all day."

Granny began to sing softly and Cassie leaned against her knee, half dozing in the somnolent heat of the morning.

> *"Shall we gather at the river,*
> *Where bright angel feet have trod?*
> *With its crystal tide forever*
> *Flowin' by the throne of God?"*

A white butterfly rose from the weeds by the porch, fluttered, and sank from sight.

"Granny? Is my mama up in heaven with Jesus and them?"

The comb hesitated and slid down through her hair again.

"Is she, Granny? And the little dead baby, is he up there, too?"

"It's four years now, child. How come you're thinkin' about them?"

"Is she? Is she up there, Granny?"

Her grandmother sighed. "I reckon so, Cassie. I reckon your mama is gettin' the rest she never got when she was in this vale of tears."

"Sing some more, Granny."

"No, child, not now." Granny pushed herself up from the rocking chair. "I got to put them beans to soak. You got your readin' to do."

"I got to fix Francine her supper."

"You don't got to do any such thing. It's your readin' time."

"Papa don't read none, and Bo, he don't even know how."

"That's as may be." Granny tugged Cassie into the front room. "But I taught your mama to read and I'm goin' to teach you, too. It's readin' that's goin' to get you out of here, missy. One of these first days I aim to get a little laid by to get you some shoes so you can go to school. They make you wear shoes there because of the hookworm."

Cassie was more afraid of school than of hookworm. "I don't want to go to no school, Granny! That man down there, he whupped Bo!"

Her grandmother turned around suddenly and her face became a stranger's, with intense blue eyes glaring from behind steel-framed spectacles. "Did he tell you about it? Did Bo tell you why the teacher whipped him?"

Cassie backed away. "All he said was that man whupped him. I reckon they whup all them little kids at the school."

"Never you mind what Bo says, child." She smiled. "He wasn't at that school but four days. Anyways, they got a lady teacher now."

"But he didn't learn to read, Granny. Why don't you teach Bo about readin', instead of me?"

Granny's face darkened. "Bo ain't goin' to learn to read. Bo's— . . . well, he's different."

"How different? What makes him different?"

Her grandmother shrugged. "I heard tell he got his head hurt when he was born, but I don't know. All I know is, he can't learn to read and sometimes it makes him act real funny."

Cassie thought of the white butterfly in the weeds and turned slowly, fluttering her hands up and down, fluttering up, fluttering down. "You mean like when he killed that old cat, Granny? Was that actin' funny?"

Granny grabbed Cassie's arm so hard that the butterflies disappeared. "How did you come to know about that, girl?"

"Granny, that hurts!"

Her grandmother released her and Cassie's eyes filled with tears.

"You answer me, missy! How come you know about that cat?"

"He told me," Cassie sobbed. "He told me hisself, when we was down to the spring. He told me how he took the hammer and some nails and—"

"That's enough! I don't want to hear no more about it!"

Cassie rubbed her eyes. "But you asked me, you was the one that asked me!"

"I said that's enough! Not one more word." She hesitated, and then she sat down on a chair and reached out her arms to Cassie.

"Come here, child. You come set on old Granny's lap. There now, it's all right. Cassie, honey, I want to tell you somethin' and I want you to listen to me real good, you hear?"

Cassie squirmed uncomfortably but her grandmother held her close.

"I don't want you to go to the spring with Bo no more, you hear? I don't want you to hang around with Bo."

"But what if I want to—"

"There ain't no 'what if' about it, missy! You're goin' to stay clear of Bo or you're goin' to answer to me!"

Cassie slipped down from her lap, but Granny grabbed her arms and held her, staring directly into her eyes.

"You remember what I said, child. You stay clear of Bo!"

Cassie looked into the cold unfamiliar eyes and shivered. "Yes'm." She hesitated. "Granny? Bo's down in the field with Papa. Can I take Francine out to my play place?"

Granny pulled Cassie close and hugged her, but her face was grim. "I don't mean to scare you none, honey, but—" She hesitated and then as much to herself as to the child, she said, "Maybe I do, after all. Maybe you need some scarin'." She laughed and gave Cassie a little push. "You want to play with Francine, do you? You tryin' to fool your old granny again? What about that readin' you was goin' to do?"

Cassie was so relieved to have her real granny back that she laughed aloud. "Yes'm! What do you want me to read, Granny?"

"Read me that paper, the new one under the window."

Cassie squatted down by the wall and ran her finger along the line of print. DUST STORM HITS OKLAHOMA PANHANDLE.

BY THE END of March the leaves on the post oak near the cabin were drying out from the sun and the unseasonably hot wind. Cassie was in her play place teaching Francine to read from a scrap of newspaper when her grandmother called from the porch. "Cassie, come get this lemonade and carry it out to your papa and Bo. It's hot work for them in that field."

Granny wrapped the quart Mason jar in a dish towel and Cassie held it tight against her chest to feel the coolness.

Bo was leading the old brown mule while Howard guided the plow. It was a hillside field where furrowed red earth climbed up to a cobalt blue sky dotted with white puffy clouds which carried no promise of rain. Captain was against climbing hills, but at twelve Bo was strong enough to keep him moving while his father handled the plow. Red earth curled up from the shining plowshare like water curling up at the prow of a ship, but there was no engine to drive the plow, there was only a man to lean into it and throw his weight against the rocky soil until the muscles in his back bulged out under the straps of his overalls.

"Whoa up there, Captain!"

Howard took off his stained felt hat and wiped his forehead with a bandana handkerchief. His face was tanned to the eyebrows but his forehead was pasty white where it was shielded by his hat.

Bo came across the furrows to join his father and Cassie. Howard sat down on the ground heavily but Bo squatted on his haunches as if he would take off at any sudden noise. His close-set black eyes darted this way and that like mice looking for a way out of a cage.

Howard passed the lemonade jar over to Bo. "Wish your granny had sent us some cookies to eat with this."

"She's plumb out of molasses, Papa," Cassie said. "Says she can't bake no more till you go to town."

"Well, I ain't goin' to get to town till I get this here field plowed. I got to get my corn in. Plant in the dark of the moon, my pappy always said. Plant your corn when the hickory buds is the size of squirrels' ears, but be sure it's in the dark of the moon. I never had no faith in them old sayin's, though, any more than I got faith in all the prayin' your granny does." He picked up a clod of dry red earth and crumbled it in his hand. "I just hope to hell we get some rain." He pulled a Bull Durham sack from his pocket and rolled a cigarette. "Don't you kids tell Granny about this, hear? She don't think I ought to spend money on no tobacco. Say, I got somethin' for you kids, too." He fished in his pocket and brought out two wrapped toffees.

Cassie unwrapped her candy and licked it, letting the sweetness fill her mouth. Sometimes she could get a piece of sugarcane but store-bought candy was a rare treat.

Her father squeezed the end of his cigarette to get one last pull of smoke and dropped it in the furrow. "Well, Bo, let's get at it. Ain't gettin' no work done sittin' here. Cassie, be careful with that jar."

"Yes, Papa." She wandered back across the field, licking her toffee and trying to decide whether to chew it or to make it last as long as possible. A black crow rose cawing from the field ahead of her, and as if the bird had made the decision for her she popped the candy into her mouth and ran for home, jumping from furrow to furrow as her bare feet sank in the warm red earth.

Chapter 2

THE RAIN CAME, but it was late and there was not much of it. When Cassie and her grandmother went blackberry picking in August the dirt road was baked hard and red dust hung in the still air. Granny carried two lard buckets and Cassie, in a shift made from a feed sack and ragged cotton panties, danced down the road ahead of her. She darted here and there like one of the white butterflies in the ditch, pausing now and again to squish her feet in a pocket of red dust or to squat down and examine a roly-poly bug.

Granny pushed aside the drooping blackberry canes. "These berries is all dried up. We better go down by Steele's, where the woods hold the damp a little."

"What's Steele's, Granny? Is it Mr. Steele's?"

"Never you mind, missy. You'll see when we get there."

They walked past a field where corn dried in the heat. Cassie lagged behind as they went through a patch of dusty scrub oak and into a clearing where dry weeds grew up close to a fieldstone chimney that stood stark and alone in the field. She hurried to catch up with her grandmother. "Granny! There's a chimney but there ain't no house!"

"It burned down long ago, child. Old Mr. Steele built it when he first come into the Indian Territory, but he'd moved his family to the new house before the fire. Folks hated that man, and they say it was a set fire, but it was only a tenant house when it burned."

"What's a tenant house, Granny?"

"Like ours, child. Like where we live. A tenant house is where you live if you farm on shares." She stopped and looked back at the chimney. "It's where you got to live if you don't own land."

Cassie squeezed her grandmother's hand. "I like our house, Granny."

"It's all you know, child." Granny looked down at her sadly. "You ain't never known what it was to have land."

There was a feeling of dampness in the woods past the clearing, and the blackberry plants were heavy with fruit. They worked their way along the ditch beside the road. Granny dropped her berries into a lard bucket, but Cassie ate hers, cramming the sweet fruit into her mouth until her lips were stained and the rich dark juice ran down her chin.

"You, Cassie, stop that! You're goin' to make yourself sick!"

Cassie stopped with a handful of berries halfway to her mouth. "Granny," she whispered, "look yonder, there's a house."

Granny straightened up and rubbed the small of her back. "Well, yes, child. It's Mr. Steele's house."

The place was set back from the road: a house, a barn, a few sheds and a substantial-looking privy. The house itself was half-hidden by sumacs that were closing in as if to return it to the forest it had displaced. In front of the house an old maple tree cast a broad shadow. The house was a rambling one-story place, sided in clapboard which had once been painted white. Tall narrow windows, still outlined with dark green trim, reached almost to the floor of the veranda, which ran around three sides of the house—curtainless windows that looked blank and threatening.

"Granny? Does Mr. Steele live there now?"

"Law, no, child. The Mr. Steele that built the place, he's been dead and gone for years. It's his son that owns it, the Mr. Steele that come to our place. He don't come often, though. He stays at his lawyerin', up there in Ballard."

"Can we look, Granny? Can we go up real close?"

The woman looked back along the road. "Well, I reckon it wouldn't hurt nothin' just to go up there and have ourselves a look."

They pushed through the wild sumac, and Granny tested the broken wooden steps before climbing up to the veranda. She stepped carefully around the holes in the floor while Cassie ran past her and cupped her eyes with her hands to peer in through a dusty window.

She saw a spacious room with more furniture than she had ever seen. There were sofas and chairs draped with white sheets, small tables with elaborately carved bases, carpets rolled in dusty canvas and a tall cherry secretary with leaded glass doors. The fireplace, however, could have been copied stone for stone from the lone chimney in the clearing. It was built of roughhewn fieldstone with a hand-adzed timber set into the stone for a mantel.

Granny looked in, too, and caught her breath. "The things! Just look at all them things! It's like they just walked out of there and never took one thing with them!"

"Did they, Granny? Did the folks just go away like that?"

"I don't rightly know, Cassie. It all happened before I come here. Your mama knew. She told me they—my land, child, look at the sofa under that sheet. Full of mice, I'll wager. Plumb full of mice!"

Cassie slipped around the corner of the last window on the veranda. She rubbed a clear spot on the glass and shielded her eyes to look into the room. "Granny! Granny, come see!"

"Merciful heaven, it's a little girl's room. It's for a little girl like you."

Cassie could not comprehend the idea of a little girl having such a room all to herself. The walls were papered, not with yellowed newsprint but with a design of small pink-and-blue flowers on a pale yellow background. The bed was a narrow mahogany four-poster with a drooping pink canopy. In the corner of the room was a child-sized desk with a matching chair that was pushed back as if a child had just jumped up to run into some other room. Next to a walnut wardrobe was a bookshelf crammed with dusty books.

"It was her room, I reckon," Granny said softly. "The little girl Leona told me about."

Cassie cried out, "Granny!" and jumped back from the window.

"What's the matter, child? What's wrong?"

Cassie buried her face in the folds of her grandmother's skirt. "It's a baby, Granny," she whispered. "There's a dead baby in there."

"Sakes alive, child, come and look. It ain't nothing but a dolly."

Cassie looked again. The thing was still there, on the dusty floor. She could see that it had a cloth body, like Francine, but the cloth was darkened by age rather than by dirt.   Where the body had been torn by rot or mice, sawdust had leaked out to make little gray cones on the wide planks of the floor.   The doll had china hands, shiny white, and white china feet in shiny black shoes, but what had frightened Cassie was the doll's round head with the remains of glued-on yellow silk hair and most of all, the face: the dead-white face with a bright red Cupid's-bow mouth, cheeks with matching pink dots, thin black lines for eyebrows and eyes as round and hard as marbles, bright blue and surrounded by short black lines of painted-on eyelashes.

She backed away from the window.   "No!   It ain't no dolly!   My Francine's a dolly.   That thing there, it ain't no dolly!"

Granny rubbed her neck.   "It's a doll, all right, and a nicer doll than any you're ever likely to have. Thrown away, just thrown away. All them things, just left to rot."   She sighed.   "Well, come along, missy.   It don't do no good to stand around here and gawp.   We got to get some more berries and get home."   She eased herself down from the veranda and walked out through the sumac.

Cassie hurried to catch up with her grandmother.   She did not want to be left behind, even if Granny was right and the thing on the floor of the little girl's room was only a doll after all.   She did not want to be alone with it.

WEEKS LATER, Cassie still remembered the day of blackberry picking. She told Francine about the vacant house.

"And there's a room for a little girl, Francine, with a little desk and toys and a—" She stopped.   She did not want to talk about the white-faced doll.   "It's scary there, Francine, real scary.   But don't you fret, your mama ain't goin' to take you to no scary place."

When she said the word "mama," Cassie had a flash of memory: a tired face and thin arms holding her.

She shook her doll.   "My land, Francine, what are you doin' up past your bedtime!   Mama better sing you to sleep!"   She rocked the doll in her arms and sang a song of her grandmother's.

> *"The years creep slowly by, Lorena,*
> *The snow is in the grass again."*

She got to her feet and watched a cloud of red dust moving toward her, then ran for the house. "Granny! There's a car comin' here!"

Her grandmother came to the door wiping her hands on a rag.

"Granny, you reckon it's Mr. Steele?"

Granny looked at Howard, who was bringing a bucket of water from the spring. "We'll find out soon enough."

The new black Packard was so shiny that each grain of red dust stood out on it, and the driver was Mr. James Steele. He loosened his necktie and nodded to Howard. "Hot for October, Taylor."

Howard took off his hat. "Yes, sir. Mighty hot."

The man turned toward Granny. "You're looking well, Mrs. Hendricks."

"Ain't seen you for a while, Mr. Steele," Howard said.

Mr. Steele frowned. "I prefer to handle my farms through my agent in San Bois." He turned as if he had felt Cassie watching him. "Well, little Cassandra, how old are you now?"

"I'm seven, Mr. Steele."

He smiled with pale thin lips. "What grade are you in at school?"

Cassie did not know why she was ashamed. With her big toe she dragged a line in the red dust and crossed it with another.

"She can't go to school," Granny said. "She got no shoes."

Mr. Steele looked at Howard. "Where's that boy of yours?"

"In the field, Mr. Steele, holdin' old Captain. I swear, that mule gets more cantankerous every day of this world."

Mr. Steele grunted. "The boy's a good worker, is he?"

"Yes, sir! He'll give you a good day's work."

"That's good. I've got to have people I can count on. Times are bad and are going to get worse, from what I hear." He looked down at Cassie. "Perhaps we should ask Cassandra if the situation will improve. Does she, like her namesake, have the gift of prophecy?"

They looked at him blankly, then with the dignity of a titled lady offering her parlor Granny said, "Will you come up on the porch and set a spell, Mr. Steele? I can send Cassie to the spring for cold water."

"No, thank you. I want to go over to the old place." He turned to Howard. "I'll need someone to patch the roof and replace the rotten boards on the veranda. Can you do that, Taylor?"

"Yes, sir!" Howard stood up straight. "I'm handy with a hammer."

Mr. Steele looked at him closely. "You staying sober these days?"

Howard flushed. "Yes, sir."

"I'll look the place over and make up a list of jobs to send out with the lumber truck. The boy can work, too. At a boy's wages, of course."

He nodded to Granny and got into his car. "Glad I can throw a little work your way, Taylor." He turned the car and eased it down the rough track to the gravel road. They watched until the caterpillar of dust began to swell, eating the road to the west.

Howard spat on the track the car had left in the dust. "Throw a little work my way! Comes out here in his big Packard car like he was some kind of a king. I ain't no by-God WPA, I'm a farmer!"

Granny watched the dust. "You ain't no farmer, Howard. A farmer's a man like my pa was, a man that farms his own land."

"His land till the bank took it! I worked for what I got, woman!"

Her voice was quiet and resigned. "You ain't got much."

"I got a truck and I got my mule. I got Captain, ain't I?"

She sighed. "That's right. You got your mule." She walked slowly to the cabin and climbed to the porch.

Cassie went back to her play place and sat down in the dust, but she did not sing to Francine, and when the Packard returned, she did not call her grandmother, not even when it stopped in the dooryard.

Mr. Steele turned off the engine and called out to her. "You, Cassandra, come here. I've got something for you."

Cassie stood up but made no move to go to the car.

"Go on, child," Granny said from the front door. "Do like he says."

Cassie picked up Francine and went to the car.

"Found this at the old place." He took something from the seat beside him and held it out the car window.

Cassie drew back. It was the doll she had thought to be a dead baby. He dangled it by a foot, so that the gold silk hair hung straight down and the hard blue eyes stared at Cassie from an upside-down face.

"Take it," he said. "Rats have been at it but your granny can mend it." He dropped the doll into her arms, and she stared at it blankly.

"Cassie!" Granny hissed. "Tell Mr. Steele thank you."

She looked up at the man. "Thank you, Mr. Steele."

He nodded and drove down the hill.

Cassie felt Granny's hand on her shoulder and looked up, but her grandmother was watching the car. They stood in the hot October sunshine and watched the dust cloud travel east toward the highway.

MR. STEELE's lumber truck went past three days later and raised a trail of red dust that hung in the air until a hot wind came up and swirled it away. Every day after that, Cassie's father trudged west with Bo trailing along behind him and watching the woods with quick dark eyes.

On Saturday morning Granny called Cassie from her play place. "I can't find Bo, honey. You fetch me a kettle of water from the spring."

Cassie took the kettle and ran back to pick up Francine. She hesitated and then she picked up the new doll, too. Granny had sewed up the holes in the body and had made a dress of sorts from a piece of flour sack. Cassie looked at the doll thoughtfully.

"You, Cassie!" Granny called from the porch. "I want that water!"

Cassie grabbed the kettle and ran. The path into the woods was deep in dried leaves, but she did not slow down until the path curved around the shaggy base of an old cedar tree. It was there that the air cooled and took on a musty smell on even the hottest of days. It was a mysterious place, just scary enough to make going to the spring an adventure. Cassie was tiptoeing by the time she reached the hollow where the spring shimmered down the shelved sides of a black slate grotto.

Someone, sometime, had split and hollowed out a log to serve as a trough, so long ago that the wood was completely covered with green moss. The water running from the end of the log had washed away the earth beneath it and formed a basin paved with flat black slate. The pool of cool water was three feet in diameter and five or six inches deep.

Cassie propped her dolls against a rock and sat down next to them to dabble her dusty feet in the water. She looked at the two dolls, the homemade one with its shapeless dirty body and the doll the man had given her, the surprised blue eyes and the red Cupid's-bow mouth. She stood up in the water suddenly and reached across to pick up the new doll.

"Mary Priscilla!" she cried. "That's your name, ain't it? Mary Priscilla Taylor!" She hugged the doll to her.

She looked down at the doll on the ground. It was old and ugly compared to Mary Priscilla with her golden hair. She turned away from it, hugging Mary Priscilla, but something pricked between her shoulder blades as if those indelible pencil eyes were looking deep into her faithless heart. She dropped to her knees in the leaf mold and snatched up the doll Granny had made.

"Francine! Oh, Francine, don't you fret. I'm always goin' to love you the best. Always!"

She hugged both dolls and then propped them against the rock again. "Now, you babies just wait there while Mama has her a little rinse-off to get cool." She pulled her faded shift up over her head and after a moment's hesitation took off her cotton panties, too. She squatted down and squealed with pleasure at the chill of the water.

A rough laugh sounded in the woods behind her, and she stood up and whirled around. "Who's that? Who's out there?"

Bo stepped out of the woods, grinning. Cassie was not surprised. He had a knack for moving quickly but quietly through the woods, like a fox slipping through a field of dry cornstalks.

"It's just me, Cassie. Just old Bo."

"What are you doin', spyin' on me that way?"

"I ain't spyin', Cassie. I just want to look."

Cassie looked down at her thin naked body. "Look at what?"

He laughed and although she did not know why she did it, Cassie slipped her shift over her head and pulled on her panties. "You better not hang around here, Bo Taylor," she said. "Granny told me I wasn't to be at the spring with you no more."

Bo took one step toward her and raised his hand. "You tellin' me what to do and where to go? I'll get—" He dropped his hand suddenly and stepped back from the pool. "What for? What for did she say that?"

"I don't know," Cassie said self-righteously. "All I know is I got to do what Granny says."

Bo snatched up Mary Priscilla and held her out over the water. "You tell me or I'll drown this here baby of yours!"

"No!" Cassie ran to him and jumped up to grab Mary Priscilla, but he held the doll high. "Please, Bo! Give me my dolly!"

He laughed and pulled away from her.

"I'll tell!" Cassie cried. "I'll tell Granny how you bothered me and stole my dolly and wanted to—to look at me!"

Bo became very still, like a cat preparing to pounce, but suddenly he relaxed and dropped the doll on the dead leaves by the pool. "Okay," he said harshly. "Take your damn old dolly. Tattletale!"

Cassie grabbed up her dolls and ran almost to the big cedar tree before she remembered the kettle. She went back to the spring on tiptoe, but Bo was gone. She filled the kettle and hurried back to the house.

She was just in time to hear the tail end of an argument. "You get them, Howard Taylor! If you drink up that money before you—"

Howard stormed out of the house, past Cassie. His pickup bounced down the track as Cassie ran up to the porch. "Here's your kettle, Granny."

"Well, it's about time! Where you been, missy? You been playin', ain't you, instead of doin' what I told you to do!"

"I wasn't—" Cassie stopped. She had started to tell her grandmother about Bo, but she suspected that Granny would be as mad at Cassie as at Bo. She put her hand to her mouth, confused. "I was just playin' with my dollies, Granny."

"Next time you do your chores before you set in to play, you hear?"

"Yes'm." Cassie walked slowly back to her play place. Granny always said she should tell the truth, but if she did she would probably get a spanking from Granny and a beating from Bo.

She hugged her dolls to her. "I love you, Francine, and I love you, Mary Priscilla," she whispered, but she was still confused.

HOWARD CAME HOME from town that Saturday with a box for Cassie.

"Is it somethin' to play with, Papa? Please, can I have it?"

Granny sniffed. "I know what it better be, Howard Taylor."

Howard gave Cassie the box and sat down while she unfolded the paper.

"Shoes! Brand-new shoes!" She jerked them out of the box and pulled them onto her feet. They were high-topped boys' basketball shoes, black canvas with white rubber soles and a white maker's seal on the ankle. "Granny, you see my new shoes? You see them?"

"They was all I could get, with the money I had," Howard said.

Granny smiled. "They're just fine, son. Now she can go to school."

"School?" Cassie sat down and untied the shoes. "I reckon I don't need no new shoes, Papa. Don't need to go to no school."

Howard laughed. "Listen to you! Say, you all seen Bo anywheres? I thought me and him might go back into town for a spell."

Bo spoke from the doorway. "I'm here, Paw. Well, look at them boys' shoes! Little old girl in boys' shoes! Ain't that a sight to see?"

"Bo, you stop that! Granny, don't let him laugh at me!"

Granny ignored her. "Howard, I don't want you takin' that boy where the men are drinkin' corn whiskey."

"Woman, you just stay clear of me!"

As the truck clattered down the hill, Granny sank into her chair and put her hands over her eyes. "Wine is a mocker, strong drink is ragin'. Lord, where's it goin' to end?"

Cassie bounced across the room. "Look how high I can jump in these shoes! Look, Granny, look at me!"

Chapter 3

ON HALLOWEEN there was a cold snap and on Monday, Cassie's first day of school, frost lay on the ground like early snow. It was bitterly cold in the cabin. Cassie huddled in bed while Granny built up the fire in the cookstove in the front room. When her grandmother's calls switched from irritation to anger Cassie climbed out of bed and hurriedly put on a faded cotton dress and a torn gray sweater which Bo had outgrown. She pulled on darned blue socks and, finally, the new black canvas shoes.

"It's about time you were up and going, missy!"

Granny held her hand tightly as they walked down the rough track and turned west on the dirt road. The sun had come out and burned away the frost on the road, but in the fields each weed and cornstalk was coated in white. They passed the woods, passed the frost-killed blackberries, passed the lone chimney in the clearing and then, as if by prior agreement, they stopped in front of the Steele place.

For all the work Howard Taylor had done, the house was not changed. There were new steps and a few new boards set into the veranda. The roof had patches of new cedar shingles, but they would soon weather.

Her grandmother snorted angrily. "Sittin' there! Just sittin' there like some old toy they ran off and left!" She gripped Cassie's shoulder.

"Granny, that hurts!"

"Never you mind that, missy, you just listen to me. You know how it is that folks can just leave a nice house like this, just walk away from it? It's because they own the land. You see what ownin' land does for a body? You see it?"

"Yes'm, I reckon so. Did they fix up the little girl's room, too?"

"Now, would I know that, child?" She jerked Cassie's hand. "Come along now, you got to get to school."

On the low wooden bridge over San Bois Creek, Cassie pulled away to hang over the rail and look down into the gray-green water. There was a skim of ice under the bridge, but a big turtle was sunning himself on a flat rock near the bank. He startled and slid into the water and his head plowed away from them, dragging behind it a widening V of ripples. Downstream a cluster of ducks with shiny green heads paddled among the weeds. "Look, Granny! Look at them pretty birds!"

"Mallards, child. Mallard ducks. Make haste, now!"

Cassie hung back. Bo had told her all about the teacher's whip and how the children would laugh at her for wearing boys' shoes.

Turner School was in a clearing halfway up the hill. The one room had windows along each side and a door with wooden steps at the end. The privies were in the woods behind the school, one for girls and one for boys, and a blue Ford coupe was parked on the dirt road.

Cassie stopped at the sight of children playing in front of the school, but Granny pulled her toward a pine flagpole set in a heap of white-washed rocks. A young woman carrying a bundled flag came down the steps. She was short and plump and wore a dark blue wool dress with a middy collar trimmed in white braid.

Granny pushed Cassie forward. "This here's my little granddaughter, Cassandra Taylor. She aims to come to the school. She can read."

The teacher smiled. Behind her gold-rimmed spectacles her eyes were dark. "Cassandra Taylor. Wasn't she supposed to start school last year?"

"She didn't have no shoes."

The teacher flushed.

Granny straightened her shoulders. "I'm Mrs. Martha Hendricks, her grandma on her mama's side. We live over yonder, on Mr. Steele's land."

"I'm pleased to meet you, and to have Cassandra in our school."

"Cassie," the child said in a tiny voice.

The teacher looked at her quickly and then back at Granny. "Will you come for her after school?"

"Yes'm. I aim to come every day till she knows the way." Granny patted Cassie's shoulder, but when the girl did not look up, she turned away and started down the hill.

Cassie was trying to hide her feet in the dry weeds. When the children made a circle around the flagpole, she let her long hair fall forward to shield her face while she looked at them. No one was staring at her feet. The girls were dressed as she was, in cotton dresses that were either outgrown or not yet grown into, and the boys wore ragged bib overalls. Their shoes were so scuffed and run-down that it would have been hard to tell girls' shoes from boys'. Two girls who looked like sisters, pallid girls with stringy black hair, wore men's workshoes that flapped unlaced around their dirty ankles.

Cassie was the only one who had new shoes. She edged her left foot out of the weeds and turned it so that the maker's seal could be seen, pristine white against the black canvas. Suddenly she saw the woman walking down the dusty road.

"Granny?" Cassie whispered. "Oh, Granny!" She crammed her knuckles in her mouth and burst into tears.

The teacher had gone inside, and the children left the flagpole to make a circle around Cassie. The smaller of the dark-haired sisters started the chanting.

"Crybaby, crybaby," she sang. "Lookit the little crybaby!"

The others took up the chorus. "Crybaby, crybaby!"

"No!" Cassie cried. "No!" She struck out at the girl.

The sister shrieked and the teacher came running down the steps.

"She hit me, teacher! That new one hit me!"

"They called be crybaby," Cassie sobbed. "That ain't fair!"

"That *isn't* fair, Cassandra." The teacher clapped her hands and the noise subsided. "Bobby Sue, I don't think you are seriously injured. Bobby Joe, see to your little sister. Come in now, and take your places in an orderly fashion."

They lined up and marched into the school. Since Cassie did not yet have a place to take in an orderly fashion, she stood by the door and had a good look at the school. The teacher's desk was at one end and a black potbelly stove at the other. Between them were two double rows of desks separated by a center aisle. On the walls were a blackboard and a pull-down map of Oklahoma. She stared at the room in wonder. Bookshelves with more books than she could count, desks with folding seats and inkwells set into their tops: it was a new world, an unimagined universe.

"Cassandra!"

Cassie realized that it was the second time the teacher had called the unfamiliar name and that the other children were staring at her. She twisted one black shoe behind the other. "Yes'm?"

The teacher smiled at her. "Come to my desk, Cassandra. I must work out what grade to put you in." The smile disappeared. "You children, this does not concern you one bit! You get to work in your workbooks, hear?"

She turned her back to the pupils and could not see that not one had picked up a pencil. They watched Cassie with avid curiosity.

The teacher smiled at Cassie again. "Mercy! I didn't even tell you my name! I am Miss Bencher. Miss Naomi Bencher."

Cassie caught her breath. Never had she heard such a beautiful name. Miss Naomi Bencher. It summoned up a world that Cassie could not have found words to describe, a world of middy collars and blue Ford coupes and books. Miss Naomi Bencher. It was even better than Francine.

Miss Bencher took a book from the shelf. "Now, Cassandra—"

"My name's Cassie." She tensed. Maybe she should not have said it. What if the teacher got out the whip?

"Is that what they call you at home? Then we shall call you that here, too. Now, Cassie, let's see if you can read this book."

Cassie opened the book, but she was so startled by the colored pictures that she did not look at the words. There was a little girl in a red dress, and a boy in a white shirt and short pants, and a white dog with a black spot. Their house was like nothing Cassie had ever seen, a white house with green shutters and a red brick chimney, flowers in neat rows, and grass, and a green car parked in the driveway.

Miss Bencher frowned. "Your grandmother said you could read."

"Yes'm. I can read." Reluctantly, she shifted her eyes from the pictures to the words. " 'See Dick. See Jane. See Spot.' "

"That was very nice, Cassie.   Continue."

Cassie turned the page and tried to ignore the new picture.   " 'See Dick jump. See Jane jump. See Spot jump. Oh, oh, oh!' "

The large print of the schoolbook was easier to read than that of the newspapers on the walls at home, but the words were not half as interesting.   There were no bank robberies, no FBI and no exciting headlines: MAN SHOOTS WIFE, SELF and BOOTLEG WHISKEY SEIZED.

"Here, Cassie, try this."   Miss Bencher handed her a more difficult book and after that, another.   "Your grandmother has taught you well."

"Oh, yes, ma'am.   My granny says readin' is real important.   She's always readin' of her Bible and she knows just about everything."

Miss Bencher's dark eyes twinkled.   "Oh, she does, does she?"

"Yes'm.   She knows to plant bunch beans on Good Friday and to tie coal-oil rags around the chickens' necks to keep off the roup and to—"

"I'm not certain that she found all of that information in the Bible. You do read well, though, and until I test you in other subjects, I think I'll put you in a grade all by yourself."

Someone whispered, "Crybaby grade!"   The room exploded in laughter.

Miss Bencher jumped up from her chair.   "Stop that! Bobby Sue, you get to work on those arithmetic problems."   She smiled down at Cassie.   "Why don't you just read while I work with the other children?"

"Yes'm," Cassie said.   She smiled, too, because school was not the way Bo had described it.   The teacher even let her read.

Later, Miss Bencher rapped a ruler on her desk.   "It's time for recess now."   While the other children ran outside, Cassie looked at her teacher for guidance: she didn't know what "recess" meant.   Miss Bencher explained, "That means you can go outside, dear, and play with the other children."

Cassie tiptoed down the steps, bracing herself against the expected wave of laughter, but the boys were running around in some wild game and the girls were huddled near the flagpole, whispering secrets. Cassie hesitated near the bottom of the steps.

"There she is!" the smaller black-haired sister cried.   "That's the one that hit me! Get her, Bobby Joe, you get her good!"   She grabbed up a rock and started to throw it, but her big sister caught her arm.

"Stop that, Bobby Sue! Teacher don't hold with no rock throwin'. You there, you new one, why'd you hit my sister?"

Cassie backed toward the steps. "She didn't have no call to laugh at me and name me crybaby."

The girl considered Cassie's complaint as seriously as a district judge would review a brief. Finally she nodded. "That's right. Bobby Sue, remember when you first come to school? You cried, too."

Cassie was not happy about the way Bobby Sue looked at her.

"Crack the whip!" Bobby Sue cried. The girls lined up with Bobby Joe, the largest, on one end and the smallest, Cassie, on the other. They clasped hands and ran laughing across the rough ground until Bobby Joe set her feet and cracked the whip. Cassie was not ready for the sudden stop or for the force that traveled down the line of girls. She lost her grip on her neighbor's hand and fell, rolling across the rocky ground to come to a stop in a thorny bush. She sat up, tears welling in her eyes, but she saw that the girls were watching her, waiting for her to cry, waiting to laugh at her.

She took her time picking her sweater loose from the thorns, and by the time she had finished, her eyes were dry. She jumped up and ran across the field, forcing herself to laugh aloud. "Let's do it again!" she yelled. "Let's crack the whip again!"

The ring of the handbell saved her. The boys and girls ran to the door, and Cassie followed them, glad to be finished with recess. They had not laughed at her, and she could go back to the wonderful new world of Miss Naomi Bencher and books.

When Granny decided that Cassie could walk to school alone, what had been a pleasant walk became a venture into foreign territory. She hurried past the woods, past the lone chimney in the clearing where Mr. Steele's house loomed over her as if the man himself were watching her.

Then came another patch of woods where black-green cedar branches hung like rags among the bare hickory trees, and pockets of darkness hid from the morning light. She ran through the woods each day, until her rubber soles thudded onto the wooden bridge. She could stop then to catch her breath and to watch the ducks sailing among the reeds before she ran up the last hill to join the circle around the flagpole at Turner School.

After a few weeks, Cassie worked up the courage to stop at Mr. Steele's house. She peered into the living room, but nothing had changed, so she edged around the corner to the window of the little girl's room.

White. There was nothing but white. Someone had covered the glass on the inside with white fabric. She looked out at the road fearfully. Had they guessed that she was going to peek?

"I wasn't goin' to hurt nothin'," she whispered. She had never even thought of going in, of touching things, but they had taken away even her right to see. She clenched her fists. "Lookin' don't hurt nothing!"

She looked into the window, and saw a child's face staring out at her. She jumped back before she realized that it was her own face, that the white backing had made a mirror of the window glass. She stared at the pale reflection of her frightened blue eyes and realized that she did not want to see what was behind that white curtain, not ever. She turned and ran, careless of everything but her need to escape.

By THE NEXT AUTUMN, September of 1933, Cassie Taylor was eight and was old enough to be aware of the fear around her. Depression and drought had combined to crush Eastern Oklahoma. Cotton and corn prices fell to the lowest level since the war and dry winds attacked the land and carried away the topsoil. The government tried with the Agricultural Adjustment Act to raise farm prices by lowering farm production. The intervention saved the landowners, but crop allotments were so low that tenant farmers could not earn enough to feed their families. They headed west in old cars with mattresses strapped on top and battered pickup trucks loaded with their few possessions: the Okies were on the move.

They left little behind: a broken chair, a burned-out pot, a rag that had once been a dress. They cooked their chickens and put them up in Mason jars for the journey, but they left their cats and dogs. The cats took to the woods and grew to twice their normal size on a diet of field mice and ground squirrels, but the dogs sought human companionship, and there were usually two or three scrawny, half-starved dogs hanging around the Taylors' dooryard. Granny ran them off to save her chickens, but Cassie liked to watch them from the safety of the porch. One afternoon a little dog kept trying to climb onto the big one's back, and Cassie laughed so hard that Granny came out to see what was happening.

"Well, I never!" She flapped her apron at the dogs. "You, sir, get away! Scat!"

Cassie was still laughing. "Oh, Granny, wasn't them dogs funny?"

Granny put her hand to her mouth but could not hold back her own laughter. "Well, I reckon laughin' beats cryin' any day. Like they say, tears put too much salt in the beans."

"What were them funny dogs tryin' to do?"

Granny's mouth became a tight line. "Never you mind, missy. Just never you mind!"

Every week Howard Taylor came back from San Bois with a report of another family heading west, and almost every week there was another vacant seat at Turner School.

One day in late September, Bobby Joe grabbed Cassie's arm. "We're goin'! After Thanksgivin', me and Bobby Sue and them, we're goin' to California! My pappy says it's a paradise out yonder! Says you can pick them oranges any old time you want. And warm! Says there ain't no winter, ain't nothin' but the sun shinin' all the livelong day!"

Miss Bencher shook her head. "Bobby Joe, I hope your father has not been taken in by exaggerated reports of California."

Bobby Joe looked up at her blankly. "What's zaggerated?"

"Overblown statements of . . . well, lies."

"No, ma'am! Pappy brung home a paper with it all printed out about the oranges and all. And there's work out there, too. It ain't no lie, teacher. They wouldn't print up no paper with lies in it!"

Bobby Joe ran outside and Miss Bencher said, "How about you, Cassie? Is your family going to California?"

"I don't reckon so. Granny says, 'Better the devil we know.' "

"Your grandmother is a wise woman." She looked at the children playing tag. "We'll be down to eleven pupils. I wonder when they'll close the school."

"Close up Turner School? Where will us kids go to school?"

"In San Bois. You'll ride the school bus to town."

Cassie looked at the school and saw boarded-up windows. No children running and yelling. No Miss Naomi Bencher.

"Teacher? Where will you go?"

Miss Bencher looked away, but Cassie had seen the fear, the same fear she had seen in her father's eyes, and in her grandmother's.

"I don't know, Cassie. I'm only twenty-one. The superintendent wouldn't say I had much seniority."

Cassie had to do something, to say something to help. "Miss Bencher! When I grow up, I'm goin' to be a schoolteacher just like you! I'm goin' to teach all them little kids to read!"

Miss Bencher laughed. "You'll have to work hard to become a teacher, dear. Before you can teach 'them little kids,' you will have to learn grammar. It's 'those little children,' Cassie. And you must improve your diction. Sound the final consonants, as in 'going.' And for heaven's sake, drop 'ain't' from your vocabulary! Now, say it again, correctly."

Cassie rolled her tongue in her mouth, trying to get the feel of a new way of speaking. "Miss Bencher, I am not going to say 'ain't' and I am going to teach those little children to read."

Miss Bencher clapped her hands. "Bravo! If you can keep that up . . ."

Cassie was too excited to sit still that afternoon. A teacher! She would wear middy dresses like Miss Naomi Bencher and drive a Ford car like Miss Naomi Bencher and live in a house like—of course! Miss Bencher's house would be just like Dick and Jane's, with a shade tree in the front yard and green grass and a driveway for her blue Ford car.

She rested her chin on her hands and watched herself park her car in the driveway and walk across the green, green grass. She opened the door and called, "Granny, I'm home from the school!"

"Cassie!" It was not Granny's voice, but Miss Bencher's. "Cassandra Taylor, you are supposed to be doing your arithmetic, not daydreaming. If you want to be a teacher, you'll have to work for it."

"Yes'm." Cassie opened her arithmetic book. "Miss Bencher? Was there a Cassandra before me—I mean, in history or someplace?"

"Yes, in mythology." She led Cassie to the front of the room.

"Look it up, dear. Cultivate the dictionary habit."

Cassie read it, stumbling over the names. " 'Cassandra: a daughter of Priam and Hecuba, a prophetess cursed by Apollo so that her prophecies, though true, were fated never to be believed.' What's a prophecy?"

"A prediction, Cassie. Telling what will happen in the future."

"How can a body know?"

"In ancient times, people believed that—wait, I have a simple book on mythology at home. You can read about it for yourself." She smiled. "Remember, Cassie, you can learn about anything on earth, if you can just get hold of the right book."

Cassie rubbed her cheek. "I can predict. I predict that sometime I'm goin'—I'm going to teach school like you and that I'm going to own land. A lot of land. Maybe even a whole farm."

The teacher looked away. "I hope you will, Cassie. I hope your prophecy comes true."

AFTER SCHOOL Cassie ran home to tell Granny about her plan.

Mr. Steele was talking to her father. Cassie edged past the men to her grandmother, who was in her rocking chair on the front porch.

"Hello, Mr. Steele," Cassie said.

"I'm glad to see that the cat hasn't got your tongue this time."

Cassie ran to her grandmother. "Granny," she whispered, "guess what I'm goin'—going to be when I grow up!"

"Not now, child. Let me hear what they're sayin' out there."

"It blossomed, but it never made no boll. Wasn't my fault."

"I know that, Taylor. The cotton crop failed all over Oklahoma."

"Yessir." Howard turned his sweat-stained hat in his hands. "Mr. Steele, without no cotton money I don't know how a fellow can make it."

Mr. Steele frowned. "A prudent farmer would have—well, I'm planning to remodel the old house into a hunting lodge where I can bring friends and business associates. I'll have a builder come out from town but I'll suggest that he take you on for day labor."

Steele drove away. "Day labor." Howard spat in the dust. "I fixed his roof for him, didn't I? How come he's got to get him a builder?"

"It's his money, Howard. He earned it."

"Earned it with his highfalutin' lawyerin'. Never had to dirty his hands. Never had to watch his crops dry up. I got half a mind to walk off this place, see what Mr. Lawyer Steele would do about that!"

Granny shook her head. "I wouldn't test him, if it was me. He's a hot-tempered man like his daddy."

"What are you talkin' about?"

"A feller that worked for old Mr. Steele let a horse get hurt, a Tennessee Walker, and the old man beat him half to death."

"Hell, this here Steele don't scare me none," Howard said sullenly.

"I reckon Leona never told you what happened to his little girl, how he—" She stopped abruptly.

"Shut up, old woman! I'm goin' to town, and there's the end of it, you hear?"

Granny braced herself with a hand on the post. "I hear it, Howard. I hear it."

Chapter 4

"YOU STAY CLEAN AWAY from Steele's, Cassie Taylor! Them workmen don't need you hangin' around and gettin' in their way."

Cassie was bursting with curiosity about the changes at the old house, but Granny's words were enough to make her run past the house on her way to school. Granny might not have been able to make a prophecy, but Cassie was convinced that her grandmother could read her mind, and would know it if she so much as dawdled as she passed the house. And it was no use asking her father what the workmen were doing.

"Damn fools," he said. "Do this, do that, and what's it for? It's so Steele can have him a play place, same as Cassie's place out there under the tree. It ain't a house where a man can live and do his work. It's just a damn toy!"

When the workmen had finished and gone back to town, Cassie persuaded her grandmother to walk down to the house to see what they had done.

"My law!" Granny said when she saw the place. "My law!"

The dingy white clapboard walls had been covered with brown-stained shingles and the green trim repainted dark brown. The crawl-space under the veranda was enclosed with round river rocks held in place by gray cement. The house no longer looked out of place. It was a part of the land and the woods, at home with the oaks and dark-branched cedars and the sumac. As if in celebration, the big sugar maple tree in front of the house had erupted in a mass of orange and scarlet leaves.

Cassie and her grandmother went up the steps to the veranda.

"Wait, child." Granny put her hand on Cassie's shoulder.

"What for?"

"I don't know. It just feels like—well, I reckon it won't hurt none if we just look."

With the windows clean, they could see the living room clearly. The fireplace was the same, but there were new black iron fire tools on the hearth. The cherry secretary was still there, waxed and gleaming, but the sheet-draped couches and chairs had been replaced with wooden-armed chairs and settees with bright flowered cushions. The late sunshine lay in squares of orange light on the polished floor.

Cassie sighed. It was such a pretty room, such a bright room. "Granny," she said, "did they change the little girl's room?"

"My land, child, how would I know that?"

"Can we look?"

"I guess so."

They went to the side window, but there was nothing to see. The white cloth was still fastened over the window.

"Well," Granny said, "if that don't beat all! A nice place like this and they got one room shut off."

"Why? Granny, why would they—"

"Come along home now, child. We've wasted too much time already."

"Please, Granny, can we go see the ducks?"

"No, child, I got work to do." Granny glanced at Steele's lodge and then at Cassie. "Well, lookin's free, ain't it? Come on."

The mallards were there, swimming up and down the pond and dipping their heads into the water to feed. Cassie stood on the bridge, holding her grandmother's hand.

"Ain't they nice, Granny? Ain't they the prettiest things? I wish they'd settle down and live here all the time."

"Looks to me like some of them is goin' to die here. Look yonder, in the reeds. Them fellows from town built Mr. Steele a duck blind."

Cassie peered downstream and finally spotted the blind, a low structure covered with the same reeds that grew around it. "What's it for, Granny? What's a blind for?"

"It's like a little room, child, with a wood floor and a wood bench. Mr. Steele and them will set out their decoys and hide in the blind."

"What's decoys?"

"My land, child, the questions you ask! Decoys is wood ducks, carved and painted to look like real. They'll put them out there to float and when the live ducks come looking for a place to rest and feed, they'll think them decoys are real and it's safe, so they'll come in to land."

"What do the men in the blind do?"

"For goodness' sake! They shoot them a mess of duck, that's what. Mallards make mighty good eatin'."

"Oh, no, Granny! They can't do that!"

Granny sighed. "Child, there's somethin' you got to get straight in your mind. Mr. Steele owns this land, don't he? He can do anything he's a mind to. Ain't nothin' you can do about it, ain't nothin' I can do. He owns the land. Come along now, we got to get ourselves home."

In spite of her hurry, Granny stopped in front of the lodge. "A shame," she said bitterly. "It's a cryin' shame. There's people hungry and run off from their homes, and Mr. Steele can make him a playhouse like this. Howard was right. It's just a toy."

THE DAY BEFORE Thanksgiving was a red-letter day at Turner School. Miss Bencher had begged treats for the children from a Ballard grocer who had Halloween leftovers, and she gave each pupil a small pleated paper cup filled with tiny candy pumpkins.

The children spent most of the lunch hour counting their pumpkins and deciding whether to eat each one slowly or to gobble all of them down in an orgy of sweetness.

Bobby Sue gobbled and then whined for the rest of the day while her big sister ostentatiously ate her pumpkins one at a time.

Cassie wanted to gobble, resisted, but at last gave in and crammed her mouth with pumpkins. She forced herself to save one to eat at home with Francine and Mary Priscilla.

She skipped across the bridge, and was almost to Mr. Steele's lodge when she smelled hickory smoke. She crossed the road and hid behind the big sugar maple near the house. A bluejay complained in metallic squawks, but Cassie was watching the smoke curl up from the fieldstone chimney.

The front door slammed open and two boys ran out. One had a shock of black hair that fell across his high forehead almost to his deep-set black eyes. The other boy was almost grown, and had light brown hair that curled above his ears.

Cassie had never seen such clothes. The big one wore dark wool trousers and a thick red sweater over a white shirt and a red necktie. The dark-haired boy was in brown knickers and thick blue socks that matched his heavy sweater. She glanced down at her torn sweater and faded print dress and bare legs scarred from chigger bites and blue-tinged from the chill in the woods.

The younger boy set a tin can on a stump near the road and they took turns shooting at it with a light rifle. The big boy fired five times before he hit the can and sent it spinning in the air.

"Huh!"

Cassie whirled around. "Bo! What are you doin'—doing here?"

"Same as you," he muttered. "Watchin' them boys. Bastards can't shoot worth a damn."

Cassie gasped. "You better not let Granny hear you talk that way!"

"Ain't fixin' to. And you ain't goin' to tell on me, you hear?"

Then it was the younger boy's turn. He was a better shot than his brother. He took his time aiming and instead of jerking the trigger he squeezed it. They argued about whose turn it was, and how many shots each should get, but neither of them seemed to be angry. They were just playing around, Cassie thought, just having themselves some fun.

She became aware that the gray November dusk was closing in and knew that she should go home, but she wanted to watch the boys. She wanted to see what made their lives so different from hers.

The door of the lodge opened and a small woman came out to the shadowed veranda. Cassie could not see her face clearly, but the lamplight behind the woman backlit her curly brown hair so that it glowed. She wore a red dress and a neat bib apron and she looked exactly the way a mother should look.

"Jimmy, Dixon," she called. "It's almost time for dinner."

The big boy propped the rifle against the veranda and went into the house, but the dark-haired boy stayed behind, gazing up at the sky. Cassie looked up, too, at a lavender sky changing to purple toward the Ozarks, but then she saw that the boy had turned and was looking right at her. She gasped and tensed herself to run until she realized that he could not see her in the woods. She could see him, though. She could see his dark eyes.

"Dixon!" Mr. Steele's voice was rough. "Your mother called you!"

The boy ran toward the house. "I'm coming, Dad!"

Cassie stared at the windows, yellow rectangles of light, and wondered what was happening inside. What would they do next? Would they go into the living room and sit around the fire? What would they eat for dinner, those boys with warm pants and heavy sweaters? Black-eyed peas and cornbread spread with lard? What would they say? Would they laugh? They were as foreign to her as Dick and Jane and Spot.

Bo grunted and for once Cassie felt a kinship for her half brother. They were together in the cold dusk, outsiders. She tugged his arm. "We got to get home!"

"Well, go on, then."

Cassie ran, but Granny met her on the road. "Where you been, girl?"

"There's people at the lodge! Two boys and a mother. I was in the woods and I seen—saw them!"

Her grandmother frowned. "You been spyin' on folks like you didn't have no bringin'-up! Missy, I'm goin' to warm your bottom for you!"

When Cassie saw Granny's angry face in the lamplight, she remembered that she still carried the little pleated paper cup in her hand. "Don't be mad. Look here what I brought you from school."

Granny sniffed, but when she opened the cup her face changed from anger to pleased surprise.

"Teacher gave us the candies, but I saved one for you, Granny."

"Well, my sweet girl. My sweet Cassie."

Cassie moved into her grandmother's arms but she was not comfortable because Granny had always said that she was never to tell lies. She had not saved that pumpkin for Granny to eat. She had meant to eat it herself. Although she did not hurt the Steeles by watching them, she almost got a spanking. Then she lied to Granny and was hugged. It was very confusing, she thought, to be eight years old.

ON THANKSGIVING MORNING Cassie woke to her grandmother's call: "Cassie! Come out to the porch and see what somebody brought you!"

Granny bent down and took something red from a cardboard carton. "Look at this sweater, child!" She turned it this way and that. "It's a mite worn, but there ain't a hole in it."

Cassie tugged the sweater on over her shift. It was the warmest thing she had ever worn. "Granny, there's more!"

Her grandmother took a book from the box. "My land, a second-grade reader. I reckon somebody brought me a book to read."

Cassie looked up, disappointed, but Granny's eyes twinkled. "I was just funnin' you, child. That book is for you."

On the cover of the book was a picture of a boy riding on the back of a giant honeybee. Cassie opened it to the first story, "The Straw Ox," facing a picture of a bear and a black-streaked cow. "Granny, I can read it! I can read this book! Did Santa Claus come?"

"More like to be Mr. Steele and them."

Cassie ran to the back room and jumped into bed. She pulled Francine and Mary Priscilla under the covers, into a dark warm tent. "You see this here book?" she whispered. "This book is mine to keep!"

After breakfast, Cassie lay on the floor, reading her book and half listening to her father and grandmother talk.

"It was mighty nice of Mr. Steele to bring them things, Howard."

He grunted. "If you like charity."

"Cassie needed that sweater, and we ain't got the money for it. We're just barely gettin' by, as it is."

"Yeah." He probed a molar with a matchstick. "I been thinkin' about headin' out for California. They say everybody gets work out there."

"They say, they say! That's all it is, just talk. How you fixin' to get the money together to take four of us out—"

"Three." He grinned unpleasantly. "Me and Bo and Cassie. No point haulin' a old woman along. They got the poor farm for folks like you."

When she heard the pickup rattle down the hill, Granny sank back in her chair. "Oh, Lord, what's there to do now?"

"Can we go to California, Granny? Can we? Can we eat oranges and—"

"Hush, missy. I got to think."

"Granny, my book says the old woman and the old man live in a little hut. What's a hut?"

Granny looked at the newspapers tacked on the wall and the bedroll in the corner and the worn-out oilcloth on the table. "I reckon you're lookin' at one, child." She rubbed her hand over her eyes. "But it's our place, where a body can stay put and not be—" She stopped, looking down at the child. "There might be a way," she said softly. She pushed herself up from her chair. "Cassie, you get yourself washed up. And do a good job on your neck, hear? Make haste now, child. We got to go visitin'."

Granny marched down the road with her faded velvet hat set square on her head. She squeezed Cassie's hand. "You remember what I taught you? Say it again so I know you got it right. I want them folks to know that you ain't half-wild like most of the croppers' children."

"Yes'm. 'Mr. Steele, sir, I'm much obliged to you for the nice sweater and the—and the *Bobbs-Merrill Second Reader*. I ain't never had a book of my own before.' "

"Don't say 'ain't.' Just say, 'I never had a book of my own.' "

"That's what Miss Bencher says, but you say 'ain't' yourself, Granny. You say it all the time."

"I ain't—I'm not tellin' you what I say, missy, I'm tellin' you what you've got to say!"

Granny led Cassie across the yellow stubble of the yard and knocked on a veranda post. The big boy opened the door.

Granny cleared her throat. "Please, is your papa to home? Me and the girl, we come to speak with him."

The boy turned, holding the door, and called, "Dad? There's a— there are some people to see you."

The mother came outside. In the shadow on the veranda, her hair was a mousy brown, but she was beautiful to Cassie. "May I help you?"

"Yes'm. We come to thank you for the them things you sent over."

Mr. Steele came out. "Happy Thanksgiving to you, Mrs. Hendricks."

Granny stood straighter. "Yes, sir, and the same to you."

"Let me introduce my wife, Amelia, and my son Jimmy." The smaller boy came around the corner of the house. "And my younger son, Dixon."

Mrs. Steele and the older boy nodded from the veranda, but Dixon came to Granny. "I'm pleased to meet you, ma'am."

Granny pushed Cassie's shoulder. "Cassie's got somethin' to say."

Cassie opened her mouth but not a word came out.

Mr. Steele laughed. "I'm afraid the cat's got her tongue again."

Cassie's face was hot, but she set her feet firmly in the stubble and said, "Mr. Steele, I'm much obliged to you for the nice sweater and for the—and for the *Bobbs-Merrill Second Reader*." She bit her lip. Granny had told her more to say, but she had forgotten it. She tried to find other words. "I already read the first story, about the little old woman and the little old man that lived in a hut like our hut yonder and—"

The curly-haired boy snorted with laughter. Cassie stared at him. She did not think she had said anything funny.

Mr. Steele smiled. "Are you a good reader, Cassie?"

Granny answered him. "Her teacher says she's the best reader in Turner School. Says Cassie's real smart."

The mother and the big boy walked to the other end of the veranda, and Granny looked up at the man above her. "Mr. Steele, Howard is makin' talk about headin' out for California."

"Foolish talk, Mrs. Hendricks. Times are bad in California, too."

"If Howard could make a livin' he wouldn't be so all-fired eager to go west. I reckon he'd stay on. Mr. Steele, a smart little girl like

Cassie here, she's got a chance to get ahead if she don't get took out of school. She's got good blood, Mr. Steele, real good blood on her mama's side. But I reckon you remember Cassie's mama, Mr. Steele, I reckon you ain't likely to forget Leona Taylor and what she did for you."

Mr. Steele flushed. "Now, look here——"

Mrs. Steele came back. "I must see to the turkey."

Mr. Steele watched her walk across the veranda and into the house. The big boy followed her. "Mrs. Hendricks," Mr. Steele said, "you're quite a gambler."

Granny looked straight at him. "No, sir, Mr. Steele. I figure you for a man that knows what's fair."

He nodded, once. "All right."

Granny sighed. "I thank you, Mr. Steele. I surely do."

"Dad? Is everything all right?"

Cassie had forgotten that Dixon Steele was still in the yard.

"Yes, son. Mrs. Hendricks has just seen fit to remind me of an obligation." He smiled at Granny, shaking his head. "By God, you've got grit, woman! There aren't many who will tangle with James Steele!"

To Cassie's surprise, her grandmother laughed softly. "Yes, sir, Mr. Steele. Yes, sir, I reckon that's so."

"Dad?" the boy said again. "Is it okay if I get some cookies for the little girl?"

"Of course, Dix. Go to your mother."

The boy ran up on the veranda and in a few minutes was back with a stack of cookies wrapped in waxed paper. "Here," he said.

Overcome by shyness, Cassie looked at the ground and then wished that she had not. She saw his sturdy brown leather shoes, but she also saw her shapeless old high-top shoes, covered with ground-in red dirt and too short for her. "I thank you," she whispered.

"You're welcome. How old are you, anyway?"

"Eight. Goin' on nine." She risked a look at him. He had a friendly smile. "How old are you?"

"Oh, I'm almost twelve, lots older than you."

"Well, that don't make me a little girl, just because you're——" She stopped abruptly as she realized that the cookies were warming her hands. "These things are hot!"

"Yeah, my mother just took them out of the oven. Go ahead, eat them while they're warm."

She glanced at Granny, who was talking quietly with Mr. Steele. "I reckon I'll wait," she said.

He laughed. "Then I guess you aren't a little girl after all. Most little girls can't wait to eat their cookies."

Cassie ran to take Granny's hand, but she looked back at the boy and smiled at him shyly. Dix, she thought. His name was Dixon Steele.

On the way home Granny and Cassie ate the sugar cookies. "Now, ain't this fine?" Granny said. "Walkin' along here, eatin' cookies, just like rich folks."

When they passed the lone chimney Cassie tightened her grip on her grandmother's hand. "Granny? Did I say it right? Did I do right?"

Her grandmother patted her shoulder. "You did fine, child. You did just fine." She said softly, to herself rather than Cassie, "I've worked, I've worked hard all my life, but I never stooped to this before."

"Granny, what was that you was sayin' about Mama?"

"Mr. Steele's little daughter died, child, from a bad fall, they said, but your mama told me she talked to the doctor afterwards and he said it was Mr. Steele that—" She stopped and looked at Cassie, measuring her. "They called your mama to help and she sent for the doctor, but it was too late. Wasn't nothin' nobody could do."

Cassie remembered the first time she had looked in the windows of the lodge, before the white cloth had been put in place, and saw what she thought was a dead baby. She knew what "too late" meant. "It was her room, wasn't it, Granny? It was that little girl's room."

"Yes, child. Yes, it was. Her name was Julia."

CASSIE DAWDLED on the way back from the spring that afternoon, kicking through the dead leaves. When she saw Mr. Steele's car she slipped into the front room to stand by Granny. Mr. Steele and her father were at the table, across from each other.

"Taylor, you've heard that I put tractors on the hill farm?"

"Yes, sir," Howard said, "I heard that."

"I've got one for this place, too, and have hired a man to drive it. He'll pull out the scrub and turn the bottom land into one big field."

"Don't hardly see how you can afford to do that, Mr. Steele. Not with cotton at five cents a pound."

Steele laughed. "You don't understand this New Deal crowd in Washington. I'll put the land to peanuts and they'll pay me for the cotton I don't grow and give me a soil conservation bonus along with it."

"Well, sir, they say you been buyin' up farms for the taxes. You want me to farm one of them other places for you?"

"No, I have a proposition for you, Taylor. I'll pay you a salary to be the caretaker for my lodge. You can live here, but I want you to watch my place, keep an eye out for tramps and that sort of thing."

Howard grinned. "Yes, sir!"

"I want you to keep the place stocked with firewood, too, and to clean it when we're coming down from Ballard. Wax the floors, wash windows and the like."

"That there's woman's work, Mr. Steele. I ain't no housecleaner. I'm a farmer. I got me a mule and—"

"You're behind the times, Taylor. Farming isn't a man and a mule these days. It's a business."

"Woman's work," Howard said stubbornly. "I ain't a man to—"

Mr. Steele scowled and his heavy brows formed a solid black bar across his face. "That's enough of that talk!"

"He didn't mean no disrespect," Granny said hastily. "Howard never meant to argue with you, Mr. Steele."

Steele stood up with his fists clenched at his sides. Cassie ducked behind her grandmother, afraid that he was going to strike out at someone and that he would not much care who it was. His voice, however, was tight but controlled. "The way things are now, no landowner is going to take on a new tenant. But if you don't want a paying job, I know damn well that I won't have any trouble finding a man who does."

Granny clasped her hands. "Howard, you just got to take it!"

Howard Taylor looked at her, and then at Cassie. "Yes, sir," he said softly. "I reckon I'll take the job, sir."

Mr. Steele smiled. "Just remember that there are good men looking for work now." He looked at Howard's torn faded overalls and ragged work shirt. "And, Howard, if you're to help out with my guests you'll have to get yourself cleaned up. I'll give you money for some decent clothes. Come to the lodge in half an hour and I'll give you a list of clothing to buy and of the work I want done."

Cassie stared at Mr. Steele. He looked like other men but, he was the one who decided whether people could stay on their farms or had to go to California. She knew why. It was because he owned the land.

Howard watched the car ease its way down the rough track. "You hear that? You hear him call me Howard like I ain't even got a last name? I ain't goin' to be no better off than a nigger slave!"

"You're better off than most men around here, Howard Taylor," Granny said sharply. "There's folks starvin' in these hills and he's givin' you a job that pays cash money and a house to live in."

"Woman's work! By God, I'm goin' to California anyway!"

"You got children to feed, man! You get yourself down there before Mr. Steele takes a notion to give that job to somebody else."

Howard grabbed his stained felt hat and went out, slamming the door.

Granny sank down on a chair. "Thank the Lord!" She hugged Cassie. "That pride of Howard's! I thought he was goin' to turn down the job."

"It's like you read me from the Bible: Pride goeth before a fall."

"There's pride and there's pride, missy. Your papa's is empty pride, like a dead branch on an oak tree. It looks fine, but the first strong wind will break it and bring it down. The other kind of pride is like a cedar tree bendin' under a load of snow. Soon as the snow melts, that cedar will stand up strong. That kind of pride is knowin' yourself, and knowin' that inside you there's strength. You got to have that, child." She held Cassie's shoulders and looked into her eyes. "God knows you're goin' to need it."

Chapter 5

BY FEBRUARY OF 1934 James Steele had sent two more boxes of clothing to the Taylor family. There were three school dresses for Cassie and a warm, if worn, winter coat. There was a dark blue mackinaw jacket and a cap for Bo. There was a black overcoat in one of the boxes, a coat that looked oddly citified over Howard's khakis, and there were two dark print dresses and a heavy purple cardigan sweater for Granny. Cassie could not remember having seen her grandmother so pleased.

"My law," she said. "My law, if that ain't the prettiest color!"

They needed warm clothes that winter. It was spitting snow on the Saturday night when Howard came back from town and slammed open the front door. The collar of his overcoat was turned up and his eyes were glittering with excitement.

"Bo! Where's Bo?"

Granny looked up from her Bible. "I thought he went into town with you, Howard."

"No, couldn't find him. But by God, I got to find him now! Me and him got to head north with the others!"

Cassie put down her arithmetic book. "Where are you going, Papa? Can I go?"

"This here is men's work, girl! We're goin' after Pretty Boy Floyd!"

Granny pushed her chair back from the table. "You been drinkin' again, Howard."

"Hell, yes! Listen, the deputies stopped me on the road, stoppin' everybody that comes by so they can keep other outlaws from gettin' up there to help Pretty Boy. They say he's holed up near Peggs, north of Tahlequah, and me and Bo, we got to get up there and——"

"Get up where, Paw?" Bo slipped into the room as quietly as a weasel.

Granny stood up. "Howard Taylor, have you lost your mind? You want to take that boy and go chasin' through the night? You'll get yourself shot, that's what you'll do!"

"Damn it, woman, I'm talkin' about Pretty Boy Floyd! They're fixin' to gun that boy down, and I aim to see it! Listen, there's cars all up and down the highway, deputies and police and somebody said the governor's goin' to call out the National Guard!"

Granny sat down and took up her Bible with shaking hands. "Then they surefire don't need you, Howard. You ain't even got a gun."

Cassie glanced at Bo, but he did not say anything.

Howard slammed his old hat on the table. "Gun or not, I'm goin'. This here's the biggest thing that ever happened around here!"

Granny looked down at her Bible. "What's Mr. Steele goin' to say? Roads full of cars, outlaws loose and roaming the countryside. What's he goin' to say if somebody breaks into his place and he finds out you was out chasin' Pretty Boy Floyd?"

"Hell, how would he know I was——" Howard stopped abruptly and scowled at her. "You'd tell him, wouldn't you? By God, you'd tell him."

Granny put her hand on the Bible. "It's my Christian duty, ain't it? 'Let the laborer be worthy of his hire.' "

Howard rubbed his face. "I know you, you'd do it. God damn it, woman, you can't run my life! Someday I'm goin' to——"

"You're goin' to what, Howard?"

"You'll see, God damn it! You'll see! Come on, Bo." He jerked the door open. "Maybe we can't go look for Pretty Boy, but we sure as hell can get down to town where they got a radio. Come on!"

Cassie heard the pickup rattle down the track, but she did not look up from her homework. It was several minutes before Granny spoke.

"I had to do it, Cassie. You can see that, can't you? If anything was to happen to your papa, you and me would be——"

"Yes'm," Cassie said.

Granny pushed the Bible away. "There's some things that ain't in the Good Book, child, and you better remember it. God helps them as helps themselves."

"Yes'm," Cassie said again. "Yes'm."

PRETTY BOY FLOYD was not gunned down that cold February night in the Cookson Hills, but in the fall of 1934 Melvin H. Purvis and his men traced Charles "Pretty Boy" Floyd to a farm seven miles north of East Liverpool, Ohio, and shot him dead. The body was shipped to Oklahoma for burial.

Granny was raveling out an old sweater for knitting wool when Howard brought the news from San Bois. "I met his poor mama down in Sallisaw, when he was only a boy. They lived out on Brush Mountain." She shook her head sadly. "They called him Choc, then, not Pretty Boy."

"But he was an outlaw, wasn't he?" Cassie said. "He robbed banks."

"Oh my, yes! But he helped a lot of folks, and when the time come, they helped him, too. Fed him, hid him from the law if they could. Folks liked Pretty Boy."

The hill people of Eastern Oklahoma liked Pretty Boy because he was an outlaw. He robbed the banks, the soft-handed men in business suits who foreclosed on land and crop mortgages. To the hill people, the law meant the hard-eyed deputies who evicted the poor from their shacks and sent them off to wander the barren land, and Pretty Boy Floyd was one of the people, a boy from Brush Mountain who grew up to be a man who fought the system. But Pretty Boy died and the system lived and the hard times continued. There were food riots in Oklahoma City in the spring of 1935, and over in Missouri three hundred farmers brandished rakes and hoes to try to keep a federal bailiff from foreclosing a farm mortgage. And in the summer of 1935, the cotton crop failed again. Depression, disorder and drought ruled the land.

With steady money coming in from Howard's job and with the boxes the Steeles left from time to time, Cassie's family was better off than most of their neighbors. Still, there were no presents for Cassie's eleventh birthday in April 1936. Her father's spare cash went to the bootlegger in San Bois.

That summer was a backbreaker. Each morning Granny went outside, looked up at the cloudless sky and shook her head. She pressed the family into hauling water for her garden, but the spring in the grotto was only a trickle. For eighty-three straight days there was no rain, and heat records were broken all over the state. In Tulsa the thermometer hit 115, but it had already been up to 120 in Nowata. Crops withered in the merciless sun, and the paved country roads cracked open when the bone-dry subsoil split and crumbled.

Granny suffered in the heat and Cassie took over more and more of the chores around the house. Bo was usually off on his own, and Howard Taylor spent his time in San Bois.

One night in August, however, Howard was sitting at the table, taking an occasional pull at a fruit jar of corn whiskey. Cassie lay on the floor reading by the yellow light of the kerosene lamp.

Granny put down her darning. "Howard? I been thinkin' on it, and I've a mind to go to the Old-Timers' reunion next Sunday."

"How was you plannin' to get there, old woman? Ride shank's mare?"

"I figure you could take me in your truck. Me and Cassie. Reckon you'd see some friends of yours there."

"Reckon I might, at that."

Cassie looked up from her book. "What's Old-Timers?"

"It's for folks that settled here before statehood, child, before 1907. They get together to talk about the old days, and have a prayer meetin' and a picnic and lots of hymns. What they call all-day singin' and dinner on the ground. Won't be just old folks, though. Everybody goes, young and old."

Cassie jumped up. "Papa, can we go? Please can we go? I never been to a singin'!"

"Might as well. Ain't nothin' goin' on around here. We'll take Bo, too."

The next Sunday morning Cassie woke to the smell of frying chicken and the discomfort of knotted rags in her hair. She ran into the front room, where Granny was already dressed in her best dress, a dark blue print from one of the Steeles' boxes, and her good shoes, laced-up oxfords that were only slightly run-over at the heels. Howard was there, too, clean-shaven and wearing the khaki shirt and pants Mr. Steele had ordained. Bo refused to go.

Cassie put on her own clothes, a pale blue dress Granny had starched stiff. She wore her school shoes, scuffed brown sandals, and clean blue socks to match her dress. She was all bones that year, but when her grandmother took out the rags, her fine blond hair curled around her face and softened her jutting cheekbones.

Howard drove the old pickup and Granny sat with her chin held high and her velvet hat as square on her head as a military helmet. Cassie bounced on the seat between them. "How far is it now, Granny? Papa, are we almost there?"

"You settle down," he said. "We'll get there when we get there."

When the truck clattered across a wooden bridge, Cassie leaned across Granny's lap to look down at the slow shallow river flowing gray-green against banks of yellow sand.

"Look yonder, child," her grandmother said. "There's the church."

Shady Grove Church stood on a rounded knoll surrounded by dried-up cornfields, a white frame building as simple as a child's drawing, foursquare and without complication.

As they climbed down from the truck, a heavyset old woman hurried to meet them. "Sister Hendricks! As I live and breathe! You are a sight for sore eyes!"

Granny answered in a shy, formal voice. "Well, Sister Campbell, we thought we might as well come on over and see how you folks been keepin'."

Howard carried their food to an elm grove where a woman added it to the dishes spread out on checked tablecloths under the trees. There were other platters of fried chicken, bowls of potato salad, jars of homemade pickles, peach cobblers and pies, shrouded against the flies with dish towels made of bleached flour sacks.

Granny pushed Cassie forward. "This here's my grandchild, Cassie."

Mrs. Campbell gathered Cassie to her large soft bosom, into the smell of warm flesh and lilac powder. "And how old is this little one?"

"Eleven," Granny said.

"Going on twelve," Cassie said.

"Well." Sister Campbell gave her a moist kiss and released her.

Granny pushed Cassie's shoulder. "You run along and play, missy, but come back when the bell rings for the first service."

Granny and Sister Campbell joined the other ladies on folding wooden chairs set in the shade of the trees, and fanned themselves delicately with paper fans imprinted *Ochuleta Funeral Home*. One younger woman sat with them, a swarthy girl with a chubby fair-haired baby. She blew in his face and he gurgled and laughed.

Cassie backed away, and someone grabbed her arm with a strong rough hand. "Hey, Cassie, what you doin' here?"

She spun around. "Bob Johnson?" She wanted to say something clever, like "What you doin' here yourself?" but she was overcome by shyness. Bob was fourteen, one of the big boys who had missed so much school for plowing and cotton picking that he was a year behind. He had a shock of red hair and a face covered with freckles. The smaller, dark-haired boy behind him also wore faded overalls.

"I come with my grandmother and my papa," Cassie said.

"Howard Taylor's your papa, ain't he? There's Taylors on my mama's side. Reckon you and me is some kind of cousins."

The smaller boy snickered. "Hey, Bob, that makes you-uns kissin' cousins! Ain't you goin' to kiss her?"

"Cut that out, George!" Bob threw himself on the other boy and they scuffled on the ground. Cassie backed away but the boys got up laughing. "This here's George," Bob said. "Come on, we'll show you around."

Cassie followed the boys. At the back of the church she saw her father talking to some men.

George ran off, and Bob and Cassie sat down on the slanting trapdoor of the storm cellar. He untied his high-top work shoes. "Let's us get rid of these."

"I think Granny wants me to stay dressed up."

"Once they get to talkin' they don't see you. Hey, look there!" A thin gray lizard with a blue tail skittered across the planks. Bob lunged and slapped his hand on the door, but the lizard was gone, a flash of blue disappearing down a crack. "Heckfire! Listen, you catch one of them little boogers by the tail and you know what happens? His tail breaks right off in your hand, just his blue tail, and his front part runs away."

"With no tail? Won't he die?"

Bob whispered dramatically, "He grows hisself a new one. Can you figure that out? Just goes off and grows hisself a new tail." He tossed his shoes into the weeds. "Come on, let's go!"

Cassie followed him, slowly at first, then faster and faster until her bare feet flew across the dry grass. They darted among the clumps of adults, as unnoticed as the flies buzzing around the food. They peeked through a crack in the wall of the church to watch dust motes drifting down the slanting beams of sunlight. They crawled up behind the ladies in the grove to listen to the hushed mysterious talk of woman things, of fevers and births and deaths.

The church bell gave a cracked, hollow clang and Bob ran to find his family. Cassie ran to get her shoes and then waited for Granny near the elm grove. Her father and a man in overalls passed her and went into the trees.

The ladies came, smoothing their skirts and setting their hats, and Granny led Cassie to a pew inside the church.

Sister Campbell arranged herself on the organ bench, pumped her feet and drew out a long, tremulous chord. A gaunt old man in a dusty black suit stepped to the lectern and raised his hands. His harsh voice rose and the congregation joined in the hymn.

> *"Shall we gather at the river,*
> *Where bright angel feet have trod . . ."*

The old man's hoarse voice carried above the others. He waved his hands and the people swayed while Sister Campbell bobbed her head and pumped her feet.

> *"Yes, we'll gather at the river,*
> *The beautiful, the beautiful river;*
> *Gather with the saints at the river*
> *That flows by the throne of God."*

The organ died with a wheezing sigh and the old man spoke. "Brothers and sisters, it's good to see your faces today, but other faces are missing, faces of Old-Timers who have gone on ahead, down that beautiful river of God. We pray that the Lord will . . ."

The preacher's voice blended with the rhythmic buzz of the cicadas outside the open door and Cassie, half dozing, leaned against her grandmother and looked around the church. There were gaps in the congregation. Two old ladies and then an empty space. An old man and another empty space.

Cassie began to see shadowy faces between the people in the pews, as if each empty space were filled with the memory of an Old-Timer. The people in the church began to look shadowy, too, as if they were already passing over into memory. The old man's voice was distant and it seemed that she could see through his face to the rough boards of the wall behind him. She looked up at her grandmother for reassurance, but Granny was an Old-Timer, too, and was fading away even as Cassie watched.

Cassie clutched at her grandmother's arm, but the flesh was soft and yielding, melting in her grasp. She felt dizzy, as if everything were floating and the safe solidity of her life were falling away. She shivered in the still, buzzing heat of the church. Her father was not there, and in her mind he, too, was shifting and changing. She wanted to cry out, to call to him, "Wait, Papa! Wait for me!" She huddled against her grandmother's side and put her hands over her eyes to close out the vision.

The congregation began the second verse of the hymn and the old man's voice, no longer harsh, rose above the others in a high sweet tenor.

> *"On the margin of the river*
> *Washin' up its silver spray . . ."*

And then Cassie saw that river. She saw it flowing gray-green against the banks of golden sand, and on the river she saw a raft. And the people were on the raft, the shadowy faces. Her father, raising his fruit jar in salute, and her grandmother and Sister Campbell, humming softly and waving their Ochuleta Funeral Home fans. The old man, leading the singing. Red-haired Bob and Cassie herself, her blond curls bouncing in time to the hymn. Even the blue-tailed lizard, even the fair-haired baby, laughing with delight at the breeze of their passing. They sang together as they floated down the river that went from here to there, from now to then and on to forever. And there was no beginning and no ending, only the water flowing down the gray-green river to the sea, rising to the clouds and falling in rain to form the river again, only the great slow turning of time.

She knew then that she was safe, a part of it. A part of everything.

"Yes, we'll gather at the river,
The beautiful, the beautiful river . . ."

Granny patted her leg and Cassie could see the hand and could feel its weight on her leg. It was solid. Liver-spotted skin, swollen knuckles. She touched the hand and felt its dry warmth. She looked up at her grandmother's face, firm beneath the square-set blue velvet hat, and she was overcome by joy.

"Granny?" she whispered. "Granny?"

"Hush, child," her grandmother said, but she put her arm around Cassie and pulled her close. "Hush, now."

TWO MORE WEEKS without rain. The evening was as hot as the afternoon, and the air was close. Even the cicadas were quiet. Only the occasional cry of a nightbird broke the silence.

Howard did not get home for supper. Bo was there, but he was as sullen as the weather and left as soon as he had finished eating.

Howard was not home at bedtime, either, but deep in the night Cassie was awakened by the sound of someone stumbling across the front porch. Her grandmother lay still beside her, but Cassie knew that she was awake.

"Bo?" Granny called. "Is that you out there?"

"It's me. Howard."

There were sounds in the front room: a clink of glass, a muttered curse and the scratch of a match. Granny raised herself on her elbow. "Howard, what are you up to in there?"

"Tryin' to light this God damn lamp, that's what."

Granny sighed and eased her legs out of bed. "Wait, I'll help you." She pulled on her wrapper, and Cassie slipped out of bed and followed her. Just as they went into the front room the lamp flared up. Granny hurried to the table and adjusted the wick. "What do you think you're doin'!"

Howard slumped onto a chair and put his head on the table.

"Howard Taylor, you are drunk as a coot! You could have burned this—" Granny turned suddenly. "You, Cassie, get back in that bed!"

Cassie ran into the bedroom but crouched by the door to watch.

Howard took a long pull at his fruit jar.

"You don't need no more of that, Howard. You had enough already. What's wrong with you? Why do you drink like this?"

He took another drink. "Ain't your business, you old bitch."

Granny's voice was low and cutting. "You never called me that before, Howard Taylor. You never called me that when you was wantin' me to stay on here after my Leona died, after you killed her. Then it was 'Please, Miz Hendricks, please stay and help me to raise little Cassie.' "

"What do you say, woman? I never killed Leona!"

"You did, sir! Sure as you took a gun to her. You heard what that doctor said, how she wasn't to have no more babies after Cassie, but you couldn't hold off your ruttin' ways and you—"

"I'm a man, ain't I? A man's got needs." He lifted the jar again.

"You don't need that," she said gently. "You got a family and a—"

"I ain't got shit!"

"You watch your language! You got work and a good landlord. Ain't many can say that these days."

He laughed bitterly. "I got me a good landlord, sure, a man that gives me old clothes and woman's work instead of land to farm. I'm goin' to get out of here, by God. I'm goin' to California!"

Granny straightened and rubbed the small of her back. "California, again. And how you goin' to get travelin' money together, drinkin' up every cent you get hold of?" She pointed to the fruit jar in his hand. "That's your California, Howard. There, in that jar. That's all the California you're ever goin' to see."

Howard shook his head as if to clear it. "Old woman, go to bed."

"I'm gone, Howard. I'm gone."

Cassie slipped back into bed and closed her eyes, but long after her grandmother was asleep she lay awake and stared into the darkness.

HOWARD AND GRANNY maintained an uneasy truce through the fall of 1936. Howard helped with Mr. Steele's hunting parties. Cassie asked him about the men from town, what they looked like and what they talked about, but he remembered only the ones who tipped him with bottles of bourbon.

The cold bothered Granny that winter. She pulled her rocking chair close to the cookstove and fussed at Bo to bring in more firewood, but Bo was seldom home. Cassie suspected that he hid out in the hills behind the lodge. And she herself was busy. Miss Bencher was pushing her at school, giving her extra homework and bringing her books from the town library.

In November Howard bought an old shotgun, and after that he was often out hunting for two or three days at a time. He was home, however, the night the car came. The three of them had just sat down to a supper of fried okra and cornbread when they heard the engine straining to climb the hill. Howard went to the door. "By God, it's Bo and he's got him a car!"

It was not much of a car, a Model A Ford that looked as if it had gone through as many wrecks as it had years. One fender was gone and another was barely hanging on.

Granny put her hands on her hips. "Did you steal that car, Bo?"

"Fine thing to say to your own grandson, old woman!"

"He's no grandson of mine, Howard. That boy's got bad blood!"

"I traded for it," Bo said sullenly. "A old boy up to Archers."

Granny took Cassie into the house. "That Bo is goin' to get us into a mess, sure as I'm standin' here. There's trouble ahead, Cassie, bad trouble." She sat down in her rocking chair.

Cassie laid a shawl on Granny's shoulders. "That's prophesyin', ain't—isn't it?" She giggled. "I reckon you're just like Cassandra."

Granny shook her head. "No, missy, it ain't prophesyin'. I'm just statin' the facts of it. The true facts."

Trouble was not long in coming. On a Saturday morning in late March, a black and white Plymouth sedan pulled into the dooryard.

"Damn," Howard said. "It's the deputy sheriff!"

Granny's hand went to her heart. "Lord have mercy! Bo!"

"Stop it, woman! Keep your mouth shut, hear? I'll talk to them."

"You, missy," Granny whispered, "whatever I say, you back me up."

Two men stood by the car, the short, scrawny driver and his passenger, a big beefy man with a red face and hard gray eyes. They wore khakis and broad-brimmed gray hats and holsters.

Howard stepped down from the porch. "How do, Skeet, Bob. Anything I can do for you boys?"

"This here's official business, Howard," the big man said. "Where's that boy of yours?"

Granny caught her breath, but she walked quietly across the porch and sat down on a straight chair. Cassie dropped to the floor at her knee.

"Well, Skeet, he ain't to home right now. Likely out huntin'."

"Mr. Deputy? What was it you wanted to see the child about?" Granny's voice sounded old and weak, not like her normal voice.

"There was some trouble down in San Bois, ma'am."

"Why, the boy don't hardly go down there, lessen he's with his paw. When was it?"

"Night before last. Thursday night, long about suppertime."

Cassie knew that Bo had not been home since Wednesday, but Granny's knee nudged her with a clear message to be quiet.

Granny laughed, an old woman's cackle. "Well, it ain't our Bo you're lookin' for. He was right here that evenin', helpin' his little sister to celebrate her birthday. Ain't that right, Cassie?"

The knee pushed her shoulder hard and Cassie knew she should not tell the deputy that her birthday was still two weeks away. "Yes, ma'am."

The deputy looked at her doubtfully. "I ought to talk to the boy."

Granny laughed again. "Little Cassie here was real mad at Bo that night because he ate so much of her birthday cake! Ain't that so, missy?"

Somehow Granny's Bible appeared near Cassie's hand and she waved her hand in its general direction. "Yes, sir. I swear it."

He laughed. "That's okay, honey, this ain't no court of law." He turned to Howard. "Sorry we bothered you."

"Hell, Skeet, wasn't no bother. Say, what was the trouble, anyway?"

"Could have been a real bad thing. This little girl was playin' outside by the porch light, girl about five years old. Somebody grabbed her and hauled her off in the bushes."

"Did he—" Howard cleared his throat. "Did he hurt her any?"

"No, she screamed like a stuck hog and it scared him off. She couldn't give much description, it bein' dusk and all, but one of the boys said it sounded kind of like your Bo."

Howard straightened his back. "Them boys in town pick on Bo because he's—" He tapped his finger on the side of his head. "You know."

"Yeah," Skeet said. "I know. Say, Howard, does Bo have a car?"

Howard's hesitation was so brief that it was hardly noticeable. "No, sir! Where would the boy get the money for a car?"

"I was just askin'." The two men drove down the hill.

Howard looked at Granny, shook his head and walked off to the shed.

"Granny? We lied to them men. You always say lying isn't right."

"Child, they was the law and Bo's your half brother. Bo's family."

Cassie stood up. "The Bible says—"

"I know what the Bible says, missy, but I know somethin' else, too. I know that God helps them that helps themselves."

Chapter 6

A DRY AUTUMN gave way to a winter of light snows that did not hold enough moisture to soften the hard ground. The sparse spring rains of 1938 ran off the land, scouring gullies in the eroded fields. The new Agricultural Adjustment Act cut farmers' allotments again, to the point where even the hardest-working tenant could no longer earn enough cash to feed his family. The lucky ones were able to get jobs with the WPA, but the others had to leave the land, and the old cars rattled west on Highway 66.

Cassie's grandmother welcomed the spring warmth, but the dry dusty winds of April made her cough until she had to fight to get her breath. On Cassie's thirteenth birthday, Granny choked until she was blue in the face. Howard took her to San Bois to see Dr. Hill.

Cassie waited for them in the dooryard. Her grandmother set pale and erect on the seat, with her old blue velvet hat and her white hair. Cassie helped her down from the truck and to her chair in the house and then ran back out to her father.

"Papa! What did the doctor say?"

"He gave her some pills, says there ain't much he can do. Ain't nothin' a doctor can do about a body gettin' old."

"She's sixty-six! That ain't so old!"

Howard shrugged. "Heart's wore out, he says. Poor food, hard work. Plumb wore out. You better take on the cookin' and whatnot."

"I will, Papa, oh, I will!"

Howard looked at her with narrowed eyes. "You're thirteen now, ain't you? Ain't no sense in your traipsin' off to school every livelong day."

Cassie caught her breath. "Give up school? But, Papa, I—"

"Gal don't need schoolin' to marry and raise a bunch of brats."

Cassie trembled with anger. For the first time, she really looked at her father: an unkempt middle-aged man with gray stubble on hollow cheeks under drink-blurred eyes, and with a belly that strained the buttons of his khaki shirt.

"Time you do some work around here, girl."

"Maybe it's time for you to do some work, too! Maybe you better put down that jug and bring some money home instead of drinking it up!"

"You, Cassie!" her father shouted. "You ain't to sass me, you hear? I'll take my belt to you!"

He grabbed at his belt buckle and Cassie turned and ran. She ran all the way to the spring, where she dropped to her knees, panting, and held her hands in the trickle of water from the hollow log. She cupped the cold water in her hands and splashed it on her burning face.

He couldn't do it, she thought. He could not make her leave school. Granny wouldn't let him. She sat back on her heels and warm tears mixed with the cold spring water on her face. The doctor said that Granny's heart was worn out. That meant Granny was going to—but Cassie could not say the word, not even in her thoughts, not even in the lonely desolation of her thoughts.

CASSIE DID NOT TELL her grandmother what her father had said about quitting school, because it would only worry her. To Cassie's relief the pills seemed to help. There was more color in Granny's cheeks, and she had fewer spells of breathlessness. Granny did not think the pills had caused the improvement. She had more faith in the spice-bush bark Cassie brought from the woods.

"My mama always said spicebush tea was good for your blood and your heart, too, child. You can see it's helpin' me."

"Yes'm, but you keep on with your pills, too."

"Oh, all right, if it takes that to make you happy."

Cassie hugged her. "Having you better, that's what will make me happy!"

IN MAY OF 1938 the student body of Turner School dropped to five students and the superintendent closed the school. The children stood with Miss Naomi Bencher and watched the workmen load the books into a truck and board up the windows of the school.

Cassie tried to comfort a first-grade boy who cried and then cried all the harder because he was not sure why he was crying.

"Billy Don, you're going to like riding that school bus to San Bois. I've seen it on the road. It will be fun, I swear it!"

There were only two seventh-graders, Cassie and Mary Martha Smith. When Mary Martha heard Cassie talking to the boy, she laughed bitterly. "It's all right for you to say, Cassie Taylor. Your daddy's got work, so you can ride that bus and go on. My paw said I got to quit school now, that I wouldn't be no help at home if I was off ridin' a bus all day long."

Cassie could not bring herself to tell Mary Martha it was not certain that Cassie would be riding the school bus. Her father had not mentioned her quitting school again, but Cassie could not be sure of anything.

Miss Naomi Bencher came up to them. "Mary Martha, I intend to have a talk with your father. You've done very good work this year, and I'm hoping that he will let you go on to San Bois School."

"Won't do no good, teacher," the girl said sullenly. "He done made up his mind. Says seventh grade's more schoolin' than a body needs nohow."

The men nailed the last board across the door of Turner School and drove away in their truck.

Miss Bencher shook hands with each of the children. "George, be sure and practice your push-pulls this summer. Your new teacher will want you to work on your handwriting." She leaned over the first-grader. "Billy Don, you'll like the new school. There will be a room full of second-graders instead of your being the only one, as you would have been here."

When she came to Mary Martha, the girl burst into tears and ran up the road.

Then there were only Cassie and Miss Bencher standing by the boarded-up schoolhouse. It was the first time Cassie noticed that she had grown as tall as her teacher.

"Well, Cassie, I must be on my way."

"Miss Bencher?" Cassie tried to think of something to talk about, anything to put off the end. "Miss Bencher, why won't you be the teacher down there in San Bois?"

"They didn't offer me a contract, Cassie. They said that I didn't have enough seniority. I have a secretarial job lined up though. It isn't teaching, but with the way things are going now, I am fortunate to find a job at all."

Cassie felt sick. Miss Naomi Bencher and her books and her blue Ford coupe were leaving forever.

"Cassie," Miss Bencher said suddenly, "get away!"

Cassie stepped back. "What?"

Miss Bencher laughed and took her hand. "I'm sorry, dear. I didn't mean to startle you. I mean, get away from here, Cassie." She waved her arm to encompass the bare barren earth of the playground, the rickety bridge over San Bois Creek and the scrub oak hills beyond it. "Get out of here. You've got the brains, Cassie." She paused and looked at the tall thin girl before her, at the blond hair braided into a long pigtail, the blue eyes and long lashes, and the faded, too-short dress. "You've got the brains, and one day you'll have the looks to go with them. Make something of yourself, Cassie Taylor."

Cassie looked down at the dusty ground. "You remember when I decided that I could prophesy, Miss Bencher? I was going to be a teacher, like you, and I was going to have my own land."

"Yes. I remember."

Cassie looked up and in the teacher's eyes she saw reflected the knowledge that was in her own. It was only a dream. It could never be more than that. There was no way that a sharecropper's daughter could go to college for a teaching certificate. The possibility of her becoming a teacher was as remote as that of her owning land.

Miss Bencher took her hand. "Cassie, think of what you have learned, of what you've done to improve your speech. At least try to get your high school diploma. And read everything you can get your hands on. Read, read, read!"

"Teacher, I—Miss Bencher—" Cassie could say no more. She turned and ran down the hill. At the bridge she looked back at the boarded-up school and the small figure of her teacher. Miss Bencher raised her hand and waved once before she went to her car. Cassie watched the blue Ford until there was nothing to see but a cloud of dust moving into the woods.

She sat down on the bridge and buried her face in her hands. It was not just losing Miss Bencher. It was not just that her schooling would probably end with Turner School. It was Papa drunk half the time and Bo getting into trouble and Granny's heart. At the thought of Granny, Cassie pushed herself to her feet.

She had to get home or Granny would try to start supper by herself. Granny needed her.

TWO WEEKS AFTER Turner School closed, Bo came in from town and told Granny that Steele had left a message for Howard at the DX station in San Bois. He was coming down to spend a few days and he wanted the lodge cleaned and aired right away.

Granny was in her rocking chair on the front porch, fanning herself. "Bo, you know your paw ain't been home for two days, and there's no tellin' when he will be here. You're goin' to have to do the job. I can ride with you in your car and show you how."

"Not me. I ain't goin' to do no housecleanin'."

Granny sighed. "You got to do it, Bo. If your paw loses his job over this—"

"Hell, old woman, I don't give a damn! I can get by. It's you that ought to be scared. It's you that's goin' to the poor farm." He laughed and climbed back into his old car.

Cassie went to the edge of the porch and watched his car go down the track to the road. "I can do it, Granny. I can clean that place up for Mr. Steele."

"Not by yourself, child. You don't know the way of cleanin' a place like that, a real house." She turned and stared out the open door as if she were looking back through the years at some other house in some other place. "But you and me together, Cassie, we can do it. Don't you let on, you hear? If Mr. Steele was to find out, he'd fire your papa for sure."

By the time they had walked down the road to the lodge, Granny was so short of breath that Cassie was frightened. She helped her to a chair at the kitchen table. "Granny, there's coffee here. I'll make you a nice cup of coffee."

Granny pressed her hand against her chest. "No, child, that wouldn't be right. That's Mr. Steele's coffee. I'll be all right. Just let me rest a spell."

She was not all right and Cassie knew it, but all she could do was clean the house and get her grandmother home to bed.

It was the first time she had been inside the house, and while her grandmother rested, Cassie explored. She had seen the living room from outside: the heavy wooden chairs and settees with flowered cushions, the tall cherry secretary and the bookshelves. She ran her hand along the spines of the books, trying to imagine what it would be like to own so many books, to be able to take any one of those hundreds of books into her hands and say, "This is mine. This is my book."

Between the living room and the kitchen there was a long dining room with an oak table and eight chairs that matched the china cabinet at the side of the room. Behind the glass doors of the cabinet were blue-and-white dishes with a Chinese scene, more dishes than Cassie had ever seen.

Four bedrooms opened off the long hall that went back to the kitchen. Three were furnished with oak bedroom suites, but the door to the fourth was padlocked. Across the hall was a bathroom, with a big tin hip bath and a rack of thick towels. Cassie stole a minute to look at herself in the first full-length mirror she had ever seen. Her long blond hair was clean from swimming in the creek. She pushed at the tendrils of hair that escaped her braid to dangle in sweat curls around her face. Her eyes were the blue of an evening sky and her long dark eyelashes gave them a look of mystery belied by the open innocence of her face. Her firm jaw showed a strong bone structure, underlying skin sunned to the color of a ripe peach. She was thin, but her hips and waist were beginning to have some shape to them, and when she pulled her scanty cotton dress tight, her small breasts pushed at the cloth. She shook her head in despair. She would never have dark hair and dark eyes and a short, womanly figure. She would never on this earth look like Miss Naomi Bencher.

Hurrying, she looked through the lodge. A beautiful house, and no one even lived in it. She remembered what her father had said long ago. "It's just a toy. Steele's toy."

Granny was still at the kitchen table, holding a rag to her mouth with a trembling, blue-veined hand. She did not look up. Cassie ached to have this be Granny's house. She would help her into one of the big soft beds and plump up the pillows and bring her spicebush tea in a blue-and-white Chinese cup. She would read to her and Granny would be her old self again.

"Cassie?" Granny tried to smile. "You'd best get to work."

To handle the cleaning supplies was a treat to a girl who had never used anything but lye soap and rags. There was a feather duster for cobwebs and a Bissell that gobbled up dust bunnies, and furniture wax scented with lavender and hand soap that smelled like flowers. She made up the beds with clean percale sheets as fine as silk. She pretended that she was making a bed for Granny, but she knew that her grandmother would never sleep on such sheets.

She went back into the kitchen. "Granny, that room, the little girl's room? There's a padlock and I can't find the key."

"Your papa told me Mr. Steele had him put on that lock and said not to bother him with no questions about it."

"But Granny, I want to—"

"No buts about it, missy." Granny straightened her shoulders. "You just put it out of your mind, you hear?"

Cassie was glad to see the color in Granny's cheeks, but she did not know how she could put the locked room out of her mind. She would bide her time until she caught Granny in a good mood, and then she would ask her about the room and about the little girl who had died.

CASSIE WATCHED Mr. Steele's car go down the road toward the lodge the next morning and felt a rush of anger, both at Steele and at her father, who had not yet come home. The walk to the lodge had tired Granny. She had slept restlessly, gasping for breath in the hot airless night. That morning she could only sit on the porch rocking and fanning herself with a tattered palmetto fan. She did not even have the strength to fuss at Cassie for doing all the chores.

When Cassie had finished the work, she made a cup of spicebush tea and took it out to her grandmother. "Granny, I reckon I'll go down to the creek to cool off. I'll be back in time to make dinner."

"You do that, child, but you just wade, hear? Don't go swimmin' in that pond, not when you're all by yourself."

Cassie was almost to the lodge when she remembered that Mr. Steele was there. She had not changed from the old dress she wore to work around the house in hot weather. It was faded and much too short, and she had ripped out the sleeves for coolness. She did not want Mr. Steele to see her looking like that. She would peek from the edge of the woods, she thought, and if she saw anyone, she would duck into the woods and bypass the lodge.

There was a car at the lodge, a green roadster with a canvas top, but no sign of life, so she walked on down the road, kicking at the dust with her bare feet.

When she was in sight of the bridge, however, she stopped. Someone was sitting on the bridge: a boy as old as Bo, seventeen or so. When he stood up she recognized him. It was Mr. Steele's younger son, the dark-haired boy she had met once on a Thanksgiving Day. He wore a two-piece bathing suit with a black-and-white-striped top cut like a man's undershirt tucked into black trunks, but his long, skinny arms and legs were bare. To Cassie he looked half naked.

She turned away, embarrassed, and started back up the hill, but he called after her. "Hey, wait up! Did you come to swim?"

Cassie hesitated, then turned back and walked slowly down the road and onto the bridge. He was watching her just as she had watched him. She smoothed her dress, very conscious of her new bosom under the thin fabric.

"The creek is low," he said, "but there are a few places where you can get wet all over." He grinned at her, his teeth a flash of white in his tanned face. "Feels great!" He jumped into the deep part of the pond and came up sputtering and flipping the wet black hair out of his eyes.

Cassie sat down on the edge of the bridge and let her dusty feet dangle in the cool water. The Steele boy sat in the shallows and looked up at her. His face was long, with heavy dark eyebrows like his father's, and the same deep-set black eyes.

"I'm Dixon Steele," he said, "but they call me Dix."

"I know. I'm Cassandra Taylor, but folks call me Cassie."

"Cassandra? Hey, that's a fancy name for a kid!"

Cassie sat up straight, forgetting her bosom. "I'm thirteen years old!" She tossed a pebble into the water. "I reckon you don't remember me. I saw you once on a Thanksgiving, when you were at the lodge."

"I remember. Dad took some things over to your house and you and your grandmother came to thank him."

"You gave me some cookies all wrapped up in wax paper, sugar cookies your mama made. They were still warm."

"Did I?" He grinned. "I remember that you said you lived in a hut."

"Still do, I reckon. My papa is your daddy's caretaker."

"Oh." He bobbed in the water. "You're thirteen? I'm seventeen, and I'll be a senior at Ballard High this fall. Where do you go to school?"

She pointed up the hill. "I did go there, to Turner School, but they closed it. I reckon I'll go on the school bus to San Bois this fall, if I'm still in school." She gave in to a sudden curiosity. "What's it like, living in town?"

Dix smiled and stood up, but only his wide bony shoulders showed above the water. "Ballard's up to twenty-five thousand people now. There are a lot of good stores and two movie theaters and some big buildings. My dad's law offices are on the sixth floor, and you can see for miles and miles. We came down this week so he can polish a brief for the state supreme court. Do you know what that is?"

"Turner School only had one room, but it had a real good teacher!"

"Okay, okay! I didn't mean to run down your school."

Cassie kicked her foot in the water. "What do you do in town?"

"In the summer I work for Dad in the mornings, running errands and stuff, and in the afternoons I hang around with the kids at the country-club pool. And sometimes I take a girl out to a movie or a dance at the club." He grinned. "But I guess you aren't interested in that stuff, since you're only thirteen."

She smiled at him politely. "I guess you know there's cotton-mouths in the creek."

"What?"

"There's cottonmouth water moccasins. Poison snakes."

In two long strides he was out on the rocky bank. "Why the heck didn't you tell me?"

Cassie smiled. "I did. I just now told you."

"No wonder you aren't swimming!"

"Oh, they won't bother you. What I do is throw some rocks in first, and make a lot of racket, and that mostly scares them away."

"Well, for Pete's sake, let's throw rocks!" He grabbed up a handful of rocks and tossed them into the water.

"Throw some over here," Cassie said. She ran down the creek to pick up a rock and throw it into the water against the far bank. "There, that's the place."

Dix threw rocks and more rocks. "Will that do it?"

"I reckon so, what with all the splashing before."

He looked at the creek and then at her. "You going to go in?"

Cassie scuffed her bare foot in the dust. "I'm not supposed to swim, unless I got somebody to look after me."

He smiled at her. "I'll look after you, Cassie Taylor."

She looked down at him, surprised. His smile was friendly and his dark eyes were steady. It seemed to her that a message had passed between them, a promise, and suddenly she felt as light as air. She jumped up and ran across the bridge. "Last one in's a crybaby!"

"Hey! Aren't you going to change to your swimming suit?"

She hesitated and then yelled happily, "Don't have one," and jumped into the deepest part of the pond. He ran through the shallow water and jumped in after her, with a splash that would scare away all the snakes in Clifton County.

Cassie came up laughing and pulling her dress down, but Dix kept an eye on the far bank. "Let's sit in the shallows and throw some more rocks."

She sat down in the shallow water. "What's the matter? No snakes in that country-club pool of yours?"

He laughed. "Okay, you win. I'll admit I don't know much about the country. I'll bet we haven't been to the lodge for four or five years. Mother doesn't much like it down here." He waded across the creek to sit down beside her and stretched his long legs out in the water. His legs were covered with fine black hair. The men and boys Cassie knew wore bib overalls on even the hottest days. She was not used to looking at male legs. She edged away, uncomfortable at being so close to him and intensely aware of the wet dress clinging to her body.

"What grade are you in, Cassie?"

"I ought to be in eighth, but Miss Bencher double-promoted me and I'll be in ninth."

He grinned at her. "You must be a pretty smart kid."

"I am."

"Gosh, modest too! Cassie—what did you mean when you said *if* you're still in school? Your father wouldn't let you quit, would he?"

Cassie's happiness disappeared. She reached down in the shallow water beside her to take up a handful of rocks and skipped a flat one across the pond. "Papa says I don't need any more schooling."

"Sometimes I wish my father felt that way! After high school it's college and then law school. I'm going to be in school forever!"

"You're lucky. I mean, that he'll let you go to school."

Dix broke the uncomfortable silence. "It must be great, living down here. When I think that Dad owns all of this and I have to stay in town and go to—I mean, I have to stay in town all the time."

Cassie squeezed the rocks in her hand until they cut into her palm. "That's right, he does own it. All of it."

"He showed me the map this morning. His place runs from the creek to that ridge behind the lodge." He waved his hand. "And all the way down to the highway."

Cassie tossed her rocks into the creek. Mr. Steele had money and power, because he owned the land. She took a clod of dirt from the creek bank and as she had seen Granny do, she crumbled it and sifted it through her fingers. "My grandmother says that owning land is all that counts."

"Dad must feel the same way. He keeps buying up farms at tax sales."

"I guess he owns land in Ballard, too, and a house. Is it as nice as your lodge?"

"Are you kidding? It's four times as big and it has—" He stopped abruptly. "Yeah, it's a nice house."

Cassie pulled her knees up and locked her arms around them. "I reckon I'm going to have my own land sometime," she said dreamily. "I'm going to have me a house where Granny can live, and Papa, too." She remembered the first book she read at Turner School, and the neat white house where Dick and Jane and Spot lived. "I'm going to have me a white house and a good garden patch with plenty of water and . . ." Her voice faded away. "Someday."

She realized that Dix was watching her, and she knew what he was seeing—the faded dress, the legs scarred by old chigger bites, the dirty bare feet. She looked up and his dark eyes were soft with pity. She jumped to her feet. "You got no call to look at me that way!"

"Hey, I didn't mean to—"

"You ain't so high and mighty, just because your papa owns the land!"

He got to his feet. "Cassie, knowing something is a way of owning it, and I'll bet you know this land a lot better than my father does."

Cassie looked up at him, measuring his words and measuring her own feelings about them. "I know it, all right. I know this land."

"So you own it, too, in a way. Will you tell me about it?"

Cassie talked about the hills and the woods and he asked so many questions that she sat down in the shallows and told him more, about the foxes and deer and the limestone cliffs and springs hidden in the woods.

"How about caves?" he asked. "Are there any big enough to explore?"

"There are some, yes."

"Where? Will you show me?"

He was waiting eagerly, ready to find out every last secret spot. She thought of the things he knew that she had never seen: big houses and country clubs and colleges. "No," she said, "I got to get home."

"Now, wait a minute!" He scowled and his black eyebrows, like

Mr. Steele's, met at the bridge of his nose. "I have the right to know what's on my father's land, don't I?"

"Your father's land? I thought I had a right to it, too. You said knowing the land was like owning it. Was it a lie?"

"Gosh, no! I mean, but it isn't exactly the same thing, is it?"

She looked at him and turned away. "I got to go now."

Dix caught up with her in front of the lodge. "Will you come in and say hello to my father?"

She looked up at the brown-shingled lodge. Mr. Steele's lodge and Mr. Steele's trees and Mr. Steele's yard. Mr. Steele's land.

And Mr. Steele's son. The promise that had been made at the creek had not even lasted as long as the sugar cookies.

"No," she said. "I ain't no town girl that can hang around a swimmin' pool and go to dances and whatever. I got work to do." She turned away and started up the road.

"Wait. Cassie, stop!" he called after her, but she did not stop. She ran all the way home.

Chapter 7

IN JUNE THE LAST great dust storm of the spring blew in from the plains. Hot winds scourged fields that tractors had harrowed to the bone of the land itself, and the dust rose and rode the wind. In the Oklahoma panhandle, the center of the Dust Bowl, the storm blew for days, raising black clouds to eight thousand feet and limiting visibility on the ground to a few yards. Children who strayed from home disappeared into the churning dust and were found later, suffocated. When travelers were caught on the road they took what shelter they could and prayed for an end to darkness.

In Eastern Oklahoma the storms were less severe, but the Taylors' tenant house creaked and groaned as the wind howled around it and drove the fine dust of the prairies into their lives.

With the drought, the water table had dropped until even the good spring in the grotto gave only a trickle of water. Cassie made trip after trip to haul water. She soaked newspapers and stuffed them into the cracks around the ill-fitting windows. She dampened clean rags for Granny to hold over her face and mouth, but still the old woman choked on the powder-fine dust in the air, choked and coughed and fought to regain her breath.

On the third day of the storm the wind blew harder than on the first. Cassie had to light the kerosene lamp at four o'clock in the afternoon because the swirling dust had blotted out the sun. After supper, Howard announced that he was going to town. "I got to get me a drink to wash down this damn dust.   My gullet's plumb coated with the stuff."

Cassie sat down at the table.   "Granny, you want me to read to you?   I can read from your Bible."

Granny nodded, stifling a cough.   "Yes, child.   Read me the Twenty-third Psalm."

Cassie ran her finger along the line of print.

" 'The Lord is my shepherd; I shall not want.   He maketh me to lie down in green pastures: he leadeth me beside the still waters.' "

"Yes.   That's it."   Granny leaned her head back.   "That's the one I want at my buryin'."

"Oh, Granny, you're going to get over this bad spell!   Soon as this storm plays itself out, you'll see."   Cassie smiled, but she was less hopeful than she appeared.   She looked from her grandmother's gray face to the Bible.   When had Granny ever had a time to lie down in green pastures?

"If you'll give me a hand, Cassie, I believe I'll get in the bed now. Seems like this wind just wears a body out."

When she was settled in bed she laid her worn hand on Cassie's. "You're a good girl, child.   I don't know what I'd do without you."

"I don't know what I'd do, either, Granny.   I love you."

Granny patted her hand.   "You get to look more like your mama every day, honey.   You're goin' to be as pretty as she was."

Cassie went to bed, too, leaving the lamp in the front room turned low in case she needed to get up in the night to tend her grandmother. Granny slept restlessly, and to keep from disturbing her Cassie took the extra quilt and made a pallet on the floor by the bed.

She was uneasy at being alone with her grandmother.   What if Granny had an attack of breathlessness?   There was no one to help, and no car to go for the doctor.   She dozed off finally, in spite of her fear.

Late in the night she was awakened by the sound of a car.   "Thank goodness!" she whispered.   Someone to help her.   Then she recognized the roar of Bo's old Ford.   She raised herself on her elbow and watched him stagger into the yellow lamplight of the front room.   He had been drinking and he had a full bottle of whiskey in his hand.

Cassie lay back on her pallet. She did not want to tangle with Bo when he was drunk.

She lay awake, listening to the roaring wind, and within that sound to creaking of the old house and to Bo's noises in the front room until she dozed again to the steady rasp of her grandmother's breathing.

How long did she sleep? Ten minutes? An hour? Cassie did not know. She was awakened by a change in the night sounds and she lay on the pallet listening, trying to figure it out. The wind was still blowing, shrieking around the house like a banshee, and the noises in the house were the same. She heard Bo thump his bottle on the table and mutter a curse.

"Granny?" she whispered but there was no answer, and then she knew what had changed. Her grandmother's rasping breathing had stopped.

"Granny?" she said again and rose to her knees beside the bed. She put out her hand, drew it back and forced herself to reach out again, to lay her palm against her grandmother's cheek. The skin was soft, but the flesh beneath it was cold.

In that first instant Cassie felt a great surge of relief. Granny had found peace. She could meet at the beautiful river with those who had gone before. She could rest beside the still waters.

Cassie took her grandmother's hand in both of hers and looked at it in the yellow light that spilled through the doorway from the front room. There were the liver spots, brown splotches on the wrinkled skin, and the knuckles swollen by arthritis, but the hand was limp and still, a hand that had always been in motion, stirring the beans, pulling a comb through the tangles in Cassie's long hair, gripping a broom handle. Cassie spread her hand upon her grandmother's, finger for finger, and saw two hands moving together along a line of newspaper print, the old finger work-worn and scarred, the young one small and pink and not very clean, pointing at each word in turn. She put her cheek against her grandmother's hand and, through the wrinkled skin, she felt the chill of death.

"Granny," she whispered, and the sharp knife of reality sliced into her heart. She clutched the old hand to her chest. "Granny!" she cried. "Don't die! Don't leave me!"

A chair clattered to the floor in the front room and Bo was in the doorway. "What the hell's goin' on? What you screechin' about?"

"Bo, it's Granny! She's—I think she's—" Cassie fought against the truth. "Go for the doctor, Bo! Hurry."

He leaned over the bed. "No point to it. Old woman's dead."

"No! She can't be—find Papa! Get the doctor!"

"What for? Dead is dead."

"How can you talk like that? Your own grandmother!"

"Not my grandma. She said it herself. 'He ain't no grandson of mine.' It ain't nothin' to do with me."

Cassie dropped to her knees beside the bed, but when Bo stood up, swaying, she jumped up and put herself between him and the still figure on the bed. "You're drunk, Bo Taylor! You ought to be ashamed of yourself, with Granny lying there—Papa's going to take his belt to you."

He laughed. "That old drunk? It's all he can do to find his damn belt, much less whup me with it." He staggered into the front room, and Cassie heard the clink of glass as he poured his whiskey.

She went to the door. "Bo, that's not respectful. If you got to drink, go outside."

He turned around and for once his black eyes were not nervous, but were as cold and shiny as black marbles. Cassie stepped back, away from his look, but his eyes followed her.

"Cassie," he said. "Little old Cassie."

He smiled with small white teeth, and something cold ran down Cassie's spine. She backed into the bedroom as if being near her grandmother would protect her, as it had always done before.

Bo followed. "Come on out here, girl," he whispered. "Come on. Want to talk to you."

She backed toward the bed, but Bo was as quick as a ferret. He grabbed her wrist and dragged her into the front room.

"You let go of me, Bo Taylor!"

She jerked her arm free and ran to the back room, but he was at the door first, barring her way.

"Ain't no use to run to Granny. She can't help you no more."

Cassie moved away from him. He wanted something from her, she knew that, but she could not think clearly, not with the black wind howling around the cabin and her grandmother lying dead. It was too much. Too much.

"I ain't goin' to hurt you none. You got no call to be scared." His soft voice curled around her like a snake.

"No!" she cried, clapping her hands over her ears. "No! I won't listen to you."

Bo clenched his fists. "Won't listen to me, huh? Ain't I a good enough talker? Didn't get to go to school like you, did I? Didn't learn no highfalutin' way of talkin'."

Cassie stared at her half brother and for the first time she saw him for what he was. It was there in the way he stood, in the way he looked at her. He was not a boy, and not a man. He was an animal, a creature with no more conscience than a wolf, with no more thought for the future than a coyote. She did not know what he wanted of her, but she knew that he wanted something and that to escape she would need to use as much animal cunning as he did. She glanced past him to the back room, but what he had said was true. Granny could no longer help her.

She backed slowly, almost imperceptibly, toward the door to the porch. "Bo, I never said you couldn't talk good. You talk real good."

"Huh. You and your granny, always readin' of them books, tryin' to talk like town folks. Listen, I had me some things to say, too. I had things to tell, but her and you, you didn't want to listen to old Bo. And she was always on my back." He raised his voice to a falsetto. " 'Bo, where you been?' 'Bo, where you goin'?' 'Bo, where'd you get the money for that car?' "

Cassie was within a step of the door. "She didn't mean anything by it, Bo. She just wanted to—" She whirled and grabbed the door-knob, but Bo was across the room before she could get the door open. He grabbed her wrist and twisted it.

"That hurts, Bo!" Cassie cried. She struck at him with her free hand, but he caught it in his own and held her wrists.

"Maybe it ain't my talkin', maybe you and her thought it was me that wasn't good enough for you."

"I never said—"

"I seen you with him. Bet you didn't know that!"

"Who? Who'd you see me with?"

"Hell, you know. That boy of Steele's, that's who. That skinny kid. Reckon you and her thought he was good enough for you, with his town ways and his fine talkin' and fine clothes. Old Bo, he ain't nothin' but a cropper's boy, he ain't no good. Ain't that what you and her said?"

"No! Granny never even knew I saw him at the creek that day! Bo, listen to me. I'm a sharecropper's girl, you know that. We got the same daddy, ain't we?"

He twisted her wrists until she was forced to look into his hard, glittering eyes. "Cassie," he whispered, "let's have us some fun. I watched you with that boy and he didn't get nothin', or I'd have seen. You ain't never had no man. You let old Bo show you what it's all about."

"You're my brother!"

He laughed. "You think it's the first time a man took his sister? Hell, I could tell you—I been watchin' you and waitin' and thinkin' to myself, I'm goin' to get me some of that. Steady down, now, girl. You let old Bo——"

Cassie bit his hand as hard as she could. He yelled and let go of her wrist, but before she could move, he slapped her face so hard that her ears rang. She cried out, and he grabbed her wrist again and twisted it behind her.

"Bite me, will you, girl? Listen, I had me a little old dog one time that I was foolin' with and he bit me on the hand just like that. I'm goin' to show you what I done to that dog, you hear? I'm goin' to give you just what I give him, but first I got somethin' to show you."

He shifted his grip until he could hold both of her wrists in one hand, in a grasp as strong as iron, and forced her to turn until she was facing him.

"Bo," she moaned. "Bo, don't——"

"I get first look, girl!" He grabbed the neck of her cotton shift and with one quick jerk ripped it down the front.

Cassie twisted away from him. She managed to get one hand free, but he grabbed it and pulled her upright.

His black eyes ran up and down her naked body and Cassie cringed, feeling as dirty as if his eyes left a smudge of filth at each spot they touched.

"Get down there, girl!" He jerked at her arm and pushed her down on the pallet of quilts in the corner of the room. Cassie bent her knees and pushed them against him, forcing him back. He dropped her wrist and slapped her, first with his right hand and then with his left, until she was dizzy from trying to roll away from his blows. One last blow was so hard that she fell back on the quilts.

He gripped her wrists again, with one hand, and with the other he fumbled at his belt buckle. "Stay down there, lessen you want me to hit you again!"

"No!" Cassie pushed herself up and Bo slapped her once, twice, three times, until tears of pain blurred her eyes. Cassie turned her face away from him. "Bo, please—please don't hurt me no more."

He grabbed her hair and pulled her face up close to his. "Old Bo's goin' to show you a good time, that's all. A real good time."

"Bo, listen, I won't tell Papa, I promise! Just—please let me go!"

"Hell, tell the old man whatever you want, I don't give a damn!" With his left hand still entangled in her hair, he used his right hand to unbuckle his belt and push his work pants down over his hips. He tugged at Cassie's hair to pull her head down. "Looky there, girl! Looky what I got for you. You want it, don't you? Tell me, hear? Say you want it!"

Cassie stared at it, at the red swollen thing thrusting up toward her face. She moaned, confused, and tried to turn away, but Bo pulled her hair until she screamed in pain.

"Say it, hear? Say you want it!"

"No! I don't—Bo, let me go!"

He pushed her head down until her face was almost on the thing. "Say it!" he snarled. "Say it!"

"Oh no, please—oh!"

He jerked her hair until it felt as if he would pull her scalp away from her skull. "Now, you bitch! Say it now!"

"Oh, God—I want it, I want—"

He twisted her wrists and forced her down on the tangle of quilts. "You're goin' to get it, girl! You're goin' to get it right—"

The door of the cabin slammed open. Bo looked back, and past him Cassie saw her father standing in the doorway.

"Papa!" she cried. "Papa, help me!"

"What the hell you doin', boy? Get up from there!"

"Papa, he——"

"I heard you, girl. I heard you screamin' when I come up on the porch. You, Bo, let her go!"

Cassie tried to pull her hands free, but Bo gripped them tight.

"Bo!" Howard yelled. "You heard me! Let that child go!"

"Get out of here, old man," Bo snarled. "Get out or when I'm done with her I'll hurt you bad! Get out!"

Howard ran to the shelves and turned back to them holding his shotgun with both hands. "Get up from there, boy! Leave that girl be, or I'll blow your goddamn head off!"

Bo froze for an instant, and Cassie could see nothing but the yellow lamplight glittering on the black barrel of the shotgun.

Bo dropped Cassie's wrists and leaped toward his father but tripped on his pants and fell on the wooden floor.

Howard laughed harshly. "Look at you, boy! Look at yourself! It's God's own punishment on you, Bo Taylor. What you was doin' was a abomination in the eyes of the Lord and you're damned, you hear me? Damned!"

Sobbing with relief, Cassie scrambled into the corner and tried to cover herself with her torn shift.

Bo rose to his knees and pulled up his pants.

"You, Bo," Howard said, "don't you get up from there till I say so! I got this gun on you and I aim to keep it there." Without taking his eyes off Bo, he called to Cassie. "You all right, girl? Did the bastard hurt you?"

"He hurt my arm, and he was going to——"

"Where's your granny? How come she let him do this?"

Cassie forced herself to say it. "Granny's dead, Papa. In there on the bed. Granny is dead."

Howard lifted his shotgun. "You done it, Bo! You killed her, didn't you? You killed Cassie's grandma!"

"No! I never!" Bo lunged at his father.

Howard jumped back, but the table was in his way and Bo grabbed the barrel of the shotgun and twisted it until it pointed at the ceiling.

Cassie scrambled to her feet and ran to the struggling men. "Papa!" she cried. "Papa!"

Bo had the shotgun and was turning it toward his father. Howard grabbed the barrel and pushed it away, and Cassie clutched at Bo's arm and then clawed at his hands, digging her fingernails into the backs of them, trying to pull his fingers away from the trigger.

Howard was shouting and Cassie was screaming, but Bo was dead silent, wrestling with his father, wrestling for the shotgun without wasting his breath in shouts.

"Cassie!" Howard yelled. "Get the——"

The shotgun went off with a dull crash that echoed in the wooden room, and at the same instant the kerosene lamp erupted in a flash of flame and Cassie saw her father's face open like a red flower against the orange flare. She saw her father's face explode.

She screamed and Bo fell to the floor and Cassie ran out of the house. She ran into the night, ran from the sight of her father's face, ran with the black wind, screaming and screaming until all thought was gone and she was no more than a shrieking hurt animal running and running and running into the howling night.

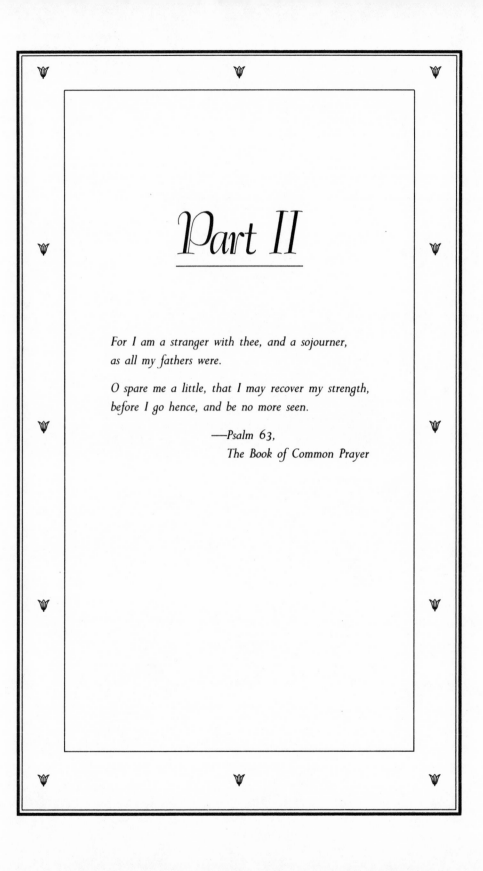

Part II

For I am a stranger with thee, and a sojourner,
as all my fathers were.

O spare me a little, that I may recover my strength,
before I go hence, and be no more seen.

—Psalm 63,
The Book of Common Prayer

Chapter 8

THE TIME FOR CEREMONY was over, at the Jesus Saves Full Gospel Church in San Bois, Oklahoma. Cassandra Taylor sat in the church parlor with her hands folded neatly in her lap and her blue eyes dull above dark shadows of fatigue.

Across the room Ella Mae Hodge, Howard Taylor's second cousin, put a pudgy hand on the arm of James Steele's chair. "And Mr. Steele, that child does not remember a thing that happened that night. Not one thing!"

He frowned. "You say the hunter found her at my lodge?"

Ella Mae smoothed the fingerwaves of her brown hair. "All huddled down on the porch, he said, and he carried her home, but the house was burned down, clean to the ground." She lowered her voice. "With Howard and them in it."

"Mrs. Hendricks and the boy, Bo."

"Yes, sir. He said there wasn't nothin' but the cookstove left, and Howard's pickup. But Cassie, she don't remember it, don't remember one thing. The doctor says it can happen to folks that's had a bad shock. Like when their mind can't stand to look at somethin' it closes it off. Says you can't tell how long it will last, neither."

Mr. Steele crossed the room. "Cassie, you know that your family is . . . gone?"

"Yes, sir. They told me." She looked down at her hands, lifeless objects resting on the skirt of the too-large dress someone had given her. They had told her, but the information was like dust motes hanging in the air around her, unrelated and unassimilated.

"And you remember nothing?"

She hesitated. She remembered the wind howling around the shack, and she remembered lamplight in the front room, but her thoughts stopped there as if a blank white curtain were draped across her mind to hide the scene. "No sir. Nothing."

Mr. Steele turned away. "Mr. Hodge, you sold Howard's truck?"

Ella Mae's husband was a tall, gaunt man with a long neck and a pronounced Adam's apple. His chest was caved in from the years of carrying a postman's bag, and his black hair was parted at the side and slicked over a bald spot. "And the mule. Wasn't nothin' else left."

"There was Bo's car," Cassie said, but no one seemed to hear.

"My wife and I want to add some money to that, so you can buy clothes for Cassie. It is good of you to take her into your home."

Ella Mae stood up and smoothed her skirt over her plump hips. "Howard was my cousin, wasn't he? Me and him was all that was left of the family. The Lord giveth and He taketh away. Me and Dale never had no children, and we're goin' to raise this girl like our very own."

Mr. Steele turned back to Cassie. "Remember this, Cassie. Your grandmother was a woman of good pioneer stock, a woman with grit. Keep her in your mind."

"Yes, sir." He patted her shoulder awkwardly and left. Cassie went to the window and watched James Steele get into the Ford roadster that had been parked at the lodge the day she and Dixon Steele swam together in San Bois Creek, a day in a different world and in a different life.

DALE HODGE'S CAR bumped across the Missouri-Kansas-Texas Railroad tracks that bisected the town of Whitman and passed boarded-up stores that had gone broke during the Depression. Farther from the tracks, the stores and offices were closed only for the night. HEPPLE DRY GOODS. BELL'S SHOES. CRUSE DRUGS. Whitman had two elementary schools, one on the north side of town, the less desirable side, and one on the south side. In the seventh grade all of the students came together at the combined junior-senior high school. Reservoir Hill, one of the town's parks, had a spectacular view of the town and the rolling country around it. It was popular for family picnics, and at night it served as the local lovers' lane.

No matter how urban it looked to Cassie Taylor, in June of 1938 Whitman had a population of 11,348 and was not much different from other Eastern Oklahoma towns. There were only four buildings of any size in the town: the hospital, the Carnegie Library, the county courthouse and the United States post office. Both the courthouse and the post office were decorated with murals paid for by the WPA arts program. The two paintings glorified agriculture with scenes of noble tillers of the soil bravely facing up to the combined forces of nature and big-city bankers, but the courthouse mural was the more authentic of the two. The artist had used Clifton County people for models and his farmers were lean, hard-bitten men who looked as if they might even recognize a boll weevil if they saw one.

If Hepple Dry Goods could not supply their needs, people could drive forty miles south to Ballard, a town of twenty-five thousand, or seventy miles north to Tulsa. In practice, northsiders usually did without, and southsiders drove to Tulsa for lunch with friends at Southern Hills Country Club and a pleasant day of shopping at Vandever's and Brown-Duncan.

Dale drove north past small frame houses in poorly kept yards. Here and there a hand-lettered sign was stuck in a front window: SYLVIA'S BEAUTY SALON or READINGS, MADAME GRACE or CHIROPRACTIC. Under the streetlights children ran across the grass, chasing lightning bugs and calling through the darkening night in high, fluting voices.

The Hodges' house was a one-story frame with a front porch half-hidden by the morning glory vines the wind had not torn down. Ella Mae opened the front door and Cassie's first impression was of grayness. When she looked more closely, she saw that there were colors after all. In the living room there were two armchairs and a couch covered in brown mohair. There was a green artificial marble fireplace with an open gas stove instead of firewood, and there were three oak tables and two black iron lamps with fringed silk shades.

The kitchen, however, more than made up for the living room. It was like pictures Cassie had seen in books: an oak ice box and a metal-topped table and a gas cookstove, and white cabinets with a porcelain sink fitted with hot and cold water faucets.

"This here's our room, Dale's and mine," Ella Mae said. "Ain't it pretty?" The bedspread was white net over pink satin, and the curtains at the windows were white net, too, and tied back with pink satin bows.

Cassie was awed. "It is pretty, Ella Mae. Real pretty."

The next door was to a bathroom with a toilet and basin and a big white bathtub crouched on clawed feet on the green linoleum. Ella Mae patted Cassie's arm. "I know Howard never had no runnin' water out there, but I'll show you how to use everything. And this here's your room."

The room had only a straight chair, a narrow iron cot and a chipped white chest of drawers, but it was Cassie's, her very own room.

"My stars, Cassie, it's like a oven in here! Open up them windows!"

"Yes'm." Cassie raised the south window and the buzzing of cicadas came in with the muggy air. She stood with her hands on the window sill, listening, trying to remember that night of the howling wind.

"You better get into your nightie and—land's sake, you don't even have a nightie, do you?"

"No, ma'am. They threw it out. It was all torn up and—" Cassie stopped, remembering the smell of smoke.

"I'll lend you one tonight, then we got to get you some clothes."

Later, Cassie lay on the narrow cot. She lifted one hand and put it on her chest, but like the rest of her body her chest felt hollow, as if her skin enclosed no tissue, no bones, nothing, so that even the weight of her own hollow hand could collapse her chest in upon itself. She tried to remember what had happened, how it had come to be this way, but there was only the blank white curtain hiding the night of the fire.

She slept, finally, but long before the first gray light crept into her room, she awakened and lay unthinking and empty on the narrow bed.

Ella Mae began the day with a burst of energy. "Cassie, honey, I got your breakfast all ready, and soon as you're done, we'll go clothes shoppin' for you. Won't that be fun?"

"Yes'm," Cassie said, but "fun" was foreign to her, a word that had no place in her mind.

As it happened, Ella Mae did not need to take her shopping. A lady from the True Word Holiness Tabernacle arrived, glowing with generosity and curiosity, and thrust a bundle of clothing into Ella Mae's hands. "And how is that poor child? Sister Hodge, tell me all about it, every single thing!"

"I thank you, Sister Conroy, and I know Cassie thanks you, too."

The woman smiled at Cassie. "Clothe them their nakedness, the Good Book says. The clothes ain't much, though." The clothes Sister Conroy wore were not much, either. Few men were as lucky as Dale Hodge, who had a government job with a steady salary.

Sister Stringer was the next to come. She brought more clothes and compliments that made Ella Mae's plump cheeks turn rosy. "You're a saint, Sister Hodge, to take this child! A saint!"

Ella Mae smiled modestly. "Suffer the little children, like they say. I ain't doing one thing but my Christian duty." She took the ladies to the front porch for lemonade, but even in her bedroom Cassie could hear their exclamations.

"And she don't remember a thing? Fancy that!"

Cassie squirmed. She was trying. She was doing her best to remember.

Later, Ella Mae sorted through the clothing. "Well, like Sister Conroy said, it ain't much, but I reckon it will do you for the summer. We'll save that money from Mr. Steele and buy you some nice school clothes in the fall." She looked at Cassie with narrowed eyes. "Cassie? You're sure you don't remember nothin' about that night? I mean, you'd tell me if you did, wouldn't you?"

Cassie rubbed her arm. "I sure would, Ella Mae."

She kept trying to remember, during the hot sultry days and the muggy nights. She went back in her memory, back to childhood, searching for a path to recent memory. She felt the comb grab in a tangle as Granny combed out her hair. She played with Francine and Mary Priscilla in her play place under the oak tree. But always, in the end, her memories washed up to that blank white curtain, eddied and stopped. She let them trickle away, then, and went back to the beginning, picking over her memories like pieces of a jigsaw puzzle. Surely she could see the pattern of it if she could find the right piece— the smell of wet winter coats in Turner School, for instance, or the way the water felt on her skin when she swam in San Bois Creek.

Ella Mae talked about going to the missionary barrel, but Cassie did not care what she wore. She did not care what she did. In fact, there were days when she was not sure what she was doing when she did it. She had a room of her own and a bed and three cotton dresses. She had a pair of white sandals that were only a little bit too small. She lived in a house with electricity and running water and a radio, but she might just as well have been living in the middle of a drought-killed cornfield for all that her surroundings affected her. There was no pain, and no fear. There was only the constant fruitless searching through the past. She went through her days dressing when she was told to dress and eating when she was told to eat, but she seldom spoke to either of the Hodges.

Ella Mae's saintly smile began to look a bit peevish, and a wrinkle pulled her eyebrows together. Doing one's Christian duty is not rewarding when it is hardly noticed by the one done unto. The Hodges began to talk together as if Cassie were not in the room.

On a hot Sunday afternoon in July, the two of them sat in the porch swing, lazily waving their palmetto fans, while Cassie sat on the steps and stared blankly at the street.

Ella Mae patted her fingerwaves into place and whispered, although it was obvious that Cassie's mind was miles away. "Dale, I'm getting to think there's somethin' wrong with you-know-who. There was this girl on the radio, she was in a terrible accident and she wasn't hurt to speak of, but she went plumb out of her mind!"

Cassie watched Dale swallow. His Adam's apple moved up and down, like a little animal trapped inside his neck, trying to climb out, trying again and failing.

"On the radio, honey?" He smoothed the hair over his bald spot. "One of them soap operas of yours, I reckon."

Ella Mae sniffed. "Well, if you got to be so smart, yes, it was on *Guiding Light*, but they have got true facts in them stories."

"She'll likely come out of it when school starts. You ought to keep her busy, get her to help you around the house and all."

"I sure could use some help. This heat, it just wears a body out to do anything."

Cassie did not mind housework. She could concentrate on rubbing a soapy rag across the kitchen floor or changing the beds or peeling the potatoes. Anything was better than thinking.

The heat wave in August reduced Ella Mae to a sweating mass. She spent most of the day on her bed, wearing nothing but a flowered wrapper while the electric fan swept over her. She tried to get Cassie to listen to her stories, but Cassie could not join in Ella Mae's comfortable weeping over Stella Dallas' sacrifices for her daughter Laurel. Anyway, the radio was so loud that even in the kitchen Cassie could hear a tinny voice cry out, "I can't bear it! I just can't bear it!" Ella Mae would cry out, too: "You, Cassie! I need something cold. We got any of that buttermilk left?"

ON THE TWELFTH straight day that the temperature had been over one hundred degrees, Dale Hodge came home from the post office peeling off his sweaty shirt. He carried a kitchen chair out to the shade at the back of the house and sat down in his undershirt and uniform pants to fan himself and drink the iced tea Cassie took to him. She dropped down in the sparse grass under the elm tree.

Ella Mae wandered out, pulling her wrapper open to dab at her breast with a damp rag. "I swear, Dale, that child there don't even feel the heat, and look at me, I got this here prickly heat all over me."

"She's skinny, Ella Mae, that's it. You know heavy people feel the heat more."

"I ain't heavy, Dale Hodge! Plump, maybe. You used to say I was pleasingly plump."

"Looks like you've put on a little—aw, honey, don't get riled up. It's too damn hot to fight."

"You watch your language, sir!" She sank down on the back steps and flapped her robe to let the air at her body. "And my back is giving me fits. I wouldn't be surprised if I have to go under the doctor."

Dale tilted his chair back. "Maybe you ain't getting up and about enough. Lying in the bed like that . . ."

Ella Mae sniffed. "You, Cassie! Why ain't you started supper? You can make us some potato salad. Oh no, I forgot. The iceman don't come till tomorrow and there ain't enough ice left to cool down potatoes." She leaned back against the screen door. "I sure wish we had one of them Frigidaires."

"Them things cost a lot of money, Ella Mae."

Cassie had stood up and was waiting for instructions like a marionette waiting for someone to pull its strings. Ella Mae tapped her finger on her lower lip. "There's that money Mr. Steele gave you, Dale. There's plenty there for a Frigidaire."

Dale looked at her. "That money is supposed to go for her, for school clothes and the like."

Ella Mae dabbed at the sweat on her forehead. "You think she's going to care what she wears to school? Look at her. You think she cares?"

Cassie was staring up at the cloudless sky as if she had forgotten Ella Mae and Dale were in the world.

"Look at her," Ella Mae said again. "She's like one of them Mickey Mouse toys, like you got to stick a key in her back and wind her up before she'll do anything. You, Cassie! Go in and get supper started!"

"Yes'm." Cassie started toward the back door.

"Stop right there!" Ella Mae said. "How you goin' to fix supper when I ain't told you what to fix?"

"Yes'm."

"We'll have that piece of cold ham, I reckon, but you might as well get some lettuce from the garden. It's all goin' to burn up anyway, in this heat."

"Yes'm." Cassie started past the garage to the garden.

"You see what I mean, Dale? No more life to her than a stick!"

Cassie knelt to pull the lettuce and also pulled a few stray weeds. Along with the housework, Ella Mae had given her the garden to tend. Dale took any leftover produce to the post office to sell. As Ella Mae said, "Every little bit helps."

Cassie had soaked the garden early that morning, but by late afternoon the earth had baked to a hard crust. She put her hand down flat to feel the heat rising from it and then she punched her fingers through the crust to see if there was any moisture beneath the surface. She took up a handful of dirt, crumbled it and let it sift through her fingers. Suddenly it was not her thin, tanned hand that she was seeing, but her grandmother's hand. It was Granny's work-worn hand, and the red earth of that other garden was trickling through the fingers and the soft voice was in her ears: "Wish you could have seen my garden when we had our own place, child. Seems like beans just don't grow as good on rented land."

The hand disappeared and Cassie could see only the white curtain in her mind. It was coming toward her, pressing against her as if it were expanding like the wall of a balloon and would split asunder and let the knowledge behind it explode and spew like acid into her consciousness: all that had happened on that night of fire, all of the memories and the anguish.

"No!" she cried. She dashed the soil from her hand and jumped to her feet. "No!" She ran past Ella Mae and Dale, ignoring their surprise, ran into the house, into the kitchen. At the sink she washed her right hand again and again, holding it under the running water long after the dirt was gone. She turned off the faucet and leaned on the sink to get her breath. "No," she whispered. "I don't want to know."

ONE HOT AUGUST morning Sister Stringer and Sister Conroy brought news that had kept even Hitler's plans for Czechoslovakia off the front page of the *Whitman Daily News*. A child had been murdered in the Cookson Hills east of Whitman, a five-year-old girl. The newspaper tiptoed around the more gruesome details, but Sister Stringer had called her friend Ila Carter, who lived near Archers, the town where the child's body was found.

Ella took the ladies to the front porch and Cassie trailed along behind and sat down on the steps. Ella Mae hitched her chair closer to the swing and said, "Now, Sister Stringer, tell me every single thing!"

"They found her in the woods, all cut up like a—" Sister Stringer lowered her voice and leaned closer to Ella Mae. Cassie did not try to hear her muttered report, because a memory was crowding into her mind, the memory of someone screaming. Was it she who had screamed? She shivered and cold sweat broke out on her forehead.

Sister Stringer said, "You all right, Cassie? You're kind of pale."

Ella Mae looked at her, too. "Cassie, go in my room and turn that electric fan on you, hear?"

When the ladies had left to spread the word, Ella Mae put Cassie back to work and turned the electric fan on herself. The radio was loud, but Cassie would rather listen to Lord Henry talking to Our Gal Sunday than to the disturbing whispers in her mind.

Ella Mae sent Cassie to her room when Dale came home that evening, but Cassie could hear her going on and on.

At dinner Ella Mae put down her fork. "Cassie, I don't want you goin' out of the yard no more, hear?"

Dale laughed. "She's thirteen years old. She ain't in no danger."

Ella Mae pursed her lips. "And what makes you so all-fired sure of that, Dale Hodge? Who's to say what a maniac is goin' to do?" She shook her finger at Cassie. "I don't even want you walkin' down to the store!"

The murderer was not captured, but the heat continued and it was too much for a heavy woman like Ella Mae to dress and walk to the store. Cassie took over the shopping again.

In the week before school started both the *Whitman Daily News* and Ella Mae forgot all about the maniac ranging the Cookson Hills. The *News* was concerned with Chamberlain's trip to Munich, and Ella Mae worried about Our Gal Sunday's latest confrontations with the English upper crust.

Cassie forgot, too, but sometimes she would wake in the night to a dream of crying. She could never remember who had cried.

Three days before school started, Ella Mae and Dale treated Cassie to her first movie. She was fascinated by the moving pictures, but the stories did not interest her. The Three Stooges talked too fast and hit each other too much. The feature was *Stella Dallas,* and from Ella Mae's radio Cassie already knew too much about self-sacrificing mothers. The movie held her attention only when Barbara Stanwyck went up in smoke.

The audience whistled and stamped its feet, and Dale told Cassie that the film had jammed in the projector and the heat of the lamp made it smoulder and break. Instead of Stella Dallas, they saw the image of the film curling up on itself and the black shadow of a wisp of smoke.

Ella Mae took Cassie to see the missionary barrel, which turned out to be three large cardboard cartons stored in Sister Stringer's garage.

She dug out a pair of school shoes for Cassie, scuffed brown-and-white oxfords, and three dresses that had lost both body and color in the course of innumerable washings.

"Now Cassie, don't you worry none about wearin' clothes from the missionary barrel."

"No, ma'am, I won't." Cassie could have told her that she had never worn anything other than secondhand clothes, but that was not what Ella Mae meant.

"We'll be real careful with everything, hear, and we'll put it back when you're done with it. It ain't goin' to hurt them little African heathens if you wear the things for a while."

The next day was hot and muggy and Ella Mae sent Cassie to register at school by herself. Cassie found her way to the office and was relieved to hear that the secretary had received a file from Turner School with her grades and a letter that strongly recommended that she be put into ninth grade instead of eighth. Cassie caught a glimpse of the letter. She knew that round, firm handwriting. Miss Naomi Bencher had written the letter.

"Cassie?" the secretary said. "Cassie!"

"Yes, ma'am."

"Copy this list and you be sure to bring your supplies to the first class. Now, go on down the hall and find Miss Cox. She'll be your homeroom teacher, and your history teacher, too."

CASSIE WAS ALMOST to the Hodges' house when she noticed the car in front of the house, a big blue car that surely did not belong to the ladies of the True Word Holiness Tabernacle. She went around the house and let herself in the back door quietly, but not quietly enough.

"Cassie?" Ella Mae called from the living room. "You come in here!"

"Yes'm." Cassie stopped in surprise in the doorway. There was a man sitting on Ella Mae's mohair couch. A big man with high, broad shoulders and heavy black eyebrows: Mr. James Steele.

He stood up. "Well, Cassie, it's been a long time."

"Yes, sir." She edged into the living room.

Ella Mae, still in her flowered wrapper, was sitting in an armchair. "Mr. Steele come by special, just to see you."

He looked at Cassie and frowned. "Mrs. Hodge, surely you could have found better clothes for the child. There was enough money, wasn't there?"

"There was that money, yes, sir." Ella Mae's voice rose to a whine. "You would not believe what it costs to keep a growing girl like Cassie here. Food has gone up a caution, a real . . ." Her voice trailed away.

Mr. Steele smiled stiffly at Cassie. "You started school today?"

"No, sir. I start tomorrow. I registered today, though, and I met one of my teachers."

"Oh? And how did you like her?"

"I guess I didn't pay her much mind."

Mr. Steele sat down on the couch as if he had found a moral position with which he could be comfortable. "Then I suggest that you start paying attention to her, young lady. A good education is available to you here, much better than at San Bois. You must gain from this experience."

He paused expectantly and Cassie said, "Yes, sir. I will."

More gently he said, "I believe it is what your grandmother would have wanted for you."

Cassie's knees went weak and she put her hand on the doorjamb to brace herself. "Yes, sir. I reckon that's so."

Mr. Steele nodded briskly. "Now, Cassie, if you will excuse us, I want to talk to your cousin."

"Yes, sir," Cassie said once more. "Good-bye, Mr. Steele."

She went to her room and sat down on her bed, but she could still hear his heavy voice. She covered her ears with her hands. His voice brought back too many memories.

The front door slammed and Ella Mae's radio went on immediately. Cassie was peeling potatoes when Dale came home and Ella Mae came out of her bedroom.

"Dale, that Mr. Steele came by here today."

"That so? What did he want?"

"He said he had business in town but I think he come to spy on us."

"Now, honey, why would he go and do a thing like that? Cassie, there any iced tea in the Frigidaire?"

"Her clothes!" Ella Mae said. "He fussed at me about her clothes!"

Dale took the iced tea. "What's the matter with them clothes, anyway? Cassie, ain't you happy with them clothes of yours?"

Cassie looked down at the limp blue cotton dress that barely reached her kneecaps, at the faded pink socks and the scuffed oxfords. "They're okay, I guess. I don't care much about clothes."

"See there?" Ella Mae smacked her plump hand on the table. "That's just what I told Mr. Steele. I said, 'That girl don't care one thing about clothes,' I said. 'She don't care about nothin' at all.' "

Chapter 9

EACH MORNING Cassie walked eight blocks to Whitman Junior-Senior High School, past the grocery store on the corner, past the Texaco filling station and past the pond in the park. She moved through the school as she moved through the Hodges' house, untouching and untouched.

It appeared that what Ella Mae had told Mr. Steele was true, that Cassie did not care about anything, but for some reason Mr. Steele's visit had affected her. It was not his sermon on doing well in school. It was the fact of his being there, in the flesh, on Ella Mae's couch. It made her remember the other times she had seen him: the day he gave her a doll that the rats had torn, the Thanksgiving Day when Granny talked him into hiring Papa as his caretaker. And there was more. In the Hodges' house he had said Granny's name and brought her into that gray living room and forced Cassie to see her, to look at memories she had packed away and was afraid to consider again. His visit upset a delicate balance between the past and the present.

It did not, however, make her pay attention to her teachers. At school she sat quietly, as if she were listening to the teacher, but her mind was back at the farm, going over and over the past. She did what she was told to do. The fact that she did not do it well was not noticed until she took home her first report card.

Since Dale's work as a mailman gave him a special relationship with official documents he checked Cassie's report card. "These ain't the kind of grades you got before. You're failing half your work, girl."

"Yes, sir."

"Well, 'yes, sir' don't quite cut the mustard, Cassie. What you got to do is work harder, ain't it?"

"Yes, sir."

Dale's normally relaxed mouth screwed itself into something that resembled Ella Mae's at its most petulant. "Well, you do that!"

Cassie tried to do better. She tried to listen to Miss Cox, her history teacher, talk about Neville Chamberlain's visit to Munich, but the past intervened, even though the people in her memories were as distant as images on a movie screen. The old woman who bent over the iron cookstove was named Granny, but was a stranger, and the little blond girl playing under the oak tree was no one Cassie Taylor had ever known.

On the first chilly morning in November Cassie put on a heavy red sweater from the missionary barrel and set off for school. She passed the Texaco station and was almost through the park when she heard the quacking of ducks. She hurried through the trees and there they were, swimming on the muddy pond. Iridescent green heads, white neck rings and gray bodies with bright blue feathers tucked in at each side. Mallards.

Cassie ripped open her lunch sack. With shaking hands she pulled out her peanut butter sandwich and tore it to pieces.

"Here, ducks, come here. I got something for you."

The mallards saw the scattered splashes and converged quacking on the floating bread, but half of it sank before they could find it.

"You ducks," Cassie said softly. "You dumb old ducks." She stood up rubbing her eyes, remembering the first time she saw mallards on San Bois Creek, remembering the wooden bridge, remembering her hand tucked safely into Granny's.

She fell to her knees and put her hands over her eyes. "Granny," she whispered. Something tore in her hollow chest and a flood of warmth rushed through her body. She let it flow, let the pain and the sorrow rush out in a gush of tears. "Granny," she cried. "Oh, my Granny."

Cassie was weak with crying when she sat up, but her eyes were dry. She was drained of tears. She had no idea how long she had been there, but in that time a change had taken place. The ducks were different, city ducks upon a city pond, in a city park that was only a symbol of the countryside: instead of woods and fields, selected trees and shrubs in regiments bordered by concrete sidewalks; instead of a fresh-running stream, a silted pond. But time and place were no longer confused. That was there and then, and this was here and now.

She looked at her discarded books with new, unclouded eyes. The history book was red, the math book blue. She picked them up and they had body and weight. They existed. She felt the rough wool of her sweater. She could see that it was red. She tried to orient herself in this new world where objects had color and bulk and weight. She turned away from the pond and ran for home.

At the sight of Cassie, Ella Mae dropped her glass of water. It landed on the linoleum with a crash, but Ella Mae did not look down. "Why ain't you in school? The maniac! The maniac's been after you!"

Cassie stopped in the doorway, confused. "No! No, Ella Mae, it's Granny. My granny is—is dead."

Ella Mae clapped her hand to her bosom. "God in heaven, you pert-near killed me! Bustin' in here like—Cassie! You remember what happened that night? Sit down here, child! You sit down and let me get you somethin' to—you think I ought to call Dale?"

When Cassie shook her head, Ella Mae hunched her chair close to the table. "Tell me what happened that night, every single thing!"

Cassie stared past Ella Mae at the stove, and it was as if a film of that hot July night were unreeling before her, projected on the white door of the oven. She saw Granny, but she was two-dimensional, like Barbara Stanwyck on the movie screen.

"Granny was sick that day," Cassie said, seeing it. "Coughing and gasping for breath." She could taste the dry bite of the dust. "From that big dust storm."

"I know, girl! Go on!"

"She was all worn out with it. Went to bed before it was full dark." Cassie stared at the oven door and saw herself, too, in the dim light of the back room at the tenant house.

Ella Mae leaned close. "And your daddy? Where was your daddy?"

Cassie looked at the oven door. "I can't see . . ." The scene shifted to the back room. "Granny was so restless, I figured she might sleep easier if she had the bed to herself so I made me a pallet and— Bo came back. I heard his car."

"You mean your daddy's truck, honey. Bo didn't have no car."

"It was Bo." Cassie watched him tilt the whiskey bottle. "He was drinking. I went back to sleep, I reckon, till something woke me up. The wind was howling outside, but there in the room it was real quiet." She saw herself by the bed, saw herself get to her knees. "Because Granny wasn't breathing anymore." She closed her eyes.

Ella Mae dabbed at her own eyes with a handkerchief. "Honey, you go on and cry it out, you hear?"

Cassie shook her head. "I felt her cheek. It was cold."

"Lord have mercy! And you there, a child all by yourself! No, wait a minute. Bo was there, too, wasn't he?"

Cassie stared at the oven door, watching herself, watching Bo. "He came in and I said to get a doctor, but he said it wouldn't do no good. He said she was dead."

"You poor baby! What did you and Bo do then?"

Cassie saw Bo reach out to her, saw him touch her wrist, and the picture was gone, the way the picture had disappeared on the screen at the movie house when Barbara Stanwyck went up in smoke. The film of Cassie's memory jammed in the projector and on the white oven door she saw a sudden curl of black, a wisp of transparent black smoke, and then there was nothing but white, the blank white of an oven door or of the curtain across her memory.

"Fire," she whispered. "There was fire."

A hard glitter replaced the tears in Ella Mae's eyes. "We know about the fire! What else? What about Bo? And what about your daddy? You got to remember what happened to them!"

Cassie stared at the oven and tried to roll the film again, but the door was white and only an oven door after all, with a chipped black handle. She shook her head. "That's all I remember." A feeling of relief crept through her.

Ella Mae was exasperated. "I don't see how you can leave a body hangin' like this—you wait till I tell Dale!"

"Can I lie down now? I feel—" Cassie stopped, unable to find words to describe how she felt. Empty, but not hollow. There was no Granny, but Granny had been, and finally Cassie was free to grieve for her.

Ella Mae sniffed. "You ought to be in school." But she looked at Cassie more closely and in spite of her obvious frustration, she said, "Yes, child, you go on in there and lie down. Sleep if you can."

THE TEARS SHE WEPT for her grandmother dissolved the barrier between Cassie and the world around her. When she could feel sorrow, she could feel happiness, too, and even curiosity.

At school she watched her classmates like an anthropologist studying a wandering band of apes. The girls gathered in the rest room at lunchtime and performed endless experiments with their hair and with a bright red lipstick Sally Green had filched from her mother's purse. Cassie hovered near the group and listened, but they conversed in giggles and catchwords that had no meaning to Cassie.

Sally Green was the leader, perhaps because she owned the lipstick. The other girls turned to her for approval of a new dress or a hairdo or a joke.

Cassie tried to edge her way into the group, giggling when she had no idea what she was giggling about, but the hard bright grins they gave her were nothing like the approving smiles they exchanged among themselves.

She knew why. She saw the difference each time she looked in the rest-room mirror. Sally Green and the others had pretty, even features and curly hair. Cassie's face, with its strong jaw and prominent cheekbones, was all planes, and her blond straight hair was pulled into braids. Her pale lips were severe in comparison with the bee-stung pouts smeared with Sally's red lipstick. They wore neat bright school dresses, and she had only missionary-barrel clothes which were sometimes too small and sometimes too large but were invariably faded and limp. Their eyes were knowing, but hers were clear and bright blue with hope until they turned away, rejecting her.

Cassie observed the boys, too, when she had the opportunity. There were a few doorways in the invisible wall between ninth-grade boys and girls. She knew that boys and girls sometimes met for sodas on the neutral ground of a drugstore near school, and a few boys went to girls' houses after school to dance to phonograph records, to "Deep

Purple" and "The Music Goes Round and Round."

One day a skinny boy with glasses broke the barrier and spoke to Cassie in the hall.

"Knock, knock," he said and waited expectantly.

"What? What did you say?" She smiled at him desperately, but when she could not break the code he shrugged and turned away.

One of the group had finally reached out to her and she had not been able to respond. She thought about it all day. If she looked more like the other girls, they might teach her their language. She would not count on dancing to "Deep Purple," but she might be able to answer a "knock, knock." To have one dress like theirs would make all the difference.

There was the usual talk at supper. Once Ella Mae had accepted the fact that Cassie could remember nothing more of that night in June, she had gone back to the drama of radio soap operas. Every night she brought Dale and Cassie up to date on her favorites.

"I already told you, Dale, it was on *The Guiding Light*. Well, like I was sayin', when Rose had to tell Dr. Rutledge about the—"

Cassie tuned her out, but then Dale was talking.

"—wouldn't even open that screen door of hers to give me a drink of water. You wouldn't believe how some of them act. You'd think I was some maniac come to their door instead of a thirsty old postman they see every dang day of their life!"

Cassie worked up the courage to broach the subject she had been thinking about all afternoon. "I heard some of the girls at school talking." She stopped to clear her throat. "They was saying that their folks give them an allowance every week—spending money . . ."

Dale stuck a toothpick in his mouth. "What for?"

"Why, so they can buy things, like a dress or—"

"Rich folks, I reckon," Ella Mae said comfortably.

"No, ma'am." Cassie took a deep breath. "They say some people pay their kids a little something for doing the chores, like the housework and all."

"Well, I never!" Ella Mae reached for another biscuit. "I reckon that's about the silliest thing I ever heard of! Why would they pay them kids for doin' what they got to? I mean, chores is chores, ain't they?"

Cassie looked down at her plate. "Yes, ma'am. I guess so."

There was nothing more to say on the subject. Cassie got up to clear the dishes and saw the Frigidaire, the one that had been purchased with the money Mr. Steele gave Dale: her school clothes money.

After that Cassie listened to the girls in the rest room, but she did not try to join them. She hunched over her stack of books as if by making herself smaller she could make herself less offensive to the others, to the insiders.

DALE AND ELLA MAE went to church every Sunday night that autumn, but Cassie pled homework and stayed home. Usually she was asleep by the time they came home, but occasionally she heard them tiptoe down the hall. Cassie's door would open and Ella Mae would peek in and whisper, "Cassie? You awake?" If Cassie did not answer, there would be other whispers and then a rhythmic squeaking coming from their bedroom.

She did not know what the squeaking was until one afternoon when Ella Mae flopped down on the bed and the springs squeaked in protest. Ella Mae looked up at her suspiciously. "What you starin' at, girl?"

"Oh, I just thought of something that happened at school today."

"Well, keep it to yourself, will you? It's time for my stories."

The next Sunday night Cassie was awake when they came home. She pulled her pillow over her head, but she heard the squeaking and she knew what they were doing. She just did not know how.

On the farm Cassie had seen Granny's Rhode Island Red rooster ride down the hens and she had watched stray dogs. She knew that human beings did it, too, but she could not figure out the mechanics of it. The insider girls probably knew but she could not ask them. In fact, she did not know what to ask.

Once Cassie began to listen to her teachers, her schoolwork improved markedly. One afternoon in early December the history teacher asked her to stay after school. Miss Cox was a gray-faced woman in her early fifties, with a long heavy jaw and piercing black eyes.

"Well, Cassie Taylor, I was about to put you back a grade. I thought your teacher at that country school had been wrong to give you a double promotion." She smiled ruefully. "Not that I would blame her. With the students those poor women get, any spark of intelligence must shine out like Diogenes' lantern."

"Whose lantern, Miss Cox?"

The black eyes bored into her. "Cassie, there are gaps in your knowledge the size of the Grand Canyon!"

"I know what *that* is," Cassie said hastily.

"Thank God for small favors! Your work has taken a remarkable turn for the better. Can you explain that?"

Cassie thought of the day she saw the mallards but she could not explain that even to herself. "I guess I'm just working harder."

Miss Cox smiled. "Indeed you are, my dear, and I want you to work even harder. I'm going to give you a list of outside reading that will plug some of those gaps in your education. You'll have to spend some time in the library, of course."

Cassie pictured the school library, two classrooms thrown together. "But it closes when school does, Miss Cox."

"The public library, dear. You have a card, don't you?"

"No, ma'am. I didn't know there was a library."

"Haven't your parents ever taken you to the—" She stopped, looking at Cassie's faded dress and worn-out shoes. She learned forward over her desk. "You must learn, child! It's the only way out!"

Cassie remembered hearing the same thing from Miss Naomi Bencher: "Get away from here, Cassie! Make something of yourself!"

"Yes, ma'am. I'll go to the public library, Miss Cox. I promise."

"Good." The teacher looked at her clothes again. "Put my name on the application for a card, Cassie. I'll be your sponsor."

The library Andrew Carnegie had given to the town, like other Carnegie libraries, was a building that looked larger outside than in. To Cassie Taylor, however, it was a refuge, a quiet place, an ordered place where she could study without the tinny voices crying, "I can't bear it!"

Unfortunately, Ella Mae was more concerned with getting the housework done than with the gaps in Cassie's education. Reluctantly she agreed to allow her three afternoons a week at the Carnegie library.

The third Tuesday in January 1939 was not one of the three after-noons, and she hurried home right after school. It was snowing lightly and the wind cut like a knife through her thin coat. When she went to the bathroom at home, she found flecks of blood on her cotton panties.

"Ella Mae!" she cried, and instantly wished that she had not, be-cause her fear was overcome by shame. Blood down there must mean that she had done something terribly wrong.

The bathroom door banged open. "What's the matter?"

Cassie blushed and pointed to the red flecks.

"Ain't nobody ever told you about the Curse? I guess your granny was too old, wasn't she? Oh, dear, that means it's up to me."

Ella Mae explained the equipment to Cassie but she could not ex-plain the physiology of menstruation. Finally she gave up and ended a conversation that was becoming as painful to her as it was to Cassie.

Cassie trudged through the park on her way home from school the next day. She did not even want to go to the library. She could think of nothing but the mysterious occurrences in her body. If only she knew more about it. If only she could ask someone, some woman. But there was no one to ask. She stopped suddenly, remembering a voice from long ago: Miss Naomi Bencher's voice. "You can learn about anything on earth if you can just get hold of the right book."

She spun around and went straight to the public library. The tall, thin librarian was on duty, the one with short gray hair. In a low voice Cassie told her what she wanted.

"A book about the—oh." The librarian leaned over the desk and lowered her voice, too. "You mean, a book about menstruation. Books of that sort are on the closed shelf and can be released only to adults. Ask your mother to come in and get it."

Cassie blushed and hurried out. She had suspected that it was shameful, but she had not realized just how bad it was. What was worse, Ella Mae said this would happen to her again and again, every month of her life. Shameful or not, she had to know.

She sat on the library steps and wrote a note in her best handwrit-ing. She could not remember the word the librarian used, so she used Ella Mae's.

To the Library.

I would come myself but I'm sick so please let Cassandra
Taylor have the book from the closed shelf that explains about
The Curse. Thank you.

Her mother, Mrs. Leona Taylor.

The tall librarian was still at the desk.

"I ran home," Cassie said breathlessly, "and I got this here—I got
this note."

The librarian read it carefully, running her finger along the words.
When the finger reached the word "Curse" the librarian looked across
at Cassie and a muscle jumped in her cheek, but she read on.

She shook her head. "I'm afraid, dear, that you have written this
note yourself, and I cannot—" She looked closely at Cassie. "Are
you sure," she whispered, "that there's no one, no woman you can
talk to about this?"

"Yes, ma'am."

The librarian sighed and went away. She returned with a thick red
book. She opened it to the right page and laid an open news magazine
on top of it. "Keep this magazine over it in case someone comes—
you must hurry, now!"

The book was written clearly and had good illustrations, but it was
tough going. Cassie was just beginning to understand it when a
middle-aged woman in a brown hat sat down at the end of the table
and opened a dictionary of musical terms. Cassie hastily pulled the
magazine over the red book. She read the magazine as intently as if
she were preparing for an examination on the article.

Secretary of the Interior Harold Ickes had made a speech denounc-
ing the Nazis, and Adolf Hitler was demanding an apology from the
United States. He in turn denounced America for prolonging the war
in Spain by sending hundred of thousands of barrels of flour to the
Spanish civilians who had suffered under Franco's bombing attacks.
The story gave a graphic description of one such attack. Explosions
gutted houses, torn and bloodied bodies littered the streets, and a baby
sat in the road and cried out to his mother, who lay dead in the ditch
beside the road. "A rain of fire, of death and destruction, fell on the
innocent victims of the—"

The woman in the brown hat left and Cassie pushed the magazine aside and turned the pages of the red book to the next section, skimming the text but paying close attention to the illustrations.

She sucked in her breath. There were drawings of the way human beings did it. It looked unlikely, but it was printed in the book, so it had to be right.

The book slammed on her hand, and she looked up into the angry face of the tall librarian. "You weren't supposed to read that part!"

"I'm sorry. I only wanted to—"

"I know exactly what you wanted to do, young lady! You thought you could trick me into letting you read it, just so you could tell all your nasty little friends. I'll have that book now, and don't you ever try to pull a stunt like that again, not in my library!"

"Please, I'm sorry." Cassie stood up. "I only wanted to—listen, I don't even have any friends."

The librarian sniffed and marched away.

Cassie dawdled in the park, thinking about what she had read. She felt better about menstruation. The book made it seem natural, even logical. There was a hint of admiration in the text, as if the doctor who wrote it wanted to give full marks to a Creator who had found an ingenious solution to a complicated problem. It was menstruation, not the Curse.

There was a proper term for the other thing, too. Marital relations. That meant it was something married people did. People like Ella Mae and Dale. She wished she had been able to read more, to discover the connection between religion and marital relations, to understand about Sunday night church and squeaking bedsprings.

———————

Chapter 10

"BUT WEDNESDAY is my library day!"

"I don't care about that, you get yourself home right after school. Brother Stoddard, he's havin' a prayer meetin' here tonight, and we got to get this house cleaned up."

It was a small group. Ella Mae and Dale, a nondescript couple named Johnson and Mr. and Mrs. Stringer. Brother Stringer was as thin as his wife was fat, a small man whose substance seemed to have been extracted by years of poverty.

Cassie opened the door for Brother Stoddard and instinctively took a step backward. Even in January, the man was wearing a white suit and white shoes and a white shirt and a white necktie. The light fell on his whiteness and he seemed to reflect it and to glow with a cold white light of his own. He was in his late thirties, taller than Dale, and broad chested with heavy sloping shoulders and a round, ruddy face under black hair parted in the center and slicked down with grease.

When he stepped through the door into the living room his small dark eyes flickered over her body. She drew back, feeling that his look was an invasion.

"Well!" he said in a rumbling voice. "I reckon you're Miz Hodge's little orphan cousin."

"Come in, brother, come in!" Ella Mae cried. She pushed him to the best armchair like a tugboat maneuvering an ocean liner. "You, Cassie! Bring in the coffee and them cookies you made."

Brother Stoddard raised a pudgy hand. "Sister Hodge, let's us have a Bible verse to start off with. Here, Miss Cassie, you stand by me. First Corinthians: thirteen." He took Cassie's hand in his and squeezed it, his damp hot flesh enclosing hers as if to take possession of it. Cassie could smell the man, the hot acrid sweat, and she felt the heat rising on her throat and her face. The others watched, and what did they see? Her blush? The shameful wad between her legs? Could they see that even as she stood there with her hand enfolded in that of a man of God, she was a woman marked with the curse of Eve?

Brother Stoddard raised his eyes as if God Himself were hovering patiently at the ceiling.

" 'Though I speak with the tongues of men and of angels, and have not charity, I am become as soundin' brass, or a tinklin' cymbal. And though I have the gift of prophecy, and understand all mysteries . . .' "

As he spoke his male power seemed to flow from his hand to hers, invading her body. Cassie trembled, listening to his heavy voice and beyond it her grandmother's soft one saying those words. She was not aware that she was speaking until she heard her own voice joining those others, her own clear voice rising above them, in passionate inspiration.

" 'For now we see through a glass, darkly; but then face to face: now I know in part; but then shall I know even as also I am known. And now abideth faith, hope, charity, these three; but the greatest of these is charity.' "

Brother Stoddard dropped her hand and stepped back, staring at her blankly at first and then with narrow suspicious eyes.

Sister Stringer screamed and then her voice called out like a trumpet. "She's got the Spirit! Praise the Lord!" And they all were on their feet, crying out their praise. Even dried-up Brother Stringer's face glowed with ecstasy.

"Amen!"

"Send down Thy Spirit, Lord!"

"Folks!" Brother Stoddard looked as if he would explode. "Now, calm down, folks. Let's us pray silently for a minute."

They were quiet then, their eyes down, until Brother Stoddard proclaimed, "Amen!"

Ella Mae turned to Cassie. "How about gettin' them cookies?"

"I'll help her," Brother Stoddard said.

In the kitchen, his smile disappeared. He waved Cassie to a seat at the table and sat down next to her, his thick thighs straining the white cloth of his pants. He looked at Cassie with cool, speculative eyes. "Well, sister, you put on quite a show. What's your game?"

"I don't know what you mean!"

"Look, kiddo, I was in the God business when you was still in your didies. If you think you got a chance of movin' in on me, you got the—" He stopped and looked at her closely. "Say, you do know what happened out there, don't you?"

Did she know? She was not sure. Something had happened, she did know that. She had heard those words and those voices, one real and one remembered, and everything had come together—the tumult of the past and the mysterious changes that were taking place in her body and the oddly exciting feeling of the hot male hand holding hers. It all came together and it lifted her, raised her from the confines of Ella Mae's gray living room to a world of passionate colors that swirled around her and carried her away. And in that one quiet moment before Sister Stringer screamed, there was a sense of a peace so broad and so deep that it could hold the whole world within it. How could she explain what had happened? How could she put it into words?

She took one look at the preacher's suspicious face and realized that she had better not even try.

She let her eyes glaze over. "I remember—I was standing back there, listening to you, and then everybody was yelling 'Amen' and 'She got the spirit.'" She smiled at him, wide-eyed. "Did I do something wrong?"

He watched her closely for a moment, then he sighed. "Oh, boy, now I seen everything."

"You mean I really had the Spirit, Brother Stoddard?"

"Yeah. Somethin' like that." He looked at her for a minute and then he put his hand on her knee, a pudgy hand with a diamond ring on the little finger. "Tell you what, let's us just forget this little talk we had, honey. Ain't no sense in botherin' your folks with it, is there?"

"Oh, no, sir!"

His eyes narrowed. "But you keep this in mind, kiddo. There

ain't room in this little old church for but one star." He put his moon face close to hers and his hard black eyes seemed to look into her mind. "You can come to church but you ain't goin' to get the Spirit. You got that?"

"Yes, sir, Brother Stoddard. Whatever you say."

He leaned back and surveyed her speculatively. "If you was to get some meat on your bones—how old are you, sister?"

"Thirteen. Almost fourteen."

"Uh-oh. Jailbait. You're right tall for thirteen." He smiled with a mouth that seemed to be crammed with big white teeth. "You know, I got a Spirit message about you, kiddo. You and me, we're goin' to get together sometime. But I ain't in no hurry. I always was one that could wait for the payoff." He gave her knee a final pat and stood up.

Cassie stood up, too, and Brother Stoddard put a fatherly arm around her shoulders and shepherded her back to the living room.

Ella Mae hurried to them. "Cassie, are you all right?"

"Sister Hodge, our little Cassie is fine, just fine. We prayed together, Cassie and me."

"Praise the Lord!"

Brother Stoddard cast a cool look at Brother Stringer. "We prayed and we got us a clear message. This here Cassie is a slender reed, the Lord told us, too weak to bear the power of His Spirit. She's got to give up on it till she's eighteen years of age and a woman grown. Yes, friends. A woman grown."

"Amen, brother!"

That time Brother Stoddard smiled upon the shouter. He smiled upon Cassie, too, and then spread his hands for silence.

"And now, let us pray."

EACH FALL during the next three years, Miss Cox's history classes could expect a sermon on the subject of current events. "Read the newspapers carefully, class. You may think that decisions made in Europe do not affect Whitman, Oklahoma, but this is history in the making." Each day, one student had to report to the class on a current event.

She could never convince her students that events abroad were as important as the current events in their own high school. In the fall

of 1939, Cassie's sophomore classmates were more interested in the
real football schedule than the Phony War, and their parents were,
too. The Nazi air war on England made people cluck their tongues,
but in 1940 it was London that was bombed, after all, not Tulsa.

To Miss Cox's students the vital questions were those which confronted them in the halls at Whitman High. Will Claremore beat
Whitman at football this year? Will Sally Green be elected homecom-
ing queen? Will Dan ask Susy to the prom?

In 1941 Marian Anderson was refused the use of Constitution Hall
by the Daughters of the American Revolution and sang on the steps
of the Lincoln Memorial, to an audience of seventy-five thousand. In
1941, fifty percent of the young Americans called up by Selective Service were rejected on medical grounds because of malnutrition suffered
during the Depression. In June of 1941 Hitler invaded the Soviet
Union and in September President Roosevelt and Winston Churchill
met on the high seas to sign the Atlantic Charter.

And in September of 1941 Claremore beat Whitman 43–6 and Sally
Green cried her eyes out because she was only runner-up for home-
coming queen. And Dan did indeed ask Susy to the prom.

Cassie Taylor dutifully presented her current event when it was her
turn, but at home the only current events mentioned were those that
took place on radio soap operas or in the Whitman post office. Cassie
went to the library two afternoons during the week and on Saturday,
but the late news from Europe was not in books and Cassie paid little
attention to magazines or newspapers.

She was as isolated from events at school as she was from those in
Europe. She belonged to none of the school-sponsored clubs, because
the after-school meetings would have interfered with either housework
or her time in the library. She had no friends. She had come to
accept herself as an outsider, as had her classmates. Although Cassie
was not aware of it, she received more attention than other outsiders.
It was not because of her grades, which were not spectacular. Her
written work was well researched, but she seldom spoke out in class.

She was noticed because Cassie Taylor had become beautiful. In
the fall of 1941, Cassie was sixteen, young for a high school senior.
She was almost five feet and eight inches tall and had long slender
legs. Her breasts were small but high and firm, and her neck was as

long as a model's. It was her face, however, that made the girls nervous about her and the boys nervous about their reactions to her. Her face had lengthened, which made her high cheekbones even more prominent, and her high pale forehead was softened by the wisps of blond hair that escaped from her braids. Her eyes were the deep blue of little springs in the hills and were set in thickets of dark eyelashes. With the proper clothes Cassie might have looked at home on the pages of *Vogue*. She did not look at home in the halls of Whitman High School.

That year the insider girls wore clothes as uniform as those of the United States Marine Corps: plaid pleated skirts and shetland cardigan sweaters back-to-front over dickies with white Peter Pan collars, saddle shoes and white socks with the cuffs turned up. Cassie wore dresses, the castoffs of the women of the True Word Holiness Tabernacle. The women had gone to fat and their dresses hung on Cassie like deflated circus tents. She tried to take them in but she did not know how, and the dresses developed a peculiar blousiness.

The boys at school talked about her and snickered, but what were they to do? Some of the outsider girls were available for outsider kinds of dates: a cheap movie and parking in the lovers' lane on Reservoir Hill, some necking, maybe some heavy petting, and if a guy got lucky the girl would go all the way. There was something about Cassie Taylor that prevented their asking her for an outsider date, but they could not take her to a party or a prom or to join the gang at the drugstore and listen to T. Dorsey on the jukebox. Not in those clothes.

Anyway, the guys said with a touch of sour grapes, anyway, the kid was only sixteen. Most of the boys were seventeen and a few, like the captain of the football team, were already eighteen, a little slow in school but capable of reading "Greetings" in a War Department telegram. The boys looked and nudged each other, but then they checked to make sure that the legs of their trousers were fashionably wide and left Cassie Taylor strictly alone.

CASSIE WAS AT the library on a sunny afternoon in late October, re-reading her favorite book, *A Tale of Two Cities*. She clutched her handkerchief, preparing herself for the beginning of Sydney Carton's speech: "It is a far, far better thing—"

She looked up with blurred eyes and saw the clock and instantly snatched up her things and ran. In fact, she almost ran over a small woman going down the front steps.

"I'm sorry!" Cassie dropped to her knees to pick up the woman's books. There was a fat novel Cassie had not read and a thin book, *The Children's Hour*, by Lillian Hellman.

She passed the books up to the woman. "I really am sorry that I—Miss Bencher!"

The woman was startled. "I don't believe I—merciful heavens, it's Cassie Taylor! I would never have known you!"

Cassie stood up slowly. She would not have known Miss Naomi Bencher, either, but for a trick of the afternoon sunlight. Her teacher at Turner School had been bright-eyed and plump, and this woman was thin, with a pale, gray-looking face and dull eyes behind bent gold-framed glasses. How could a woman change so much in just three years? And how could a girl get to be so much taller than her teacher?

"Cassie Taylor," the woman said, shaking her head. "I can't believe it. Are you visiting in Whitman?"

"No, ma'am, I live—" Cassie stopped abruptly. Miss Bencher must not have known about the fire. "It's kind of a long story."

"Well, I'd like to hear it sometime. You were my best student, you know, and how you loved to read!"

Cassie laughed. "I still love reading! Listen, I'm real late today and they're going to be mad at home." She hesitated, wanting to ask Miss Bencher to come to see her, but she thought of the tinny cries from the radio: "I can't bear it!" It just would not do. "Miss Bencher, maybe I could come see you Saturday."

Miss Bencher was as hesitant as Cassie. "It's such lovely weather, dear, let's meet at the park. About two o'clock, say, by the pond."

"By the pond. I'll be there!" Cassie ran for home.

"Cassie, you're late!" Ella Mae called from the bedroom.

"I'm sorry." Cassie tried to forestall the tirade that she knew by heart. "Guess who I saw at the library!"

Ella Mae sat up on her bed. She had been a plump, vaguely pretty woman, but since she had Cassie to do the work, she had become obese. Cassie did the housework and gardening, and except for her weekly trip to church and an occasional movie, Ella Mae spent her days lying on her bed, listening to interminable radio stories and snacking on food from the Frigidaire. Her eyes looked smaller in a moon face, and more suspicious. Her isolation had made her broody and her irritability had increased in proportion to her weight. She complained of a bad back, but Cassie suspected that Ella Mae's back ached because she lay on it so much.

"Who'd you see at the library, Errol Flynn? You took long enough!"

"My teacher from Turner School. You know, from down by San Bois."

"Well, hoo-ray," Ella Mae said sarcastically. "And I bet you two had so much fun gossipin' about old times that you plumb forgot about gettin' supper ready."

"No, ma'am, I didn't forget. I stopped by the store and picked up a chicken to fry."

Ella Mae's eyes narrowed. "And where'd you get the money to do that, Cassie Taylor? You been at my purse?"

"Oh, no! Remember, you gave me the money this morning since it was a library day."

"Oh, I guess that's right. Well, you better get at it. Turn that radio up a mite before you go."

ON SATURDAY Cassie told Miss Bencher what she could remember of the hot night in June of 1938. As she talked she stared blindly at the duck pond, and a white butterfly rose from the reeds and fluttered away. Miss Bencher seemed to withdraw while Cassie told her about Ella Mae and Dale and Whitman High. "Miss Bencher?" Cassie said finally. "Do you remember what you told me on the last day of school?"

"How would I remember a thing like that?"

"Well, I remember it. You said, 'Read, read, read!' You said learning was the way for me to make something of myself."

The teacher's voice was bitter. "I must have been out of my mind."

Cassie looked down at Miss Bencher's hands, twisting a white handkerchief this way and that. "You said I had the brains and that someday I would have the looks and that I was to work hard and read."

"Brains! What do brains have to do with it?" Miss Bencher's eyes flashed as they had when she fussed at Bobby Sue for tattling. "Look at me, child. Does it look like reading has done me any good at all?"

The teacher wore a long gray sweater over a calf-length gray skirt, and a broad-brimmed brown felt hat. Her clothes were clean and they were neat, but they were worn and faded. Cassie tried to find the right words. "I thought you—that last day at Turner School, you said you had a job lined up, that you were going to be a secretary."

Miss Bencher laughed sharply. "Oh, I was a secretary, all right. Yes, indeed. Until the boss decided to give the job to his—his girl friend. I was demoted to typist and my pay was demoted, too."

"Couldn't you quit? Couldn't you just get another secretary's job?"

"In 1938? I was lucky to have any job at all."

Cassie remembered a current event from Miss Cox's class. "But business is picking up now, isn't it? With the war in Europe and all?"

"Oh God, I hope so. But there's more to it than the job. I had to have an operation last year. My boss held my job for me, but I had to sell my car." She looked across at Cassie and gave her a brittle smile. "Why am I going on like this? Look at you, sixteen and a senior in high school. You don't want to hear an old woman almost thirty talk about her problems. Tell me about your classes and your boyfriends."

Cassie moved uncomfortably. "I don't exactly have any boyfriends, but I'm going to be a secretary, too. I'm in second-year typing now, and next spring when I graduate I'm going to look for a job and—"

"You're going to apply for a job as a secretary?" Miss Bencher looked her up and down, and Cassie blushed, knowing that she was seeing the shapeless rayon dress and the scuffed brown oxfords. "Cassie, you must get some better—" She stopped and shook her head. "Oh, Lord," she said, "do I have to take them to raise? Don't they ever graduate?"

"Next spring," Cassie said quickly. "I'll graduate in the spring."

"That wasn't what I meant, Cassie. That wasn't it at all." She sighed, but when she stood up she smiled at Cassie with some vestige of the old sparkle in her eyes. "Well, come along, girl. It's high time we got to work on you."

Although Cassie had not given it conscious thought, she had kept intact her picture of Miss Naomi Bencher going home each day to the little white house with the green shutters and the grass and the shade tree and the blue Ford parked in the driveway. Dick and Jane's house.

Miss Bencher lived in a two-story rooming house with a wide front porch that had listed to the right as the foundation settled. The white paint had long since flaked away, and the yard was a gray patchwork of bare ground and dead weeds. Five rusty black mailboxes were nailed up in a row next to the bellied-out screen door.

Miss Bencher led the way into the hall, but Cassie was stopped in the doorway by the gray smell of the place, a pervading odor of stale cooking and decayed wood, as if the walls had soaked up the smell of every pot of cabbage, of every strip of slightly rancid bacon and of the slow demise of the house itself.

It was the smell of poverty.

Chapter 11

MISS NAOMI BENCHER'S apartment consisted of one room with an alcove for a stained sink and a gas cookstove. The furnishings were a narrow iron bed with a yellow chenille spread, a brown armchair and a scratched hotel dresser with a mirror. She removed her brown felt hat and laid it on the dresser. "Well, Cassie? I'll bet this isn't what you expected."

"No, ma'am." Cassie giggled and said hastily, "I'm not laughing at your apartment. It's just that—when I was little I thought you lived in Dick and Jane's house!"

Miss Bencher raised her eyebrows. "In Dick and—oh! *That* Dick and Jane! Oh, my God!" All at once they were laughing uproariously, although neither of them could have said why it was so funny.

Miss Bencher wiped her eyes and hugged Cassie. "Cassie, you are a breath of fresh air! I haven't laughed like that since I don't know when!"

"Me neither!"

The room looked brighter and the smell of poverty was less oppressive. They saw themselves in the mirror, the small woman in the neat gray sweater and skirt and the gawky girl in the shapeless dress.

"Where on earth did you find that getup?" Miss Bencher said.

Cassie blushed. "In the missionary barrel."

"I might have known it. What Christians will do to the poor in the name of charity." She gathered a wad of Cassie's dress and pulled it this way and that. "I'm good with a needle, but I can't do much with this mess. Cassie, did you really think you could wear clothes like this to apply for a job? I know you don't have money, but you don't have the first idea about style, either. Don't you ever look at what the other girls wear?"

"Yes, ma'am. But there aren't any shetland sweaters in the missionary barrel, or any plaid skirts."

"What do you wear to school?"

"Well, I usually wear—" Cassie laughed, giddy with happiness at having someone care about her. "Usually, I wear this lovely garment."

Miss Bencher pursed her lips. "Being poor is not a laughing matter."

"No, ma'am, but my granny used to say that laughing beats crying. Tears put too much salt in the beans."

"Well!" the teacher said briskly. "Do you have any money at all? Does your cousin pay you for doing the housework and gardening?"

"Oh, no! They took me in when I had no place to go!"

"I understand that. But shouldn't they pay you a little?"

"I thought they might, but they give me food, and a bed, and—"

"Never mind." Miss Bencher looked at Cassie as if from a great distance. "Cassie, you are such an innocent. Well, I guess we have to rely on the missionary barrel. Sit down and let me tell you about clothes. To begin with, remember two words: 'neatness' and 'simplicity.' "

By the time Cassie left she had specific instructions as to what to look for in the missionary barrel.

Sister Stringer helped her go through the boxes. "I don't know what you want with them plain old skirts, Cassie Taylor. They're real old-fashioned, and a mile too big for you. Look here at this nice purple dress. It's a mite sweat-stained under the arms, but that don't hurt it none. Cassie, that's a boy's sweater. Don't you see how plain it is? Here, take this pretty one with the big pink roses on it. I bet that stain will mostly come out."

Cassie was tempted by the purple dress and the big pink roses, but she was under orders. She took a bundle of clothes to Miss Bencher's apartment on Saturday.

The teacher sniffed. "I've seen better clothes torn up for cleaning rags. Well, try them on, and I'll see what I can do."

On the following Saturday, Cassie saw a stranger in Miss Bencher's mirror, a girl who looked neat and trim in a white blouse, a brown skirt that fit her small waist snugly and a plain beige sweater.

The teacher smiled at the girl in the mirror. "It's just like the movies, when the mousy librarian takes off her glasses and instantly becomes a raving beauty."

Cassie giggled. "Oh, Miss Bencher, I'm not even pretty, not like the girls at school."

"Of course you aren't pretty. You are beautiful." She looked away. "Do you know, I think the boss's—girl friend is about your size. I'll ask her if she has any castoffs." She tugged at Cassie's arms. "All right, now, that's enough gawping at yourself. You have some idea of how a secretary should look. Now, let's get to work on how she should act."

Changing her actions, Cassie discovered, was much more difficult than changing her clothes.

"Stand up straight! Look people in the eye when you talk to them, and speak up! Cassie, take pride in yourself."

"My granny used to say that pride goeth before a fall."

"She meant vanity. Cassie, you are beautiful and intelligent and good. You have the right to be proud of yourself."

Saturday afternoon with Miss Bencher became the highpoint of Cassie's week. During the warm days of Indian summer they met at the duck pond in the park and strolled through the yellow light, talking about everything under the sun. Cassie felt more grown-up, but Miss Bencher seemed younger each week, with color in her cheeks and a ready laugh.

One afternoon Cassie brought along a sack of dry bread crumbs. As she scattered them for the ducks she felt a sudden pang of loneliness.

Miss Bencher touched her shoulder. "Are you all right, dear?"

"Yes." Cassie dusted the crumbs from her hands. "I was thinking about Granny."

"And your mother?"

"I don't hardly remember her."

"Cassie! You must improve your grammar. When you go to the movies, study the women, what they wear and how they move and how they speak. Not everyone has an Oklahoma twang, you know. And listen to that history teacher of yours. Train your ear to hear correct usage."

"Miss Cox says we're going to have to get into the war in Europe. Do you think that's true?"

"I'm afraid it is. We'll go to war and it will change everything."

"I guess it won't be for the better."

Miss Bencher's mouth was a thin straight line. "Things couldn't be much worse than they are now, could they?"

A week later the boss's girl friend sent a sack of clothes for Cassie: a skirt, two blouses and a pair of almost new black oxfords. Cassie walked through the school like a new person. As Miss Bencher had taught her, she looked at her classmates' faces instead of their feet.

There was no Hollywood miracle in her life. She was not invited to the drugstore to listen to T. Dorsey, but she was no longer invisible. Students nodded to her and once Sally Green said, "Hello, there."

Cassie spoke up in class and surprised both her teachers and herself with the depth of her knowledge. Her grades improved somewhat, but she had long since been classified in her teachers' minds as a good B student.

NOT EVEN WHITMAN could ignore the Japanese bombing of Pearl Harbor. After the first news came over the radio, people gathered downtown, and moved aimlessly through streets normally deserted on Sunday afternoon. A small crowd formed outside the offices of the *Whitman Daily News*. They could have listened to their radios, but there was a general feeling that something had to be done, even if it was only hanging around the newspaper office to wait for the latest bulletin.

Ella Mae and Dale and Cassie clustered around the radio in the bedroom. They found Pearl Harbor in Cassie's school atlas, but they could not figure out how far it was from Whitman, Oklahoma, or why the Japanese would want to drop bombs on it. That evening they went to church.

Cassie had never been to the True Word Holiness Tabernacle, but she joined the other members to say over and over again, "Ain't it awful?" and "Them dirty Japs!"

Brother Stoddard took as his sermon text Matthew 24:6: "And ye shall hear of wars and rumors of wars."

A girl put her face against her young husband's shoulder and cried softly, and a mother held her son's hand until he said, "Ma, cut it out!"

Brother Stoddard waited out the muted chorus of "Amens" and "Praise the Lords" and then gripped the lectern with both hands and shouted, "ARE YOU SAVED?"

"Amen, brother, amen!"

"Praise Jesus!"

The preacher hushed them, patting the air with flat hands.

He glanced at Cassie, sitting between Ella Mae and Dale, and stopped in midsentence as if the sight of her had made him forget his words. She sat up straight and looked right at him, as Miss Bencher had taught her. Her hair was in a blond coronet and she was wearing her gray skirt and the boss's girl friend's sweater, which was not shetland but which buttoned up the back and was the exact blue of her eyes.

A stray "Praise God" recalled Brother Stoddard to his duty. He thumped the lectern twice and preached his sermon, making an unassailable case for the Japanese being in the direct employ of Beelzebub himself.

"Amen!"

"Oh, Lord Jesus!"

Brother Stoddard stood by the door afterward, to bless his flock, wiping his sweaty moon face with a blue bandana handkerchief. He took Cassie's long thin hand in his pudgy one. "Well, little girl, you're growin' up, ain't you?"

"Yes, sir." She looked down. No matter what Miss Bencher said, she did not like to look into the preacher's glittering black eyes.

Holding her hand, he smiled at her with teeth as white as his suit. "Yes, sir, Cassie. All of a sudden you've just gone and grown up."

EMBOLDENED, PERHAPS, by wars and rumors of wars a boy spoke to Cassie at school. Teddy Karp was a second-string tackle on the Whitman football team, a stocky boy with pimples and straight brown hair oiled until the comb marks were as distinct as furrows in a freshly plowed cornfield. He cornered Cassie by the water fountain and waited until a group of insider girls had passed.

"Cassie," he muttered.

"Yes?"

He cleared his throat. "Can I walk you home after school today?"

Cassie was speechless in astonishment and Teddy said, "I'll buy you a walkin' sundae."

"Well, okay."

"Meet you on the northeast corner after school."

Cassie waited on the corner, huddled against the cold north wind.

"Uh, Cassie?"

Cassie quivered with embarrassment. "Hi, Teddy."

He glanced at the students scurrying to the drugstore where the jukebox played T. Dorsey. "Let's get goin', okay?" He led her to another drugstore with no jukebox and no insiders.

"Walkin' sundaes," Teddy muttered to the druggist. "Two."

The man put scoops of vanilla ice cream into paper cups and drizzled chocolate syrup over it. He stuck a flat wooden spoon into each cup and pushed them to the edge of the counter. Teddy plunked down a dime.

"Thank you," Cassie whispered.

They stopped in the park to eat their walking sundaes and Cassie shivered in the cold wind. Did the girls in the shetlands do this? Did they eat ice cream in the park, no matter how cold it was?

"Uh, Cassie. This here is good ice cream." Teddy stopped as if he had exhausted his stock of conversational ploys.

Cassie tried to think of something equally interesting to say, but "It is a far, far better thing that I do" did not seem to be appropriate.

"You like school?" he said.

"Oh, yes! Especially Miss Cox's history class."

"Old Boxy Coxy."

"What?"

"That's what they call her."

"Who?"

He waved his hand to encompass the world. "Them. Everybody."

"Oh." Cassie licked the last chocolate from her wooden spoon.

"Come on, let's walk. It's colder than a witch's tit!"

Cassie bent over her books. Should she laugh, or should she just ignore his language? Oh, Miss Bencher, she thought, you haven't taught me enough, not nearly enough. As they walked, Cassie looked over at him and as quickly looked away from the big purple-ringed eruption on the left side of his nose.

"Uh, Cassie? I'm goin' in the navy."

Cassie stopped and stared at him. "Are you old enough?"

"I'm seventeen now, be eighteen when I go in. After graduation."

"But you weren't even drafted! You enlisted!" The pimple on his nose disappeared into an aura of heroism.

"Yeah."

Cassie clutched her books to her chest. "Teddy, that's so brave!"

He seemed to grow an inch or two. "Ain't nothin' much."

They walked on and Cassie was very much aware of his body moving along beside hers. His strides were longer and more positive than hers, a boy's strides. He blew to watch his breath steam in the cold air and it seemed to her that it was an especially male thing to do. She ducked her head in delight at the differentness of him.

She stopped at the corner to avoid taking him into the house to meet Ella Mae. She waved her arm vaguely. "I live over there." The silence stretched out. "With my cousins," Cassie said desperately. "He's a mailman."

Teddy's eyes brightened. "My dad's a policeman."

"Well." Cassie shifted her books. "I read a lot, do you?"

"No. I like movies, though."

"So do I!" Cassie said. "Did you see *Stella Dallas?*"

"Not on your life. I don't like them weepies. I like action. Like *Jesse James.* That was a good movie."

"I didn't see it."

"How about *Gone With the Wind?*"

"I just loved it! It was one of the best books I ever read!"

"I mean the movie. You know, Clark Gable and all."

"I didn't see it." Cassie looked down. "It cost too much."

"Yeah." He took a step backward, toward the curb. "You ever go to any of the dances at school?"

"Well, no. I don't know how to dance."

He took another step back and then another, and Cassie realized what was happening. He was finding out just how much of an outsider she was. No *Gone With the Wind*. No school dances. She tried to think of something to say that would make her appear knowledgeable and desirable.

Teddy bounced his book from one hand to the other and laughed nervously. "I guess you never went up on Reservoir Hill, either. To look at the lights and all."

Cassie had heard Reservoir Hill mentioned in the girls' rest room, but she did not remember hearing anything about lights. She had thought it was only another catchphrase, like "Do not pass Go." A girl would say the words "Reservoir Hill" and the other girls would dissolve in giggles.

So Cassie giggled. "Sure. Reservoir Hill."

Teddy looked surprised. "You been up there?" He moved toward her and Cassie sighed in relief. She had finally said the right thing, the insider thing.

"Uh, Cassie, you want to go to the show Saturday night? I can get my dad's car, and they got John Wayne at the Ritz. I seen it twice already, and it's real good."

"Why, I——" Cassie tried to look as if boys invited her to the movies every day of the week. "I'll have to ask. Can I tell you tomorrow?"

"Okay. I got to go now."

"Teddy? Thank you for the ice cream."

Cassie smiled at Ella Mae and Dale that evening and she even smiled at herself in the bathroom mirror. A date. She had a date!

The world lay before her, wrapped in a pink haze of happiness. She and Teddy would go to the movie and once they were on a real date, she knew that conversation would flow in a cascade of fascinating talk. They would talk about the movie and about school, and when they went on the second date, they would have the first date to talk about.

The second date. She propped her elbows on the edge of the basin, rested her chin on her hands and stared into the mirror as if it were a crystal ball. And then the third. And in the spring, he would take her to the senior prom. Miss Bencher would help her fix up a dress and teach her to dance. And after graduation, Teddy would go into the navy and she would write to him every single day. She would come home from her job as a secretary and sit down at the kitchen table. She would have a picture of Teddy in his uniform and she would prop it against the sugar bowl and look at it while she wrote. "Dear Teddy," she would write, and somewhere, in some foreign place, he would read her letter while the bombs were falling all around him, and he would think of her and be terribly, terribly grateful that he had chosen her, not an insider, but Cassie Taylor, who was faithful and loyal and . . . She sighed. "Dear Teddy."

Ella Mae was on her second helping of meat loaf. "What do you mean, go out with a boy? You're only—merciful heavens, child, you're sixteen now, aren't you?"

"Almost seventeen. I'll be seventeen in four months."

Dale looked at Cassie as if she were a stranger. "A boy asked you to go out?" His eyes moved to her chest. "Where'd you get them clothes?"

"Oh, Dale!" Ella Mae shifted her bulk on the chair. "She's had them things. Trouble with you is that you never look at people."

Dale turned to her. "I look at people, all right. Sometimes I ain't all that crazy about what I see."

Ella Mae's cheeks turned pale and it occurred to Cassie that she had not heard the squeaking of bedsprings for months.

"What boy?" Dale asked Cassie. "What boy wants to take you out?"

"Teddy Karp. He says his daddy is a policeman."

Dale tilted his chair back. "I know Ed Karp," he said grudgingly. "What's this Karp boy want to do? Go dancin'?"

"We'd go to a movie," Cassie said hastily. "A John Wayne movie."

Dale tucked a toothpick into his mouth. "Preacher don't hold with no dancin' but I reckon John Wayne's okay. I want you home early, you hear?"

"Yes, sir," she said. "I'll come home right after the show!"

Cassie caught up with Teddy in the hall at school. "Listen, I can go Saturday night. I can go to the show with you."

Teddy blushed and Cassie realized that he was with another football player. "Uh, I'll pick you up at seven, okay?"

"Sure, Teddy. Listen, I wanted to tell you—"

But they were already walking away. The other boy poked Teddy's arm and Teddy said something that made both of them break into rough laughter. Cassie smiled. Boys were so different.

Cassie could hardly wait to tell Miss Bencher, but the teacher was less excited than Cassie expected. "Just imagine, Miss Bencher! I mean, it's my very first date! He walked me home from school and he bought me a walking sundae and—oh, and he's already enlisted in the navy! Right after graduation, he'll go into the navy."

"A hero," Miss Bencher said.

"Oh, yes! And he likes movies, especially John Wayne."

"A paragon!" Cassie was glad that Miss Bencher was laughing, and she laughed, too, in delight.

Cassie met Teddy on the front porch. He walked her to the car and helped her into the front seat of his father's Chevrolet. Cassie felt as if she were two people: the girl sitting in the passenger seat and staring straight ahead, and that other girl, the invisible one who floated along next to the car to observe this strange new Cassie, this girl on a date.

The sense of being two people persisted during the movie. One Cassie ate popcorn and watched John Wayne saddle up, but the other Cassie watched Teddy take her hand in his and later slip his free arm across the back of the seat and let it slide down until it was around Cassie's shoulders.

When they were in the car again, Teddy turned the Chevrolet left instead of right, and the two Cassies came together.

"I'm supposed to go straight home from the movie, Teddy."

"Hell, let's us take a ride up to Reservoir Hill to see the lights."

Cassie knew that she should argue, but she was entranced by riding in the car. There were only the two of them, engaged in a night passage through a silent town: darkened houses and streetlights haloed with the settling frost and, occasionally, another car, round headlights flaring and gone, other wanderers in the night. She watched Teddy's hands on the steering wheel, so confident, so much in control. He coughed once and it was a boy's cough, a male sound.

The car climbed a winding road, and then Teddy spun the steering wheel and the car bounced down a rutted lane. Just as he cut the headlights Cassie saw two other cars parked under the trees.

She leaned forward to look down at the valley below, where scattered yellow lights were like warm reflections of the stars in the winter sky. "It's beautiful! I never imagined—" She hesitated. "Teddy, listen, I told you a fib. I never came up here before."

"Sure," he said. "Sure." He grabbed her so suddenly that she bumped her head against the windshield.

"Teddy! What are you doing?"

"Come on, kid, let's get with it!" He crowded her against the door and his hands ran over her body.

"Stop that!" She struck out at him, but he grabbed her wrist.

"What's wrong with a little smoochin', for Christ's sake. Why'd you come up here with me, anyway?"

"The lights!" She pushed him away. "To see the lights!"

He laughed. "Oh, sure! What are you, anyway, some kind of teaser? Why'd you think I'd take you out, a girl like you? Come on now, give!"

"Teddy, take me home!" she cried. "You take me home right now!"

"Later, kid, later. I didn't know who you come up here with, but I bet he wasn't as big as me." He grabbed her left hand and pushed it down into his lap. "Have a feel, baby. Just feel what Teddy's got for you."

Cassie felt it, the hard thing under the rough wool of his pants. He pushed her hand against it and the feel of it traveled up her arm and into her brain like an electric shock. The curtain, the white curtain at the back of her mind billowed like a white sheet whipped in a gale.

"No!" she screamed. Her blouse ripped, and she struck at Teddy with her fists, pounding his arms, his face. "No!"

"Hey!" Teddy raised his arms to shield his face. "Cut that out! Are you crazy?" Teddy rubbed his face. "God! You're plumb crazy!"

"I want to go home," she whispered.

"Don't you worry none about that! I'll take you home, all right."

The car roared back up the lane and the tires squealed as it sped down the winding road to the valley.

Cassie sat up and wiped her eyes, but Teddy stared straight ahead, both hands clenched on the steering wheel. He brought the car to a screeching stop in front of the Hodges' house and reached across her to shove the door open. "Get out! You're home now. I said, get out!"

She pulled her sweater around her and climbed out of the car. She started to say something, but he grabbed the door handle.

"You're crazy! You know that? You ought to be up in Vinita with the other nuts! They ought to lock you up in the loony bin and throw the goddamn key away!" He slammed the door and took off from the curb with squealing tires.

Cassie stared after the red taillights until they went around a corner and disappeared. She pulled her sweater close and stumbled up the sidewalk to the house.

Chapter 12

 ELLA MAE WAS WAITING in the living room with her arms crossed on her ample bosom. "Well, it's about time you was gettin' home! I told Dale, I said—"

The toilet flushed in the bathroom and Dale came and leaned against the kitchen doorjamb, a gaunt slumped figure scowling down at Cassie.

"Yeah," he said. "Where you been, girl?"

Cassie was still too shaken to talk. She pulled off her sweater.

"Look at that!" Ella Mae cried.

Cassie looked down and saw that her blouse was ripped to the waist.

"You, Cassie!" Dale crossed the room in two strides and gripped her shoulders. "What you been up to, Cassie Taylor?"

"Dale, I didn't—he—" She pulled herself free and dropped to her knees to bury her face in Ella Mae's lap. "Teddy tried to—oh, Ella Mae, it was awful!"

Dale jerked her shoulder. "What did he do, girl? Tell me!"

"We went up to the hill. Reservoir Hill. He said we were going up there to look at the lights, but—"

"By God, I'll horsewhip that boy!"

"Wait, Dale!" Ella Mae said. "You tell me, Cassie Taylor. What did that boy try to do to you?"

Cassie looked down. "I'm not sure."

"Did he take off his clothes? Did he undo his pants?"

"No, but he wanted to—he put my hand on his—oh, Ella Mae!"

"And what was you doin' all this time, missy?" Ella Mae's eyes were like black rocks. "Just what did you do? Tell me that!"

Dale smacked his fist on his skinny thigh. "By God, I'm goin' over there right now! I'm goin' to tell Ed Karp what his boy's been up to!"

"No!" Cassie cried. "Please don't!"

"Dale," Ella Mae said, "you ain't goin' to do no such thing! You want everybody in town to know she goes up on that hill like some tramp?"

Cassie sat up. "Ella Mae, that isn't it at all!"

"Why'd he take you up there if you didn't give him the idea he could play around with you?" She pushed herself up from her chair. "You been up there before, that's it. You been up on that hill with some other boy. Sinner! The wrath of God will—"

"No! I told him I'd gone up there before, but that was just to—"

"Just to what?" Ella Mae leaned over her. "Everybody in town knows what goes on up there!"

"I didn't!" Cassie cried. "I swear on the Bible, I didn't know!"

"Don't you take the word of the Lord in vain, you sinner! Don't you talk about the Bible! Goin' up to that hill with boys and—"

"Ella Mae, I never went up there before, I swear."

"You hush up, missy, I don't want to hear one more word out of you! You led that boy on and you know it!"

Cassie turned desperately to Dale. "I didn't lead him on, Dale, I just didn't know . . ." Her voice trailed away when she saw the odd half smile on his face.

"Sure, Cassie. Sure." He swallowed and his Adam's apple jerked in his thin neck. He turned to Ella Mae. "We got to face it, honey, our little Cassie's turnin' into a right pretty girl. It's only natural that boys is goin' to take a interest in her." He smiled at Cassie, but she looked away uncomfortably. "I don't think Cassie would lead a boy on, honey. She wouldn't go and do a thing like that."

Ella Mae glared at him. "I don't care what you say. You, girl, you get to you room, you hear? And let me tell you, that's the last time you're goin' out with a boy! That's the last time you're goin' to bring shame on this house!"

Cassie started to protest, but Dale winked at her behind Ella Mae's back. "Go on, do like she says."

In her room, Cassie jerked off the torn blouse and her other clothes and threw them into the corner. She pulled on her flannel nightgown and got under her covers, but removing the offending clothes had done no good at all. She still felt dirty.

Her door squeaked open and Dale's gaunt body was silhouetted against the light in the hall.

"Ssh," he whispered. He pushed a piece of paper into her hand. "Wait till I'm out of here, honey, then you read this. Don't tell her, hear?"

When the door closed Cassie got out of bed and turned on the light.

It was a piece of notebook paper with a Bible verse copied out in Dale's angular handwriting.

> He that is without sin among you, let him
> first cast a stone at her.
>
> > John 8:7
>
> Pray for forgiveness.

She turned off the light and climbed back into bed, relieved. Dale was kind, she thought. Suddenly she sat up in bed. That verse was about a women taken in adultery, in sin, and Cassie had not sinned. She had been sinned against. She put her hands over her face. No matter what he had said in the living room, Dale agreed with Ella Mae. Cassie was the sinner. Only Cassie.

THE NEXT DAY, Sunday, the house was foggy with accusation and suspicion. Ella Mae would not look at Cassie, but Dale watched her with that same little half-smile. Cassie did not talk to them, because she was coming around to their way of thinking. She was not sure how she had sinned, but they knew their religion, and they made it crystal clear that she was one of the ungodly.

She went to church with Ella Mae and Dale that night and prayed ardently for forgiveness. God knew what her sin was, as He knew all.

She hoped that He was the forgiving God of the Old-Timers' church, because the Hodges' God would probably strike her down with fire.

After the service, Brother Stoddard waited at the door to bless his flock. He put his hand on Cassie's hair and called down a special blessing. "And free, O Lord, Thy servant Cassie Taylor from temptation and deliver her out of sin."

Cassie stiffened. Could Brother Stoddard tell that she was a sinner just by looking at her? She was confused as to what she knew, what Brother Stoddard knew and what God knew. She felt abased and at the same time chosen, set apart from the innocent.

At school that week, Cassie was sure that everyone was staring at her, insiders and outsiders alike, and that her guilt was manifest as surely as if she wore a scarlet *A* embroidered on her breast.

All week she tried to find a way to atone for her sin and finally she realized what it would be. On Saturday she went to see Miss Bencher.

Cassie put her back against the door for support. "Miss Bencher, I came to tell you—"

"Wait, dear. Come over here by the heater and get warm."

"Miss Bencher, I can't come here no more."

"Anymore," Miss Bencher said automatically. "What? What are you—"

Cassie clasped her hands like Brother Stoddard and her voice rose to the fervent singsong of his prayers. "You helped me. You took me in when I was in need and you nurtured me and you gave me hope. You fixed up my clothes and all and you taught me how to stand and how to talk to people and I—and I betrayed you."

Miss Bencher went white and sat down abruptly. "You mean, you told someone I was—how did you know?"

Cassie was startled by her reaction, but she plodded on with her confession. "You taught me and I used your teaching for evil. I lured Teddy Karp with my sinful ways and I went up on Reservoir Hill with him. Not much happened up there, but I know that I have sinned against God and against you. So—" Even in her fervor she realized that she had overshot the climax. "So I can't come here no more. Anymore."

Miss Bencher covered her face with her hands and her hunched shoulders shook. Cassie was horrified. She had not meant to make her cry. But when Miss Bencher looked up, Cassie backed away. The teacher was not crying. She was laughing. She was laughing at Cassie.

"Oh, my dear!" Miss Bencher put her arms around Cassie. "You poor child! What has your idiotic cousin done to you now?"

Cassie stood stock-still. Ella Mae? A woman who did nothing but lie in bed and listen to the radio? A woman who accepted soap-opera triviality as the gospel truth? Idiotic? Yes. And she herself was just as idiotic to accept Ella Mae's sin-seeking God as her own. Her mouth twisted. "Idiotic!" She burst into laughter. "It's me that's the idiot!"

Miss Bencher laughed, too, and pulled her across the room to the heater, but the comforting warmth changed Cassie's laughter to tears and she sank down on the side of the bed. "Oh, Miss Bencher, I'm so—so—"

"There, dear, it can't be as bad as all that."

In a torrent of words, Cassie told her about Teddy and the date and what happened in the car on Reservoir Hill. Not everything, because she could not find words to describe the billowing of the white curtain in her mind. "So that's why I thought I was a sinner."

"No! You listen to me, Cassie Taylor. You are not a sinner, do you hear? You have not done one thing wrong. If there is a sinner, it's that stupid boy."

Cassie sobbed in relief.

Miss Bencher hugged her. "You go ahead and cry it out, dear. I'll take care of you."

The relationship between Cassie and Miss Naomi Bencher changed during the winter. At first Miss Bencher was pure teacher and seemed to relish the job. "No, Cassie, you may not read Chaucer in translation. Look, this edition has excellent footnotes. You'll soon get the hang of the Middle English."

"But why bother? It would be so much easier in modern English."

"Because that's the way Chaucer meant it to sound. Not like this." Miss Bencher grinned wickedly and began to read from the translation. The broad Oklahoma accent she used made the words twang like a banjo string. "When Ayprul weth its swait shahrs . . ."

Cassie roared with laughter. "Okay, okay! I see what you mean."

At Cassie's insistence, Ella Mae invited Miss Bencher to come for coffee, but the two women were worlds apart. Ella Mae tried to explain the latest episode of *The Guiding Light* and became so entangled in the various plotlines that she was as lost as Miss Bencher. Afterward, Ella Mae grunted at Cassie: "Dried-up old stick! She ain't nothin' but a old-maid schoolteacher." Miss Bencher was more polite. "The coffee was good," she said.

Just before Christmas Cassie walked two miles out of town to cut holly for Miss Bencher's room. On the Saturday before Christmas Miss Bencher gave her a carefully wrapped package: a minuscule bottle of cologne.

As the weeks went by, Cassie began to realize that their Saturday afternoons were as important to Naomi Bencher as to her. When Miss Bencher opened the door her dark eyes lit up. "Cassie, you're here!"

"I always come, Miss Bencher."

"But sometime you might not."

In February a delicate shift took place in their relationship. Miss Bencher began to defer to Cassie. Instead of teaching, of doing all the talking, she asked for information. "Tell me about your school friends, Cassie."

"Oh, Miss Bencher, you know I don't have any."

"Well, tell me about your history teacher, that Miss Cox. Are you—fond of her?"

"Fond! Well, I like her. I guess I admire her, but I don't feel—"

"Are you fond of anyone?"

Cassie grinned. "You, Miss Bencher. You know that, don't you?"

Miss Bencher smiled and touched her arm. "I suppose I do, Cassie."

March of 1942 came in like a lamb. The first Saturday was so warm that they decided to go for a long walk. A frail old woman, the downstairs renter, was rocking in a sunny spot on the front porch.

Miss Bencher leaned over her. "Mrs. Butterworth, let me introduce my friend Cassie Taylor."

The old woman put her cupped hand to her ear. "Say what?"

Miss Bencher raised her voice. "My friend Cassie Taylor!"

"Oh, yes." Mrs. Butterworth nodded. "Does look like May, at that. None too soon for old bones."

"Yes," Miss Bencher said. "Well, good-bye for now."

"Oh, don't you worry, honey. I like it real well."

Cassie and Miss Bencher restrained themselves until they turned the corner, then they giggled like schoolgirls. Their meeting with Mrs. Butterworth set the tone for the day. Everything they saw was funny, even when a north wind came up and they went back to the apartment. Miss Bencher made tea and Cassie sat down on the bed and began to rebraid her hair to catch up the windblown strands.

Miss Bencher laughed. "It's a rat's nest, Cassie! Let me brush it for you." She stood over Cassie and brushed her long hair gently. Cassie closed her eyes and remembered the way she had stood between her grandmother's knees and how the comb tugged when it caught in the tangles.

"You have lovely hair, Cassie," Miss Bencher said. "When you have a job and some money to spend, do get it cut properly. Come over here to the mirror." She bunched Cassie's hair at the sides. "About this length, I think. See what that does for your face?"

Cassie looked in the mirror. The fullness at the sides of her face softened her strong cheekbones and made her look older and at the same time more womanly. "Yes, I see." She put her hand over the teacher's. "Miss Bencher? May I brush your hair now?"

"Yes. I would like that." The teacher laughed. "But not if you call me Miss Bencher! Can't you bring yourself to call me Naomi?"

Cassie grinned at their reflection in the mirror. "I'll try, teacher, but it ain't goin' to be easy."

"Cassie!"

"Yes'm. Naomi. Here, give me that hairbrush."

Brushing each other's hair became a Saturday ritual. Like girls in the high school rest room, they experimented with hairstyles, studying the results until they dissolved in laughter.

Another, less pleasant ritual began that March. Brother Stoddard fell into the habit of visiting the Hodges on Tuesday evenings.

When the preacher first asked Ella Mae if he might drop by, she and Dale were flattered. Cassie came home early to clean the house from top to bottom and Ella Mae herself got out of bed and made oatmeal cookies.

The gray room dimmed Brother Stoddard's whiteness, but Ella Mae was flustered by his visit. Dale looked uncomfortable wearing his suit on a weeknight. Cassie sat in the corner, trying to be invisible. Ella Mae watched the preacher with open admiration while he ate cookies and regaled them with stories about his days in the seminary.

By the third visit, however, Brother Stoddard's focus had shifted from them to their young cousin. "Well, Cassie." He smiled with teeth as shiny as his white satin necktie. "Tell me about your studies."

"I go to the high school. I'm a senior."

"And what subjects are you studyin', my dear?"

"Typing and shorthand and history and—"

"Sounds like you're figurin' on a career in the business world."

"Yes, sir. I hope to get a job as a secretary when I graduate."

Brother Stoddard turned to Dale. "Brother Hodge, how fares your work down at the post office?" The preacher listened to Dale's stumbling description of his job, but Cassie noticed that he kept looking back at her. Ella Mae noticed it, too, and did not look happy about it. Finally even Dale realized that the preacher's attention was on Cassie, and he scowled at both of them.

The Tuesday visits deteriorated into idle talk and wary looks shooting back and forth across the room. Brother Stoddard watched Cassie and Dale watched the two of them. Ella Mae watched the two men watching Cassie and frowned impartially at them and at Cassie. Cassie was afraid to look at anyone.

On the first Tuesday in April, Brother Stoddard stopped at the front door to give Ella Mae and Dale his blessing. He turned to Cassie and rested his pudgy hand on her head. "And may God watch over you, my dear." He paused, and in his resonant preaching voice he said, " 'Thou hast doves' eyes within thy locks: thy hair is as a flock of sheep that appear from mount Gilead.' " He smiled at her. "Good night, little girl."

Cassie took a bath that night and washed her hair and scrubbed every inch of her body. She was in the tub so long that Ella Mae yelled at her through the locked door.

"You going to stay in there all night?"

Cassie found a note on her pillow. It was in Dale's handwriting.

Behold, thou art fair, my love; behold, thou art fair; thou hast doves' eyes within thy locks: thy hair is as a flock of goats, that appear from mount Gilead."

The words "goats" was underlined three times. Cassie laughed softly. Dale had caught the preacher making a mistake in a Bible verse! Something about it, however, made her uncomfortable. She crumpled the paper, but after a moment's hesitation, she tucked it into the pocket of the skirt she was going to wear to school the next day.

There was nothing to hide, of course, but she did not think it would be a good idea to leave the note where Ella Mae might find it.

IN THE FIRST WEEK OF April the park was a cloud of dogwood blossoms and an Eastern Oklahoma spring was in Whitman to stay. Cassie dawdled in the park on the way home from school on Wednesday, wandering across the new grass. The ground was soft under her feet, as if it were swelling gently in the warmth of the sun. The warm sweet scent of early jasmine hung in the air like haze. Everywhere she looked green shoots were fighting their way up through dead leaves and sun-warmed soil. It was like the poems they studied in English class: submerged meanings pushing up through a clutter of ordinary words.

In one week she would be seventeen years old, and a month after that, she would graduate. There were new meanings emerging in her life, and new emotions rising from the phoenix from the ashes of her childhood.

She bent down in the reeds at the edge of the pond to see her face rippling in the gray-green water. Her reflection shimmered as if she were looking up from the sea. "Behold," she whispered. "Behold, thou art fair, my love." She laughed and tossed a clod of dirt into the pond to break the reflection into splinters of pale color.

Cassie did not think of Dale's note again until that afternoon, when she found the crumpled paper in her skirt pocket. She smoothed it out. In the light of day it was only a note, only a Bible verse: Dale's way of poking fun at the preacher for misquoting the Bible. Cassie tucked it into her pocket and forgot it.

That night, however, there was another note on her pillow.

Thy teeth are like a flock of sheep that are even shorn, which
came up from the washing; whereof every one bear twins, and
none is barren among them.

Cassie's hand shook. Surely it was only a game, but it was not a
game she enjoyed.

The note on Thursday night had nothing to do with games.

Thy two breasts are like two young roes that are twins, which
feed among the lilies.

At supper Friday night, Cassie did not look at Dale, but she was
aware that his eyes strayed frequently to her chest. She was sure that
Ella Mae would catch him, but her cousin talked on and on about her
radio stories as if there were nothing else in the world.

Friday's night note was the last straw.

Thy lips, O my spouse, drop as the honeycomb: honey and milk
are under thy tongue.

Cassie put the note in her skirt pocket with the others and hid the
skirt at the back of her closet, but the notes seemed to glow with a
heat of their own. She pulled the covers over her head. She had to
stop Dale before Ella Mae found out about it.

On Saturday Cassie stayed in bed until she heard Dale leave the
house. She hurried through the housework because she wanted to
talk to Naomi Bencher about the notes. Naomi would know what
to do.

Mrs. Butterworth was rocking on the front porch of the house, and
Cassie smiled and ran up the stairs. She knocked and shoved the door
open before Naomi had time to answer it.

Naomi looked up from her book. "You're early, Cassie. How
nice!"

"Naomi, I need help! It's Dale. He's been writing these notes and
leaving them on my pillow."

Naomi read them slowly, one after the other, and read the last one twice. "How dare he! A married man, and your own cousin! We ought to call the police! Or better, I'll go over there and straighten him out!"

"Oh, no! What if Ella Mae found out?"

"Cassie, this has gone past the point where you can worry about Ella Mae's reactions! Dale could—he might—"

"Wait, Naomi." Cassie remembered the way she had felt in the park, free and grown-up, and capable. "Look at me, I'm a big strapping girl. I can handle old Dale."

"You, Cassie?" She smiled. "Yes. I suspect that you can."

"I guess I could—wait, I know. I don't know why I didn't think of it before. I'll just tell Dale that I have all his notes and that if he writes another one, I'll show them to Ella Mae! I should have thought of that right away. It's so simple!"

Naomi looked down. "Blackmail often is."

"Blackmail! The way he's been acting? Listen, you were ready to call the police!"

"Cassie, I didn't say that a little blackmail is not called for in this particular situation. I just want you to know what you are doing. From time to time, each of us has to do something that is not quite— not what we would prefer. We have to know it, though, and put a name to it, so that we can make peace with our gods or with ourselves. We can't give our acts fancy names like 'fair' or 'just' so that we can hide from them. Cassie, don't you see? If you call a skunkweed an American Beauty rose often enough, you might forget that it stinks."

"No," Cassie said sullenly. "I don't see."

"You're growing up, Cassie, and like most of us grown-ups, you'll see only what you want to see." She laughed. "But let's not worry about that now. I'm sure your plan will work, skunkweed or rose. From what you have said, I don't think Dale will take a chance on Ella Mae's finding out."

Cassie hugged her. "Naomi, I'm sorry I was so—"

"My dear, you were only full of yourself. And when you're sixteen—"

"Almost seventeen!"

"When you're almost seventeen and it's spring, it is all right to be a little full of yourself now and then." She looked toward the open window. "April can get to be too much for anyone. 'April is the cruellest month—' But you haven't read Eliot yet, have you?" She seemed to withdraw into some past life of her own, and it made Cassie nervous.

"No, ma'am. Naomi, I have an idea for a new hairdo for you! Can I brush your hair?"

Naomi's face lit up. "*May* I brush your hair. Of course."

They did each other's hair, finding one more ridiculous style after another until they were breathless from laughing. Cassie sat on the side of the bed, giggling, and plaited her hair into a long thick braid that hung down her back.

"Cassie, I almost forgot. The boss's girl friend gave me a blouse for you." Naomi took a brown paper bag from the dresser drawer.

Cassie unfolded the blouse, a print cotton with blue and green flowers on a yellow background. "It looks like April! *May* I try it on?" She peeled off her old white shirt and, in her white cotton brassiere, she slipped one arm into the new blouse.

"Wait," Naomi said, "let me hold your braid out of the way."

She lifted the braid and ran her fingers lightly across Cassie's bare shoulders. Cassie shivered and glanced at the mirror, then she closed her eyes. She felt light and airy, as if she were floating, as if she and Naomi were floating together, floating with all the others on a raft, drifting slowly down a gray-green river that flowed between golden sands. She felt safe, so safe. She opened her eyes and looked into the mirror, looked at Naomi.

Naomi was facing the mirror, but her eyes were closed and her head was tilted back. Her lips were slightly open, and she was smiling.

"Naomi?" Cassie said softly.

Their eyes met in the mirror and Cassie's smoky blue eyes looked into Naomi's brown ones. Naomi's eyes widened and she turned away, raising Cassie's braid with a jerk. "There," she said breathlessly. "There, now, it's out of your way."

Cassie turned away to hide a blush she could not have explained and hastily buttoned the new blouse. "Look, it's a perfect fit!"

Naomi's face was pink, too. "I don't know, it might need to be taken in a little in the bosom." She reached out, but snatched her hand back as if from hot metal. "No," she said, and then again, more firmly, "No! It's perfect. It's exactly right."

Cassie tucked the tails of the blouse into her skirt and twisted to look at her back. "It's so pretty. Thank you, Naomi, and thank her for me, too, will you? Can I—may I wear it home?"

Naomi had gone to the window. With her back to Cassie, she said, "Of course. Wear it home if you like." When she turned around she was holding her Big Ben alarm clock. "Mercy, look at the time!"

"We have plenty of time, Naomi. I don't have to be home until—" She realized that Naomi's face was pale and drawn. "Are you all right?" She started toward her, but Naomi waved her back.

"It's nothing. A headache."

"Let me get you some aspirin. Or shall I massage your temples?"

"No!" She put her hand over her eyes. "You'd better go, Cassie."

"Well, if there's nothing I can do. If you want me to go."

Naomi did not look at her. "Yes," she said, "I want you to go."

"Well." Cassie hesitated in the doorway. "Well, good-bye then."

Naomi took her hand away from her face. She was very pale and her eyes were moist. "Yes. Good-bye, Cassie Taylor. Good-bye."

Cassie walked home through the park, but her mood had changed since Wednesday afternoon when she had dawdled on the new grass on her way home from school. Where she had seen the beauty of the new life thrusting up through the litter of the old, she saw the pain of birth, instead. She saw only sadness.

Dale was in the backyard, raking leaves. Cassie stuck her head in the kitchen door, and the sound of the radio told her that Ella Mae was safely in the bedroom. She hurried across the yard.

"Dale," she said. "Dale, I want to talk to you."

He turned around and looked down at her, looked directly at her breasts. Cassie clutched her fists behind her.

"Well, hello there, honey. That's a pretty shirt you got. New?"

"I don't want to talk about shirts. I want to talk about those notes you've been leaving in my room. You've got to stop, you hear?"

"Why, Cassie, them little old notes don't mean nothin'."

"Well, I don't want you writing any more of them."

Dale smiled so openly that Cassie was afraid she was wrong about the whole thing. She fingered the top button of her blouse.

Dale's eyes followed her hand. "Young roes," he whispered. "Young roes among the lilies. Honey and milk are under thy—"

"Stop that, Dale! You stop it! Listen, if you leave one more note, I'll tell Ella Mae, you hear? I'll show her those notes!"

Dale moved back. "Hell, Cassie, them notes wasn't nothin' but a joke, that's all. They was just my little joke."

Cassie spat the words like snake venom. "I don't want any little jokes!" She looked him up and down. "And if I did, if I wanted that kind of joke, I sure-fired wouldn't want it from a man like you!"

Dale gripped his rake handle so hard that his knuckles turned white. "Cassie, you didn't have to go and say a thing like that."

"Oh, yes, I did! You leave me alone, Dale Hodge, you hear?"

She stalked across the grass toward the house, stiff with self-righteousness. As she took the handle of the screen door she glanced back at Dale. He was leaning on his rake, and his hunched shoulders looked tired and old. What if she had hurt his feelings? He had it coming to him. It was only fair.

She remembered what Naomi had said about skunkweed and roses, but she was sure that she had done the right thing. She was almost sure.

Cassie pulled the screen door and shivered. Had the wind changed? It was strange, how all of a sudden the warmth could go out of an April day.

_____

Chapter 13

TUESDAY NIGHT the preacher watched Cassie as usual. Dale watched her, too, but with angry eyes. Ella Mae stared intently at Dale as if she too sensed a difference in him. Cassie thought that the visit would never end, but finally they were at the front door.

Brother Stoddard rested his heavy hand on Cassie's head. "And bless this here girl, O Lord, as she passes out of the halls of education next month and into Thy great world of commerce. Make her, O Lord, a woman like the Good Book says, whose price is above rubies. 'The heart of her husband doth safely trust in her—' and so forth."

He gave Cassie's head one last pat and grinned. "Of course, the first question the Good Book asks on that subject is, 'Who can find a virtuous woman?'"

Brother Stoddard laughed richly, but the others stared at him.

"As Senator Claghorn says, 'It's a joke, son!'" No one laughed and the preacher looked peeved. "Just one of my little jokes, that's all. Well, good-night, all."

Ella Mae headed for her bed, but Dale caught Cassie's arm and held her back. His face hard with anger, he whispered, "I bet you liked that. I bet you liked the preacher's little jokes real fine!"

Cassie pulled away and hurried to her room. She sat down on her bed and propped her chin on her hand. There was a new problem, something to discuss with Naomi. Besides deciding whether an action was skunkweed or a rose, there was the question of what to do when that action created an enemy.

WEDNESDAY WAS CASSIE'S seventeenth birthday, but she was the only one who noticed it. While she braided her hair she leaned close to the bathroom mirror and whispered, "Happy birthday, Miss Cassandra Taylor!" She stuck her tongue out at herself. Naomi would help her celebrate her birthday, if only with a walking sundae in the park. Cassie wound her braids into a coronet. Saturday seemed far away, but after all a woman of seventeen should be able to wait a few days for a celebration.

As Cassie walked home Thursday afternoon, she thought about the serious part of being seventeen. In a month she would graduate and become an adult. One month. She would apply for a job, like any other adult. She would take charge of her own life and of her own money. She would pay the Hodges room and board, of course, but she would have the cash for some clothes and other things. They had not discussed it, but she knew Ella Mae and Dale would not expect her to do the housework when she was paying for her keep.

The future was upon her, and the more she thought about it the more she liked it. She could buy brand-new clothes! She could go to the movies anytime she wanted to! She danced her way through the park, and was near the duck pond when someone called her name. She whirled around and saw a white form among the trees. "Brother Stoddard?"

"Yes, my dear." He stepped out into the open and waved his white Panama hat toward a picnic table. "Will you sit and visit a spell?"

"Were you waiting for me?"

"Yes, indeed. I keep an eye on you, my dear. I watch you comin' and goin'. Let's sit down here."

Cassie shivered. How many times had he watched her when she thought that she was alone? What had she been doing, or thinking? She went around the table to sit, but he followed and sat down right beside her.

"I watch you at church, too, Cassie, and when I come to the house."

"I know," she said.

He raised his eyebrows. "Well, sure you do." He fanned himself with his hat. "You're a pretty smart cookie, Cassie Taylor. I bet you're even smart enough to remember a little talk we had the first night I saw you. I showed you a side of myself that night that nobody at that church ever saw." He smiled with long white teeth. "I've thought about it, sister, and I figure I learned some stuff about you that nobody knows, too."

"About me!"

"You got talent, girl. You had them folks in the palm of your hand!"

Cassie ducked her head in embarrassment. She remembered that night and the fever that had taken her. Had the Holy Spirit really possessed her? She did not think so. "I don't know what you're talking about."

"Call me Vance, baby." He narrowed his eyes. "And there's another thing about you. You're one of the hungry ones. Most folks will just sit and take what comes, but you're goin' to go after what you want."

"I don't understand."

He grinned. "Hell you don't, sister! I don't know what it is you want, but I know you want it bad. Money, or whatever. I can help you get it."

From deep in Cassie's mind one word rose and fluttered on top of her thoughts like a dragonfly larva emerging on a pond and breaking free of the surface tension. She whispered it. "Land."

"Land!" The preacher laughed. "Hell, that's easy!"

"How could it be easy?"

"You just listen to your old Uncle Vance, kiddo. I got a little proposition for you that's goin' to get you land and anything else you want. Like I say, I been watchin' you, girl, and I reckon you're ripe. I been thinkin' for some time about movin' on, see. There ain't enough money here for Vance Stoddard. Well, a pal down in Texas, in a little place called Grand Prairie, he got himself in some trouble with the wife of the—well, he had to get out fast. But he says there's goin' to be a lot of money in Grand Prairie. They're buildin' a aircraft factory and the hillbillies are pourin' in. I figure a good team of evangelists could make it big. A preacher and a pretty girl to call down the Holy Spirit. I aim to get myself down there, Cassie, and I aim to take you with me."

"You're crazy!"

Cassie jumped up from the bench, but the preacher grabbed her wrist.

"Don't you say that, girl! Don't you ever say that to me!"

"You're hurting my arm."

"Don't fool with me, sister! Now, you just calm yourself down and think about what you got here in Whitman, and let old Vance tell you what's goin' to happen if you don't go, what's goin' to happen to you here in Whitman."

"I'll tell you!" Cassie said rebelliously. "I'm going to get my high school diploma and I'm going to get a job as a secretary and—"

"Sure! And live with Ella Mae and Dale, right? And Ella Mae will get fatter and fatter while you do the work and someday old Dale is goin' to get his pecker up and corner you in the woodshed."

"No!" Cassie cried. "Who told you Dale was bothering me?"

"Them old biddies at church love to dish the dirt to the preacher."

"Dale wouldn't—"

"Hell he wouldn't! He just ain't wanted it bad enough yet. And if Ella Mae don't cotton onto it, Sister Stringer will decide it's her Christian duty to tell her all about it." He laughed and slapped his fat thigh. "Oh, that's goin' to be the day! Which one you think Ella Mae'll go for first, you or Dale?"

Cassie covered her face with her hands.

"Hey, now, little lady, I didn't go to upset you." He patted her shoulder. "You come on down to Texas with me and we'll set up the damnedest little evangelism shop anybody ever saw. I'll do the preachin' and you can do the prayin' and we might get into some healin', too." He nodded like a businessman considering a new line of soft goods. "I reckon faith healin' is the comin' thing."

Brother Stoddard raised his fat hands and his voice lifted as it did when he preached. "Cassie Taylor, we will have us fine clothes and a big house and a big white Cadillac car! And old Vance will get you your land, yea, verily, a real-live Texas ranch!" He put his hand on her head as if he were calling down God's blessing upon her. "And we will live as man and wife, and you won't have to take nothin' off of nobody!"

Cassie caught that part. "You mean, get married? You and me?"

"Well, not in the strictest sense. I mean, I got this wife up to Joplin—but we'll be married in the eyes of the Lord. I've got strong feelin's for you." His voice took on a pleading note. "A man's got needs, Cassie."

She caught her breath. Her father had talked about needs long ago, in that other life. She had not known then what those needs were, but she had read the library book and she knew. She had seen the look in Dale's eyes when he stared at her breasts, the same look she saw in Brother Stoddard's glittering black eyes. Did women have needs, too? Did they have the right to needs, or were needs only for men?

"Do you hear me, Cassie? Do you hear what I'm tellin' you?"

"Yes, I hear," Cassie said, but she wanted nothing to do with it. All she wanted was to get away from Brother Stoddard. She managed to smile. "I guess—let me think it over."

Brother Stoddard slid his hand up her bare arm and she had to force herself to be still, to keep from shuddering. "Now, that's what I like to hear, baby! I can show you a good time, kiddo."

Cassie looked at the hand on her arm. "I can't decide it right now."

"Sure, honey." He took his hand away. "Now, we can't chance bein' seen together, so you meet me right here at three o'clock on Saturday, okay? And we'll make us some plans." His eyes narrowed to slits with a hard black glitter behind them. "Now, while you're doin' all this here thinkin' you ain't goin' to talk to anybody about it, right? Because if you do, old Vance will have to preach about you in the church and say things that'll get you thrown out of your cousins' house and make sure you never get work in this town."

Cassie moved back, frightened.

"You go ahead and think, but you better come up with the right answer, hear?" Suddenly he laughed. "Oh, hell, kid, I ain't worried about you! That first night I said to myself, I said, Vance, that little lady has got a touch of the con in her, too. Yes, sir, I said, she's got an eye for the main chance. I tell you one thing, sister. You and me, we're goin' to set the world on fire!"

CASSIE WALKED HOME from the park in a daze. She tried to sort out all of the things that the preacher had said, but there was too much.

That night at supper, however, she found herself watching Ella Mae and Dale. Ella Mae was talking and talking about her soap operas while she buttered a hot biscuit. Dale hunched round-shouldered over his plate.

"—and so Lord Henry, he says to Our Gal Sunday, he says, 'Now, if you're goin' to—' "

"Ella Mae?" Cassie said.

With a fat finger Ella Mae poked a stray biscuit crumb into her mouth. "I was talkin', Cassie."

"I'm sorry, but it's important. Something I need to ask you."

Ella Mae sighed. "Well, all right."

"When I graduate, Ella Mae, and get a job—"

Dale laughed. "*If* you get a job, that's more like it."

Cassie did not look at him. "My shorthand teacher says there are plenty of jobs now, with the war and all, for a girl with a high school diploma. When I get my job, Ella Mae, I won't have time to do all the housework and the gardening and—"

"Whyever not?" Ella Mae said in surprise. "There's the evenings, ain't there? And the weekends. Cassie, you know I can't do housework with my back!"

Cassie continued doggedly, "But I thought you would want me to pay you room and board when I got a job, and that—"

"I hope to tell you you'll pay for your keep!" Ella Mae smiled at Cassie and helped herself to another biscuit. "I figure you can just bring your paychecks home to me and then I can give you spendin' money. Ain't that goin' to be nice? You'll have money of your own to spend any old way you want to spend it!"

A sour taste rose in Cassie's mouth. She suspected that once Ella Mae got her hands on a paycheck there would be little left for her. "But I'll have to buy clothes for work and they'll cost a lot."

Ella Mae's plump face wadded into a scowl. "You think runnin' this house don't cost a lot? The way groceries been goin' up since the war started is a caution! Besides that, I reckon you owe us a little somethin' for all these years we kept you like our own child." She shook her finger at Cassie. "You never brought one dime into this house, missy, not one dime!"

Cassie clenched her fists under the table. "There's the Frigidaire. You bought that Frigidaire with money that was supposed to be for me. And there's the garden stuff I grow in the summer, that Dale sells at the post office."

Ella Mae put her hand to her chest. "That Frigidaire is almost four years old and you know it! And that garden truck don't bring enough to—oh, sharper than a serpent's tooth is a ungrateful child!" She heaved herself up from her chair. "All this here talk about money has put me clean off my supper! I got to lie down a spell." She left the kitchen.

Dale grinned at Cassie. "She got you then, didn't she?" He leaned across the table. "You ain't goin' to put nothin' over on Ella Mae."

"Oh, Dale, I wish—"

"If wishes was horses, beggars could ride. No sirree Bob," he whispered. "You ain't puttin' nothin' over on me, neither. You'll see!"

Ella Mae called from the bedroom. "What's all that whisperin'?"

"It ain't nothin', honey. I was just tellin' Cassie she better get at them dishes." He grinned at Cassie again and left the room.

Cassie automatically began to stack the dishes. Her life stretched out before her like a bleak, dusty road. Working at an office, coming home, cooking the meals, cleaning the house. There would be no money for new clothes, no money for movies, only the same endless grind of work and poverty that she had always known. How could she have been so innocent as to expect things to change? How could she have been such a fool?

She set the dishes on the drainboard and leaned on the edge of the sink to look out at the April night. Brother Stoddard had known what would happen. He was right.

But if he had been right about Ella Mae and Dale, did it mean that he was right about her, too? He said she was like him, with an eye for the main chance. What had he called it? "A touch of the con."

"No," she whispered. "No!" She washed the dishes, but she could not wash away her disappointment. No money for movies and no money for clothes. And there would never, ever be money for land.

Chapter 14

CASSIE WOKE EARLY on Saturday morning to hear birds singing in the gray April dawn. Far away a rooster crowed once
and then again, and in that instant, the solution to all her
problems came to her. Naomi, of course. She and Naomi would take
an apartment together.

The more she planned, the happier she became. Even with their
two salaries, they would not have much money, but it would be enough
to rent a two-room apartment or a small house. Cassie sat straight
up in bed. Yes! A little house with a garden. They could sell the
produce they didn't need. There would not be much money for clothes,
but Naomi was good with a needle. And if they did not have money
for movies, they could talk about books and hairdos and take long
walks. It would be perfect!

Cassie hummed while she cleaned the house that morning and even
sang a little while she was changing the beds.

> "And if that mockingbird don't sing,
>   Papa's going to buy you a diamond ring."

Ella Mae's suspicious face appeared in the doorway. "I'd like to
know what you're so all-fired happy about."

"Have you looked outside? It's such a beautiful morning!"

"Beautiful for them that ain't wracked with pain in their backs."

In her happiness, Cassie could even sympathize with Ella Mae. "I just put clean sheets on your bed. Why don't you lie down for a while?"

"Well!" Ella Mae said as if it were a brand-new idea. "I believe I might just do that."

At two o'clock, Cassie was free to go to Naomi's. She was so caught up in her plans that she was halfway through the park before she remembered that Brother Stoddard expected her to meet him at the picnic table at three that afternoon. She shivered, remembering his threats. She would ask Naomi to go to the park with her. Between the two of them, they would put Brother Stoddard in his place.

She ran lightly up the stairs and tapped on the door. She waited and knocked again. "Naomi? It's me, Cassie. I mean, it is I!"

There was no answer. Cassie tried the door but it was locked. She hesitated and then ran down to knock on Mrs. Butterworth's door.

The old woman opened the door a few inches.

"Mrs. Butterworth, it's me, Cassie Taylor."

"Say what?"

"Cassie Taylor!"

"Oh, yes." Mrs. Butterworth waited as if she were prepared to stand there for the rest of her life.

"Do you know where Miss Bencher is?" Cassie pointed upward. "The lady upstairs?"

"Up there? She's gone." A spark of recognition lit her eyes. "You're that girl Kathy, aren't you?"

"Well, yes, ma'am. I'm Cassie Taylor."

"She left a note for you." Mrs. Butterworth shuffled away from the door and Cassie heard her moving around her room and muttering to herself. She reappeared in the doorway and with obvious relief handed an envelope through the gap. "There, that's done!" she said, and closed the door.

Cassie looked down at the envelope in her hand, and it seemed to grow in weight and importance as she held it. "For Cassie Taylor," it said in Naomi Bencher's handwriting, but Cassie did not want it. She wanted to go back in time five minutes, back to the point where she had not even known that the envelope existed. She turned it in her hand, delaying the reading. Inside was one piece of stationery, folded over once.

> My dear Cassie,
> When you receive this, I will have left Whitman. I will be gone forever. I am sorry to leave without seeing you, but a clean break is the only way. You will not understand my going like this. I almost hope that you never will. Your innocence makes you vulnerable, but it also shields you against the world.
> Perhaps someday you will realize that my leaving is an act of love. "For now we see as through a glass darkly." Try to forgive me, and to remember me as I shall remember you, with gratitude that you were part of my life. Good-bye, Cassie Taylor.
>   Your friend, Naomi Bencher

"No!" Cassie cried. She crumpled the letter in both hands and burst into tears. Blindly she ran down the steps and away from the house, ran until she was at the library. She sank down on the wooden bench outside and read the letter again. She could read the words, but the meaning was as obscure as if they were written in Greek. She could understand only that one incontrovertible statement: "I will be gone forever."

Forever. Cassie hunched down on the bench and curled her body around the pain. After a time, she went up the library steps and down the hall to the rest room. She washed her face with cold water and dried it on the roller towel. She was careful not to look in the mirror.

At a table in the corner of the library Cassie took up the letter once more. She prayed silently, Please, let the words be different this time. But they were the same final words. Gone forever.

Cassie wrapped her arms around her body. Why had Naomi deserted her? Why? That last day at her apartment, Naomi had said that Cassie was a grown-up. But grown-ups discussed their plans. They talked over decisions, like whether to leave, forever. Naomi had not treated her like a grown-up but like a careless child.

She looked at the letter again and took a Bible from the shelf.

For now we see through a glass, darkly; but then face to face: now I know in part; but then shall I know even as also I am known. And now abideth faith, hope, charity, these three; but the greatest of these is charity.

Cassie's grandmother had once explained the passage to her. "It means faith in the Lord and hope for the future." Cassie covered her eyes with her hands and saw Granny's wrinkled face. "Child, it means there ain't nothin' that matters a hill of beans if you ain't got love."

She put the Bible back on the shelf and went out to sit on the bench. Faith. Granny had faith in God, and what had that faith done for her? She had hope, too, a hope for land that was never fulfilled. And love. Cassie knew that her grandmother had loved her, just as she had loved Granny, but could love exist when it was not returned? She touched the letter in her skirt pocket. There was no love.

And nothing mattered a hill of beans.

Naomi Bencher had said Cassie's innocence was a shield against the world, but she was wrong.

THEY ALL WANTED SOMETHING from her, it seemed, and they took what they wanted. Ella Mae liked being the saint who brought a lone orphan into her home, but she was not satisfied with that. She wanted someone to do the housework while she lay around and ate and listened to the radio. Dale's notes made it crystal clear that he wanted her body, and if the preacher was right he would get it, and there was not one thing Cassie's innocence could do to prevent it. And Naomi. Cassie had thought that they were friends, almost sisters, and that they gave each other great happiness. She never suspected that Naomi, for whatever reason, was ready to toss her aside like a worn-out rag doll. Even Brother Stoddard was more honest with her than Naomi had been. He came right out and told her his plans. He wanted her for her body and for her brain, and because he thought she could help with his schemes to con the true believers of Grand Prairie, Texas. To her, at least, Brother Stoddard did not pretend to be saintly or a good Christian or a friend. And at least he was not a hypocrite.

Her innocence was not a shield, Cassie thought, but was pollen to the bees instead. So much for innocence. Cassie straightened her shoulders. There was one more thing her grandmother had told her: "God helps them that helps themselves."

She wiped the last of the tears away with the back of her hand and stood up feeling tall but insubstantial, as if the slightest breeze could carry her away. She shoved the crumpled letter into her pocket and set off for the park.

Cassie stood by the picnic table and stared out at the muddy pond. Winter was over and the mallards were gone. She had cried at the library, but there by the pond she felt nothing, as if the body organ that had the capacity for happiness or sorrow had been excised by two sharp words: Gone forever.

Brother Stoddard stepped out of a grove of cedars. His white suit was so brilliant in the sunshine that Cassie closed her eyes. "Hey, little lady, you been cryin'? You ain't sad about leavin' are you?"

She shook her head and forced herself to smile at him. "Not me! I'll be glad to get out of here."

He looked at her closely, then nodded and wiped his face with a white handkerchief. "God, but it's hot! I hate to think what it'll be like in July. But me and you don't have to worry about that, do we?"

Cassie managed a weak laugh. "That's right, Brother Stoddard."

"Call me Vance, honey, and I bet you'll call me sweeter names when we get to know each other better." He pulled her down on the bench with him and patted her leg with his meaty hand. "Okay, let's make our plans. I got to see Brother Stringer this afternoon. Don't want him to get onto the idea that I'm skippin' out, see?"

"Yes. I see."

"The bus to Dallas goes out at ten o'clock tonight and—"

"Tonight! You didn't tell me it would be tonight!"

He squeezed her thigh. "I wasn't takin' no chances, sister. What if you got it in your head to tell somebody?"

"I didn't tell anyone. I just didn't think it would be so soon."

"Why not? You got any reason to hang around here?"

Cassie reached in her skirt pocket and touched Naomi Bencher's letter. "No. There's no reason at all."

"All right, then! Now, I got a little job for you. I'm takin' along a little souvenir of the True Word Holiness Tabernacle." He laughed. "The church treasury, all $236.50 of it."

Cassie stared at him. "You stole the church's money?"

He grinned. "It's for the Lord's work, ain't it? And who's better than the preacher to say what the Lord's work is? Maybe it's the Lord's work to send you and me down to Texas. No tellin' how many souls we'll save down there."

"But the police! They'll come after you—after us!"

"I got a trail laid out that even hick cops can't miss. I'm goin' to meet a rummy at the hobo jungle tonight and hand him my white suit and a train ticket to Kansas City. The cops can follow this suit all the way up there, right into the pawnshop where he'll cash it in to get himself some rotgut whiskey. They'll be lookin' for a preacher in a white suit, and they won't pay no attention to some old boy in overalls and a straw hat gettin' on the Dallas bus. I'd like to see their faces when those old birds at the church find out that their preacher disappeared in a pawnshop in Kansas City!" He laughed and wiped his eyes with his white handkerchief.

Cassie could imagine Ella Mae's face when she discovered that Cassie had disappeared. She giggled and then she laughed, too, until Brother Stoddard had to lend her his handkerchief.

"Take it easy, girl! We got to get serious now." He gave her a folded paper. "You copy this off when you get home. You got to leave a note, so your cousins don't get the cops after you." Cassie put the paper in her pocket with that other letter.

"Now, the money's already at the bus depot, in a little brown suitcase in one of them lockers. You go down there about eight-thirty tonight, and get the suitcase. Take some money out of it and go up there to the window and say, 'Two tickets for Dallas.' That's all you got to do. Then you get on the bus, and I'll show up at the last minute. You got that?"

"Get the money and buy two tickets to Dallas and wait on the bus. Will I need a key for the locker?"

Brother Stoddard slapped his forehead. "Damn if I wasn't about to forget that! You're a pretty smart cookie, all right."

Cassie smiled innocently. "I try to be."

The preacher nodded. "Just don't get too smart, sister, if you know what I mean." He looked at her for a moment and seemed to come to a decision. "Okay, here's the key, and the locker number's on it, see? Number 4. Give me a kiss now, baby, and I'll get goin' to Stringer's."

He reached out, but she ducked away. "Watch out! Somebody's coming!"

"Where? Oh, hell, they ain't close enough to see what we're doin'."

She opened her eyes wide and smiled at him. "Later . . . Vance. There'll be time for that later."

"Those are some peepers you got, kiddo!" He ran his hand down her arm. "I bet you got some other goodies, too. Okay, I'll see you at the bus depot, right?"

"Right," Cassie said. "Right."

CASSIE WATCHED Ella Mae and Dale eat the supper she had cooked, but she felt detached, as if she were watching them from the back window of a bus that was taking her farther and farther away from them. It might be the last time she ever saw them. She thought she should feel either delight in escaping or sadness at leaving them, but she felt nothing.

Ella Mae and Dale settled down in the bedroom to listen to their evening radio programs. Cassie changed into her nightgown and went to the door of their room. "I'm going to bed now. Good-night."

Dale looked up. "It ain't even full dark."

"I know, but I'm tired tonight. Real tired."

In her room Cassie changed quickly to the least worn of her skirts. She hesitated and then, defiantly, she put on the flowered blouse Naomi had given her that last day. She picked up another blouse but looked at it and put it back in the closet. After almost four years with the Hodges, she had no clothes that were worth taking into a new life.

She read again the note she had copied from Brother Stoddard's paper.

Dear Ella Mae and Dale,
The time has come for me to go away. My girl friend has a car and we are leaving tonight for California. Don't try to find

me. I'm going to change my name and anyway I won't ever
come back, no matter what.

Yours very truly,
Cassie Taylor

Cassie hesitated, holding the note, then took up a pencil and scrawled
one phrase across the bottom of the page. "God bless you." She put
the note on the pillow and took one last look around the room, and
then she unhooked the window screen and climbed out.

On the sidewalk, Cassie stopped and looked back at the house and
the lighted window of Ella Mae and Dale's bedroom. A dog barked
somewhere in the night, and she turned away from the house and
started walking.

The depot was gray and dirty, and was empty at eight-thirty on
Saturday night except for a rheumy-eyed old man dozing on a bench.

Cassie took the small brown cardboard suitcase from locker 4 and
carried it to a bench across the room from the old man. She shielded
it with her body while she raised the lid.

It was packed with money. There were a few five-dollar bills, but
most of it was in dollar bills that were soiled and crumpled, is if the
earning of them had been a hard, dirty job. Cassie tucked a stack of
them into her purse and closed the suitcase.

She studied the schedule on the blackboard next to the ticket window.

Destination	Departure	Notes
Tulsa	8:35 p.m.	1 hr. late
Ballard	9:05 p.m.	On time
Dallas	10:00 p.m.	On time

That was it. The ten o'clock bus to Dallas. She looked again at
the schedule and at the clock next to it. She waited until a group of
people had gathered and then went to the ticket window. The clerk
was busy and did not even look at her face.

Cassie climbed the steps of the bus and looked back at the door of
the depot, half expecting to see Brother Stoddard coming through the
doorway in his overalls and straw hat.

She took the seat behind the driver and tucked the little brown suitcase between her hip and the armrest. She sat there staring straight ahead, not thinking, just waiting.

The driver climbed on and started up the engine, but Cassie did not look at the door of the bus. In a few minutes the bus was moving, rolling slowly through the streets of Whitman and then faster and faster as it escaped the lights of town and sped into its own tunnel of light in the muggy April night.

Brother Stoddard still had plenty of time to catch the ten o'clock bus to Dallas, but Cassie Taylor and the little brown suitcase were riding the 9:05 bus to Ballard, Oklahoma.

Part III

Deliver the outcast and poor;
save them from the hand of the ungodly.

They know not, neither do they understand,
but walk on still in darkness:
all the foundations of the earth are out of course.

—Psalm 82
The Book of Common Prayer

Chapter 15

BALLARD, OKLAHOMA, was set in a wide valley among gently rolling hills. The business district was twelve blocks long and three wide. Most of the stores were still home-owned in 1942, but they looked tired, as if the grinding poverty of the Depression years had exhausted not only the merchants' purses but their spirits as well. The stores near the bus depot were down-at-the-heels, with smeary windows displaying limp, flyspecked merchandise.

Ballard's residential areas were shaded by trees: elms and maples and catalpas. On the west side, the white-collar side of town, there were large comfortable frame houses with wide front porches decorated with Victorian gingerbread work, and west of that the land rose to Ballard Heights and a few mansions built of stone or brick. They were set well back from the streets, and the mowed equivalents of moats separated the castles from the commoners on the city streets.

IT WAS AFTER eleven o'clock at night when Cassie Taylor got off the bus, bone-weary from the ride through the April night. She spent the rest of the night sitting straight up on a wooden pew in the bus depot, clutching with both hands the little brown cardboard suitcase that contained the worldly wealth of the True Word Holiness Tabernacle of Whitman, Oklahoma.

When the hand on the depot clock crept around to seven Cassie ventured out to the streets of Ballard, heading instinctively for the sections of town where the poor clung to the last shreds of respectability. She stopped on East Twelfth Street, at a house with a hand-lettered sign in the front window: ROOM AND BOARD.

It could have been Naomi Bencher's house in Whitman, the same two-story frame building with flaking white paint and a sloping front porch, but there were no black mailboxes by the front door and there was no Mrs. Butterworth rocking in the April sunshine.

The landlady was as tall as Cassie and as thin and, like her house, she appeared to have come down in the world.

Cassie's story sounded thin even to her own ears: an orphan, whose suitcase had been stolen at the bus depot. The woman nodded coldly, however, and said, "Second floor back. Bath down the hall."

The room was small and the walls and ceiling were covered with gray, flaking paint. The iron single bed was covered with a faded pink chenille bedspread. The white curtains were frayed but clean, and there was a small mirror over the battered dresser.

"Change of sheets and towels once a week. Breakfast at seven sharp, supper at six. No lunches and no cooking in the room." The woman looked at Cassie's remade missionary clothes. "Pay in advance."

"Yes, ma'am." Cassie counted out the limp one-dollar bills, and the touch of cash sweetened the woman's disposition. She doled out one tight smile with the room key.

Cassie looked down at her right hand, the hand that had paid out the money. It was not the tabernacle's money, or even Brother Stoddard's. It was God's money. She rubbed her hand on her skirt as if to erase a stain.

When she lay down on the chenille bedspread and stared up at the cracked ceiling the events of the last few days unrolled before her again and again, like a loop of film moving around the reels of a projector. Mrs. Butterworth peering through her half-closed door. Naomi's letter. Brother Stoddard in the park. Ella Mae and Dale at the supper table. The tunnel of light reaching out ahead of the bus. Mrs. Butterworth. Naomi's letter.

Finally she slept, and when she woke, she felt a tingle of excitement. The past was past and there was a new world out there. In Ballard the only connection with her past was through the Steele family: Mr. Steele, the man who had owned their farm, his wife, and their sons.

She remembered the younger son, Dix, swimming in San Bois Creek. She remembered his laugh and his long skinny legs. But she remembered his wanting to see the caves, too, his demanding to see them because they belonged to his father. Mr. Steele had owned the land and, in a sense, he had owned Howard Taylor and Granny and Cassie, too.

She sat up on the bed. The first thing she had to do was find a job. From what her typing teacher had told her, that would be easy. She would work hard, she would succeed, and she would show Mr. Steele and his fine son Dix that they did not own Cassie Taylor and they never would.

Neatness and simplicity, Naomi Bencher had said. Cassie bought three cheap blouses, two cotton skirts and a sweater at Gorman's Cut-Price Store. After careful thought, she also selected a pair of black pumps with Cuban heels, and two pairs of rayon stockings and a garter belt to hold them up. Her last purchase was a leatherette handbag large enough to hold the rest of the tabernacle's money.

In the cracked mirror over the dresser, she was a woman: Cassie Taylor, adult. The short black skirt emphasized her long legs, and although the cheap blouse skimped on material, it looked good on her small-breasted figure. She smiled at herself, a big open smile that enlivened and illuminated her strong, sober face. She laughed in delight, at the sight of herself in her first brand-new clothes.

After two weeks of looking for a secretarial job, however, Cassie's delight had disappeared. No one wanted to hire a lanky country girl who had no high school diploma and no experience. She considered writing to Whitman High to ask that they send her diploma, since she had done all of the work, but what if the school told Ella Mae, or worse, the tabernacle? She could not risk it. People said there were more jobs since the war had started but there was no job for Cassie Taylor.

Cassie was too involved in her own problems to notice, but the war was not going well in May of 1942. Corregidor fell, and within a few weeks Admiral Yamamoto's fleet was steaming toward Midway Island. The Nazis had Stalingrad under siege and Rommel was close to Cairo.

Although Raeder's U-boats were sinking American ships within sight of the East Coast, to the people of Ballard the war was at a distance.

There was no war industry in Ballard and, as yet, no shortages. Individual families were affected when a father or a husband or a son
went into the armed services, but the town as a whole rocked along
as it always had.

Cassie was learning her way around Ballard. During the day she
trudged through town, looking for work, and at night she took long
walks on streets that were almost deserted on the warm spring nights.
Occasionally she met a few high school boys, who shoved at each other
and laughed as they passed her. Once a little dog came out to yap at
her and retreated to its doorstep panting in triumph at having de-
fended its master's 50-by-125-foot portion of the globe. June brought
a heat wave, and families sat on their front porches on the hot, still
evenings with only the glow of a cigarette or occasional soft laughter
to show that they were there in the dark. Once Cassie walked past a
house where a ukulele plinked in the muggy night and a man's voice
sang softly.

> *"Love, oh love, oh careless love,*
> *You see what careless love has done."*

People left their windows open to catch the breeze, and as Cassie
walked along Maple Street and Oak and Spruce, she saw scenes like
frames cut from a reel of movie film. A fat woman with her hands
poised in midair over the keyboard of a piano. A man bending down
to adjust an electric fan. A boy and girl at a window, two silhouettes
against the light of the room, his short hair and protruding ears and
her fluffy curls backlit at the edges. Children doing their homework
under the light of the dining room fixture. A mother holding a plate
of cookies. A father lifting his small daughter high, in a frozen moment of laughter. If they argued and screamed at each other, they
did it in the kitchen or the bedroom, away from the street. Cassie
saw only the good scenes, the homey scenes. In the dark, she wrapped
her arms around her chest and passed by, alone.

As the summer began Cassie walked farther and farther from the
rooming house, as far as Ballard Heights. The houses there were so
far from the street that there was not much to see, but sometimes she
could hear something of the lives going on inside the houses: a girl's

high-pitched fluting laugh or the rich music of an expensive radio—classical music or war laments, "As Time Goes By" or "I Don't Want to Walk without You."

Cassie kept a careful record of her expenditures and knew to a penny how much of the tabernacle's money she had spent, but it was the middle of June when she laid the remaining dollar bills on her bed and counted them. She had paid her room and board. She had bought clothes. For lunches, she had bought peanut butter and crackers to hide in her suitcase in the closet. She had lived frugally, but there was only $102.25 left of the $236.50 that two months earlier had seemed to her to be all the money in the world.

She folded the money into her purse and sat down on the bed to stare blindly out at the broad green leaves of the catalpa tree outside her window. The money was running out. She had to find work. She lay back on her bed, and in her mind the words repeated themselves in a sullen circular refrain. She had to get work. The money was running out. She had to get work.

No money, no work and the cotton didn't make, got to get out of here, got to go, got to go to California. She looked up, half expecting to see walls covered with faded newspapers, but she saw only the scabrous gray ceiling of her room. She shut her eyes and saw another scene: a sunny Thanksgiving Day. Granny, in her blue velvet hat, looking up at a tall, heavy man. Mr. Steele. Mr. James Steele, the man who owned the land. The man who had power. She laughed bitterly, but it was at herself, the girl who had sworn to show Mr. Steele that he did not own her. She had tried and she had failed. She would have to go to him and ask him, beg him, for a job.

What if he turned her down?

Cassie went to the window and stared unseeing at the jumble of trash in the backyard of the rooming house. What was it that her grandmother had done to get a job for Papa? What was it that she said? "I reckon you ain't likely to forget Leona Taylor."

She went down to the pay telephone in the front hall and shuffled through the phone book until she found it: Jas. Steele, Jr., Attorney-at-Law, Rm 610, First National Bank Bldg. Phone 2880. She put her forehead against the cold metal of the telephone. She had to do it. She no longer had a choice.

———————

CASSIE CHECKED her appearance in the mirrored wall of the elevator. Neatness, simplicity. Blond hair in a neat coronet. A pale blue blouse with a black skirt. Rayon stockings, neat black pumps, a leatherette handbag that was softening after only two months' use but was still presentable. She looked seventeen and not one day older, but she could not change her face. She set her lips in a friendly but respectful smile.

The door was open. On the frosted glass a sign was lettered in gold leaf edged with black paint.

JAMES R. STEELE, JR.
ATTORNEY-AT-LAW

Cassie took a deep breath and went into the office.

A tall, broad-shouldered woman was typing at a large desk facing the door. She glanced at Cassie, seemed to see all that she needed to see and continued typing to the end of a paragraph. Cassie thought she was in late middle-age but her hair, a neat doughnut shape around her head, was as black as ink. She wore small gold pince-nez, but then her whole face looked pinched, as if ten years before she had smelled something unpleasant and had not relaxed since then. She threw the carriage across to the right and looked up again.

"Yes?" she said in a tight voice.

"Can I please see Mr. Steele?"

"Do you have an appointment?"

"Well, no."

"Mr. Steele is a busy man."

"Yes, ma'am, but it's real important."

Obviously the woman had heard that one before. "Are you a client?"

"No, ma'am. Not exactly a client."

"Then may I know the nature of your business with Mr. Steele?"

"I guess you could say I'm a friend of his. Yes, that's it. An old friend."

The woman's fingers darted to her pince-nez, and her stare made it clear that Mr. James Steele was highly unlikely to have as an old friend a seventeen-year-old girl in cheap clothes.

Neatness, Cassie thought desperately. Simplicity. Couldn't the woman even see it? She took a deep breath. "If you would just tell him—tell him Cassie Taylor is here. Ma'am, he knows me. He really does."

The woman sniffed, but she stood up. She was as tall as Cassie, about five feet eight, and she wore an elegant teal blue shantung dress with one long string of crystal beads. She started toward a door at the back of the office.

"Just tell him, Cassandra Taylor from San Bois."

The woman hesitated as if waiting to hear all of Cassie's aliases, then went through the door and closed it firmly behind her.

She came back looking surprised. "Mr. Steele will see you. Knock first."

Three walls of Mr. Steele's private office were covered in oak paneling and floor-to-ceiling bookshelves, but large windows in the fourth wall filled the room with light. On the wall behind the desk was a large black-and-white map with a number of areas colored in red.

Mr. James Steele had put on weight in the four years since she had seen him. He looked like a rich man should look, Cassie thought, not like that skinny Mr. Rockefeller in the newsreels, handing out his dimes.

"Cassandra Taylor," he said in a heavy, rasping voice. He laughed. "The prophetess of San Bois. What strange design of the Fates brings you to Ballard?"

Cassie noticed the gray mixed into his black hair and the deep vertical creases in his face. She clutched at her handbag for support. "I wanted to talk to you, Mr. Steele. Sir."

Steele raised his heavy dark eyebrows. "Sit down then."

"No, sir, I'd rather stand."

He shrugged, sat down and put his big hands on the wooden arms of his swivel chair. "Well?"

Cassie dug her fingernails into the leatherette of her purse. She had to say it quickly before she lost her nerve. She had to say it just the way she had memorized it. "Mr. Steele, sir, please will you give me a job?"

He looked at her, and Cassie hurried on to fill the silence. "I did real well in my typing classes, and in shorthand, and I didn't get my diploma, but I did all the work and . . ." Her voice trailed off.

His face was as hard and blank as a slab of gray Ozark limestone. "How old are you?"

Cassie hesitated, wanting to say nineteen, but afraid to lie to him. "I'm seventeen, Mr. Steele. I was seventeen in April."

"And you have not finished high school? You still live with your cousins in Whitman, don't you? I forget their names."

"Ella Mae and Dale Hodge. I finished my high school work this spring, Mr. Steele, but I didn't get my diploma. I had to leave before graduation day."

He raised his heavy eyebrows. "Had to leave?"

"Yes, sir." She took a deep breath. "Ella Mae, well, she worked me like a slave, never gave me money for clothes or—"

"Yes." Steele looked uncomfortable. "I suspected something of the sort that time I visited the house."

"Well, then I found out that when I got a job she was going to take all my pay and I was still going to have to do the housework and the gardening. It wasn't fair, Mr. Steele. It just wasn't fair."

"I suspect you have some of your grandmother's grit, but less of her common sense. Why didn't you wait until you received your high school diploma?"

"It was Dale, Mr. Steele. He was all the time, well, he was . . . after me." She dropped her eyes, because he was looking at her in a different way. "So I left in the night and I came to Ballard and I can't find a job, because of no diploma or experience and—"

"Seventeen, in April." The limestone cracked into what might have been a smile and to Cassie's surprise he laughed, a deep grating sound like the rattle of stones in a landslide. "Seventeen!" He rubbed a big hand across his face and his laughter stopped as unexpectedly as it had begun. "I'm afraid a law office can use only experienced employees, Cassie, but I wish you well." He stood up.

She knew what she had to do, but she put it off. "Mr. Steele? That map over your desk? What's it a map of?"

"It's a map of Clifton County. The red part is my land."

Cassie's mouth slipped open. At least a third of the eastern part of the county was colored red. "You own all that?"

He chuckled. "Yes, I do." He pointed at a spot near the right-hand border of the map. "That's my lodge, do you remember it?

And the farm where your family lived." He took out a gold watch.

"I met your wife down there," Cassie said hastily. "Down at your lodge. How is she doing, Mr. Steele?"

He glanced out the window toward Ballard Heights. "I'm afraid she's rather lonely with the boys gone. My elder son, Jimmy, is twenty-seven and something of a playboy, but he should graduate from law school next spring. And my younger boy—"

"Dix," Cassie said, remembering the tall thin boy who was afraid of snakes.

"Dixon is twenty-one now. In a burst of misguided patriotic fervor, he refused to allow me to arrange a commission for him. He enlisted in the army and is training in the tank corps." He glanced at the papers on his desk. "Well, Cassie, good luck to you."

Cassie had no choice. It was all going away from her, like the taillights of a bus disappearing into a tunnel. She would not be able to get a job and she would run out of money and she would have to go back to Whitman, back to nothingness.

"Mr. Steele." She cleared her throat and said it again, more firmly. "Mr. Steele, you said one time that you had an obligation to my mother."

He was very still. "Did I?"

"Yes, sir. It was one Thanksgiving. And you gave my father a job because of it."

His face was getting red, but his eyes were cautious. "And you feel that I owe you a job because of that obligation?"

"Yes, sir," she said in relief that he had put it into words. "I sure do need work, and if you could see your way clear to—"

"Do you know the nature of that obligation?"

"I . . ." she hesitated. Her grandmother had never told her the whole story. Cassie had added facts and suspicions together, and thought that Mr. Steele was involved in his daughter's death, but what if she had arrived at the wrong answer? Her mind raced, caroming off the little money she had, off the probability of her having to go back to Whitman, and came to rest at the one certainty in her life: she had to have a job. "I know, Mr. Steele. I know all about little Julia's death and what you did."

"So what?"

"Does Mrs. Steele know?"

He stood up abruptly and clenched his big hands into fists. Cassie wanted to run from his sudden anger, but she could not. She was afraid to face him and afraid to turn her back to him.

"You—you little—" His effort to control himself was obvious. He flexed his hands and let them fall to his sides, but his face was still dangerously red. "You think you know everything, don't you? Well, you don't. You can't. Your grandmother reminded me of an obligation, but there was more to it than that. I respected her. I do not respect you. You are no more than a blackmailer and a clumsy one at that. In your foolish questioning, however, you might destroy . . . something that is very important to me."

Cassie backed away from the desk. "Mr. Steele, I never went to—"

"Stop. I don't want to hear any more from you. And if you ever speak to anyone about these silly suspicions, I will crush you, I swear. I will crush you. Do you understand?"

"Yes, sir. I sure do. I promise, I'll never say one word about—"

"That's enough!" He stared at her for a moment, his eyes coal-black with anger. "All right. All right, God damn it, I will give you a job, but that is the end of it. Any obligation I might have to your mother is discharged. You will never get another favor from me, Cassie Taylor. Never!"

Cassie's knees went weak with relief. "Thank you, Mr. Steele! Thank you! I promise you that you won't regret it!"

"I already regret it." He looked at her coldly. "And you may come to regret it, too. I'll talk to Miss Whirter, and she will give you instructions. Now, get out of my office."

God helps them that helps themselves, Granny had said, but she did not tell Cassie how guilty she would feel afterward. She lay on her bed that night and vowed to make it up to Mr. Steele. She would work so hard that he would forgive her. She did not allow herself to think of Naomi Bencher's voice saying, "Skunkweed."

She soon discovered, however, that it was Miss Verna Whirter she had to please. Miss Whirter gave her only short, unimportant letters to type and even those rarely met with her approval.

"You must retype this letter, Miss Taylor. In *our* office, Miss Taylor . . ." she said, but to Cassie the *our* sounded more like *my*. "In *our* office, we do not countenance erasures."

"Yes, ma'am."

"And, Miss Taylor, you must learn to work more quickly. In our office, the work must be done correctly and it must be done on time."

"Yes, ma'am."

"What are the peculiar spots on this letter, Miss Taylor?"

Cassie did not want to admit that the spots were from her tears. "I'll retype it, Miss Whirter."

Miss Whirter stopped Cassie as she was leaving to go home. "In our office," she said, "typists do not dress in skirts and blouses like schoolgirls. They wear proper shirtwaist dresses. And they wear foundation garments at all times."

"Foundation garments, Miss Whirter?"

Miss Whirter flushed. "Girdles."

Cassie thought first of the money a girdle would cost and second of her hips, which were so slender that they hardly could hold up a garter belt. "But I'm skinny, Miss Whirter. I don't need a girdle."

Miss Whirter peered over her pince-nez.

"Yes, ma'am," Cassie said meekly, but she gritted her teeth. "In *our* office, do we prefer print dresses or solid colors?"

Miss Whirter looked at her sharply, as if weighing the question for insubordination, but she answered it. "Muted prints are acceptable. Very muted prints."

Two dresses and a girdle used up Cassie's first two weeks' salary and she had to pay her room and board from the tabernacle money. She liked the dresses, but the only thing she liked about the girdle was taking it off at night.

Nevertheless she had a job. Instead of going out, money was coming in. It was not much money, but there was enough to live on and even enough for an occasional movie.

During that hot summer, Cassie was more interested in seeing Air-Cooled on a theater marquee than the name of the feature attraction, but alone in the cool darkness she found herself more and more involved with the faces on the screen. Afterward she walked home past islands of light where June bugs swirled and drove themselves to sizzling death against the streetlamps, but she could think only of the story she had seen.

In that war year of 1942, men were brave and women waited, sad but courageous, for their men to come home from war. It was a time of sadness, and yet a time of shared glory, even for seventeen-year-old secretaries in Ballard, Oklahoma.

In September Miss Whirter grudgingly gave Cassie more important letters and a few briefs to type. One day she sent her in to take Mr. Steele's dictation. Cassie was nervous, but he paid no more attention to her than he did to the other office machines.

The second week of October was as hot as August. Mr. Steele was grouchy, but then so was everyone in Ballard. October should be cool and crisp, not a soggy repeat of summer.

Miss Verna Whirter was impossible. She made Cassie work late one night to retype a sixteen-page brief that was not quite up to her Olympian standards. Cassie missed her dinner at the rooming house and was as grouchy as everyone else by the time she delivered the brief to Miss Whirter's apartment.

Miss Whirter left Cassie to wait in the hall while she took her time inspecting the brief, but Cassie could see in through the half-open door, and what she saw depressed her. Miss Whirter's apartment was larger than her one room, but the furnishings were just as shabby. The woman must have spent her entire salary on the dresses she wore to the office.

Miss Whirter came back to the door. "I suppose that this will do, Miss Taylor. You must be more careful next time."

"Yes, ma'am. Good-night."

The door closed firmly in her face.

At the foot of the stairs Cassie stopped, caught by an odor that hung in the hot stale air of the front hall. She remembered that odor from Naomi Bencher's rooming house and from her own place: the smell of stale cooking oil and decaying wood.

In her room that night Cassie tried to recapture her dream. She would be a success, with a good apartment and elegant clothes and maybe even a convertible like the rich people in movies. She would drive through the summer night with the wind whipping her hair and the scent of honeysuckle would be heavy on the air and there would be someone beside her, riding with her through the night.   Someone.

But a question wound through her dreams, a coil of doubt as cold as a water moccasin slithering through a swamp.   Would she never escape the smell of poverty?

Chapter 16

THE HEAT CONTINUED. Cassie kept a clean rag in her desk drawer to blot her fingertips before touching a freshly typed page, and even Miss Whirter's perfect doughnut of hair was frazzled. An electric fan whirred constantly, back and forth and back and forth until the rise and fall of its sound imposed a rhythm on the typewriters.

Mr. Steele left his office door open for a better circulation of air and Cassie discovered that she could hear every word he said either to a visitor or over the telephone. His interests were more varied than she could have imagined.

"Joe, tell that loan officer that we aren't in banking to play Santa Claus. I don't want to see any more marginal loans."

"I had to talk with the boys at the M-K-T, Charlie, and the railroad will go along with us on this."

Cassie's curiosity about some of the terms Mr. Steele used led her to the Ballard Public Library, which she discovered was cooler than her room and cheaper than the movies. Each term she looked up led her to another reference. In an agricultural state like Oklahoma, she learned, the large landowner was at the foundation of power, but the dirt farmer with forty acres was no more than a pawn, an example of the family farming system to be brought out and displayed when legislation was before Congress. One book led to another and lured Cassie into unexplored forests of banking and law and politics.

The heat broke, but Cassie continued her trips to the library on

East Main Street, and when she had the chance she studied the map that showed how much of the county Mr. Steele owned. She began to see a pattern in the letters she typed and the telephone calls and conferences she overheard, another sort of map leading to the acquisition of more power.

Cassie's quick grasp of legal language pleased Mr. Steele and by April and her eighteenth birthday she was handling most of his correspondence and learning even more about the uses of power. A favor done for a judge, for instance, might be repaid indirectly by a banker in another part of the state. A land deal or the transfer of oil leases could become as complicated as a spider web and could depend on whose deposits were in which bank and even on who could call a man by his college nickname.

She also learned how Mr. Steele dealt with his opposition: a foreclosed mortgage or a withheld business license or an unfavorable mention on a golf course.

That summer, Cassie went to movies often, searching out cheap theaters where she could sit in air-cooled comfort through two showings of the feature for a dime. Her favorites were the movies about secretaries in broad-shouldered suits, women who typed like concert pianists, in spite of fingernails the length of stilettos, and flipped their steno pads like weapons. The message was always the same, as black and white as the images upon the screen: true happiness lies in true love, and marriage to the boss.

Gradually she began to see the clothes, too, and the furniture, and that there was a shine about them: a halo of success.

After the movies, she lay on her pink chenille bedspread and stared out at the flickering lights of Ballard. She would make it, she swore. She would be part of that glittering success.

But there was no movie hero in the office. There was only Mr. Steele, to Cassie a man as old as Methuselah, and from what she had heard of his telephone conversations with his wife, being married to that boss would be no fun at all. Cassie heard a conversation in July of 1943 that was even worse than the others.

"There is nothing wrong with the swimming pool at the club, Amelia, and I see no reason to tear up our back lawn. . . . Amelia, Dixon is in Africa and will hardly benefit from a private pool installed in

Ballard, Oklahoma. . . . Jimmy is going to have to work when he gets home, not lie around a pool all day. . . . All right, all right, do what you want, but let me get back to work!"

Cassie went back to her desk in a daze. A private swimming pool. It was impossible to imagine such a thing.

Such a thing existed, however, and in a very short time it existed in Mr. Steele's back lawn. She typed several letters to the Dallas company that had done the installation. Mr. Steele refused to pay one cent of the bill until the changing rooms were finished to his satisfaction.

Cassie recognized Mrs. Steele when she came to the office, but the brown hair was gray and frowzy and she looked frail for a woman of fifty. They talked in Mr. Steele's office.

"Couldn't this have waited until tonight, Amelia?"

"James, the manager at the club—I have to make the reservations for Saturday night—and dear Jimmy—"

Her voice was soft, and she began and ended her talk in the middle of sentences as if her thoughts surfaced like water bugs on a pond, fighting their way through the surface tension that separated her mind from whatever was going on in the real world of hard edges and hard decisions. "—poor dear Jimmy has worked so hard this summer and—"

"If poor dear Jimmy had done any work at all, he would have finished law school with his class and begun practice a full year ago. Just what is it you want to do?"

"—A little swimming party for Jimmy and his young friends—to the country club for dinner and dancing and—"

"Do what you like, Amelia."

Cassie stared at the papers in her hand, but what she saw was a big house with a swimming pool: a confused version of Katharine Hepburn's house in *The Philadelphia Story*. Pretty girls and handsome young men laughed and splashed in the pool. Distinguished white-haired men and their fashionable wives sat at little tables and smiled while an old darkie passed a tray of mint juleps and chuckled at his white chillun's antics.

And Cassie was there, too, leaning down to splash someone in the pool, diving into the cool water, down, down to the pale blue bottom of the pool. If Mrs. Steele would only—Cassie snatched the letter she had just finished typing, took a deep breath and marched into Mr. Steele's office.

"Mr. Steele, I believe this is the letter you wanted to—oh, I'm sorry!" She gave Mrs. Steele a two-hundred-watt smile. "I didn't realize that you were busy."

"My wife is just leaving. Amelia, I told you Cassandra Taylor works in the office. Her father was my caretaker down at San Bois."

Amelia Steele looked up at Cassie with soft, unfocused eyes. "Of course. How nice."

"It's nice to see you again, ma'am," Cassie said, and smiled.

Mrs. Steele dropped a white glove. Cassie picked it up and handed it to her with another big smile, but the woman did not seem to see her. "James—about Jimmy—if you could be more patient—"

Mrs. Steele left and Cassie slumped over her desk, watching the scene at the swimming pool, hearing the joking and the calling back and forth when it was time to dress and move on to the country club for dinner and dancing. But she was not in the picture. Would it have been so difficult for Mrs. Steele to invite her? "—A little party on Saturday—do join us, dear—"

Cassie leaned over her Underwood, but instead of the white paper she had rolled into it, she saw the plain truth staring her in the face. Mrs. Steele had not given one thought to inviting her to the party. Why would she? Cassie Taylor was not a person. She was a girl who worked in Mr. Steele's office. She was the caretaker's daughter.

Why was she marked, she thought, why? Was it God's punishment because she had stolen the tabernacle's money? No, it was not the money, because God had begun her punishment long before that. He had set her down on a poor dirt farm, in a sharecropper's shack, and then he had taken from her what little she had. He had sent her to Whitman and afflicted her with Dale Hodge and Brother Stoddard.

God was punishing her for something she had done earlier in her life. Or for what she was. Or for being born. But Granny had told her God created her. How could He punish her for being what He had made, for being a sharecropper's daughter?

Perhaps punishment and victim were created simultaneously, by whim. Mrs. Steele was born with a swimming pool in her future. Jimmy Steele would have a party at the country club. Mr. Steele, of course, deserved land, the best gift of all. And Cassie Taylor? Why, Cassie received what she deserved: the absolute right to smell poverty every day of her life.

CASSIE WORKED until noon Saturday, as usual, but as she walked home though the baking heat, the thought of the Steeles' swimming pool rode with her like a vicious little bird pecking away at her brain. They would not be sweating in girdles and stockings. The girls would be cleaving the cool water like nymphs and the boys would be lounging by the pool, drinking from tall frosted glasses and saying the smart things that insiders said to each other, things Cassie would not understand but that she was certain she could learn if she ever had the chance.

That night Cassie walked farther than she ever had, past the comfortable frame houses on the west side, past the stone mansions on Ballard Heights, all the way out Section Lone Road. It was dark when she reached the Ballard Country Club.

The entrance was lighted by a streetlamp and marked by two stone posts, each with a weathered signboard. One said BALLARD COUNTRY CLUB and the other, MEMBERS ONLY. There was no physical bar to access, but the power of the members locked out Cassie and her kind as securely as a wrought-iron gate. She looked in at the lights of the clubhouse, which was set back in a grove of trees. A breeze riffled the muggy night air, and the rising call of a trumpet escaped from the country club.

" 'Stardust,' " she whispered. "They're playing 'Stardust.' "

There was a patter of applause and then the wind changed and carried the music back to the clubhouse and the people who owned it.

Cassie turned away to start home, but two round lights detached themselves from the glitter of the clubhouse and came toward her. She ran to the side of the road and dropped to her knees behind a clump of weeds. The car slowed to pass between the stone posts, and like a photographic flash the streetlight overhead imprinted a picture on her mind. The car sped up and rushed away, trailing behind it a scatter of loose gravel and a swirl of laughter.

Cassie stood up and slowly dusted her skirt, but the picture was locked in her mind. The car was a convertible, a long white Packard convertible with the top folded down. There were six people in it: three girls in pastel linen dresses, with their hair flying in the wind, and three young men in white shirts and neckties and lightweight summer suits. One of them was waving a bottle and all of them were laughing. The driver had curly brown hair and a smile like a slash of white across his tanned face.

She watched the red taillights of the car get smaller as they went toward town and disappeared.

Cassie dusted her hands and started down the long road toward town, and the breeze rose and brought her one last wisp of music. She stopped and raised her head and listened until the wind changed and carried it away.

ON FRIDAY MORNING Cassie was at her Underwood when she heard a sound so foreign to the office that she stopped typing in midsentence. Miss Verna Whirter was laughing.

"Mr. Jimmy! Let me be the first to welcome you to the firm!"

Cassie turned around. It was the man from the country club, the man who had driven the white convertible. He was tall, with a round boyish face, light brown curly hair and wide-set brown eyes, and so clean-cut that he might have stepped out of an Arrow shirt advertisement.

"Thanks, Miss Whirter. Is Dad in his office?"

Cassie felt a quiver of excitement. Jimmy Steele. Mr. Steele's older son. His voice was a light baritone that suited his looks.

He stopped at Cassie's desk and smiled. "Well, hello there!"

Cassie tried to speak but her lips were numb. Her skin felt clammy and at the same time, burning hot. She half rose from her desk, and his eyes narrowed and ran down her body as if they saw right through her clothes, caressing and at the same time evaluating. Suddenly he smiled at her, a ready smile with lots of bright white teeth, and turned away to the door of Mr. Steele's office.

"Well, Dad, here I am!"

Mr. Steele's voice was cool. "It's about time, Jimmy."

When the two of them came out, Mr. Steele stopped at Cassie's desk. "Jimmy, this is our typist, Cassie Taylor. You may remember that her father, Howard Taylor, worked for me down at San Bois."

"Oh, yes." Jimmy smiled at Cassie and her hands trembled. "Sharecropper, wasn't he?"

Cassie stood up. "My father was the caretaker at your father's hunting lodge."

Mr. Steele gave her a sharp look, but Jimmy snapped his fingers. "Cassie Taylor, sure! You came to the lodge once with your—was it your grandmother? But you were just a little kid then." He looked down at her body. "And now you're all grown up, aren't you?"

Mr. Steele said curtly, "Jimmy, we have work to do."

"Yeah, Dad. Sure." He followed his father, but at the door of the small office he looked back and winked at Cassie. She put her hand flat on her desk for support.

"Miss Taylor," Miss Whirter said, "what are you mooning about? I want you to move the supplies out of Mr. Jimmy's office and put them in the stockroom next to the elevator."

For the rest of the morning Cassie moved boxes, sweating more with each trip. Jimmy Steele watched her come and go and she was all too aware that she did not look anything like an efficient girl Friday. She reached up to get a box of stationery from the top shelf and he said, "Hey! Let me help you with that."

When he reached for the box his arm brushed her right breast. Cassie blushed. "Thank you, Mr. Jimmy."

"Listen, call me that in front of old Whirter if you want to, but when we're alone, make it Jimmy, will you?"

She turned and looked at him. "Yes, Mr. . . . uh. Yes, Jimmy."

It was then when she said his name that she knew that the visible world of work and poverty was the lie and that everything she had seen in the movies was true.

Something was happening to him, too, she could tell. A muscle jumped in his left jaw and his brown eyes narrowed and ran down her body until she felt that they were looking into the most secret parts of her. She stood up straight, proud to present her body to his survey. He smiled at her then, and she knew that he felt it, too.

It was what she had hoped for and waited for and despaired of finding. It was love.

CASSIE STOPPED in the park on Stigler Avenue, near her rooming house, and leaned against an oak tree. There were other people in the park— a fat old lady with a fat old dog, two boys playing catch—but Cassie paid no more attention to them than to the heat of the evening. She basked in the glow of an inner fire. Scenes from the movies passed before her eyes: a lifted champagne glass, fingers dancing over the keyboard of a grand piano, a woman waltzing in a swirl of chiffon, a lighted cruise ship sailing away on a moonlit sea. And the movie scenes became confused in her mind with a fantasy closer to home: a swimming party by a private pool, a strain of music on the evening breeze, a white convertible rushing through a summer night.

And two people wandered through the scenes: Jimmy Steele and Cassie Taylor, hand in hand, heart in heart.

Cassie was back in her room when a thought crept into her mind that jumbled the pictures into meaningless scraps of film. What if he doesn't love me? Why should he love her? A tall skinny girl off the farm, a sharecropper's daughter.

She took out her few dresses, held them up to her while she looked in the mirror and one by one discarded them. They were not right, not for a woman in love. To be fit to love Jimmy Steele and to be loved by him, she needed more. She dug out her old leatherette purse, took out the $83.79 that remained of the treasury of the True Word Holiness Tabernacle, and weighed it in her hand.

MISS VERNA WHIRTER noticed the difference in Cassie the moment she walked into the office on Monday morning. "Miss Taylor, have you lost your mind? A pageboy haircut! And that dress! It is too short and it is entirely too low in the . . . in the front. And those shoulder pads, and black patent sandals! Miss Taylor, in our office, we dress like ladies, not like showgirls!"

Cassie blushed. "I thought this might be cooler, Miss Whirter."

"Cooler! And what have you done with"—she leaned forward and lowered her voice—"with your foundation garment?"

Cassie opened her eyes wide. "It wore out, and I can't get a new one. There's a war on, you know."

Miss Whirter gritted her teeth. "I know there's a war on. Well, see that you try to find one."

When Jimmy came into the office Cassie got all the approval she could want. "You look like a million dollars, Cassie!"

Her eyes lighted with love. "Why, thank you. You're very kind to say so."

Later, she carried a statute book into Jimmy's office.

"Say, Cassie, wait a minute, will you?"

She glanced at the open door. "I better not. Miss Whirter . . ."

His eyes wandered down her body. "How come I never even saw you till last week?"

"I've been here for over a year, but you were at law school."

"If I'd known Dad was hiding a gorgeous girl down here . . . Listen, Cassie, how about letting me take you to dinner tonight?"

"Me? You mean me?"

Jimmy laughed. "Who do you think, old Verna? Will you come?"

"Well, I suppose . . ." Her heart pounded because it meant he— that he loved her, too! "Yes," she said. "Yes!"

"Great. I'll pick you up at six."

"That will be . . ." Cassie hesitated, remembering the smell in her rooming house. She gave him the address and said, "But don't come in. I'll be watching for you."

"Okay, baby, and say—wear that dress, will you?"

Miss Whirter sniped at Cassie all afternoon, but nothing could touch her. The country club, she thought. He would take her to dinner at the country club and the band would play "Stardust" and they would dance together in the warm night.

Cassie was waiting on the porch when the white Packard convertible pulled up in front of the rooming house.

"Hey, kid, you look even better outside of the office!"

Cassie was too much in awe of the automobile to answer him. The seats were covered with red leather that smelled the way money should smell. As Jimmy steered through the poor streets, she sat back luxuriously. Cassie Taylor, sharecropper's daughter, sitting on the red leather seat of a Packard convertible, going to dinner at the country club with the man she loved.

"You like catfish, Cassie?"

"Oh, yes." At that moment Cassie liked everything.

"Good. There's a place out on Highway 12 that does a great job on catfish."

"But I thought we would go to the country club for dinner."

Jimmy looked over at her and Cassie saw surprise in his eyes, but something else, too. "That boring dump?" he said quickly.

Cassie thought of the night she had seen him driving out between the stone posts. He had not looked bored then. "I've never been there and I thought—"

"Baby, you take old Uncle Jimmy's word for it, you're going to love the Riverside. It's a great place!"

The Riverside was a dilapidated frame building with six battered wooden tables inside, and a bar running down one side of the room. The wall was cluttered with photographs and postcards and newspaper clippings. A flyspecked sign over the cash register said, IN GOD WE TRUST, ALL OTHERS PAY CASH. At the end of the room a jukebox flashed green and purple lights but instead of "Stardust" a twangy male voice belted out "Pistol-Packin' Mama."

Jimmy pushed Cassie to a table near the bar and a slovenly waitress came over to take their orders for catfish.

"And a couple of Pearls, honey," Jimmy said.

The waitress brought two brown bottles and a couple of smeared glasses. "Don't tell me you don't like beer, baby."

"I've never tasted it."

Jimmy laughed. "Sure! And my mother hides a bottle of sherry in her closet to keep out moths! Drink up, kid, and let's dance."

Cassie told him she did not know how to dance, but he pulled her up from the table. "You just let your old Uncle Jimmy teach you."

Jimmy laughed at Cassie's stumbling attempt to jitterbug but Cassie didn't mind. He was laughing with her, not at her. When the jukebox switched to "Paper Doll," Cassie discovered that dancing was no more difficult than walking, and a lot more fun. Jimmy held her close, and she buried her face in his shoulder and his male, slightly acrid smell.

Jimmy drank four beers while she had another half, but the River-side began to look better to her.   Late in the evening Jimmy leaned back in his chair and Cassie watched the lights from the jukebox play across his face—purple, green, purple, green.   His brown eyes were dark and he was no longer smiling.

"Come on, Cassie," he said suddenly.   "Let's get out of here."

Outside, the night air was fresh and cool, but Cassie was woozy from the beer and the music and the dancing.   The high heel of her black patent sandal caught in a rut in the moonlit parking lot and she grabbed Jimmy's arm to keep from falling.   He helped her into the car, laughing.

Cassie pulled her sweater around her shoulders.

"Want me to put the top up, baby?"

"Oh, no, Jimmy.   The moon is beautiful tonight."

He ran his hand down her bare arm.   "You're the one that's beautiful, honey.   God, so damn beautiful."

She looked at him quickly.   "You keep saying that."

His eyes were shadowed.   "Because it's true, baby."   He drove only a few hundred yards and turned off on a side road and let the Packard roll to a stop on the riverbank.   "Look down there, baby, at the river.   This is one of the best spots I know for moonlight."

Cassie shivered, not from the chill in the night air but from the memory of that other time she sat in a car at night and looked down at lights.   She smiled.   James Richard Steele III was no Teddy Karp.

Jimmy whispered into her ear.   "What's so funny, kid?"

"Oh, nothing, just—"

He blew gently into her ear, and his right hand moved slowly, easily up from her waist to the side of her breast.

"Jimmy, wait, I—"

His lips covered hers and pressed her head back against the cold leather of the seat and at the same time his hand dropped to her ankle and then slid up her leg, under her skirt, to the soft flesh of her inner thigh.

"No," she said against his mouth.   "Please don't—"

But his warm hand moved higher and Cassie felt her flesh rising to meet it.   A slight, pleasant shiver moved up her body and she caught her breath in surprise.

"I—Jimmy, I—"

His mouth opened over hers and his strong wet tongue moved along her lips, prying at them, and Cassie shivered again, but the shiver became a shaking inside of her mind, where a white curtain quivered, the curtain that she had almost forgotten. The quaking curtain expanded, taking in her chest and then her arms and her legs until she was shaking from head to toe.

"What the hell!" Jimmy wrapped his arms around her. "Cassie, you're shaking like—what's the matter?"

Cassie shook her head from side to side. She could not speak because she was screaming silently at that blank white curtain in her mind. "No! You can't do this to me! Not now! I won't let you ruin it for me!"

"Baby!" Jimmy pulled her up from the seat. "Cassie, are you all right?"

"Yes," she whispered and then she said it again more loudly. "Yes, I'm all right."

"What the hell happened to you?"

"I don't know. A chill, maybe."

"You scared the hell out of me!"

"Oh, Jimmy, I—I don't know what happened. I'm sorry I—" She squeezed his hand. "I don't know what came over me. Maybe it was the beer."

"The beer!" He sat back and looked at her in the moonlight. Suddenly he laughed. "My God, what a little—okay. Okay, baby. I'll take you home now, but next time, listen, next time you get coffee and that's it! You got that?"

Next time. Cassie made her answer light and snippy, like Ginger Rogers. "Sure, big boy, if that's the way it's got to be!"

Jimmy gave her a bear hug. "You're something, kid. You're really something!"

On the way home, Cassie sat very close to him, enthralled by the promise in the words: next time.

Cassie did not notice the smells in the hall that night, nor the washed-out chenille spread on her bed. Her room was dusted with the magic that had sprinkled the evening. "Next time," she whispered.

She lay back on her lumpy mattress and let herself float away into a dream of music and moonlight on the river and Jimmy's strong arms holding her. That moment of terror would not come again, she knew. Fear could not exist, not in a world of love.

Chapter 17

CASSIE TAYLOR floated through the days of August. She spent the days typing and the nights dancing with Jimmy Steele. He did not take her to the country club, but she thought he wanted to be sure of her love before he took her into his world. She would have told him not to worry, but she was shy of saying it aloud, of making a clear statement of love. She was sure that he knew from the way she watched him at the office and from the way she trembled when he took her in his arms. She loved him and she was almost certain that he loved her, too.

Their evenings fell into a pattern: riding around in the white convertible, dining and dancing at a roadhouse and, inevitably, parking the Packard in a dark lane. There was a pattern to Jimmy's lovemaking, too. Each time they parked, he tried to extend the frontier of his exploration of her body. He loved her, Cassie knew. He must love her to want her so much.

Cassie wanted him, too, more than she had thought she could, but she fought it, trying to block her sensuality just as she blocked that portion of her mind where the white curtain lurked, waiting to rip apart and to rip her apart.

It was an unseasonably hot night in late September when Jimmy took her again to the Riverside. They were trying to dance to "Flat-Foot Floogie" when Jimmy winced and said, "Oh, Christ!"

"What's the matter?"

"Just some people. Let's get out of here."

Jimmy paid the check, but the people had seen him, too.

"Hey, Jimbo!"

They surrounded Cassie and Jimmy. The two men wore light-weight sports jackets and slacks and the women wore pale linen dresses that made Cassie's rayon look sleazy.

Jimmy mumbled introductions. "Cassie Taylor, Fran Jordan, Joanie Smith. And these guys are Biff Latham and Todd Larson." Jimmy laughed uncomfortably. "Hey, what are you kids doing here?"

Fran Jordan, the red-haired girl with a sharp face and green eyes that reflected the flashing green lights of the jukebox, was the one who answered him. "Just slumming, Jimmy darling." She looked at Cassie's cheap rayon dress. "What about you?"

"Hey, wait a minute," Biff said. "Don't tell me this is the famous Cassie, in the flesh!"

In a fake Southern accent Fran said, "Why, Jimmy, darling! How come old Biff knows all about Miss Cassie and you've never told little old me one word about her? No secrets now, you hear? You just tell us every single thing."

"Cassie is my father's secretary."

Biff laughed. "And that ain't all, right?"

The girls giggled, but Cassie blushed and tugged at Jimmy's arm.

"Listen," he said, "we were just leaving."

Fran laughed sharply. "I'll just bet you were." She looked Cassie up and down. "Well, we don't want to keep you from your short-hand or whatever."

Cassie hurried to the door. Jimmy caught up with her in the parking lot.

"What's the big idea, baby? Why did you run out like that?"

"You didn't answer her question, Fran's question. What were you doing there, Jimmy? Why were you with me? Just slumming?"

"I used to date Fran, that's all. She didn't mean anything."

"I know what she meant! I know exactly what she meant! And what have you told Biff about me? What does he think I am?"

"Now, wait up there. I told Biff that you're a beautiful girl. What's wrong with that? Come on, now, get in the car."

In the car, Cassie asked him sadly, "What do you think I am?"

"Look, don't get all in a snit about what that loudmouth said."

"You'd better take me home, Jimmy. Right now."

He swung the wheel and let the Packard roll down the dirt road toward the river. "Listen, they didn't mean to—anyway, I want to talk to you, Cassie. I want to tell you something important." He stopped the car and turned off the engine. There was no moon, but the lights on the bridge cast a faint yellow glow on the open car. Jimmy leaned over and put one hand on Cassie's waist. "Cassie—"

He hesitated and Cassie's anger melted instantly. This was it. He was going to tell her, finally, that he loved her as she loved him. "Jimmy," she whispered.

"It's about Dad." He sat back and put both hands on the steering wheel. "He called me into his office this morning."

Cassie was startled. "But he calls you in there every day."

"Not to talk about you."

"Me!"

Jimmy turned on the seat to look at her. "He made quite a speech about his plans for me and how I have to think ahead if I'm going into politics and about my reputation and—"

"Your reputation?" Cassie's breath caught in her throat. That was it! Mr. Steele thought Jimmy should quit running around and settle down, even get married.

"Yeah. Listen, Cassie, you know how the old boy is always harping on family and position? He wants me to stop dating you."

Cassie felt as if she were falling. She covered her face with her hands. "Oh, no. No!"

"Hey, baby, don't cry! You know how I feel about you! Listen, you know what I told the old man? I told him to go to hell!"

Cassie dropped her hands from her face and looked straight at him. "You did? Did you really say that?"

Jimmy looked away. "Not in so many words, but that was what I meant. I told him he wasn't going to break up our . . ." He hesitated.

Say it, she urged him silently. Break up our what? Friendship? Romance? Love affair?

"I told him I'm a grown man and I'll date anybody I want to."

Cassie sank back on the cool leather. Even if Jimmy had not come right out and said "Go to hell," he had stood up for her. There was no question about that. He had stood up to Mr. James Steele and that was not easy. "Thank you, Jimmy."

"Well, all right!" Jimmy put his arms around her.

He does love me, she thought. She kissed him tenderly.

Instantly, Jimmy kissed her, hard. He groped for her breast and opened the front of her dress, and then he was kissing her breasts, panting, and Cassie was breathing hard, too, and pulling his head to her. He pushed her down on the red leather seat and slipped his other hand inside of her rayon panties.

"No, Jimmy! No!" Cassie fought to regain control of herself.

"Christ, Cassie, you drive me nuts!" He pushed himself up from her. "Let's get in the backseat. Please!"

"No, I can't, Jimmy, I just—" Suddenly she had to know, she had to hear the words. "Jimmy, do you love me?"

"For God's sake, Cassie, you know I do!" He grabbed her hand and jammed it against his fly. "Feel that, for Christ's—I've got to— please, Cassie, get in the backseat!"

Cassie felt it, the hard thing pushing itself against her hand, and in her mind a white curtain fluttered, but she forced it back.

"A man's got needs, Cassie! Please, get in back with me!"

Cassie's heart skipped a beat. A man's needs.

She knew all about a man's needs from her father, who had made her mother pregnant and had caused her death, and from Dale Hodge, who had helped to drive Cassie out of Whitman.

Confused, she pushed Jimmy away. What did a man's needs have to do with love? Were a woman's needs the same? "Oh, Jimmy," she cried, "does it have to be like this?"

"What the hell are you talking about?"

"I love you, and I think I want you, too."

"Oh, Christ! Let me—"

"No! I can't."

He pulled back. "Your time of month? I might have known it!"

"No, it's just that—Jimmy, I've never done it before."

"Oh, sure. A girl like you? Look, there's a name for girls that lure guys on, that tease—"

"That's not so! It's wrong but I can't—I want you, too."

Jimmy ran his hand through his hair. "Oh, hell!"

"You'd better take me home now."

In front of her rooming house, he said, "Cassie, look, I'm sorry if I—well, if I was too rough on you."

She sighed in relief and touched his arm. "It was my fault, too. Another time, maybe we could talk about it and—"

"Oh, Cassie!" He pounded his fist on the steering wheel. "You drive me crazy! What the hell do you want, anyway?"

She got out and went around to his side of the car. He got out, too, and stood looking down at her.

"I don't know what I want, Jimmy. I have to think. Can we see each other tomorrow night?"

He stepped back. "This is kind of a bad week. Tomorrow night there's a thing at the club and then there's a family dinner and the club dance is Friday—get the picture?" He grinned at her, cocky again. "Let's make it Thursday night. That ought to give you plenty of time to think."

Cassie bit her lip. "Sure, Jimmy. Thursday night." She ran up to her room and stared out the window at the empty street below.

Get the picture? That was what he said. Get the picture?

She was slow, but yes, now she got the picture. There were two kinds of girls in the picture of Jimmy Steele's world. There were the girls you took to a thing at the country club or to a family dinner or to a dance where "Stardust" floated on the evening breeze. Girls like Fran Jordan, girls in linen dresses. And there were those others, the girls you took to roadhouses, the girls you got woozy on beer and jukebox music and took out for a necking party and for anything else that you could get from them. Typists. Sharecroppers' daughters. Girls like Cassie Taylor.

She jerked down the torn window shade. But she loved him. In spite of everything, she loved him. What if he was not perfect? What if he was a man like other men, like Dale and Brother Stoddard. Did that mean he could not love her? Was it Jimmy's fault that he was not a romantic movie hero?

Cassie had pulled down the window shade, but she could not hide from the truth. Jimmy Steele wanted her and, God help her, she wanted him. Of all the books she had read, of all the movies she had seen, not one had told her how to deal with physical desire.

MISS VERNA WHIRTER was waiting when Cassie went into the office. "Mr. Steele wants to see you immediately, Miss Taylor."

Mr. Steele was reading a V-mail letter.

"Is that a letter from Dixon, Mr. Steele? Is he all right?"

Mr. Steele looked at her but he seemed to be looking far past her. "As well as anyone can be when he's in action."

Cassie sat down and flipped her notebook to a fresh page.

"I do not want to dictate a letter. I want to talk to you."

A trickle of sweat rolled down her back. "Yes, sir."

Mr. Steele tilted his chair back and stared at the ceiling. "You have spent a number of evenings with my son Jimmy."

Cassie swallowed hard. "Yes, sir."

"It must stop."

"I beg your pardon?"

Mr. Steele laid his big hands flat on his desk. "You heard me. It must stop."

Cassie gripped her steno pad with both hands. What right had he to talk to her in that flat insulting tone? "Mr. Steele, Jimmy told me you talked to him about me. Did he tell you he loves me?"

"What Jimmy said has nothing to do with it. I will put my position simply, Cassie. I have constructed an edifice and I fully intend to leave that edifice in the hands of my son, with the expectation that he will maintain it and moreover will add to it."

"You have two sons," Cassie said.

"Dixon is an idealistic fool. He will never build anything more than castles in Spain. I plan to make Jimmy an important man in the political structure of this state." He leaned forward and lowered his dark eyebrows. "And you do not figure in that plan."

Cassie gripped her steno pad. "How can you say that? Jimmy and I love each other!"

"Love?" Mr. Steele leaned back in his chair. "Love has nothing to do with it. Jimmy must settle down, but he needs a wife who knows how to entertain graciously, how to talk to important people and . . ." He shrugged. "I am hardly describing a sharecropper's daughter."

Cassie jumped to her feet. "Don't say that to me!"

"It's the truth, isn't it?" He frowned at her. "I'm thinking of your happiness, too, Cassie."

She laughed bitterly. "I can see that you are."

"Would you be happy in Jimmy's crowd, with young people who have had everything? Imagine it, girl. Be honest with yourself."

Cassie found herself doing just that. She tried to picture herself at the country club, chatting with Fran Jordan, dancing to "Stardust," but she could not. They were insiders and she was an outsider. She did not know the right jokes, she did not know the right laugh for rushing through the night in a convertible. From her family she had inherited blond hair and height and smoky blue eyes and what James Steele called grit, but girls like Fran Jordan had inherited a way of life.

"You need not worry, Cassie." Mr. Steele's voice was oily with kindness. "There is, after all, such a thing as *noblesse oblige*. That means—"

Cassie glared at him. "I know what that means."

Mr. Steele raised his eyebrows. "You surprise me. Since it will be awkward for you to work here after this, I am prepared to help you leave Ballard."

Cassie stiffened her back. "Why should I leave? I can get another job."

"No," he said softly, "not in my town, and not in Oklahoma."

"You can't do that!" But she knew that he could. She could hear the telephone calls to Oklahoma City and Tulsa, even to Guthrie and Muskogee and Tahlequah. "I won't give up Jimmy. I love him."

Mr. Steele smiled. "And does he love you with equal fervor?"

Fervor! She almost laughed. "I believe he does, Mr. Steele. But he told you that, didn't he?"

"What do you want, Cassie Taylor? What do you really want?"

Instinctively Cassie's eyes flicked to the map on the wall behind him. She looked back to him quickly. "Just Jimmy, Mr. Steele. I love him."

He shook his head, smiling. "No, not just Jimmy. It's land, of course. I suppose it is your grandmother's influence."

Cassie was surprised. "My grandmother? How do you know what she wanted?"

"Your grandmother and I had some interesting conversations, Cassie. It's a pity she never told you about them. Perhaps you would realize how foolish you are to oppose me." He leaned forward. "I am prepared to make you a very generous offer. If you promise not to see my son again, I will arrange for you to have a good job in Tulsa and I will give you one thousand dollars. In cash."

Cassie's notebook fell to the floor with a clatter. "You're trying to bribe me!"

"Of course. I'm sure you can see that such an arrangement would be far more suitable than an alliance with my son. Think about it, girl. You could have a good job, a nice apartment, new clothes, possibly even a sturdy used car. Wouldn't you be more comfortable among people of your own sort?"

Cassie bit her lip. She could see the life he had offered her: a nice apartment, good solid furniture with bright throw pillows, a little kitchen of her own. But then she looked across the desk at James Steele and he was smiling. He was so sure that he had hooked his fish. He was so sure that she would jump at the chance.

She compared the images he put before her. Cassie the career woman, on her own in an exciting new city, in charge of her own life. Or Cassie the wife, trying to be a country-club girl, trying to break the code of the insiders' jokes.

"I have to talk to Jimmy about this. I'll try to see him tonight."

"No, you won't. I sent him to Oklahoma City. He won't be back until tomorrow afternoon and I want you out of Ballard by then."

"You planned all this!"

"Of course. In any deal, planning is of the first importance." He looked at his watch. "You may go now, Cassie."

THAT NIGHT, Cassie went to the park near the rooming house. Fall rains had filled the pond, and when she sat down on a bench a duck quacked in protest.

Cassie was reminded of the bridge over San Bois Creek and her grandmother's soft hand holding her own small one. That was love, she thought, not something to be run through an adding machine, but not the romantic love of the movies, either.

She wished she were in Jimmy's arms. They would hold each other and reaffirm their love, and they would face James Steele together.

Who cared if Jimmy was not Cary Grant and she was not June Allyson? Their romance was just like the movies. They met, the boss's son and the secretary, and fell in love, but there was an obstacle: James Steele's opposition. There was always an obstacle, because that made it exciting. And in the end, they would marry and the church bells would ring and they would live happily ever after.

Cassie looked out at the dusk gathering over the pond. If only Jimmy were home, she thought, and then she remembered that even if he was home, he would not be with her. He would be at "a thing at the country club." She moved restlessly on the bench. Mr. Steele had made it clear that she was not "Jimmy's sort." Could they live happily ever after? She would give herself to Jimmy and she would try to become a country-club wife. The movies did not say so, but every woman had to submit herself, in the long run. Some women got land, some got wedding rings, some got cash, and some settled for fried catfish and a few Pearl beers. In the real world they had no choice.

But she did. Cassie stood up slowly. She had a choice. She could marry Jimmy and try to fit in, or she could take the job Mr. Steele had offered her and make it on her own. Her choice might not be the right ending for a movie, but it could be the right beginning for Cassie Taylor.

Yes, she thought, yes! She would take the job and she would take Mr. Steele's money, but she would not buy new clothes and rent a fancy apartment. She would save her money, and she would buy land not with her body but with her own hard work. And it would be her land, and no one could take it away from her, ever.

And Mr. Steele would be happy and, in time, Jimmy would be happy. He would be with his own kind. He would marry Fran Jordan or someone like her, someone who knew the score, and he would forget Cassie in time. He might think of her sometimes, she thought sadly, when moonlight was on the river or when he drove through a summer night, but he would be happy. She stifled a sob at the sweetness of it, of sacrificing one's own happiness for true love. Like Irene Dunne giving up Charles Boyer.

She smiled then, in the darkness, and took one step and then another, lightly, until she was skipping. Her own apartment, and one day, her own land! Her relief at finding the solution was overwhelming. Granny would be proud of her.

She hurried across the park. She could see it: a farm near Tulsa. She could keep working until she got the place built up. A little farm with a white house that looked like Dick and Jane's. In the house, there would be comfortable chairs and books, and in the evenings she would come home from work—she stopped short at the corner of Stigler and Guthrie because at the edge of her vision, something moved.

A dark figure detached itself from the shadow of the catalpa tree on the corner and stepped into the cone of light under the streetlamp. Even before he spoke, she knew. She knew by the way he moved, like a fox gliding into a spot of sunlight in a shadowed forest.

"Hi, Cassie," he said.

Cassie stepped back and put her hand to her mouth. She tried to speak, but no words would come. She cleared her throat and managed to whisper his name.

"Bo?" she said. "Bo Taylor?"

"Yeah, Cassie. Yeah. It's me."

"No!" she cried, but even as she did, she knew it was true. They had told her he was dead, but deep in her soul she had known, had always known that he was alive, as alive as the memory of an unresolved sin. The thought of Bo had been pushed deep into her unconscious, but it had always been there, waiting.

An unruly shock of straight black hair fell down over his low forehead and his eyes were hidden in the shadows under his heavy black eyebrows. The bridge of his nose was flattened and slightly off-center, as if it had been broken at some time, and his mouth, loose and with full, damp lips, was no longer the mouth of a boy. Bo was a man of twenty-three and very much alive.

"Where have you been, Bo? Why didn't you get in touch with me?"

He laughed. "What for? You never had nothin' I wanted. Knowed you was with them cousins up to Whitman." He raised his chin and laughed, and the light glinted in the quick black eyes she remembered all too well. "Seen you up there, lots of times."

Cassie's flesh crawled at the thought of those eyes watching her from some hidden place. "I never saw you."

"Didn't aim for you to." He glanced over his shoulder like a wild thing uncomfortable at being in the open. "Hey, ain't you even goin' to ask me to come up to that room of yours?"

"You know where I live?"

"Sure. I been watchin' you. Know where you live and where you work for that bastard Steele and where you go with that curly-headed boy of his." He snickered. "How'd you like it, down there by the river? Him and you, you sure go at it, don't you?"

Cassie flushed. "That's none of your business, Bo Taylor, and it's certainly not your business to spy on me!"

"My, don't you talk fancy, sis? Still got a temper on you, ain't you? Didn't do you no good the night the shack burned, though."

At his words, Cassie began to shake, first her hands and then her entire body. The night the shack burned. The night that had re-played itself in her mind like an endless loop of movie film, with the soul-searing pictures appearing again and again. Howling wind, Granny lying cold and dead, Bo in the doorway, a black threatening figure against the yellow lamplight. Other scenes played, too, scenes that could not be seen or heard, but that had lurked for years beneath conscious memory: a flare of orange, indistinct shouts, screams that went on and on and on.

Cassie clenched her fists and her nails dug into her palms, bringing her back to the here and now.

"Come on, girl, we'll go up to your place and you can fix me some chow."

He had not watched her in her own room, Cassie realized, and he did not know everything about her after all. She regained some of her equilibrium. "I don't have any way to cook in my room."

His eyes darted toward her suspiciously. "There's a joint down the street. Least you can do for your brother that's rose up from the dead is buy him a hamburger."

In the bright light of the café, Cassie could see that it was not only his nose that had taken a beating in the last five years. There was a small, J-shaped scar on his right cheek, and when he put his hands on the table she saw that their backs were covered with small white scars. They were also very dirty.

She asked him again: "Where have you been?"

His eyes skittered away. "Around. I been around."

"Around! I remember Granny saying you—"

"Don't talk to me about that old bitch! Give me that ketchup."

Cassie did not want to eat. She took a paper napkin from the dispenser and pleated it between her fingers.

"Why did you come back?"

He grinned. "Why'd you think? I want money."

"I don't have any money. You saw where I live."

"Sure. Seen you with that Steele boy, too. There's money there, lots of it."

"That doesn't have anything to do with you, Bo Taylor."

"The hell it don't!" He swallowed the rest of his hamburger in one gulp and washed it down with coffee. "I got it all figured out. You got to get money from him and send it to me every month. That ain't askin' much from a guy's own sister that's gone and caught herself a rich man."

Cassie folded the paper napkin into smaller and smaller pleats. What Bo did not know about her was more important than what he did know. He had no way of knowing that she was going to leave Ballard.

"Get me another one of them hamburgers, Cassie."

"Get it yourself, Bo Taylor. I'm not going to wait on you, and I'm not going to give you one penny. You have no claim on me."

"Hell I don't." He leaned toward her. "That fancy-boy of yours gettin' any lovin' from you? I bet that boy ain't gettin' shit. What's he goin' to do when he finds out about me and you?"

Cassie was cold, suddenly, cold to the bone. "What is there to find out, Bo?"

"Get me a hamburger like I told you."

Cassie walked to the counter as though she were walking in her sleep. She paid for the hamburger, and if the counterman spoke to her, she was not aware of it. She gave the plate to Bo, and went back to work on the paper napkin, unfolding each pleat as meticulously as she had folded it.

Bo took a bite of his hamburger.   "That's more like it, girl.   You got to treat me nice, hear?   Real nice."

"What is there to find out about you and me?"

"That I was first.   That I was the first one that had you."

"That's a lie!   You never——"

"You think your fancy-boy's goin' to want you when he finds out you been with your own brother?"

"No!" Cassie cried.

"Hey," the counterman called.   "You okay, sis?"

"Sure," Bo said and jerked Cassie's arm.   "Come on!"   He pulled her up Stigler to the park and shoved her onto a bench by the pond.

"Tell me," Cassie sobbed.   "Tell me."

He laughed.   "Okay, but first you got to ask me nice."

She crumpled on the bench.   "Tell me, Bo.   Please tell me."

In the yellow light she saw that he was watching her closely.   "You don't remember nothin' about the night of the fire, do you?"

"How did you know that?"

"They was all talkin' about it, down there at San Bois."

"You went to San Bois after the fire?   But someone must have seen you or——"

"Didn't go myself, sent somebody else.   You don't remember?"

"Nothing that happened after I . . . after I found Granny dead." Cassie put her hands to her hot face.   She could not bear to know about it, but neither could she bear not knowing, and Bo was the only living person who had been there.   "What happened, Bo?   Tell me!"

"Sure, I'll tell."   He leaned back on the bench.   "I went into town that night and got me a bottle to carry back to the shack."

"I remember that.   You were drinking in the lamplight."

"All of a sudden you set in to screechin' like you seen a panther and I run in the back room and sure enough, the old woman's dead."

"Granny.   Yes."

"Well, pretty soon me and you, we go in the front room and——" He glanced at her.   "Well, we get down on that there pallet in the front room and we have us a little party."

"You mean we . . ."

"I mean I fucked hell out of you, girl, and you loved it."

Chapter 18

THE TERRIBLE WORDS reverberated like thunder in Cassie's brain. "No!" she cried. "I was only thirteen!"

"So what? Girls been with their brothers when they was a hell of a lot younger than thirteen." He put his hand on her arm.

"Don't touch me!" Cassie jerked away from him. "Did Papa know?"

"Paw. Now, that's somethin' else, ain't it?" He laughed harshly. "Sure. I'll tell you. Paw come in there while me and you was still down there on the pallet, see?"

Cassie could see the front room and the yellowed newspapers on the wall and the rough gray planks of the floor, but the room was askew, like a room in a dream, with a sloping ceiling and no square corners. As he told her what happened, Bo and Papa and Cassie moved through the misshapen room but their movements were dream-like, too, and surreal.

"Paw commenced to yell like that never happened in the whole world, a boy havin' his sister that way, and he grabbed up that no-account old shotgun of his and waved it around, so I wrestled him for it." Bo leaned close to look at Cassie in the yellow light. "You still don't remember nothin'? It ain't comin' back to you?"

"No," she said dully.

He grinned. "Well, you had to get in it, too, so you was there wrestlin' for the gun and all of a sudden the goddamn thing went off and Paw went down. The coal-oil lamp got hit, too, damn thing blew up and, God almighty, there was burnin' coal-oil all over the place!

You run out screechin' and I run right after you, but you got to the woods. I took my car and lit for the Cookson Hills. Later on somebody told me it was in the paper that I was dead and all that. And that's the way it was."

Cassie pushed her knuckles against her teeth. "Bo?" she said. "Bo, who pulled the trigger?"

He hesitated, looking at her closely. "You did it, Cassie. You was the one."

"Oh, God." She bent down over the pain in her stomach and covered her face with her hands. "Dear God in heaven."

"Hell, it wasn't nothin' but a accident. He didn't have no call to wave that old—"

"I killed my father?" she whispered. She stood up slowly.

"Hey, where you goin'?"

"I don't know. To my room."

Bo grabbed her wrist. "Hell you are! We got business to do!"

Cassie looked at him blankly. She felt removed from the scene, as if she were watching two strangers talk, the wiry, dark-haired man and the tall pale girl. "Business?"

"Hell, yes! You get me some money or I'll tell that curly-headed boy of yours about me and you."

"I don't care about that. I'm going away."

"What the hell you talkin' about, girl?"

"I'm leaving Ballard," she said absently.

Bo slapped her. "You ain't! Where you think you're goin'?"

Cassie rubbed her cheek. The slap pulled her back to earth. Her mind was numb but it was working again. "I won't tell you. You'll never find me again, Bo Taylor, do you hear? Never!"

Bo laughed. "Me? It's not me you got to worry about, girl, it's the law. Them cops is goin' to come after you so fast it'll make your head spin!"

"But you told me it was an accident!"

"Maybe that ain't what I'm goin' to tell the law."

She sank down on the bench. "You wouldn't do that to me."

"I want money, girl, and you got to get it for me. So long as the money comes regular I'll keep my mouth shut."

"I've got to think about it."

Bo took her wrist again and squeezed it just to the threshold of pain. "Sure, Cassie, but you ain't got no choice, hear?" His voice dropped to a snarl. "I'll tell the law, but first I'll hurt you, girl. I'll hurt you so bad won't no man ever want you." He jerked her arm and she cried out. "Shut up! You got till day after tomorrow, understand? And that's all!"

"For God's sake, how can I get hold of money that fast?"

"That's your look-out, ain't it? You get it, or I won't mess around with you no more."

Without another word he melted into the shadows and was gone.

In her room, Cassie lay on her bed and stared at the ceiling, watching the action in the tenant house unroll itself like a movie. Granny's cold figure on the bed, Bo in the doorway with the lamplight behind him. Cassie and Bo on the pallet in the front room, Papa in the doorway, Papa with the shotgun, Bo wrestling with him, Cassie fighting with both of them. The shotgun explosion. The fire.

She heard the shotgun go off. She saw the lamp burst into flame, but she did not feel the heat of the explosion and her fingers did not feel the cold steel of the trigger.

She reached for the feelings, but the white curtain still hung there and blocked her memories of that night. She could not go back and be that girl, she could be only the one who lay on the iron bed, the girl whose body was defiled by the act it had shared with Bo, the girl who had killed her father.

She was sick in body and sick in mind. The sickness whirled through her and around her and became a great wheel that carried her up from the burning tenant house and around and down to the street corner where Bo had waited for her in the dark, from the farm to Bo, again and again and again. And the wheel rolled on and carried with it everyone she knew: Bo, the Steeles, all of them were caught up in the same great turning of fate. The life that she wanted, the hopes she had built, were beyond her grasp and always would be.

She rolled onto her stomach and buried her face in her pillow to stifle the bitter laughter. She had set her sights high. She had worked hard to raise herself above her beginnings, and for what? For what?

For nothing. They had seen her for what she was—Mr. Steele, Jimmy, Miss Verna Whirter. Only she, only Cassie had stubbornly refused to look in the face of truth. What was she? A bright, hard-working girl who would make something of herself? No.

In the end she was what she had been and what she always would be: a sharecropper's daughter.

CASSIE WAS ON TIME for work the next morning, but Miss Verna Whirter was there before her and was already irritated with her.

"Mr. Steele came in early, Miss Taylor. He wants to see you." She sniffed. "Again."

"Yes, ma'am." She closed the door of the private office behind her.

Mr. Steele looked up from his desk. "Well?"

Cassie knew what she had to say, but with those cold black eyes staring at her, she could not do it. "Mr. Steele, I need more time."

He looked as irritated as Miss Whirter. He had told Cassie once that a banker who could not make quick decisions was not a banker with a quick mind. "How much time?"

"One day." For one more day, she could pretend that she had a future.

He moved a paper on his desk. "Jimmy will be back in the office this afternoon."

"Yes, sir."

"I do not want you to discuss my offer with him."

Cassie shrugged. "I won't."

He looked suspicious, but he nodded. "All right. Tomorrow morning. Now, bring your book. I have work to do."

JIMMY STOPPED BY Cassie's desk at a few minutes after four o'clock. "God, what a waste of time! Dad insisted that I hand-carry a brief to the Supreme Court when the damn thing could just as easily have gone by registered mail. And it was a hell of a hot drive over there yesterday and a worse one back today!"

Cassie spoke softly so Miss Whirter would not hear. "I have to see you tonight."

"I'd like to see you, too, but I'm dog-tired after that drive and my mother's expecting me home for dinner. How about tomorrow night instead? We have a date then, remember?"

"Jimmy, it's important."

"Important?" He grinned. "You mean—what we talked about— okay! If it's *that* important, I'll pick you up at six."

Cassie was waiting at the curb. She had planned to tell him then, at that moment, but Jimmy was wearing a white polo shirt that set off his deep tan and the convertible was long and shiny and the leather seats were red. Once more, she thought, just one more time. Surely she deserved that much.

"What do you want to eat tonight, Cassie? I heard about a new steak place out on the Muskogee road."

Cassie put her head back on the leather seat and let the late sun soak into her face. "I'm not really hungry now. Could we just ride around for a while?"

He glanced at her. "Sure. Open up that glove compartment, though. I want a drink."

She took out the pint bottle of bourbon and opened it for him.

He took a long pull. "God, that's good. Want some?"

Cassie took the bottle and looked at it. She had never tasted hard liquor before. "Why not?" She tilted the bottle back and the whiskey went down like liquid fire. She coughed, but when she took another drink, it did not hurt as much.

She realized that Jimmy was watching her with curious eyes.

"Hey, kid, you watch that stuff. What's with you tonight, anyway? You don't act like the same girl."

Cassie laughed bitterly. "I'm not the same girl, Jimmy. Here, you want another drink?"

"Damn right I do!"

The convertible, Cassie realized, was on the road that ran along the riverside. Just then Jimmy swung the steering wheel and cut off onto a dirt road that ran back into the woods. "Where are we, Jimmy?"

"Just a place I know."

It was getting dusky in the woods when he stopped the car and turned toward her. "Come here, baby, come to papa."

Papa. The word turned like a knife in Cassie's heart. She tilted the bottle and took another long drink.

"Hey, you going to leave some of that for me?"

She handed him the bottle, but he propped it on the dashboard and put his arm around her.

"Hell, I'd rather have you than liquor, kid, and that's saying something."

The pattern began, as it had before, with his left hand moving up her leg and his right gripping her shoulder and then her breast. She felt nothing, no response from her body. "Give me the bottle, Jimmy," she whispered.

He raised his face from her breast. His eyes were surprised at first and then calculating. "Sure, baby. Sure." He reached for the bottle but suddenly he looked up. "Oh, shit, It's sprinkling rain. Let me put the top up." He hesitated. "Damn, we can't stay here."

"Why not?"

"Because if this goddamn road gets muddy we can't get out." He raised the top of the car and started the engine just as it began to rain in earnest. "Oh, shit!"

Cassie giggled. "Jimmy, honey, don't get all upset. We'll get out before it gets too muddy."

"That's not what's bothering me and you know it."

She felt the giggles bubbling up again. "I reckon I do, Jimmy, honey. I reckon I do know."

Jimmy laughed suddenly. "Boy, it doesn't take much booze to get you tight, does it?"

The convertible swung onto the gravel road and Cassie was bounced across the seat. She took his arm. "Could I have just a sip more, Jimmy?"

He grinned down at her. "Sure, Cassie, all you want."

The whiskey was tasting better and better to her. She felt warm, glowing. Jimmy took a long pull at the bottle and gave it back to her.

"Hey," he said, "I know where we can wait out the rain."

"You have friends out here, Jimmy?"

"Not exactly. You'll see."

Jimmy turned left on the blacktop highway, and it seemed to Cassie that they had only driven a few miles before he pulled the car to a stop at a huddle of buildings. Jimmy was out of the car and running through the rain before she had time to read the rain-streaked sign.

"Oh!" she said aloud, and tears welled up in her eyes because she knew where he wanted to wait out the rain. And why.

The Rock Springs Tourist Court looked like a tourist court in a movie, not the kind where Clark Gable and Claudette Colbert stayed, but the kind where the feds came gunning for Bonnie Parker and Clyde Barrow.

Jimmy came back, and before Cassie could say anything, he parked the car and pulled her from it. "Jimmy! We can't—"

"Hey, baby, it's okay, just trust your old Uncle Jimmy. Look, I got another bottle from the manager. We'll just go in here and have a few drinks till the rain stops. There's nothing wrong with that, baby, nothing at all."

There was plenty wrong with it, Cassie thought, but she had lost the will to argue with him.

The room was awful. The mattress on the rusty iron bed sagged suspiciously to the middle and the one chair had a broken rung. The green linoleum was torn and stained and through an open door Cassie could see that the bathroom was just barely serviceable and was very dirty.

Jimmy made drinks in chipped tumblers and handed one to Cassie.

Cassie drained her drink in desperation, and Jimmy set his glass on the bedside table.

"Come here, kid," he said, and when she did not move he went to her and put his arms around her. "Let's just sit down on the bed, so we'll be more comfortable. Come on, now. I swear I won't do anything."

She let him lead her to the sagging bed and pull her down beside him. She knew she should not be there with him. She should not be in the room, even, but somehow that was not important. All that mattered was the way she felt. So the room was cheap and dirty. Laughter rose within her, but it turned into a choked sob. Who was she to complain? She was cheap and dirty, too. Now that she knew about Bo, now that she knew everything about herself, about incest and patricide, there was no point in saving herself. There was nothing to save.

Jimmy reached up and pulled the string of the ceiling fixture and the room went dark except for a streak of yellow light that came through a torn window shade and lay across the bed. "No, Jimmy!" she cried. "I don't want to—"

"The hell you don't! You want it as bad as I do, and you know it." He pulled at her dress until she said, "Wait, you'll tear it! Let me—"

He waited while she pulled it off and then he pushed her back on the pillows and jerked at her slip.

She tugged at his big hands, but he pulled her slip over her head and was tugging at her rayon panties before she could get her arms untangled from the slip. "No, Jimmy, we can't—"

It was too late. The cheap material ripped at the waist and he cast them aside. Her brassiere tore as easily and was tossed aside and then he was on top of her. There were none of his usual moves, no hand starting out at the ankle, no wet mouth over hers, no hand groping its way to her bosom.

"Oh, Christ," he cried, "I can't wait!"

"Stop, Jimmy, you're hurting me!"

He was beyond caring. He grabbed her hips and entered her with one fierce thrust. Again he thrust into her, and again, then ejaculated and fell across her body.

Cassie screamed. "Oh, God!" The tearing agony in her body ripped the white curtain in her mind, the curtain which for all those years had dammed the stream of memory, and a flood of pictures broke through and engulfed her in a sea that burned at her soul like acid.

She saw it all: Bo dragging her across the room and throwing her on the pallet, Bo slapping her again and again, Bo thrusting his red engorged penis into her face, Papa shouting, Bo falling on the floor, Papa and Bo fighting for the shotgun, the gun shooting, the gun blasting, Papa's face exploding, the lamp flaring, Papa's face exploding, the shotgun blasting, Papa's face exploding, and all the time she could see it and she could feel it, she could feel the flare of heat on her face when the lamp exploded, she could feel her fingernails, the fingernails of both hands digging into the dirty flesh on the back of Bo's hands.

"He lied to me!" she screamed. "Oh, God, it was all a lie!"

Jimmy clamped his hand over her mouth. "Cassie, for Christ's sake! They'll hear you a mile away! Who lied? Oh, Christ, did I hurt you that bad? I never meant to—I just couldn't stop myself. God, Cassie, you're bleeding!"

She clawed his hand away from her mouth. "I won't scream, I promise, I won't scream anymore."

"Christ, baby, you said you were a virgin, but I never thought—oh, God, Cassie, I hurt you. I know I hurt you."

She pushed herself up on one arm and saw the bloody sheet between her legs and she began to cry, in great racking sobs that shook her whole body.

"Cassie, Cassie!"

"It's all right," she sobbed. "It's not you, Jimmy, I swear it. It's all right."

"But you're bleeding! I'd better get a doctor."

"Just get me a towel from the bathroom."

He ran for the towel, he brought her water and he apologized over and over again. "Oh, God, Cassie. What kind of a man am I?"

"It's all right."

Their roles had changed. He thought he was a man, but she knew that he was only a child, a willful child who was angry and upset because he had broken his toy. She was eighteen and he was twenty-eight, but she felt years older than he. She felt older than time.

Jimmy apologized again, and it was Cassie who was comforting him, who was soothing him. She did not tell him that it was not only the physical pain that had caused her to scream. She could not.

He offered her bourbon, but Cassie no longer wanted to drink. He sat on the chair with the broken rung and drank the bourbon himself. "Cassie," he said in a slurred voice. "I'll make it up to you, I swear. I'll make it up to—" He stood up so suddenly that he almost fell. "By God, I'll marry you! We'll get married."

"No, Jimmy. Your father would never let you marry me."

"Oh," he said, "I guess that's right." He sank back down on the chair, but then he stood up again and banged his fist on the wall. "I don't care what he'll let me do or not let me do, I'm a grown man. Cassie, come on, let's get married!"

Married? Cassie turned the idea in her mind, examining it. Married. But what if Bo told James Steele—she realized that if she married Jimmy she would have money to buy Bo off. She would have money for a house, a real house, and for clothes and maybe, someday, enough to buy land. And she loved Jimmy, in a way. Well, she had loved him until tonight, but surely he would not do that again. They would be married, yes, and have a nice house, and children, and she would never again be Cassie Taylor, the sharecropper's daughter. She would be Mrs. James Steele III.

"Didn't you hear me, Cassie? Come on, now, get yourself fixed up. We're going to get married, by God!"

"Jimmy, if you're sure you want—yes!"

It was not by God that they were married, but by a surly justice of the peace in the one county in Eastern Oklahoma which empowered judges to issue a license and perform the ceremony without a waiting period. After the ceremony, they went back to the tourist court, and it was Jimmy who drank the half pint of bourbon he had bought, along with a tin wedding ring, from the justice. He passed out on the bed.

It was Cassie who lay awake that night with Jimmy's head against her shoulder. It was Cassie who watched the sun come up in the cold gray dawn while she asked herself the same questions over and over again. What have I done to Jimmy? Dear God, what have I done to myself?

DAWN FADED into a dark October morning. It was misting rain when Cassie woke Jimmy. They avoided each other's eyes as they dressed and they hardly spoke at all. In the bathroom, Cassie discovered that the bleeding had stopped, but she was so hurt that it was painful to walk.

The rain was heavier on the Ballard highway. Cassie huddled on her side of the front seat and watched the windshield wipers beat back and forth. Questions beat back and forth across her mind. What would she do about Bo? Would she tell Jimmy about him? Would she see Bo again or would she just try to forget that he had come back and that he had ever existed? And what would Mr. Steele do?

When they stopped at a roadside café for breakfast; Jimmy said, "I'm sorry, Cassie. I mean—for what happened, not for getting married. I was drunk. It won't happen again, I swear it."

She looked across at him. Brown eyes that would not quite meet hers, brown curly hair, tanned round cheeks, soft self-indulgent mouth. This was the face that she would look at every morning and every night for the rest of her life. She forced herself to smile. "Jimmy, it's all right. Let's just forget about it. Let's pretend that last night never happened at all."

He laughed tentatively. "Well, we better not forget everything that happened, baby. There was a little matter of a wedding."

Cassie glanced down at the tin ring on her finger. "We won't forget that."

The waitress brought them bacon and eggs and hash browns, and Jimmy tucked into his food like a hungry boy. Cassie held her fork, watching him. A boy. She could see her whole life laid out before her, her whole marriage. Jimmy would err, like a thoughtless boy, and she would gloss over it and soothe his pain. Their ages did not matter. He would always be the child needing reassurance and she would be the mother, the one who had grown up because she had to.

When they were back in the car, Cassie felt a little better. There was a certain coziness to being with Jimmy in the Packard, with the rich smell of leather in the air and the rain beating down on the canvas top. There were just the two of them then, the two of them together.

Jimmy seemed to sense it, too. "Hey, Mrs. Steele, how about getting over here next to your loving husband?"

Cassie tried to laugh as she slid across the seat. "I don't know this lady. Who is she, this Mrs. Steele?"

He put his arm around her shoulders and pulled her close to him. "She's my wife, that's who. She's my own Cassie Steele." Suddenly he put his head back and laughed. "Dad! My God, I'd almost forgotten about Dad. What do you think he's going to say when he finds out that we're married?"

Fear surged through Cassie's mind, and some guilt. No matter what else he had done, James Steele was the man who had given her a job when she was desperate. "I don't know, Jimmy. I just don't know."

Chapter 19

CASSIE'S NERVOUSNESS increased as they drove back into Bal-lard. Jimmy waited in the car in front of the rooming house while Cassie washed and changed clothes, but as they rode up in the elevator of Mr. Steele's office building, she felt as soiled as if her very skin were stained with the experiences of the night.

Miss Verna Whirter smiled obsequiously as she said, "Good morning, Mr. Jimmy," but the smile disappeared when she turned to Cassie. "Do you have any idea what time it is, Miss Taylor? Mr. Steele asked for you two hours ago. Two hours ago!"

Jimmy took Cassie's hand. "Not Miss Taylor, Whirter. Miss Taylor is now officially Mrs. Jimmy Steele."

Miss Whirter's pince-nez fell off of her nose. She replaced them hastily and looked from Jimmy to Cassie. "You mean you are—are you telling me that you two are—"

"Married." Cassie felt no guilt at all about Miss Whirter. "Yes, Miss Whirter. This morning."

"Well, I never!"

Cassie became aware that James Steele was standing at the door of his office, a bulky figure against the light.

"Dad!" Jimmy's grip on Cassie's hand tightened. "I was just telling Whirter that Cassie and I—"

"I heard you," Mr. Steele said quietly. "Come into my office, both of you."

He sat at his desk and waited until they had sat down, too. "I will have the marriage annulled," he said calmly.

"The hell you will." Jimmy slouched in his chair and grinned at his father. "Remember me, Dad? I'm the guy who just spent three years in law school. There aren't any grounds for annulment."

"Four years in law school," Mr. Steele said contemptuously. "It took you four years to complete a three-year course."

Jimmy flushed. "I learned enough to know you can't set aside this marriage!"

Mr. Steele started to get up from his chair but he sat back as if the action required superhuman control. "I hope that you do not expect me to congratulate you." He looked at Cassie. "You got what you wanted, didn't you?"

Cassie blushed. "Mr. Steele, I'm sorry if we——"

"I doubt that." Mr. Steele scowled at her and moved a paper on his desk. "Jimmy, take her to the house now. I will call and prepare your mother for the shock."

"Wait a minute, Dad! I want to talk to you."

"I will want to talk to you also, but this is neither the time nor the place to do so."

The rain lessened as Cassie and Jimmy drove up the hill to Ballard Heights, and by the time the Packard swung into the circular driveway it was no more than mist trailing down from low sullen clouds. The house loomed over them, a tall two-storied house of rain-streaked red sandstone. The roof slanted off in eccentric directions and the corners of the building rounded into a suggestion of turrets.

Cassie bit her lip. In the mist the house was closed and forbidding, a dark castle barred to a girl who had grown up in a two-room share-cropper's shack.

She remembered James Steele standing in the dooryard of that shack and her grandmother offering him the hospitality of a chair on the rickety porch and a glass of cool water from the spring in the woods. When he left the shack that day he had come home to this. He had let her grandmother live in squalor while he lived in a mansion. In that moment any last trace of guilt toward James Steele vanished. He lived like a king in his castle on the hill, a king who gave no mercy and should not expect to receive any. She pushed open the door of the Packard.

"What are we waiting for?" she said angrily.

"Hey, what's up?" Jimmy said, but he hurried around the car to escort her up the concrete steps. As they crossed the porch the front door opened.

"Jimmy!" Mrs. Steele stood in the doorway, wringing her hands. "Your father called—so angry, so terribly angry. I just don't know what—"

Jimmy hugged her. "He'll get over it, Mother. He always does. Now let me introduce my wife, Cassie. Cassie Taylor Steele."

"I hope this isn't too much of a shock for you, Mrs. Steele."

"Oh, yes! I mean, no! Oh, dear. I've met you before—"

"Yes, ma'am. I was a typist in your husband's office."

Mrs. Steele stared at Cassie as if she were trying to translate the words into a language she could understand.

Jimmy took his mother's arm with one hand and Cassie's with the other. "Why are we standing here? Mother, I'm sure the occasion calls for champagne, or at least a glass of sherry."

Mrs. Steele brightened. "Oh, of course. Do come in—my dear." She hurried them into the room on the right of the hall. "Oh, Jimmy, you'll never guess who's here. Dear little Frannie Jordan just happened to drop by a few minutes ago."

Jimmy laughed. " 'Dear little Frannie'! My God, how did she find out so fast?"

"Jungle drums, darling," a voice drawled from across the room. Fran Jordan was leaning on the mantelpiece, stylishly angular in a lightweight suit. She smiled at Cassie with very white teeth. "So this is the new Mrs. Jimmy Steele. I simply couldn't place the name when I heard it, darling, but now that I see you, I know that we've met. Was it at the club?"

"Fran," Jimmy said warningly, but Cassie stopped him with a gesture. She had learned long ago, from Ella Mae's soap operas, that the poor girl who married a rich man was in for big trouble if she tried to conceal her background.

"Oh, no. It was at the Riverside. Maybe you don't remember meeting me because I am so much younger than . . . than most of Jimmy's friends."

Fran flushed and set her sherry glass on the mantel. "Now, listen here—"

Jimmy laughed. "Match point, girls! Here, Cassie, have a glass of sherry. More for you, Mother?"

"Well, I might—just the teeniest drop, dear."

"Fill mine up, Jimmy," Fran said. "I need it."

Jimmy filled Fran's glass and stayed by the fireplace, bantering with her, but Cassie was more interested in the room than in their conversation. The living room was huge, reaching from the leaded bay window in the front of the house to the french doors at the back. A gleaming ebony grand piano was draped with a fringed silk scarf and weighted with a group of silver-framed photographs. A white marble fireplace was centered in the long side wall of the room and over it hung a large marine painting. There were sofas scattered around the room and armchairs covered in pale brocades, and spindly-legged straight chairs with carved backs. There were tables everywhere, low dark ones in front of the sofas and smaller, more ornate ones next to the chairs. Some of the bookshelves held books and others were full of vases and figurines. The polished hardwood floor was covered by richly colored Oriental rugs.

Cassie realized that they were watching her, and took a hasty sip of her sherry.

Fran smiled. "Do you like your new hubby's little home? It's a bit overwhelming, isn't it?" She laughed lightly. "But what am I saying! I don't know a thing about your background. I'm sure your own house is much grander than this."

"Fran, dear," Mrs. Steele said nervously, "I really think—"

"It's all right, Mrs. Steele." Cassie smiled. The soap operas had been right. It would be easier to live with the truth than with Fran Jordan's clever guesses. "I think this is a beautiful room. And to answer your question, Miss Jordan, I was a typist in Jimmy's office, as you probably know, and I lived in a cheap rooming house on the east side of town."

Fran clasped her hands together. "Darling! Surely you don't think that I was prying into your background! And you must call me Fran. I'm sure you and I are going to be close friends, every bit as close as Jimmy and I have always been."

Jimmy set his glass down hastily. "Come on, Cassie. I'll show you the house."

He led her through the front hall, past the wide stairway that swept up to a broad landing with a leaded glass window, through the dining room with mahogany breakfronts filled with china and crystal and a gleaming table that seated twelve, to the big dark kitchen where two black women were working, and through so many bedrooms that she lost count. There was one first-floor room, however, that they did not enter. Jimmy opened the door and stopped in the doorway.

"This is Dad's study."

Two walls were covered by bookshelves and a third by black-framed certificates and awards and group photographs. At the center was a map like the one in Mr. Steele's office, the map that showed his landholdings. The fourth wall was almost all windows. Through the mist Cassie saw the swimming pool, the trees at the bottom of the rolling lawn and beyond them the dim shapes of the buildings of downtown Ballard. There were several leather armchairs but the desk dominated the room, a large walnut desk with neat stacks of papers and files and a desk lamp with a green glass shade.

Jimmy laughed uneasily. "God, how we hated it when we were told to report to him in here."

"We?"

"Dix and me. You know, my brother. This is where we got yelled at, but yelling wasn't as bad as that cold silence of Dad's. I hated it!"

Dinner was tense, four people at a table for twelve. Jimmy and his father exchanged an occasional remark about the office, but Mrs. Steele seemed to be far away and Cassie had to concentrate on choosing the right fork at the right time. A young black maid served them efficiently, but spoke only once, to acknowledge her introduction to Cassie.

Mr. Steele said, "This is our maid, Luella. Luella, Mr. Jimmy's wife."

"Yessir. Yes'm, Miz Jimmy."

At last Mr. Steele laid his napkin on the table. "Jimmy, I would like to see both of you in my study in fifteen minutes."

Cassie glanced at Jimmy, but he was looking down at his plate. "Yes, sir," he said.

Mr. Steele waved them to seats and sat down at the desk. The lamp lit the lower half of his face but his eyes were in shadow.

"Well, Dad," Jimmy said with some bravado, "what's up?"

His father frowned at him. "About this marriage of yours, Jimmy: what's done, it appears, cannot be undone."

Jimmy leaned forward. "It's about time you—"

"Please do not interrupt. There is a lot of ground to cover. First, the matter of your expenses. You will live here, of course, so your household costs will be minimal."

"Live here?" Cassie said. "In this house? But I thought we would have our own—"

"There is ample room here. As a married man, Jimmy, you will have certain increased expenses, your country-club membership and so forth. Although you are not yet bringing money into the firm, I will increase your salary." He looked at Cassie with obvious distaste, taking in her wrinkled rayon dress and her cheap shoes. "I will give your wife a personal allowance, also, and I highly recommend that she immediately purchase more appropriate clothing."

Cassie bit her lip, but she spoke softly. "You are very generous, Mr. Steele."

He looked directly at her for the first time. "It is not generosity, but necessity. I cannot afford to have my son's wife looking like a . . ." He hesitated.

Cassie laughed bitterly. "Like a sharecropper's daughter?"

Mr. Steele scowled at Jimmy. "That kind of talk is uncalled for, either in public or in the privacy of my house. I wish to hear no more of it, from your wife or anyone else."

Cassie stood up. "And I wish you would stop talking about me as if I were only an object. I have a name, Mr. Steele."

He nodded. "That is a reasonable request. Cassie." He looked back at Jimmy. "These arrangements will be satisfactory for the time being. If you have children, of course, I will make other—"

"Children?" Jimmy grinned. "Aren't you jumping the gun, Dad?"

"I do not see why I should not plan for all eventualities. Jimmy, you may leave now. I want to talk to Cassie alone."

"Wait a minute. She's my wife and I——"

Mr. Steele looked at him. "Jimmy."

"Oh, all right. I'll be in the living room with Mother." He closed the door hard, but he did not slam it.

Mr. Steele's face was as stony as the gray slabs on the San Bois farm. "Contrary to what our fledgling lawyer believes, Cassie, I can have your marriage annulled."

"But you said——"

"It would cause talk, however, so I have decided to make the best of the situation." He stood up and looked down at her coldly. "But I give you fair warning, Cassie Taylor, if you ever bring disgrace on my house or on my name, I will ruin you."

Cassie sat forward on her chair. "Mr. Steele, I promise I wouldn't do a thing to——"

"You promise?" He laughed harshly. "You promised me that if I hired you I would never be sorry. I have no more faith in your promises, Cassandra Taylor, than her contemporaries had faith in the prophecies of your namesake."

Cassie had to clear her throat before she could speak. "But she was right, you know. It was just that nobody ever believed her. Mr. Steele, I'll be a good wife to Jimmy, I swear it!"

Mr. Steele sat down and looked at her thoughtfully. "You are clever, Cassie, and you are ambitious. You got what you wanted when you married Jimmy, didn't you?"

"No! You make it sound like——"

"Don't try to pull the wool over my eyes. You think that with Jimmy you will get money and position and, eventually, my land."

"I love Jimmy! That's why I married him!"

"Nonsense." His voice was low and intense. "I know what you are after, but you will never get it. Do you hear me, Cassie Taylor? You will never get my land."

IT WAS ALMOST nine o'clock when Jimmy drove Cassie to the rooming house to pick up her clothes and her ration book. He started toward the porch, but she stopped him.

"I want to do it alone, Jimmy. Can you come back in an hour?"

"Sure, if that's the way you want it. Hey, do you have any cash for your landlady? Here, you better take this."

He drove away, and Cassie stood on the sidewalk looking down at the two twenty-dollar bills in her hand. She had not expected, some-how, that he would be kind.

She gathered her few personal possessions in her room, set the boxes on the front porch, and ran down the street to the little park. Bo was waiting in the shadows near the pond.

Cassie hesitated. Seeing him there was like seeing a part of herself, a shadow on her soul. Their father's blood ran in both of them. What else might they share, what darkness of the heart?

"About time you showed up, Cassie."

"Bo Taylor, you're a liar!"

He grabbed her wrist. "Hey, you ain't callin' me no—"

"You lied to me about the night of the fire! I remember everything now! I'm not going to give you money, not one red cent. You can't set the law on me and you can't—I never want to see you again, you hear? Never!"

Bo's laugh was low and insinuating. "Okay, Cassie, I won't bother you none."

Cassie stepped back in surprise. "You won't?"

"Hell, no. I'll just go talk to your new papa-in-law."

"How did you know I got married?"

He sat down on the bench by the pond. "There's ways. I reckon the old man will fix me up with a room in his big house, seein' I'm your brother and all."

"Oh, God!" Cassie sank down on the bench beside him. "You don't know him, Bo. He's a dangerous man."

"Dangerous? Hell, Cassie, you're ashamed of your own blood, I know that." He picked up a straw from the ground and stuck it between his teeth. "Reckon if you give me money like you said you would, I ain't goin' to have to bother the old man."

Cassie felt Jimmy's twenty-dollar bills in her dress pocket. "If I give you money will you go away?"

"Sure. I ain't lost nothin' in Ballard. Won't come back, neither, so long as you send me money."

"Here!" She pushed the money into his hand. "Take these and go, for God's sake!"

He held the bills up to the light. "You carry this much in your pocket? You did marry rich! Reckon I ain't in all that big a hurry to light out. Might stick around awhile, see what turns up."

Cassie had suspected that Bo might want to stay near the goose that laid the golden eggs and she was prepared. "No. You can't stay in Oklahoma, Bo."

"A lot you got to say about it, girl!"

"What I've got to say, I'll say to the police." She hoped she sounded more confident than she was. "If you don't get out of town this very night, I swear I'll turn you over to the law."

He laughed nervously. "Hell, you ain't goin' to go and do a thing like that, not to your own brother."

"I will, Bo. Believe me, I will."

"It would be in the papers and all, you know that, and old man Steele, he'd have him a fit!"

"He might get mad, yes, but it would be all over for you. I've been working for a lawyer and I know something about the law. Murder in the first degree, attempted rape of a minor child. You'd get the chair, Bo. You would die in the electric chair!"

Bo was pale. "Wasn't no murder, by God! I was defendin' myself from Paw. You was there, Cassie. You seen it all!"

Cassie hesitated. She knew that she had to convince him, even if the words she used haunted her forever. "That's right, Bo," she said. "I was there. I saw it. I saw you take the shotgun from the shelf and lie in wait till Papa came home. I saw you take aim and shoot him. I saw you murder your father."

Bo sat very still for a moment, and when he spoke, his voice was low and venomous. "All right, you bitch, I'm goin' and I'll stay gone, long as you keep the money comin' to me." He stood up and stuffed Jimmy's twenty-dollar bills in his pants pocket. "This'll get me to California, but how'm I goin' to get the rest?"

"I'll send it to you, I swear. When you get out there, get some-body to write your address on a postcard. No name, just an address." She gave him the Steeles' address on Ballard Heights. "I'll send a money order the first of every month."

He looked down at her and the light glittered in his small dark eyes. "You do that. But I'll tell you somethin'. I'll be back, hear? I'm comin' back someday."

CASSIE'S LIFE as a country-club wife began earlier than she had expected. Amelia Steele suggested a party for the newlyweds, but James Steele vetoed the proposal. "We will treat their marriage as casually as they did."

That meant that Cassie's introduction to Ballard society would be at a regular country-club dance.

Cassie was nervous. "But what should I wear, Jimmy?"

"Oh, any old thing. It's only a dance at the club."

"I don't have any old thing! I'll have to buy a dress."

Jimmy was not interested in her problem, nor were Luella and Cornelia, the fat cook. They were polite to Cassie but distant, and she suspected that when she was out of earshot they talked about poor white trash.

Amelia suggested that she see Miss Margie at the Bon Ton Shop, and then wandered away, perhaps to check her hidden supply of sherry.

On the night of the dance, Cassie twisted around, trying to see her back in the full-length mirror in her dressing room. Her evening dress would not meet Miss Naomi Bencher's criteria of neatness and simplicity, and it was not like anything Cassie had seen in the movies, but Miss Margie had assured her that it was just the thing for a dance at the Ballard Country Club. It was pale blue tulle, with a full skirt and half sleeves that were masses of ruffles. Each tier of the skirt was edged in a narrow ruffle trimmed in white lace. Cassie twirled in front of the mirror in a surge of excitement, and the tight curls the beauty operator had given her bounced and glittered in the light.

The others were waiting in the front hall when she went down the wide stairway. James Steele looked distinguished in a dinner jacket, and in his well-cut evening clothes Jimmy looked almost like a movie star. Amelia seemed to be startled when she saw Cassie, but kept on looking for her white gloves. When Luella helped Cassie with her evening wrap, however, there was a malicious glint in her dark eyes.

The clubhouse was a rambling shingled building painted dark green. Country club or not, Cassie thought it had a down-at-the-heels look about it.   The big, shabby room inside was crowded with older couples seated at tables around the walls and young people dancing to the music of a five-piece band.

One look at the other women was enough to tell Cassie how wrong Miss Margie had been.   No woman over the age of fifteen had ruffles on the sleeves of her evening dress and no woman under forty had a full skirt.   The women in Jimmy's set wore dark dresses that clung like skin by necessity, since the dresses were strapless, and their hair styles were divided about evenly between sleek pompadours and Veronica Lake's sweep over one eye.

Cassie's head was a mass of tight curls, and she was the tallest woman in the room.   She stood at the entrance and she could see herself as they were seeing her: a gigantic plaster dolly, first prize from a carnival game of Pitch the Baseball.

The friends who came to greet them and to be introduced were polite, but something in their eyes told Cassie that they would gossip all evening about Jimmy's bride, the girl who looked like she just got off the bus.

Jimmy danced once with his mother and once with Cassie and disappeared into the locker room with his cronies.

James Steele did not ask Cassie to dance, nor did any other man. She was not surprised.   Who would want to dance with a beruffled five foot eight carnival dolly?   Finally she escaped to the ladies' room and sank down in an armchair in the corner.

She covered her face with her hands.   "This isn't the way it's supposed to be," she whispered.   "It's all wrong."

"What's all wrong?" a voice asked sharply.

Cassie took her hands away from her face.   It was Fran Jordan, as sleek as a panther in a black satin dress secured at one shoulder with a narrow strap.   Her red hair was combed down over one side of her face like Veronica Lake's.

"Oh, God!"   Cassie sobbed.   "It had to be you!"

"What now, darling?   Guess the Song Title?   Kay Kyser's Kollege of Musical Knowledge?   And you're crying?   Surely not because of that truly remarkable dress of yours.   Wherever did you find it, darling?"

"At the Bon Ton Shop.   Go away, Fran.   Just leave me alone."

Fran laughed and perched on the chair next to Cassie's. "But that's just the problem, darling! Everyone has left you alone to make every dreadful mistake you can." Cassie pulled her dress to one side and Fran shrieked. "Those shoes! They're even worse than the dress! Don't tell me you let Miss Whatsit at the Bon Ton sell you those, too!"

"Well, yes. She suggested—"

"She would!" Fran raised her slender arms toward the ceiling. "O Lord, let this cup pass from me."

"What on earth are you talking about?"

"I've been nailed to a cross of gold or whatever, darling! I'll never sleep again, not even with someone yummy, if I don't do my duty by this poor innocent lamb."

"What poor—"

"You, you idiot! Let me think . . . Okay. You be ready at the very crack of dawn on Monday. We shall flee to Tulsa to Miss Jackson's and Vandever's and a few nifty little shops known only to me in all the world. We shall dress you stylishly and terribly expensively and if I ever hear you utter the words 'Bon Ton Shop' again, I shall wash out your nasty little mouth with Fels Naphtha."

Cassie sat up. "But, Fran, I don't have the money to—"

"My God!" Fran cried. "You still don't know, do you? Why in God's green heaven did you marry Jimmy, if it wasn't for his father's money? Child, James Steele is one of the richest men in Oklahoma. We'll charge it to him, dear. We'll charge everything!"

"But what if Mr. Steele says—"

"What would he say? Do you think he would send you back to Miss Jackson's to say, 'My dear pa-in-law just can't afford this dress'? You really haven't a clue, have you? Well, fear not, you are my very own cross to bear and I'll soon have you spending Pa's money with wild abandon."

"Oh, Fran! How can you be so good? You must have a heart of—"

"A heart of gold, like the legendary old whore? Not on your life, baby. Fran is out for Fran, period. I'll get something out of this, you can bet on it. I'll get something."

Chapter 20

FROM THE FIRST JOURNEY to Tulsa, Cassie loved the shopping trips. Fran seemed to know everyone in the state of Oklahoma. Sometimes, however, Cassie turned suddenly and caught Fran watching her, with a secret little smile on her sharp face. When Fran dropped her off at the Steeles' after one of their expeditions, Cassie felt let down but relieved, as if she had passed through a battle unscathed.

What Fran Jordan got out of them Cassie did not know, but what she got from the shopping expeditions and the lunches and the shared visits to the hairdresser was a new wardrobe and a sense of how to wear it with some style. Fran's advice was close to that which Naomi Bencher had given Cassie so long ago. "Stick to the classic," Fran said. "Simple design, with all the work in the cutting and sewing." There were no more evening gowns with ruffles and tiered skirts.

James Steele never mentioned the charge-account bills, nor did he comment on Cassie's new clothes.

Jimmy and Cassie settled into the social life of Ballard. With Fran's help Cassie began to look the part of a young country-club wife. With her height she could wear the styles of the autumn of 1943, the broad-shouldered suits and free-swinging coats and, above all, the slinky evening gowns. Her stylish haircuts dramatized her long face and high cheekbones, and Fran made sure that she chose colors that would emphasize her deep blue eyes. She knew she looked good, not just from the mirror but also from the envious looks of other women and from the sometimes frankly lustful looks of the men. She learned which fork to use and how to get into a car gracefully, but the country-club set spoke a foreign language. "They just joined Southern Hills." "She's a Pi Phi, of course." "His mother was an Appleton." It was insider talk and meant nothing to Cassie, nothing at all.

Cassie found herself wishing for a map. She had known her way through the swamp of poverty, where quicksand lurked to drag down the unwary. The movies had taught her that the country of the rich was bright and open with broad paved roads, but real life was not like the movies. Life among the wealthy was a dark forest in which she consistently took the wrong turn.

She kept up with the war news, but Ballard people were not interested in the landings on Tarawa. They clustered around the couple who had seen *Oklahoma!* in New York City, and they complained about red points and A stickers for gas and the fact that the OPA required roadhouses to post the prices of bootleg whiskey.

Occasionally she went to church with Mr. and Mrs. Steele, but Episcopalians were insiders, too. Polite, white-gloved parishioners worked their way through the prayer book, conversing with an equally polite and white-gloved God. She could not sing the complicated hymns. She longed for her grandmother's hymns of a loving God, or even to hear the tabernacle people shout out their fear of a vengeful, fiery one. She giggled to herself at the thought of anyone getting the Spirit in that mannerly place. Would Amelia cry out "Amen!"? Would James Steele shout "Praise the Lord!"?

Jimmy was the center of parties at the country club, but when the inevitable moment came and men and women separated into two groups, Cassie was no more comfortable with talk of the servant problem and childbirth and rumors of infidelity. The truth was that Cassie was still an outsider.

The evenings at home were even less interesting than the parties. James Steele sat in his armchair by the fire delivering himself of an occasional opinion on the basic stupidity of an electorate that would keep that man Roosevelt in the White House, and reading aloud tidbits from the local newspapers.

One evening in early October, he snorted. "The military mind is the eighth wonder of the world. Listen to this. There's a detachment of the Women's Army Corps at Fort Sill, near Lawton."

Cassie looked up from her book. "What's wrong with that?"

"Nothing, per se. I concede the value of hiring women for noncombatant duties as typists, cleaning women and the like, but to give such women the rank of field-grade officers is absurd. Listen. 'Fort Sill's newly appointed chief librarian, Major Naomi Bencher, announced today that the historic military post's archives will be——' "

Cassie stared at him. "What did you say?"

James Steele looked annoyed. "I said that they are giving these women field-grade——"

"I know. The name! Read the name again!"

He held the paper to the light. "Major Naomi Bencher. Why? Do you know the woman?"

"Yes." Cassie felt again the overwhelming sense of loss with which she had read Naomi Bencher's letter that April day in Whitman. Gone forever. Those were the only words she could remember from the letter, the words she had never been able to forget. Gone forever. Why hadn't Naomi told her that she was going into the WAC? They could have kept in touch. Cassie would have had a friend, someone she could count on for love and advice. Instead Naomi had walked out of her life as if they had never meant a thing to each other. She had deserted Cassie. Gone forever. She clenched one hand into a fist and looked up at James Steele. "She was my teacher at Turner School, down at San Bois."

Steele raised his eyebrows. "I would be inclined to say that the woman has bettered herself considerably, to go from teacher in a one-room school to the position of major in the United States Army. I still say, however, that I think such a designation is ridiculous."

Cassie sighed. "I suppose so."

"And everyone knows," he continued, "what those women in the army are. If they aren't the worst kind of loose women they are——"

"James!" Amelia said, and the subject was dropped.

Sometimes James Steele and Jimmy discussed a case and Cassie listened carefully. With her background of work in Steele's office and the reading she was doing, she could usually follow their reasoning.

Amelia Steele sat in her own chair in the evenings, stabbing vaguely at a needlepoint cushion cover that never seemed to change by as much as one stitch. There was always a glass of sherry on a small table at her elbow. Cassie thought of it as the magic glass. Amelia drank from it, but the glass was always precisely half full, as if refilled invisibly by helpful elves.

Cassie dreaded the moment each night when she and Jimmy went upstairs. Their bedroom was spacious, with large chests and closets big enough to hold her new wardrobe comfortably. They had a bathroom of their own, done in black and white ceramic tile, which connected with another, smaller bedroom. The setting was fine, but the actors left something to be desired.

"You ready, Cassie? Old George is chomping at the bit!"

"Old George?" Cassie asked the first time, and wished that she had not when she realized that theirs was a marriage of three: Cassie, Jimmy and the insatiable Old George.

Jimmy's technique of slow advances had ended with her loss of the right to oppose them. He would roll on top of Cassie and give her breast a rub as automatically as if he were turning on the ignition of his car. He would enter her abruptly, ease himself with a few deep thrusts and roll off with a grunt. Within minutes he would be snoring, while Cassie lay awake feeling cheated. Was this the love the movies had promised? Was this romance? There was no happy-ever-after with Jimmy Steele.

The Christmas season in Ballard was more about parties than about Christ's birth. Everyone was merry, there was plenty of liquor and even the young officers on leave obviously wanted to forget for a while that there was such a thing as war. On the rare evenings that Cassie and Jimmy spent at home, however, Cassie saw that Amelia was becoming depressed as Christmas approached. The magic sherry glass had to be refilled by human hands.

One night at dinner, Amelia burst into tears. "But why can't he come home? Why won't they let him come home for Christmas?"

James Steele sighed. "Be reasonable, Amelia. If our army let the young men come home, the war would come to a halt and the Axis powers would win."

"I don't care who wins!" Amelia cried. "I just want my son home!"

"Luella," Steele said, "would you please help Mrs. Steele up to her room? Perhaps a cold cloth for her head . . ." With unusual gentleness he helped Amelia. "My dear, let Luella take you upstairs. You are not yourself tonight."

Steele's kindness to his wife touched Cassie. She said softly, "Is her . . . condition recent, Mr. Steele?"

He looked at her coldly. "No, it is not. I have work to do in my study." He left the room.

Jimmy raised his eyebrows. "Curiosity killed the cat, baby."

Cassie felt as if James Steele had slapped her in the face. "Well, is it recent, Jimmy?"

"Hell, no. I can't even remember her without her little glass of sherry. I think it started when my sister was killed. Oh, Christ, let's not talk about it! Let's go out to the club and see if anything's cooking."

"Wait, Jimmy. I want to ask you something else. Why don't you all ever talk about your brother Dixon?"

"You ought to be able to figure that out. We don't talk about him because it upsets Mother."

"But do you hear from him? Do you know where he is?"

"Oh, sure. He writes but he can't say where he is. Somewhere in Italy, we think." He threw his napkin on the table. "Come on, baby, let's go!"

Cassie folded her napkin slowly. "It will be a lonely Christmas for him."

JAMES STEELE gave Cassie a car for Christmas, a blue 1941 Chevrolet convertible. "It is used, of course," he said, "but I've had it painted and had the canvas top replaced."

Cassie was stunned. A car! She jumped up from her chair and ran to hug him. "Mr. Steele, I don't know what to say!"

He stepped back before she could touch him. "It is only appropriate that Jimmy's wife should have a car."

"Oh," she said, letting her hands fall to her sides. "I see. Well, thank you, Mr. Steele. Thank you very much."

Jimmy was as excited as a child with a new toy. "Come on, I'll give you your first driving lesson!"

Cassie was a quick learner but Jimmy was bored with teaching after the third lesson. She made arrangements with a driving instructor, a gray-faced man who taught with gray efficiency. Thankful for an excuse, Cassie gave up luncheons and teas to practice with him, and within six weeks, she had a driver's license.

There was an A sticker on the front window of the car and Cassie had a book of ration coupons, but she rarely used them. Behind the garage, concealed in the shrubbery, was a large metal tank on struts, and the yardman kept Cassie's tank filled from that. Cassie asked James Steele where the gas came from, but she did not get an answer and she was not encouraged to ask again. She began to notice, however, that everyone the Steeles knew had seemingly endless supplies of gasoline, and of tires and standing rib roasts and bourbon whiskey and cigarettes.

"I don't understand it," she told Fran the day she first drove her blue convertible to Tulsa. "I read in the papers about all these terrible shortages, but no one we know seems to be short of anything at all."

"Sssh!" Fran put her finger to her lips and peered dramatically over her shoulder. "The walls have ears! Loose lips sink ships!"

"Oh, Fran!" Cassie giggled. "What on earth are you talking about? Nazi spies?"

"No, rationing-board spies. The OPA's people. We'd all go to the Bastille for two hundred years if they found out." She shook her head in sorrow. "You simply must learn something about the power of money. It's such fun, darling!"

Cassie did not think it was fun at all. At that moment she saw wealth as a swamp: a bog that could suck you down into degradation so deep that you could lose your very soul.

Degradation? Cassie remembered the money she had stolen from the tabernacle, God's money. Who was she to talk about degradation?

"Fran!" she said suddenly. "Let's pick a marvelous place to have lunch today. I'm in the mood to spend lots and lots of Mr. Steele's money!"

Fran laughed. "You're learning, darling! You're learning."

SINCE NO ONE in the Steele family had appeared to notice that Cassie was no longer going to the teas and luncheons at the club, when her driving lessons ended she saved the daylight hours for herself. She took long drives through the countryside and found the gray January days and bleak fields soothing after the artificial glitter of the Christmas parties. Sometimes she stopped the car to climb through the barbed-wire fence and walk in the whitened stubble of a cornfield, kicking at the rock-hard frozen furrows and watching a flock of crows rise like crying black demons against the heavy winter sky. She drove past tumbledown shacks as squalid as the one where she herself had lived, past dooryards scattered with rusty farm equipment and abandoned cars, where poorly clad children, bowlegged with rickets, stopped their play to watch her passing.

In February, a heavy snow blocked the country roads and rather than spend her days in the lonely cavernous house, Cassie went to the Ballard Public Library. Those things that she had seen on her drives through the country aroused her curiosity. How much money did farmland produce and how was that money divided between the owner and the tenant? Which crops depleted the land and which replenished it? The big question, however, was the most complicated. Why was there such a vast gulf between the man who owned the land and the man who farmed it?

Cassie discovered that she had to go beyond books on agriculture, to economics and the more technical fields of banking and lease law and meteorology.

During the long quiet evenings in the Steeles' living room, Cassie mulled over what she had read each day, trying to fit the information into the matrix of her experience and planning the route to pursue in her studies.

One raw March night Jimmy roamed the living room like a tiger pacing out the measurements of its cell.

"Cassie," he said suddenly. "Cassie!"

She looked up. "What? Did you say something?"

"My God, you're getting as vague as Mother. Have you been at her sherry bottle?"

James Steele rattled his newspaper.

"For Christ's sake," Jimmy said, "let's go out to the club. Maybe Biff's there, or Fran."

"But it's so cold and windy! I don't want to go out tonight."

"Suit yourself, baby. I'm going, with or without you."

She smiled, refusing to react to the implied threat in his voice. "All right. I'll go to bed early and read. Have a nice time, Jimmy."

He slammed the front door when he left.

Amelia looked concerned, but James Steele lowered his *Wall Street Journal* and smiled at Cassie thinly. "So the honeymoon is over?"

Cassie dozed off to sleep with a Department of Agriculture pamphlet titled *Soil Conservation Management* on her stomach. She was awakened by the crash of the bedroom door against the wall.

"Jimmy! Is that you?"

"Yeah. Who were you expecting?"

Cassie raised herself on her elbow to look at the clock on her bedside table. "It's after two."

"So what?" His voice was thick and his words slurred. He stumbled into the dressing-table bench. "God damn it, why do you keep moving everything around?"

Jimmy moved into the light from the bed lamp. His jacket was halfway off one shoulder and his collar was open. His eyes were glazed and his mouth was loose and misshapen.

"You're drunk!" she cried.

"Damn right! Had me a good time for once. Didn't have my darling wife standing around looking bored out of her mind."

"Jimmy, that's not fair! You know I always try to——"

"The hell you do!" He weaved across the room and stood at the foot of the bed looking down at her. "They all asked about you, everybody asked about you."

"That was nice of——"

" 'Where's Cassie been?' That's what they said. Doesn't come to lunch anymore, didn't even come to the silver tea at the club." He tried to straighten up. "What the hell was I supposed to say? Hell, I don't know where Cassie's been. My own wife, and I can't tell them shit about the way she spends her time."

"Jimmy! Don't say——"

"Shut up." He raised his hand and managed to clench it into a fist. "You tell me, baby. You give it to me straight or I swear I'll beat it out of you! Who is he?"

Cassie pushed herself back against the headboard and pulled up the blanket. "Jimmy, there's no——there's never been another man!"

"Sure. Sure, what the hell. You been sitting around the house every day, is that it? My mother's company is so delightful that you simply can't drag yourself away to go to the club. Don't give me that!"

"The library! Jimmy, I swear it. I go to the library every day of the week. Look, I can prove it!" Cassie fumbled for the government pamphlet and held it up for him to see. "Look, it's stamped right there, 'Due Date: March 21, 1944.' "

Jimmy leaned down and tried to focus his eyes on the title of the pamphlet. *"Soil Conservation Management.* Christ, what are you trying to pull?" He raised his fist.

"It's true! So help me——" She slipped under his raised arm to get her purse from the dressing table. "Look, Jimmy, it's my library card. See, 'Mrs. James Steele III, Ballard Public Library.' "

Jimmy sat down on the side of the bed. "I don't feel so good."

Cassie ran to him. "Are you going to be sick? I'll get a basin."

"No." He reached out and grabbed her wrist. "No, I'm not going to—come here, you." His voice broke and tears welled in his eyes. "Little Cassie, my little Cassie. You never told me you liked to read all that much. Why didn't you tell me you liked to read? I would have bought you books, all the books in the world."

Cassie tried to move away, but he pulled her toward him.

"I guess . . . maybe you never asked me, Jimmy."

"Well, I'm asking now! Come here, I said." He tried to get up, but he fell back on the bed and pulled her down with him. "Hey, baby, what you doing in bed with Jimmy? You want to get fucked? That it? You want me to put Old George in your——"

"No!" She tried to make her voice calm and reasonable. "You've had too much to drink."

"Hell, I never had too much to drink! Baby, you snuggle up here by me, and I'll show you." He fumbled at his pants and rolled on top of her. "Okay, baby, get ready to have yourself some fun." After a moment, he rolled off and lay back. "Shit. I can't get it up."

Cassie sighed with relief and edged away from him. "It's just the liquor, Jimmy," she said soothingly.

"Hell it is! I never had so much to drink that I couldn't get a hard-on. It's you, God damn it! It's you, the way you lie there like you were a million miles away. Why the hell don't you get with it? Why can't you—"

"I try!" Cassie sat up on the bed. "I swear it, I try. But you just get on top of me and you hardly touch me except to—"

"Wham-bam," he said and laughed drunkenly. "Wham-bam, thank you, ma'am. Hell, that's the way I like it!"

"Well, I don't."

Jimmy looked down at her with hard eyes. "Okay, then, suppose you tell me how you do like it? And suppose you tell me who's been giving it to you the way you like it."

Cassie drew back nervously. "I didn't mean—you're the only one, and you know it. Remember that first night, and how I bled?"

He looked at her. "There've been lots of nights since then."

"I'm here, every night! I'm with you!"

"How about the days? This stuff about the library—"

"But it's true! You can ask the librarian!"

Jimmy sagged down on the bed. "Okay. Okay, maybe I believe you." He grinned suddenly. "Anyway, Old George believes you. He's all ready to go to work. Come here!" He pulled her down on the bed with one heave. "And God damn it, put some life into it, hear?"

He entered her with one thrust. Cassie cried out at the pain, but she wriggled beneath his heavy body, back and forth, back and forth. He came almost immediately and fell back on the bed, jerking his still-large penis out of her with a tug that pulled painfully at her dry tissues.

"You better get you some kind of a book at that goddamn library of yours. You like to read so damn much, read about how you can be a good wife to a man."

Cassie lay there for a few minutes and then got up and went into the bathroom. When she came back she stood by the bed looking down at him. He had passed out, still in his clothes. She thought about the hangover he would have the next morning and how bad-tempered he would be, how ready to blame it all on her. A child. A child who would strike out at someone if he did not get his own way and who would pout when he got it and did not like what he got. She had known that he was a child when they were first married, but she was only beginning to realize that he could be a dangerous child.

She tugged at his clothes until he was nude except for his shorts. She covered him and lay down on her own side of the bed and turned off the bed lamp, but she could not sleep.

JIMMY SPENT more and more evenings at the country club that spring, while Cassie stayed at home.

One evening at dinner, however, James Steele said briskly, "Remember, Jimmy, that I want to see you in my study after dinner."

Cassie looked up quickly, remembering how Jimmy had dreaded after-dinner talks with his father, but Jimmy was grinning.

"Sure, Dad," he said. "I remember."

Jimmy told Cassie nothing about his conference with his father, but from that night the two men spent two or three evenings a week in the study. Afterward, James Steele would join Amelia and Cassie in the living room, but Jimmy would go out. Cassie thought he was going to the country club, but many nights he did not tiptoe into their bedroom until long after the club had closed. He began to take trips, too, and was sometimes gone for three or four days at a time. Cassie felt only relief that he had lost interest in her. Old George left her alone.

It was from James Steele that Cassie discovered the reason for the changes in Jimmy's life. One evening when Jimmy had gone to the country club, James asked her to go to his study for a few minutes.

"Cassie, Jimmy has no doubt told you about his political plans."

"No, he has not. Is that why he has been away so much?"

"Yes. I want him to run for Congress two years from now."

"But why should he start now?"

He turned his swivel chair and looked up at the pictures on his wall. "I doubt that you would understand, but we must build a political base before the actual campaign. The congressional election in Oklahoma will be settled, of course, in the Democratic primary in April of 1946, but Jimmy must become acquainted with local politicians long before that. Later, you will need to travel with him."

"Why?"

He looked at her carefully and nodded as if in confirmation of an earlier decision. "You will make an attractive appearance as the candidate's wife. Perhaps a short speech, something from the woman's angle. We'll work that out later." He leaned back in his chair and snipped the end from a cigar. "We will apprise you of the travel schedule, of course. Jimmy was somewhat worried about your enthusiasm, but I told him that any woman would like to see her husband achieve a high governmental position. I told him that you would cooperate fully."

Cassie smiled for the first time. "Did you, Mr. Steele? Did you indeed."

Chapter 21

THE ALLIES invaded Normandy on June 6, 1944. Amelia Steele was frantic with worry about her son Dixon, but within a few weeks she received a V-mail letter that reported he was safe and had received a battlefield commission. James Steele, for once, was proud of his second son. Jimmy was less enthusiastic.

"Isn't that kind of commission given for exceptional bravery?" Cassie asked him that night.

Jimmy said reluctantly, "I suppose so."

"Then you must be proud of him!"

"Yeah, sure. You saw how Dad carried on about it."

Cassie grinned at him. "Jimmy Steele, I think you're jealous!"

"Look, just because I have this trick knee and the army wouldn't take me—"

"You're jealous! You want to be the star of the family, don't you? You can't stand the idea that Dixon is a hero. You want all your father's attention."

"The hell with it. I'm going to the club." He slammed out of the house and did not come home until very late.

Jimmy was away more and more that summer, but Cassie resisted James Steele's attempts to get her to go campaigning. She dreaded the thought of nights in hotel rooms with Jimmy and Old George.

Old George was not in retirement, however. Cassie heard the news when she had lunch with Fran Jordan.

"Cassie darling, everyone at the club knows what Jimmy's been up to! I can't think why no one has told you about it!"

Cassie blinked to clear her eyes and swallowed hard. "I don't even know why you're telling me now."

Fran became very busy with her silverware. "Darling, I've never bought the idea that the wife should be the last to know."

"Then you left it too long, didn't you? If everyone at the club already knows—Fran, is anyone even speaking to him?"

Fran looked surprised. "Why wouldn't they? Everyone plays around a little, you know that. Jimmy's just more open about it. The men envy him and the women—well, I wouldn't want to say that they're all lining up, but—"

"Fran, who is she?"

"You mean, 'Who are they?' "

Cassie rubbed her eyes. "I just can't believe Jimmy would—"

"Darling, Jimmy is nothing but a child, you know that. When Old George gets going—" She stopped abruptly and fumbled in her purse.

Cassie looked at her steadily. "And what do you know about Old George, Fran?"

Fran pulled out her cigarette case and tamped a Camel on the silver top. She flashed a brilliant smile at Cassie. "Oh, you know how the boys talk!"

"Fran, it's you, isn't it? You're the one Jimmy is—"

"Certainly not!" Fran appeared to be honestly indignant. "Listen, would I tell you what he was doing if I—and anyway . . ." She smiled maliciously. "You know I don't like crowds."

"I'm sorry, I shouldn't have said that."

Fran reached across the table to pat her hand. "Darling, you're just upset. Don't give it a thought, hear?"

"Yes," Cassie said absently, already thinking ahead to the evening, when she would see Jimmy. What would she say to him? What would she do?

In the end, she said nothing, she did nothing. She could threaten to divorce him, but she knew that James Steele would not put up with the scandal of divorce when Jimmy was beginning a political career. It would cause talk. Jimmy's behavior was causing talk enough, she thought bitterly, but in this strange new world that sort of talk was acceptable. She would not say anything, but if Jimmy even tried to come near her she would risk going to James Steele.

Jimmy did not come near her. In fact, when she told him that she was not sleeping well and would move to the smaller bedroom that shared the bath with theirs, he did not object.

"Yeah, Cassie. That's fine. I'll probably sleep better, too."

Cassie loved having her own room and doors she could lock. She could read as late as she liked, but best of all she no longer had to live with the unsettling knowledge that at any time Jimmy could come home from his partying and want her.

When she saw Fran she asked about Jimmy's affairs, but Fran said that nothing had changed, that he was still playing the field.

JAMES STEELE called Cassie into his study one night. "You have not yet made any trips with Jimmy. May I ask why not?"

"No, Mr. Steele, you may not ask."

He looked away, and Cassie realized that he did not need to ask, that he knew exactly what Jimmy was doing.

"I have found a better car for you, Cassie. An Oldsmobile convertible, prewar and used, of course, but with very low mileage. It will be delivered day after tomorrow."

Cassie laughed. It was such an obvious bribe. She started to refuse, but then she thought, Why not? If she had to stay with Jimmy she might as well get a bonus for it.

"Thank you, Mr. Steele," she said lightly. "An Oldsmobile is more appropriate for a candidate's wife."

He was obviously startled. "Yes, of course. You may go now."

She left the study angry at him and angry at herself for accepting his dismissal like a child sent out of the principal's office.

To celebrate the new Oldsmobile, Cassie drove Fran Jordan to Tulsa for shopping and lunch. On the way back, Cassie idled along the back roads, enjoying November foliage. Fran was unusually quiet.

"Cassie, pull over for a while, will you?"

"Well, sure. I'd like to stretch my legs, too."

But when the car rolled to a stop, Fran made no move to get out. "Cassie," she said, and hesitated.

"It's Jimmy, isn't it? What's he up to now?"

Fran took a deep breath. "More of the same, but it's so much more of the same that everyone at the club is talking about it." She patted Cassie's arm. "I know it must be terribly upsetting, darling, but I thought you should know."

The talk bothered Cassie, but she realized that the idea of Jimmy being with other women did not. It had nothing to do with her.

"I don't care," she whispered and then she said it clearly, loudly, like a declaration. "I don't care!"

Fran turned quickly. "You mean about the talk?"

"I mean about the talk and about what Jimmy is doing. I don't care about either of them."

"But you must care, Cassie! You're his wife!"

"I mean it. I don't care what Jimmy Steele does, just so long as he stays away from me."

Fran's eyes narrowed. "You don't mean . . . bed?"

Cassie gripped the steering wheel so tightly that her knuckles whitened. "Bed is exactly what I mean."

"Well, what do you know?" Fran tapped her finger on her chin thoughtfully. "What is he like, Cassie . . . well, in bed?"

"He's the only man I ever—I mean, I know I don't have much experience. And of course, I'm his wife and he doesn't have to—but if what we do is all there is to it, I sure can't see why people get so worked up about it."

CASSIE WENT DOWN to dinner one night and found James Steele and Jimmy huddled on a couch in the living room, talking intently.

". . . might be a big help to agriculture, Jimmy. After all, he comes from the Midwest."

"I don't know, Dad. You know Kansas City politics. God, the man's a machine politician, and a bankrupt haberdasher to boot. What can he do for us?"

"I just feel sorry for his poor wife," Amelia said, touching a handkerchief to her eyes. "And after all the trouble she's had with those boys—"

"Amelia, Mrs. Roosevelt can certainly look after herself."

"Yeah," Jimmy said. "She can always go off and kiss an Eskimo!"

Cassie stepped into the living room. "What on earth has happened? What are you talking about?"

"President Roosevelt is dead," James Steele said. "Jimmy and I are discussing this Truman fellow."

Cassie gripped the back of a chair. "The president! But how . . . when . . ."

"Just a short time ago. It was on the radio," Amelia said. "Luella heard it in the kitchen and she came in and——"

"I believe," Steele said, "that he suffered a cerebral hemorrhage, but the facts are not clear yet." He turned back to his son. "Now, Jimmy, in that speech that Truman made in . . ."

Cassie ran out of the room and upstairs. She could not believe that the president of the United States, the man who had seen the country through four years of war, had died and that all her husband and her father-in-law could do was speculate on the effect the new president would have on their business and political affairs. She had to do her crying in private.

At dinner they were still at it, but Cassie did not listen to them. Just once did she feel some warmth in that cold dining room. She looked up at Luella, who was serving dinner, and saw that she had been crying, too. For the first time she and Luella looked at each other as human beings, as two people who shared a sorrow.

CASSIE'S COUNTRY DRIVES increased in April, both in distance and frequency. She drove the Oldsmobile restlessly, turning at random, passing along roads she had never seen before, searching for something she could not define and might not recognize even if she found it. She drove into the hills east of Ballard to see the redbud in bloom, and along back roads where white dogwood blossoms hung over spring-fed creeks, casting shadow patterns on the shallow ripples. It was after a drive to Tahlequah that she pulled the Oldsmobile to a stop in front of the Steele house and Luella came running down the front steps screeching like a banshee. "Miz Jimmy, Miz Jimmy! Miz Steele say come quick!"

Cassie's first thought was of President Roosevelt's death. Who now? she thought. "Luella, what is it? What's wrong?"

Amelia met Cassie at the door, laughing and crying at the same time. "Dixon! Cassie, it's Dixon! He's in Washington! James just got the telegram! Dixon is safe!"

"Oh, Amelia!" Cassie grabbed her and they whirled around the hall, able for once to be happy together like all women whose men have come home from war.

"Amelia, I'm so happy for you! When will he be home?"

"I don't know. The wire didn't—he just said he was—he's safe, Cassie!" She burst into tears. Luella came and helped her up the stairs, shushing her.

Dixon Steele called his parents several times during the next few weeks, but there was some confusion about when he would be allowed to come to Oklahoma. While they were all still excited about the news of Dixon, even greater news came.

On the eighth of May, 1945, Germany surrendered. The war in Europe was over. James Steele came home from the office as soon as he heard the news and he, Amelia, Cassie, and even Jimmy, went straight to St. Luke's Episcopal Church to join in the impromptu service of thanksgiving. The service was anything but restrained that day. The congregation sang hymns of thanksgiving with as much fervor as the members of the True Word Holiness Tabernacle. Middle-aged gentlemen in sober business suits stood next to ladies in print dresses and flowered spring hats and the tears rolled down the faces of women and men alike. In a pew near the front a young woman, the wife of a soldier, collapsed in sobbing relief while her six-year-old son awkwardly patted her shoulder.

After the service, Jimmy got ready to go to the club. "There's going to be one hell of a party tonight!"

"'Don't you want to go with him?'" Amelia asked, but Cassie shook her head firmly.

James Steele opened a bottle of champagne and the three of them celebrated quietly. Amelia was so happy that neither he nor Cassie mentioned the fact that the war was still going on and that Dixon Steele might well be sent on to the fighting in the Pacific.

CASSIE CAME HOME from the library one afternoon and Amelia called to her from the living room. "Yes, Amelia," Cassie said, balancing her stack of books on the hall table. "I'll be right in."

Amelia was standing in the middle of the room, beaming with joy, and with her was a tall man in uniform, holding a cane and a garrison cap. A man with cropped black hair over a long thin face. A man with dark, tired eyes under black eyebrows as heavy as his father's.

"Dixon," Cassie whispered. "Dixon Steele."

"Yes." His voice was deep and well modulated, but it sounded tired, too. "And you are Cassie, Jimmy's wife." When he smiled his eyes were more alive. "We went swimming together once. Do you remember?"

"Yes," Cassie said. In the barely perceptible pause, she had remembered more: the shy gawky boy, all arms and legs, who had been afraid of snakes. She remembered, too, the girl in a too-small dress, self-conscious of her budding breasts, resentful of the boy's knowledge of the world. "Yes. I remember."

He took her hand and she trembled. "You were thirteen, weren't you? And I was seventeen. And now we're all grown up." He grinned, but his eyes acknowledged the fact that she had grown up to be beautiful. There was a quick flash of—was it desire? Cassie caught her breath, but the light left his eyes as suddenly as it had come. "And sister and brother of a sort."

He released her hand and Cassie felt that she had lost her mooring and was floating away from shore. Nothing had been offered, nothing taken away, but she was drowning in a sense of loss.

"Dixon!" James Steele was in the room. "Welcome home, son!"

Soon the whole family was gathered in the living room. Dixon Steele took off his Eisenhower jacket, but not before Cassie noticed a captain's insignia and an impressive display of ribbons.

Amelia sat with Dixon on one of the couches. "Dixon, dear? You haven't told us what's wrong with your leg. Is it . . . serious?"

Dixon put his arm around her shoulder. "No, Mother, it will be fine." He looked over at his father. "I didn't want to worry you, but that's why I was in Washington. They did a little operation, and now the doctors say it will be okay."

"Then you're on leave to recuperate," James said. "You'll have a long stay at home, won't you?"

"No, sir. Just a week."

"A week!" Amelia cried.

"I'm sorry, Mother. I'm assigned to teach a tactics course at Fort Benning, Georgia." He laughed. "I guess they figure that a teacher can sit around all day, so my leg won't be a problem. I'll get a longer leave later, before I rejoin my outfit and we—" He stopped suddenly, but Cassie knew what he had left unsaid: "Before we invade Japan."

"Jimmy," James Steele said quickly. "Will you make drinks?"

Jimmy said, "Oh, hell, let's go to the club. We're going out there for dinner, aren't we?"

"We are not!" Amelia said firmly. "It is Dixon's first night home and we are all going to stay right here! As soon as Cornelia found out he was home, she said she was going to make his favorite—oh, Dixon, dear, there is so much I want to ask you!"

Jimmy made drinks and handed them around, then dropped into an armchair and swung one leg over the arm. Amelia did not ask Dixon about the war but about what he had eaten and if he had been warm enough: a mother's questions. Cassie listened with interest, but gradually she found herself looking from one brother to the other. Jimmy was better-looking, really, when you compared his tanned boyish face to Dixon's gaunt, exhausted one. Jimmy was thirty and Dixon was only twenty-four, but he seemed older than Jimmy, more mature, as he answered his mother's questions gravely and lovingly. When he patted his mother's arm Cassie saw that the back of his hand had a light cover of fine black hair. It was a good hand, Cassie thought, gentle. She watched it as it gestured or smoothed Dix's short black hair, as it picked up a glass and set it down again. She wanted, suddenly, to feel that hand patting her arm, touching her skin.

Jimmy lit a cigarette, and Cassie turned toward him. He looked sullen, a bored child thwarted in his plans.

It was the war, of course, that made the difference between the brothers. The experiences of war had matured Dixon. Idly, Cassie created a mental picture of the brothers in which Jimmy was the one in uniform, the man who had just returned from war, and Dix the one who sat by while his brother described his life in the army. But in her picture Dix leaned forward in the chair, interested in his brother and everything that he said, and Jimmy the soldier was on his feet, restless at being cooped up in the house, wanting to go to the club and show off his captain's insignia and his campaign ribbons and his wounded leg. Cassie thought of that Thanksgiving Day so long ago, when Dixon had given sugar cookies to a sharecropper's child and Jimmy had laughed at her.

Perhaps war did not change people after all but only, like pain, intensified the characteristics with which a man was endowed in childhood or even before his birth. On the heels of that insight came another so strong and so certain that Cassie gasped.

"Are you all right, dear?" Amelia said.

Dixon looked concerned. "I hope I haven't upset you. Believe me, it wasn't as bad as it sounds." He laughed lightly. "But what's an old warrior to do, if he can't shock the home folks with his gory tales?"

"Are you comparing yourself to Ulysses?" James Steele asked with an unaccustomed smile.

They laughed, but Cassie's laugh was hollow. She realized that she had made a wrong decision, a hideously wrong decision.

She smiled at the Steeles, but behind the smile she was praying. God help me, she thought, because she knew then, as surely as she had ever known anything in her life, that she had married the wrong brother.

CASSIE MANAGED to avoid Dix for most of the week, but at breakfast on his last day at home, he said, "Look, I've thought about the lodge a lot during these past few years. Is there any chance I could get down there today?"

"You can't drive yet, can you?" James Steele said. "Your mother doesn't drive, of course, and Jimmy and I must be in court this morning, but Cassie can run you down to San Bois."

Cassie looked up quickly. "But I was going to—"

"To take a long drive?'" James Steele did not smile. "You usually do. Why not make it to San Bois?"

Amelia said, "I'll have Cornelia pack a nice lunch for you. There's the chicken from last night and . . ."

By nine o'clock, Cassie was dressed in a sleeveless blouse and white shorts covered by a blue wraparound skirt and was driving the Oldsmobile convertible down Highway 12 toward San Bois. She had both hands on the wheel and was looking straight ahead, but she was very much aware of Dixon Steele in the passenger seat. He had dug out some prewar clothes for the trip to the country, stained khaki pants that were too short, a worn cotton polo shirt and battered tennis shoes.

He stretched his long arms in the sunshine. "Cassie, thanks for hauling me around like this." He laughed. "The guys in my outfit would never believe this. Old Dix Steele riding along in a convertible with a pretty girl! I'd almost forgotten that pretty girls and convertibles existed."

"It was terrible, wasn't it? Worse than you've been telling us. You've only told us about the good times and the funny things."

He turned in the seat. "You know how upset Mother gets."

"Yes," she said. "I know."

"When it's all over I can talk more about it—" He laughed shortly. "Oh, hell. When it's all over, I won't even want to think about it again."

"What are you going to do, Dix, when the war is over?"

He was silent for a moment. "I think I'll go to law school."

She was slightly disappointed. "And go into your father's firm, I suppose. And into politics, like Jimmy."

Dix laughed softly. "I don't think Dad and I would make a happy partnership, since we are on opposite sides on almost everything. I think I'll try to get a job with the ACLU."

"The civil liberty lawyers? Your father says they're a bunch of radicals."

"They are, Cassie, they are! They believe in the rights of the individual, and the Constitution and all sorts of Bolshie ideas. I would be defending the rights of black people and the poor and—"

"Your father would have a fit!"

"I'd hope so. If he was happy with my choice, I would know I'd picked the wrong outfit."

Again, Cassie found herself comparing the brothers. Dix was an idealist, perhaps, but he had a strong sense of helping people. Jimmy, like his father, was interested in public service, but in his case it was private service, paid for by the public.

They drove along in a comfortable silence. When they went through San Bois, Cassie saw that the town had grown. There were a few more stores, a few more houses and a small clinic. The name on the sign was familiar. Dr. Hill was the doctor who had not been able to get to the tenant house in time to help her mother through a difficult birth, in time to save her life. He was also the doctor, she remembered, who had treated little Julia Steele.

South of town they rode past green fields of corn and cotton, past scrub oak hills gouged with red dirt gullies, past weather-grayed shacks and occasionally a white farmhouse with hollyhocks along its fence.

"It's all so peaceful," Dixon said quietly. "So untouched."

Cassie laughed abruptly. "Untouched? What you are seeing, Captain Steele, is some of the most tortured, farmed-out land in this part of Oklahoma."

Dix waved his hand. "Come on, now. Look at those stands of corn. And that cotton is as healthy as any I've ever seen."

"Sure, Dix, but come back and look at it in a couple of months. If we get a dry summer or, for that matter, even if we get a fair amount of rain—do you remember the summer of 1935, when the cotton crop failed?"

"Because of the drought."

"Not just the drought. The land was worn out then, and it has had ten more years of plowing since then, and ten more years of crops. Look at the color of that dirt."

Dix shaded his eyes with his hand. "Red. It's always been red, as long as I can remember."

"But it's light red now, and getting lighter in color every year as it loses its organic materials and reverts to minerals. What you're looking at is not much more than powdered sandstone, Dix. Even if we get some good rains, the water will run off this stuff as fast as it runs off of a gravel road. There aren't any organic materials left to hold it in the earth."

Dix was staring at her. "How the hell do you know all this?"

She blushed. "I like to read."

"About dirt?"

"Well, about soil and conservation and crops and—"

"Do you talk to Dad about it?"

"Heavens, no!"

"I seem to remember—you told me one time that you were going to get your own land. Do you remember it? That day we went swimming in the creek."

Cassie concentrated on watching the highway. "Dix, that was seven years ago. I was thirteen years old. Look, we're almost there. Help me watch for the turnoff."

They spotted it at the same instant and laughed together. Cassie eased the convertible down onto the narrow gravel road, where a jungle of greenery overflowed the ditches. "Blackberries," she said softly. "Won't be ripe till August, though."

Dix looked at her and then away, as if he did not want to interrupt the flow of her memories.

Cassie stopped the car. There was no longer a track climbing the hill, only a faint tracing of a road, a place where the undergrowth was less thick than it was on the surrounding hillside. She looked up the hill. The privy was still standing, its door hanging open on one rusty hinge, and one rough post stood where the shed had been. Her knuckles were white on the steering wheel. "It was up there. Our house was up there, on that hill."

"Want me to walk up there with you?" Dixon said.

"No!" she cried and then she said softly. "No, Dix. There's nothing there to see, not now." She shifted gears and drove on, past a patch of woods. She slowed the car again at the clearing where the fieldstone chimney stood. The sumac had grown so tall that she had to look carefully to see the lone chimney. She laughed. "Lord, how I used to run past this clearing! I was so scared!"

"Why? What scared you?"

She shrugged. "I don't know. I never did know." She drove into that other clearing and saw James Steele's lodge. Cassie switched off the engine. "This place scared me, too."

"The lodge? Why on earth would it—"

"I always felt like it was watching me." As she spoke, however, she realized that the house was no longer frightening. Had the place changed or was it something within her that had changed?

Dix laughed. "It's just a house, and a house that needs some work at that."

"You're right," she said, with a slight sense of loss. "It's just a house, isn't it?"

Chapter 22

 JAMES STEELE'S lodge looked seedy, but the outbuildings discreetly tucked away behind it were in good condition, with heavy padlocks on the doors of the barn and toolshed.

Dixon Steele shaded his eyes to look past the house. "Dad said his contract farmer keeps his equipment in the sheds and barn. Looks like he takes good care of that part of the place." He grinned at Cassie. "Let's see how the house looks inside."

The lodge had been changed since Cassie had last seen it. At some point during the past seven years James Steele had hooked onto the REA electric lines and had put in a well and plumbing. Instead of kerosene lamps, there were electric ones that looked like discards from the house in Ballard. The tin bath had been replaced by a porcelain tub with chrome faucets, and in the kitchen, a new linoleum-covered counter supported a wide shallow sink.

"The place is dusty," Dix said, limping from one room to the next, "but it's in pretty good shape."

Cassie followed him, trying to sort out her confused impressions of the place. That day when she and her grandmother had walked down the road to clean the place, when they came from the tenant shack, she thought that the lodge was a mansion. But she had lived in James Steele's house in Ballard for almost two years, and now the lodge was no more than a tatty old house.

In the hall she noticed the dusty padlock on the door of the room that had belonged to a little girl, and turned back to ask Dixon, "What happened to her? What happened to your sister?"

"I was just a little kid then, three years old."

"But you know, don't you?"

"Yes. And you're in the family now, aren't you? I'll tell you, Cassie, but wait till we're outside."

Cassie shivered. Even in the May heat the house felt clammy. "Let's open some windows to air the place out."

"Good idea. Do you want to have lunch in here?"

"No, let's go down to the creek."

Cassie offered to drive the Oldsmobile to the creek, but Dix insisted on walking, so she got their towels and lunch basket from the car. She stopped to drop her wraparound skirt on the veranda steps and with it she seemed to drop her claims to being an adult. She felt like a child again, on old familiar territory. She wanted to skip down the dusty road to the creek the way she had skipped to Turner School, but she paced herself to Dix's slow uneven gait.

When Dix lowered himself onto the rocky bank of San Bois Creek, his face was gray with strain and his forehead glistened with sweat.

Cassie wet the end of a towel in the creek. "Here," she said calmly. "Wipe your face with this."

He looked up at her and smiled. "Yes, ma'am, Miss Nightingale."

"I didn't mean to—"

"I know you didn't." His eyes were so warm that Cassie had to look away.

Dix leaned back on his elbows. "It's quiet, isn't it?"

"Yes. Quiet."

"Wasn't your school somewhere around here?"

Cassie pointed up the hill. "Up there. I might walk up after a while and see if it's still standing."

"Okay." He lay back on the rocks and closed his eyes. "Wake me when it's over."

"When what's over?"

"Anything. The war. Rationing. The human race."

Cassie lay back to soak up the sun's warmth and listen to the creek chuckling its way over the rocks in the shallows. "Dix?"

"Mmm?"

"Tell me about your sister. What happened to her?"

He sat up and stared down at the water. "It was an accident," he said slowly. "That's what Dad told me later. A stupid accident."

"It was your father who told you about it? Not your mother?"

"Yes. I was fifteen and when he called me into his study, I was scared!" He laughed. "Usually, a call to his study meant—"

"I know. Jimmy told me."

He turned and looked at her blankly. "Jimmy. Sure. Anyway, Dad said I should know about it. Julia was seven that summer, Jimmy was nine, and I was about three, as I said. The folks lived in Ballard but they liked to come down to the old house now and then for a few days in the country. Dad had rigged up a board swing for us kids, in that big maple tree in front of the house. It was hung on a high branch, I remember, so high that it scared me, but Julia loved it. When Dad called her for lunch that day, she threw a temper tantrum. They said she always was a stubborn little thing. Anyway, she kept on swinging, and maybe she wasn't holding on tight or she went too high or the seat slipped . . . Anyway, she fell off and hit her head on a rock or something."

"Oh, the poor little thing!"

"It knocked her out, but they thought she was all right. Dad had some first-aid training in the army during the first war, so he checked her over. A few bruises, he said, but nothing broken. He thought that she might have a mild concussion. Mother wanted to go home and get Julia to the doctor, but Dad said it wasn't necessary. They would watch her, he said, and if anything worried them, they would drive home in the cool of the evening. Then he left for town."

"For Ballard?"

"For San Bois. He had an appointment to go over the contract on a farm he was trying to buy. He had to see the man that afternoon or the deal would fall through. Well, it took a lot longer than he had anticipated. The farmer brought his lawyer along and, knowing Dad, I bet he wrangled with the lawyer over every comma in the—"

"Julia, Dix! What about Julia?"

"She was conscious when he left, he said, and Mother kept her quiet, but later she started running a temperature. Mother was scared to death, but she expected Dad at any minute. Julia's fever kept rising, and finally Mother sent Jimmy to get a farm woman who lived in the neighborhood."

"My mother. It was my mother."

Dix was surprised. "I never knew that. Your mother must have been pretty sharp, Cassie. From what Dad said, she took one look at Julia and sent Jimmy out to the fields to find her husband."

"My father, Howard Taylor."

"Yes. I remember him. Your mother sent him to town for the doctor, and she did what she could to keep the fever down. By the time Dad got home they were afraid to move her and the doctor was too late. She was dead."

Cassie pushed a knuckle against her teeth. All those years ago. Nineteen twenty-four, a year before Cassie herself was even born. She remembered the little girl's room, Julia's room, as she saw it when she first peeked in the window. The child-sized chair was pushed back from the desk, and on the floor lay the doll that Cassie had thought was a dead baby, the doll she named Mary Priscilla. "Dix?" she asked abruptly. "What caused the fever?"

"A skull fracture. When Dad told me about it, when I was fifteen, he was under control. You know how he looks sometimes, like the great stone face. But he was holding a pencil while he talked and when he said 'skull fracture,' the pencil snapped. It didn't look like he moved a muscle, but that damn pencil just broke in half." He looked down at the water. "Like Mother. She broke, too. Some kind of nervous breakdown. I don't think she ever got over Julia's death."

"Was that when she started the sherry?"

"Yes. She's been better this week, though, than in years."

"She's so glad to have you safe, Dix." Cassie picked up two rocks and rubbed them together. There were things about Julia's death that she still did not understand. If James Steele had only made a mistake in judgment, why would he feel guilty after all those years? "Dix, did your father get the farm that day? Did he get the land he wanted?"

"Yes. Oh, yes, he got the land."

Cassie jumped up and threw her rocks into the creek, as hard as she could, and the splashes broke the spell.

"Good arm, for a girl," Dix said.

"For a girl!" she said indignantly, but then she laughed. "Do you remember when I told you that there were cottonmouth water moccasins in the creek?"

"Do I ever! I'll bet I jumped ten feet straight up!" He looked around at her. "Cassie? Were there poisonous snakes in this creek?"

Cassie dropped down on the bank next to him and dug into the picnic basket. "Maybe. I never saw one."

He grabbed her arm and spun her around. "You . . . by God, you scared me half out of my mind that day!" He leaned back and roared with laughter.

Cassie laughed, too, at the memory they shared, at the beauty of the spring day and at the pleasure of being there by the creek with Dixon Steele. She laughed until she was weak and leaned against his shoulder to catch her breath. Still laughing, he automatically slipped his arm around her to support her. The weight of his arm on her shoulders stopped Cassie's laughter instantly and at the same moment, Dix slowly withdrew his arm.

"Well," Cassie said hastily, "shall we eat our picnic?"

"Let's wait a while. I want to have a swim in that creek, now that I know it's not alive with snakes. I've got my trunks on under my pants."

Cassie pulled her swimming suit out of the basket. "I'll go back to the lodge to change."

"No, don't do that." He grinned at her. "Change on the other side of the bridge. Remember, I'm an officer in the U.S. Army and by definition a gentleman. I won't peek."

"By whose definition?" Cassie said. She carried her things to the upstream side of the bridge and peeked to make sure that Dix was gazing steadfastly downstream. She undressed and stood up to feel the sun's heat on her naked body. She stretched, feeling young and free and happier than she had been since the days of Turner School.

"Hey!" Dix called. "I like the color of that swimming suit!"

Cassie dropped into a huddle on the creek bank. "You—"

"Always was crazy about red swimsuits."

She peeked over the bridge again and saw that his back was still to her. "Darn you, Dix Steele, you had me believing you for a minute!

I thought that you really had looked!"

He laughed without turning around. "Always keep them on their toes, that's what my C.O. used to say. Keep the enemy off balance."

"The enemy? You bet!" Cassie pulled on her blue swimming suit, but she did not take off her tennis shoes. The days when Cassie Taylor could run barefoot over sharp rocks had long since passed.

Dix had stripped down to black swimming trunks. As Cassie waded downstream toward him, he pushed himself up from the bank with an obvious effort and braced himself with his cane as he turned to face her.

Cassie stopped short. On the inside of his left leg was an angry red scar that ran from the edge of his trunks almost down to his knee. She forced herself to move again and to look up at his face.

His dark eyes were cold and blank. "Ugly, isn't it?"

Cassie wanted to weep, but she forced herself to speak in an angry voice. "So what? It's just a scar. Am I supposed to pretend that I don't see it?"

His eyes widened and he laughed. "By God, Cassie Steele, you don't ask for quarter, but you don't give it either, do you?"

"Am I all that tough?"

"I like you just the way you are. You don't treat me either as a cripple or a little boy with a skinned knee."

"You aren't a boy, Dixon Steele. You're a man."

"Yes," he said quietly, looking at her. "Yes."

She looked back at him just as openly. He carried his broad shoulders high, but his body had the bony look of illness. The hair of his chest was black and curly, a wide patch that narrowed to a thin line before it disappeared under the waistband of his swimming trunks. She raised her eyes to his face.

His dark eyes glinted and he held out his hand. "Madam, will you be so kind as to help an old soldier into the water?"

"Of course, brigadier," she said. "And aren't the dahlias lovely this year?"

Dix braced himself on her shoulder and she squatted down slowly, helping him lower himself into the shallow water. His hand jerked on her shoulder. "My God, that's cold!"

She laughed. "I know, I know."

He stretched out his bad leg and sat down on the rocks of the stream bed. "How come it's so cold when the day is so hot?"

"San Bois Creek is spring-fed, Dix. The hills back there are limestone, with lots of little springs."

"And how come you're so much fun, Cassie? No one ever told me that you had a silly streak."

She looked at him quickly. "I guess I never had anyone to act silly with, until today." She picked up a flat rock and skipped it across the surface of the creek. "Hey! I got five skips! Try to beat that, city slicker!"

"Is that any way to talk to a poor wounded lad?"

She grinned at him. "Poor wounded lad, my foot!"

"Now you've got my dander up. Watch this, sister. This city slicker has skipped rocks on rivers from the Rhône to the Rhine."

His rock skipped once and sank.

Cassie crossed her arms on her chest. "I'm watching, captain. Now, was that the Rhône technique for rock skipping, or the Rhine?"

He jammed the heel of his hand against the water to splash her.

"Hey! No fair! I wasn't expecting that!"

"Oh, I'm sorry," he said innocently. "I didn't know we were playing by San Bois Creek splashing rules."

Cassie jumped up and ran around and around him, kicking water at him until he was spluttering. "No fair," he gasped, "no fair! I can't get away from you! I'm helpless!"

"Too bad, too bad!" She kicked higher and his hand darted out to grab her ankle. She fell flat on her back in waist-deep water. Her head went under and she came up gasping for breath.

"Cassie! Are you all right?"

She went limp and let her mouth fall open. He jerked her body toward him. "Cassie!"

She pursed her lips and blew a thin stream of water into his face, then opened her eyes and grinned at him wickedly.

But he was no longer smiling and his dark eyes were serious.

"Cassie. Oh, God, Cassie."

He pulled her to him slowly, and put his arms around her. He looked into her eyes, searchingly, and then be bent over her and kissed her.

It was the first time he had held her like that, the first time he had kissed her, and yet it seemed to Cassie that it had happened again and again in some far country of her memory. She was so comfortable, so at home in his arms that she might have spent her whole life there, in that place, with that man. She was alive in every nerve ending, conscious of the gray-green water rippling over her bare legs, of the warm sunshine on her arms and the slight breeze ruffling her hair, conscious of his strong, thin arms around her, of his breath on her cheek and of his lips on hers.

He raised his head and looked down at her with eyes so sad that Cassie almost cried out.

Gently he shifted his hands to her shoulders and moved her away from him. She let him do it, but behind her own eyes she felt tears building. They sat there together in the water, not touching, not even looking at each other.

"I'm sorry," he said quietly.

"No, Dix," she said as quietly. "Don't be sorry. I'm not. I never felt that way before."

He looked down at the water. "I never felt it either."

Cassie put her wet hand to her cheek. It was warm, almost feverish. "What are we going to do?"

Dix cupped water in his hand and let it dribble out, watching it as if he were studying the attributes of a newly discovered element.

"Dix?" Cassie said it again. "What are we going to do?"

He sighed, a long slow, sigh, and then he used his arms to heave himself out of the water and onto the rocky bank of the creek. "Well, Cassie, we're going to eat our picnic and we are going to get back in your car and we're going to drive back to Ballard."

"That's all?"

"That's all. There is nothing else that we can do."

Cassie stood up in the water. "But you were——" She could not seem to form a coherent sentence. "I know you were—and I was——"

"I know. I was out of line. You are my brother's wife. I'm sorry, Cassie."

"Sorry about what?" she cried. "Sorry because you kissed me or sorry because I'm your brother's wife?"

He looked at her soberly. "Which do you think?"

She put her hands on her hips. "And now we just forget about it, is that it? We just pretend it never happened?"

"I wish I could." He tried to laugh. "Say, you better get some clothes on before I give you the splashing of your life!"

His attempt at lightness fell as heavily as a stone in water, but Cassie waded to the bank. "All right," she said. "I'll get dressed and bring the car down to get you."

"I thought you wanted to eat lunch down here by the creek."

"Not now."

When Cassie came back with the car, Dixon had changed into his polo shirt and khaki pants.

They had their picnic in the shade on the steps of the veranda. The land was spread out before them like a pastoral painting: the creek off to their right, the rich bottomlands thick with dark green cotton plants, the high, rolling fields with stands of spring-green corn, and beyond the fields, the dark foothills rising to the hazy blue of the Ozarks. Cassie did not look at the view. She looked at the food on the red-checked cloth she had laid out on the top step. Fried chicken and deviled eggs, a jar of pickles and bowls of potato salad and celery and tomatoes. She tried not to look at Dix's hands as they reached for food or poured out iced tea. She did not want to see. He was not looking at her, either, but she felt that both of them were being watched. It was the house again, she thought, the house looming over them like a presence.

Cassie picked at the lunch, but food could not fill the emptiness within her. Dix did not eat much either, and they ended by packing most of the food back into the basket. Dix stowed it in the backseat of the car while Cassie went through the empty, dusty house closing windows and locking doors. She paused at the door of the little girl's room, of Julia's room, and then she went out the front door and pulled it shut behind her. As she got into the driver's seat she looked up at the lodge one last time. It was, after all, just a house.

They drove slowly along the rough gravel road, past the overgrown clearing where the lone chimney stood, past the track that had led to the tenant house. Like a harbinger of the dry summer to come, a dust devil rose in a cornfield and whirled to the east, spinning red with the dust it carried.

Dixon cleared his throat. "From your reading about soil conservation, Cassie, what would you say would be the best way to handle land like this?"

When Cassie glanced over at him, he was facing straight ahead. He obviously wanted to return them, if not to their earlier light friendship, at least to some sort of patched-up relationship that would serve to get them through the day. He was a good man, she thought. He was such a good man. Her hands trembled on the steering wheel, but when she spoke her voice was flat and practical.

"Grazing. This land should never have been plowed. The Cherokees grazed hundreds of cattle on it long ago, and they had no trouble with used-up soil and wind and water erosion. I'd plow the organic material back into the land, and I'd plant it to Bermuda grass and clover. With the creek it would make first-class pasturage."

"That makes sense," Dixon said thoughtfully. "I wonder if Dad has ever considered that idea. He probably has."

Anger seeped into the void Cassie was trying to ignore. "That's right, it's his land, isn't it? I guess I lived here so long that I think I have a stake in saving it. Thanks for reminding me."

"Cassie, I didn't mean to—"

"No, Dix. Don't apologize. I appreciate your being so ready to remind me of things. This is your father's land. I am your brother's wife. Everything has to belong to someone, doesn't it? We possessions must not forget that. We can't get the idea that we have the right to make choices of our own."

"Hey, now, I didn't say that!"

"You didn't have to, did you? I sort of wonder, though, how your attitude jibes with your wanting to work with the ACLU. Didn't you say something about the rights of the individual?"

Dixon hesitated, then said calmly, "There's an old army saying: Never apologize, never explain. If you are going to misinterpret everything I say, there is little point in my saying anything at all." He crossed his arms on his chest.

Cassie nodded sharply. "Okay," she said. "Okay."

Chapter 23

 CASSIE DROVE through San Bois in angry silence, but three miles north of town the steering wheel jerked in her hands and the car veered sharply to the left.

"It's a blowout!" she cried.

She jerked her foot off the accelerator and gripped the wheel until the car slowed and she was able to brake gently and ease it off the paving to the gravel shoulder.

Dix let out his breath. "You handled that like a motor-pool sergeant!"

"We'll have to change the tire."

"I can do that for you, Cassie."

They opened the trunk and Dix thumped the spare tire. "Plenty of air. Where are your tire tools?"

Cassie stared at the trunk blankly. "I'm afraid—I don't think I have any."

"Oh, God, deliver me from women drivers!"

"Don't you say that to me! If the dealer didn't put them in, it's not my fault, is it?"

He scowled at her. "Whose car is it? Anyone with any sense at all would make sure she had a damn lug wrench in her car!"

"What is it they say in the army? Never apologize, never explain? So what do we do now, captain, sir?"

"We wait for someone to come by and we hope like hell that he has sense enough to carry a few basic tools."

They got back in the car and Dix looked at his watch. "Oh, God.

This could take hours, and Mother and Dad want to take me to the club for my last night home."

"You and your precious club! That's all I ever hear from Jimmy—the club, the club, the club!"

They sat in stony silence for almost an hour until a car came, a black-and-white car with Sheriff emblazoned on the door in gold letters. It made a lazy U-turn and pulled back across to park on the shoulder nose-to-nose with the Oldsmobile.

Two men got out, a stocky gray-haired man from the driver's side, and from the other, a big red-faced man with a beer belly. They wore khakis and broad-brimmed gray hats. When the fat man came to her car Cassie recognized him as the deputy sheriff who had come to the tenant house once, looking for Bo Taylor because a little girl had been dragged off into the night.

"Deputy Beasley?" Cassie said. "Do you remember me?"

"I reckon I do." He planted a meaty hand on the door. "Where'd Howard Taylor's girl get her a fancy car like this? You and the boyfriend stop to do a little necking?" He peered at the basket in the backseat. "Little drinking, too, like your papa."

Dix half rose in his seat. "Now, look here, you can't talk to her like that!"

The deputy stepped back from the car and put his hand on his holster. "I said, where'd you get this car, girl? You steal it?"

Dix started to open his door.

"Bill," Beasley said, "get your gun on that boy! Like as not a deserter, hanging out with Howard Taylor's girl."

Dix got out of the car and raised his hands. "Deputy, we'd better straighten this out before someone gets hurt. If you'll let me get out my wallet, I can prove to you that I am Captain Dixon Steele of Ballard. This lady is my brother's wife, and you probably know my father, James Steele."

The deputy immediately yelled at his assistant, "God damn it, Bill, put that gun away! Captain, I'm mighty sorry for this here little misunderstanding. Say, you got car trouble or something?"

Cassie and Dix and Beasley watched while Bill brought tools and changed the tire. When he finished, Beasley walked over and kicked it. "That ought to do it, Captain Steele."

"Thank you, Deputy Beasley," Cassie said softly.

"Don't need no thanks, Miz Steele." He grinned at her but his small eyes were hard and watchful. "Say, what do you hear from that brother of yours?"

"Bo?" She was startled. "But he's—Bo's dead. He died when our house burned."

"Yeah, that's what they all said, but I never could figure out what happened to that old Ford of his."

"Bo's car? He didn't—I don't—" She bit her lip.

The deputy laughed. "I was just wonderin', Miz Steele. Never knew what that Bo would get up to next, did you?"

Without speaking, Cassie started the engine and drove away.

Dix laughed. "What a fool! Did you see how he changed when I told him who we were?"

"He didn't change," Cassie said absently. "I was the one who changed."

"What are you talking about?"

"One minute I was Cassie, Howard Taylor's daughter, someone who would steal a car and park on the highway so she could neck with a deserter. The next minute I was a different person, James Steele's daughter-in-law, who would have her own car, of course, and who would never stop on the highway unless she had car trouble."

"Now, Cassie, the man's just a fool. He's nothing but a—"

"A dictator. What's the difference between a Deputy Beasley and an Adolf Hitler? Beasley would put me in jail just because I was a Taylor and Hitler put people in concentration camps—"

"Because they were Jews." Dixon drummed his fingers on his knee. "And all my high-flown ideas about the rights of man are so much eye-wash if we are willing to put up with the Beasleys."

"Or if we use them," Cassie said, "as we used him to get a flat changed. We're on top because of your father's position, so we use Beasley and he uses the sharecroppers and—"

"And they use the next lower echelon."

Cassie jerked at the steering wheel. "There's nobody lower on the scale than a sharecropper!"

"Negroes, Cassie. And in Germany it was the Jews. Tell me, how many Negroes do you know socially?"

"I don't need to know them," she said softly. "I am them."

Dix leaned back and stretched. "Oh, sure. With your own car and a big house and——"

"Once you've been there, you don't forget." Cassie sighed. "And no one else forgets, either. Deputy Beasley very carefully reminded me that I was only a sharecropper, that I wasn't a dyed-in-the-wool Steele, didn't he?"

"By asking about your brother? Cassie, consider the source."

"I am considering the source. Maybe he's had news of Bo."

"I don't understand. Dad told me your brother was dead." Dix touched her shoulder. "Do you want to tell me about it?"

Cassie hesitated, but since the deputy's probing, the pressure had brought her to the bursting point. She had to tell someone. She told Dix about her father's death, about Bo's attempt to rape her, and that although she had paid him to stay away, recently the money orders had begun to come back from California uncashed. She did not, however, tell him how Bo had lied about the night of the fire. That was too painful still.

When she finished, she sneaked a look at Dix. How would he react? Bo was her brother. Was she to be tarred with the same brush? When he spoke, however, there was nothing but honest indignation in his voice.

"Cassie, you should be glad to be rid of him!"

"But he's like a snake, Dix, a copperhead that will come out of the rocks and strike when you least expect it. I know he'll hurt me. Just by being alive, he'll hurt me." Tears blurred her eyes.

"Pull over," Dix said. "You can't drive like this."

"But what about the club? You'll be late."

"The hell with the club! Pull over."

Cassie stopped the car and Dix put his arms around her and pulled her to him. "Go on," he said. "Cry it out." She leaned into his shoulder and let the tears flow.

When her weeping subsided, Dix poured some cold tea from the Thermos onto a red-checked napkin. "Hold this on your eyes so the folks won't see that you've been crying."

"Thank you," she whispered. "Thank you, Dix."

He put his arm around her and gratefully she leaned her head against his chest. She could hear the beat of his heart, steady and solid. "Cassie, I don't know where I am going to be, but I want you to call me if Bo shows up. Will you do it?"

"You promise you won't tell anyone he's alive?"

"Of course."

"I'll call, Dix, I will! But why are you willing to do this?"

He held her shoulders and looked into her eyes. "Because I . . . what I feel for you is so large, so grand——"

"Oh, darling, I feel the same way about——"

"No! I can't let you say it. It isn't right."

She drew back. "Is that so, Dix? Do you have a compass with a needle that points to absolute right?"

His black eyes were desolate. "It's a question of honor."

"Honor." It took all of her strength to pull away from him, but Cassie moved back to the driver's seat and held on to the steering wheel. "I'll tell you something, Dixon Steele. Some people can't afford luxuries like honor. They've got to survive. You fought the war, you ought to know that. They've—we've got to survive. You want to help everybody, but you can't help anyone until you learn what it costs, just to survive."

CASSIE BEGGED OFF going to the club for dinner. A headache, she said, from the day in the sun. When they returned she was reading in the living room. Jimmy had stayed on at the club, and she could understand why. The tension between James Steele and Dixon was as taut as a wire. Amelia was wringing her hands and eyeing the cabinet where the sherry decanter was kept.

"I tell you, I've counted on this for a long time, Dixon," James Steele said angrily.

"Do we have to go into this now, with Mother and Cassie here?"

James Steele ignored him. "I told you, I've planned it for years. Law school at the University of Oklahoma, of course, and then the firm, and then politics. As a war hero, you can——"

"War hero! It could be a long time before the war is over. You know that! But do you honestly think I would stoop to using my war record for political gain? It would be dishonorable even to——"

"Come now, Dixon, let's not get carried away by abstract notions of honor and that sort of thing."

For once Cassie could agree with James Steele, but she was afraid to speak or even to move from her chair.

"I must warn you," James Steele continued, "I will not support you through law school if you insist on opposing my wishes. To throw away an opportunity like—"

"An opportunity to be a money-grubbing lawyer like your old pal in the office next to yours? Or a venal judge like your fraternity brother? Or maybe an opportunity to be a two-faced politician like your friend in the—"

"That's enough of that!" his father roared. "I will not have you insulting my friends!"

"And I will not have you insulting my integrity!"

Cassie had heard enough, too much. She slammed her book shut with a bang and ran up the stairs.

In her own room she dropped on her bed to catch her breath. Two grown men, yelling at each other like children. Two stubborn men. James, power-mad but practical, and Dixon, honor-mad and idealistic. It was so ridiculous that she wanted to laugh, but she could not. It was so ridiculous that it was not funny.

AT DIXON STEELE'S last breakfast at home, everyone except Amelia maintained an air of polite formality. Amelia dabbed at her eyes at the same time that she smilingly reminded them that Georgia was not really all that far from Eastern Oklahoma and that dear Dixon would at least be safe there.

Cassie told Dix good-bye at the breakfast table. "I hope you have a safe trip."

Dix was as formal as she. They shook hands without quite looking at each other.

Upstairs, Cassie went into Jimmy's room, at the front of the house, to watch them in the driveway below.

Amelia stood in the driveway to hug Dix, and James Steele gave him a stiff handshake.

Jimmy stuck his head out the front window of the Cadillac.

"Hurry up, Dix! You want to miss your train?"

With his hand on the car door Dix looked up at the house. Cassie ducked behind the curtain and peeked past the edge. He stood there in the driveway in his uniform, with his chin held high, soldierly and brave and very, very honorable.

She watched the car roll down the driveway, watched it pass between the stone posts and roll into the street.

As she let the curtain fall into place she remembered something her grandmother had said. "A clean break heals faster."

Granny was wrong. This was a clean break, and it would never heal. Never.

JAMES STEELE'S house felt even larger to Cassie after Dixon left, larger and lonelier. Amelia seemed to feel it as much as Cassie, but they had never talked together and it was too late to begin.

Cassie had not seen Fran Jordan for several months. Time and again she had called her, but the messages seemed to get lost or be forgotten. One morning in July, Fran answered the telephone herself.

"Fran! Will you have lunch with me at the club today?"

"I suppose—"

"Fine," Cassie said. "I'll meet you there at twelve sharp."

Fran was not herself. There was no sparkle in her eyes and her voice was flat and dull. Cassie ordered a martini for Fran and a Tom Collins for herself and laughed nervously. "I was beginning to think you were avoiding me."

Fran glanced at her and then away. "Why would I do that?"

"Oh, just a notion."

A tall woman in shorts ambled over from her table. "Well, if it isn't Fran. Haven't seen you in months, darling, simply months. How's Jimmy?"

Cassie answered automatically. "Oh, he's fine. He's been out of town a lot lately."

The tall woman raised her eyebrows slowly. "Has he? How nice!"

She ambled back to her own table, but the minute she sat down the other two women at her table put their heads close to hers.

And at that minute, the pieces fell into place as surely and as solidly as tumblers falling in a lock.   Jimmy's coming home late, long after the country club had closed.   Her calls to Fran and the messages that were always lost or forgotten.

Cassie's blush seemed to begin on her chest and move right up her throat to her face, but she did not care.   All she cared about was getting away from that table and getting away from the club as quickly as she could do it without looking like an idiot.   But it was too late. She had already made a complete fool of herself when she had asked her husband's mistress to have lunch with her.

Fran looked worried.

Cassie reached across to touch her hand.   "I'm sorry, Fran."

Fran's eyes opened wide.   "You're sorry?   What do you have to be sorry about?"

"That I got you to come out here today."   Cassie took a deep breath.   "And about you and Jimmy.   I can't give him a divorce.   You have to understand that.   James Steele would never permit it."

"A divorce!   You mean, you think that I want to marry Jimmy? You are too much, Cassie Steele.   You are just too much."   She swallowed half of the martini in one gulp.   "Waitress," she called.   "The same again."   Suddenly she threw back her head and laughed.   "Too much!"

Cassie gritted her teeth.   She had already made a fool of herself and to top that, she had made a ridiculous mistake that she did not even understand.   Fran was quick to explain it to her.

"You've got it all wrong, darling!"

"But you looked so worried, Fran, that I thought you—"

"I was worried, darling, but not because I was in love with Jimmy Steele.   In lust, maybe; never in love.   Anyway, it's all over now." She grinned.   "I guess you could say that I gave him up because of your esteemed father-in-law."

"James Steele?   What has he got to do with it?   Did he make you break up with Jimmy?"

"Lord, no!"   Fran leaned toward her.   "You said that you didn't care what Jimmy did or whose bed he did it in.   Remember?"

"Yes," Cassie said bitterly.   "But I didn't think my best friend would—"

"I didn't think I would, either," Fran said, "but we had too much to drink one night and before I knew it . . . Cassie, I've had other affairs with married men, and part of the fun was the game—you know, going to lunch with the wife and to bed with the husband. But I couldn't play it that way with you. I told Jimmy that I wanted to break off and he said his father had already told him to end it. Cassie, why does he have so much power over Jimmy?"

"I don't know," Cassie said slowly. "But if it was all over, why did you avoid me?"

"Because I knew I had to tell you about it, and I hated it. If I just waited till you found out there would be no way on earth of patching up our friendship. Strange as it may seem, even old Frantic Fran needs a friend. A friend like you."

"Me? But I'm not even an insider."

Fran raised her eyebrows. "An insider? Oh, you mean here at the club." Her quick laugh sounded more like the old Fran. "Cassie, that's the best thing about you. You don't play the country-club games, and I am not talking about golf and tennis!"

Cassie smiled. "I want to be your friend, too. I don't care about you and Jimmy."

Fran put her hand to her breast and sighed dramatically. "What a relief!" But she looked at Cassie directly and said, "I'm glad, Cassie. I am very glad of that. Thank you."

Cassie asked the question that bothered her. "Fran? Why did James tell Jimmy to break up with you?"

"Politics, of course. James thought gossip about us might get out and hurt Jimmy in the southern part of the district. Would you believe it, he even told Jimmy to go to prostitutes if he had to!"

"He didn't!"

"He sure as hell did. And Jimmy thought it was funny."

"Jimmy would," Cassie said grimly.

"Jimmy would take his dear papa's advice, too. After all, what are little things like fornication and the possibility of catching a disease, compared to a seat in—" She stopped suddenly, looking uncomfortable. "I'm not one to talk about fornication."

In the parking lot, Fran gave Cassie a quick hug. "Thank you, darling. I do want to keep you as a friend."

Cassie hugged her back. "And I want you to be my friend."

Fran laughed and crossed her heart with one manicured finger. "I solemnly promise you that I won't have one thing to do with your husband, Cassie, whether you care or not." Her eyes sparkled. "But that handsome brother-in-law of yours, Dixon Steele, he's up for grabs, isn't he? When will he be home on leave again?"

Cassie forced herself to smile. "I don't know. Fran, I must run now!" She hurried to her car, leaving Fran looking puzzled.

She had driven through the country-club gates before she allowed her face to relax from that fixed grin. Fran and Dixon. It could happen, and if it did, she would have no right to interfere.

AT 9:15 A.M. on August 6, 1945, the *Enola Gay* dropped an atomic bomb on Hiroshima. The word went around Ballard at the speed of light, but no one was sure what the word meant. "Atom bomb? What's a atom bomb?" The radio issued a steady stream of information, but it did not help. The atomic bomb had the destructive force of so many thousand tons of TNT, but no one in Ballard had ever seen even one ton of TNT. The radio gave the casualty figures, too, but one hundred thousand dead or wounded had as little meaning to Ballard people as a thousand tons of TNT. One dead had meaning, great meaning. One Ballard boy was killed at Anzio. "Tommy Ray Jackson, sure, you remember him. Used to deliver groceries for Riggs' Market. His mother was a Kendall, her sister married that yahoo from Tulsa."

When another bomb was dropped on Nagasaki the meaning of the atomic bomb began to sink in. "Old Harry's going to drop them things till them dirty Japs yell 'Calf rope!' " It meant that the war would end and the boys would come home.

Dixon Steele did not come home. He called to tell his parents that he had managed to get a leave but would go to New Haven and register at Yale's law school. He would pay for it with the aid of the GI Bill and a legacy from his grandmother.

James Steele was angry, but Amelia was desolate, even when James promised to take her east that fall so that she could see her son.

Cassie was both desolate and relieved. She wanted to see him terribly, but she knew that if he came to Ballard it would be a toss-up between her throwing herself at his feet and screeching at him in anger. It was better not to see him at all.

A FEW NIGHTS LATER, James Steele asked Cassie to come to his study after dinner.

She sat down in front of his desk, irritated at herself for being nervous. James Steele lit his after-dinner cigar, and twirled the end in the flame of a match. "Cassie, I want you to go with Jimmy to an evening political meeting in Muskogee Saturday."

"Why?"

"Surely even you realize that it is important for a candidate's wife to be seen with him." He laughed pleasantly, which seemed to startle him as much as it did Cassie. "Especially when the wife is as attractive as you."

"Mr. Steele—"

"Don't you think you should call me James?"

Cassie hardly knew what to think. James Steele laughing? James Steele being friendly? "Yes, of course. James."

"We'll make sure it's a pleasant trip for you, my dear. You might even like to buy a few new dresses."

Cassie was recovering her wits. New dresses, a pleasant trip: he was like a father bribing his child with an ice cream cone. "No, James, I don't want to go with Jimmy."

He scowled at her. "You must go. It is important."

She watched him struggle to control his temper. For once, she had the upper hand. "That's too bad."

"You will do as I say, Cassie Taylor."

"Steele, remember? Cassie Steele."

His face was red with anger, but he smiled at her, coldly. "As long as you live in my house, you will do as I say."

In those words Cassie could see the future, her future: the empty life, the aimless drives through the countryside, the hours killed at lunch or at the country club, the pointlessness of being married and not a wife.

"Then I will leave your house," she said softly.

James Steele raised his eyebrows. "What's this, a display of your grandmother's grit?"

Cassie stood up. "I am free, you know. I don't have to do what you tell me to for the rest of my life. I'll go to Tulsa or Oklahoma City, I'll get a job, and I'll—"

"No." He shook his head slowly. "You will stay here, Cassie, and be a fit wife to Jimmy, and you will help with his campaign."

"I will not! You don't own me, James!"

"Perhaps not, but I can keep you from getting another job."

"Oh, you used that threat once, didn't you? You would call around the state, you would keep your pals from hiring me. Well, I've learned a thing or two since then, James Steele. Not everyone in this state is under your control."

He took up a paper from his desk and put on his glasses. "I have received a report that might interest you."

"Why would a report of yours have anything to do with me?"

He looked at her over his glasses. "Because it is about your brother."

Cassie sank down on the chair and her courage drained away. "My brother. What about my brother?"

He smiled. "This is taken from a file in the California courts. Bo Taylor, case number 836423, is in San Quentin prison, convicted of indecent liberties and endangering the life of a minor child."

"Oh, God," Cassie whispered. "No! It's a lie! Bo's dead!"

"I won't ask you why you have pretended he was dead, but you know this is the truth, don't you?"

Cassie nodded, unable to speak.

"Who would hire the sister of a convict? Especially of one who had raped a child? You understand why you must stay here, don't you, Cassie? And now you understand why you must do as I say."

She put her hand to her mouth and nodded, once more.

"Fine. I will tell Jimmy that he can plan on taking you to Muskogee with him."

CASSIE LAY AWAKE late into the night. Bo had come back, not physically, but like a dark shadow, the representative of the dark side of her family, of herself. He had come back to prevent her escape into a life of her own. Why? Why?

Beneath her anguish, a whisper of doubt crept from the back of her mind and pushed itself forward. How had James found out that Bo was alive? And how had he known where to look for him? Who else had known that Bo Taylor was in California before he disappeared? Cassie had known. Only Cassie. No, she thought, that was not quite true. She had told one other person. She had told Dixon Steele.

Chapter 24

THE MEETING ROOM in Muskogee was small, the evening was hot and humid and the room was crowded. Cassie stood at Jimmy's side, a fixed smile on her face, and wished that politicians smelled better.

Dutifully, she shook every hand that was thrust at her and passed out smiles as freely as Jimmy's young aide passed out campaign buttons that said STEELE: THE MAN OF IRON.

Back at the Severs Hotel, Cassie kicked off her high-heeled sandals. Jimmy had reserved the twin-bed room that she had insisted upon. On the dresser was a frosted silver bucket with a bottle of champagne.

Jimmy closed the door behind the bellboy and grinned at her. "How about that? Dad must have had a bootlegger bring it in."

They sat down with their champagne, Cassie on the one armchair and Jimmy on one of the beds. He raised his glass to her. "I really appreciate this, your coming to the meeting and all."

Cassie wiggled her tired feet and sipped her champagne. It was strange to be in a hotel room with a man who was her husband and yet was not. It would be the first time since their wedding that she had not slept under James Steele's roof. For once he was not there to supervise her every move, to shape her life. Even James Steele, she thought, could not come into a married couple's hotel room. She laughed softly.

Jimmy looked up, startled, but smiled. "Cassie, listen, I've been acting pretty rotten, I know." He leaned forward, holding his glass in both hands. "But I want to change. I want us to get back together."

It was Cassie's turn to be startled. Could he finally be growing up? She doubted it. More likely, he had tired of his new toys and wanted to play with an old one for a while. She finished her champagne and without speaking held the glass out for more. The wine was the only thing in her life that had any sparkle to it.

Jimmy wanted to come back to her. Maybe he even meant it, about wanting to change. She looked into her glass as if she could find the answer there. Could she be any worse off than she was?

She looked up from her glass. He was watching her, but she could read nothing in his eyes. "Why not?" she said. "We could give it a try."

"Cassie!" Jimmy set his glass on the table and pulled her up from her chair. "Oh, Cassie!" He grabbed her and kissed her, thrusting his tongue into her mouth.

Cassie remembered the kiss she and Dixon Steele had shared when they were together in the cool water of San Bois Creek. She trembled as the memory surged through her body and then she was back in a hotel room with Jimmy and he was pulling her toward the bed.

"Let me . . ." she said breathlessly. "Jimmy, my dress!"

Jimmy pushed her down on the bed. Cassie tried to enjoy it. She thrust her pelvis up to him, but it was over almost before it had begun. Jimmy grunted and rolled over on his back.

"Shit! This fucking bed's too narrow."

"Stay with me, Jimmy! I'll make room for you."

"I've got to get some sleep."

Within five minutes he was snoring in the other bed. Cassie was exhausted but too keyed-up to sleep. Eventually she dozed, only to be awakened by Jimmy rubbing her breast roughly. "Again? Jimmy, we don't have to—"

"Hell, yes, again!"

He entered her as abruptly as before and ejaculated as quickly. He was soon snoring again, and Cassie lay alone in the darkness.

He would not change. He would never change. He took her like a thing, an object that existed only for his gratification, only to relieve his needs, and each time that he took her it diminished her. She could not go back to that.

It was not that she was so wonderful. She was no more than a woman-shaped doll who goose-stepped through the life of a country-club wife. She was not wonderful, but she was all that she had.

Unless. Cassie sat up in bed and looked across at Jimmy, a bulky shape in the dim light from the street. They had not used birth control that night. She could get pregnant. The idea was like a flare of light in a dark room. A baby. Her baby. Cassie lay back on her pillow and allowed the idea to grow and become hope.

Jimmy was sulky as they drove back to Ballard the next morning, but Cassie ignored him. She would be using him, but hadn't the Steele men used her again and again? She went to his room that night, and the next. Their night and day relationships had nothing to do with each other. He was gone during the day, at work or playing tennis. He spent the evenings at the country club but was always home by bedtime. She went to him every night for the next two weeks, until the day he left to defend at a murder trial in McAlester. She was tired and sore by then but it would be worth it to have a baby. It would be worth anything.

Jimmy had been gone for three weeks when James told her that the trial would last for two more weeks, but Cassie was almost certain that she was pregnant.

She was so happy that she thought sure someone would notice, but not even sharp-eyed Fran Jordan suspected it. Fran was involved in plans of her own.

"I would have told you earlier, Cassie, but you've been out of circulation."

Cassie smiled inwardly. "Yes, I have. What is this big news?"

Fran ordered drinks for them.

"I'm going to Dallas this week."

"For a vacation?" Cassie asked, although she could not imagine what Fran would need to vacation from.

"For good! I have a job lined up with an interior decorator and I've rented a house—"

"Why, Fran?"

Fran looked down at her drink. "I've got to get out of Ballard, that's why. That business with Jimmy—well, it made me think about what I'm doing with my life. She pushed the glass away and looked directly at Cassie. "I saw what I am becoming, and I didn't like it. A lunch time lush. The club slut. That's not good enough. Maybe I won't make it in the big city, but by God, I'll have tried!"

"Fran, I'll miss you so much." It was true, but Cassie was comforted by the thought of the new life within her. She would have her baby. "I will miss you terribly."

Cassie saw Fran again only once before she left, and she could tell that Fran was already halfway to Dallas. Her eyes sparkled and the bitter lines around her mouth had disappeared.

IN LATE SEPTEMBER, Cassie asked Amelia for the name of her physician and went to see Dr. Mathers, a tall distinguished-looking man with gray hair and cool gray eyes that seemed to weigh her and find her wanting. He greeted her with a bright professional smile. He glanced at her chart. "You are twenty years old? Well, well! You youngsters are certainly keeping me busy these days. Go into the examing room now, my dear, and I'll be with you in a few minutes."

Later, Dr. Mathers stood up and looked at her over the tent of sheets. "You can put your legs down now."

"Am I pregnant?"

"Yes," he said shortly. "You're about six weeks along."

He was no longer smiling, but Cassie was too happy to care.

Jimmy came home from McAlester that evening, and at dinner Cassie told the whole family the news.

"Hey, that's great," Jimmy said.

Amelia came around the table to hug Cassie. "Won't it be lovely to have a baby in the house!"

James sat back in his chair at the head of the table and smiled like a man who had just completed a highly satisfactory business deal. "That is indeed good news, Cassie. Jimmy, my hearty congratulations."

Jimmy came out of James's study an hour later and went upstairs to his bedroom. Cassie ran up after him.

"Jimmy?" she said.

He turned around, grinning, and she saw that he was half-drunk.

"You've been drinking!"

"Sure. Dad and I had a few brandies to celebrate the good news." He pulled on a sports coat.

"Are you going out?"

"Yeah. Want to go out to the club. Haven't seen the old gang for over a month."

"You haven't seen me for over a month either, Jimmy."

He leered at her. "Don't have to see you anymore, baby. I've done it, haven't I?"

Cassie put her hand on the back of a chair. "You've done what?"

"Got you knocked up. Got you pregnant. That's what he told me to do."

Cassie gripped the chair back. "I don't understand, Jimmy. Who told you to—"

"Christ, you're dumb! Dad, of course! Dad said you were about ready to break out but that if I got you pregnant it would probably settle you down. I tell you, Cassie, he's a pretty smart old boy!"

Cassie covered her face with her hands. She didn't know whether to laugh or to cry. For once she and James Steele had been working toward a single aim. And what did that make Jimmy? What on earth did that make Jimmy Steele?

"You bastard," she whispered and then she screamed it: "You bastard!"

"Wait just a damn minute!" Jimmy raised his fist. "You can't call me that!"

Someone knocked hesitantly at the bedroom door. Cassie looked at Jimmy and then crossed the room and opened the door. It was Amelia, red-faced and not quite looking at Cassie.

"I'm so sorry to . . . disturb you, children, but your father just now took a message on the phone in his study. Cassie, Dr. Mathers wants you to come into the hospital tomorrow morning. He wants to examine you again under an anesthetic."

Cassie's hand flew to her abdomen. "Why? Is something wrong? Did he say that something was—"

"I don't know, dear. James just said that Dr. Mathers wants you there at eight."

"JUST A PRECAUTION." Dr. Mathers said before the anesthetic took effect. "Just a precaution."

When Cassie came out of the anesthetic she was in a hospital bed and a nurse was leaning over her. Cassie's tongue was thick, but she asked, "Is the baby all right?"

The nurse hurried out of the room.

Cassie dozed and woke later to find Dr. Mathers standing at the end of her bed, watching her.

"Oh, Dr. Mathers! Tell me, please! Is the baby all right?"

"The baby has been taken care of."

Cassie pushed herself up on her elbow. "I don't understand."

The doctor straightened his vest. "I have performed a therapeutic abortion."

"What? Why would you—"

"The foetus has been removed surgically."

Cassie fell back on the pillow. "But you never said—you didn't ask me! You can't just—"

"I had the signed permission of your husband and moreover I discussed this matter with your father-in-law on the telephone last night. He was in full agreement with the course of action."

"An abortion." Cassie shook her head, rejecting the words. "But why would you want to take my baby from me?"

Dr. Mathers raised his chin and glared at her. "It was not a matter of wanting to do it, young woman! It was a clear-cut case, well within the established guidelines of medical practice. The baby could have been born blind or deformed. At the very least, it would have been diseased, and even with the so-called wonder drugs, the prognosis for treatment of a newborn is guarded."

Cassie tried to make sense of his words. "Why would my baby have a disease? I'm not sick. I take good care of my body."

He looked down at her with undisguised contempt. "That may be so. But you certainly are sick, Cassie Steele. You are sick in body and, I would suspect, very sick indeed, in your mind. A woman who would allow herself to become pregnant when she was infected with a venereal disease is beyond my comprehension."

"What did you say? I don't have a—"

"Oh, yes. You have a veneral disease. You have gonorrhea."

CASSIE STAYED in the hospital for a week. She did not want to go home to the Steeles' house on Ballard Heights.

Each time Amelia and James visited her she pretended to be asleep until they went away, whispering.

Fran Jordan wrote from Dallas. "I am so sorry about the miscarriage."

So that was what they were calling it, Cassie thought.

Jimmy did not visit her, but he came to drive her home. He flirted with the women on the hospital staff and did not quite look at Cassie. They were driving up the hill to Ballard Heights when he finally spoke. "I'm sorry, Cassie. I mean it. I'm really sorry about this."

Cassie looked straight ahead. "You knew, didn't you, Jimmy? A night nurse said that women don't have visible symptoms but that men do. You knew all the time that you had gonorrhea."

"Hell, Cassie, a little dose of the clap, that can happen to any man. I swear I didn't think you'd get it, and I didn't have any idea that it could hurt the . . . hurt a baby."

Cassie stared out at the hood ornament. "You didn't think. Of course. You never think. You aren't a man, Jimmy Steele. You're a stupid careless child, and this time you have gone too far. Jimmy, I want a divorce."

His hands jerked on the wheel. "Cassie! You don't mean it! Not now, when I'm running for—"

"I do mean it." Cassie laughed softly. "As soon as I can get to a lawyer I'll file for divorce."

"On what grounds?" he said sullenly.

"Come on, Jimmy, I'm sure there are legal terms for it. I'll tell the lawyer that you knowingly infected me with gonorrhea and got me pregnant and told that doctor to do an abortion without discussing it with me. A good lawyer can surely come up with a name for it."

"Listen, Cassie, I didn't do that, about the doctor! Dad's the one who talked to Mathers."

Cassie did look at him then. "Oh, God, Jimmy, can't you do anything on your own, even accept responsibility? You were the one who signed the permission for surgery."

Jimmy pulled the car to the curb and stopped. His brown eyes looked soft and wounded. "Cassie, you wouldn't do that to me. God, just think what it would do to my political chances."

"I don't give a damn about your political chances and I care even less about you. You killed my baby, Jimmy Steele! You can burn in hell, for all I care."

He started the car and sped down the street. "You better talk to Dad before you get yourself in a mess!"

"I don't want to talk to your father, Jimmy. I want to talk to my own lawyer."

In the house, Cassie started up the stairs.

"Where are you going?" Jimmy said.

"To pack. I'll move to the hotel."

Cassie had almost finished packing her overnight case when Amelia knocked timidly on her bedroom door.

"Cassie, dear, I am . . . I am so sorry." Her eyes were full of tears but she was still able to deliver a message. "Jimmy telephoned James just now, at his office."

"I thought he would."

"James wants you to come downtown."

"Why? What good would it do?"

"I don't know, dear. I just know that he told Jimmy that it was very, very important." She wrung her hands nervously. "I do hope you'll go see him, Cassie."

Cassie sighed. "Oh, Amelia, I know it's not your fault. I'll go see James. I'll go by his office on the way to the hotel."

"Thank you, dear." Amelia put her hand on Cassie's arm. "My dear, I am so very sorry that it worked out this way."

Cassie patted her hand gently. "So am I, Amelia. So am I."

Miss Verna Whirter jumped up from her chair so quickly that she dropped her shorthand pad. "He's waiting for you in his office!"

Cassie closed the door of James Steele's office and leaned back against it. "Well, James."

He looked up from his papers. "Sit down."

"Why? We have nothing to talk about."

"I believe we do. Jimmy tells me that you intend to file for divorce." He leaned back in his chair. "No lawyer in Ballard will get mixed up in this."

"Who says I have to find a lawyer in Ballard? I've read in the papers about a lawyer in Tulsa, a Bernard Smithson."

James Steele stood up abruptly. "That damned radical? He's expensive as hell!"

Cassie sat down and relaxed. "You gave me an Oldsmobile, remember? Perhaps Mr. Smithson would accept that as a fee. And if he's as liberal as you say, he might take considerable pleasure in ruining Jimmy's political future."

James Steele sat down and turned his chair to look out the window. When he turned back he had regained control.

She said quietly, "You told me once that I had a lot to learn. I've done my homework. I'll ask my attorney to subpoena Dr. Mathers so that the whole story will come out in court. Jimmy's political career will be over before it even begins."

James scowled so that his heavy eyebrows came together at the bridge of his nose. "And I will make sure that your brother's criminal record is revealed."

She laughed. "So what? It won't be my reputation on trial, but yours and Jimmy's. It's all over now."

James smiled thinly. "Not quite." He shuffled among the papers on his desk. "I've done my homework, too. Ah, here it is." He put on his reading glasses. "I have here a private detective's report on a certain Naomi Bencher of the Women's Army Corps, who is currently an officer stationed at Fort Still, Lawton, Oklahoma."

Cassie sat forward. "What on earth are you trying to—"

"Hear me out. There was a nasty little incident at Fort Sam Houston, Texas, a few years ago, an incident involving this Naomi Bencher. A young corporal wanted to file charges of a sexual nature against Major Bencher and was only dissuaded by the commanding officer, who felt that such an action would be deleterious to the reputation of the Women's Army Corps. They tell me it was hushed up but could be reopened."

"This has nothing to do with me!"

He looked at her over his glasses. "No? My man also made a little trip to Whitman, Oklahoma, to interview Mr. and Mrs. Dale Hodge. He did not reveal my interest, of course, but when he informed them that their expenses would be reimbursed on quite a handsome scale, Mr. and Mrs. Hodge became extremely cooperative. He says that they are willing, even eager, to testify in court that their cousin Cassie Taylor spent every Saturday afternoon in the apartment of a Miss Naomi Bencher."

Cassie twisted her hands together. "This doesn't make sense."

He took off his glasses and smiled. "Oh, but it does, it makes perfect sense. You see, the young corporal I mentioned before was also a WAC. The corporal was a woman."

"I don't believe it! Naomi was never a . . ."

"Is it so difficult to say the word? A lesbian. Yes. An unpleasant term for an unpleasant person. And what did you two do, all those Saturday afternoons? I will admit to a certain salacious interest. I've never quite been able to understand what they—"

"Nothing!" Cassie cried. "We didn't do anything! Naomi was my friend. She taught me how to do my hair and dress and—it was all innocent! I was only sixteen, James! I didn't even know about that kind of thing!"

He chuckled. "Innocent. She brushed your hair and helped you to dress and—"

"No!" Cassie said, but she remembered that last Saturday afternoon, when Naomi had helped her with a new blouse, when Naomi had brushed her fingertips across Cassie's bare shoulders. "It's not true," she whispered.

She put her hands over her eyes to shut out the sight of that afternoon, of the way she had looked at Naomi in the mirror, of the way Naomi had looked at her. In her innocence, in her abysmal innocence, she thought that Naomi Bencher offered only friendship and wanted nothing more in return. She did not realize that Naomi was using her, just as James did, just as Jimmy did. They used her and when they had what they wanted of her, they left. Everyone left her in the end. Even Granny.

She pushed herself up straight and said it again, trying her best to believe it. "It's not true. You're taking a friendship and trying to make it filthy and—"

"Not I, Cassie." James raised his eyebrows and looked the picture of falsely accused innocence. "I am merely warning you of the construction that the public will put on your relationship when it is revealed. Major Bencher, apparently, is planning on a peacetime career as a WAC, but if this comes out the army will be forced to discharge her on moral grounds."

"They couldn't prove—"

"Surely you learned something when you worked in this office, Cassie. Proof is not necessary. Rumor is enough to ruin a career." He put both hands flat on his desk. "I want my son to win the primary and I will do anything that is necessary to achieve that goal."

His words were like blows, each one beating Cassie farther down in her chair. Naomi had left her, but could she ruin Naomi's life, even to save her own? James would win, as he always had, and she would lose. She would lose everything and James Steele would win because no matter how many lives it would ruin, he would do what he had to do.

Cassie took a deep breath. "Have you no decency, James? And no love? Don't you love anyone, anyone at all?"

His eyes darkened but his voice was hard. "Love? Love has nothing to do with it. This is business."

"No," she whispered. "I won't let you do this to me, James. Not again."

"I beg your pardon? I didn't quite hear you."

She sat up straight. "You heard me, all right. I said no! You have blackmailed me, James Steele, and you have manipulated me. You have controlled my life from the first day I ever laid eyes on you, and now you have killed my baby. No more, James. No more!"

"I don't know what you are talking about."

"The hell you don't!" Cassie jumped up from her chair and went over to the window. There it was, hazy in the September mist, but solid as a rock: Ballard Heights. From the time she went to work in James Steele's office and discovered that there was a life beyond grinding poverty, she had wanted it. She had wanted Ballard Heights and she had gotten it. But she had paid too much for it, and she was tired of paying. She was tired of being the only one who had to pay. She would be ruined, but Jimmy Steele would be ruined, too, and James, and Naomi Bencher, everyone who had used her. This time, they would pay, too. She turned and faced him. "James, I am going to divorce Jimmy."

"My God, girl, you don't know what you're saying! You'll go down in disgrace!"

She smiled at him. "I know. But I'll take you down with me, James. And you have more to lose. After all, I'm nothing but a sharecropper's daughter."

James sat back in his chair. "You're bluffing. You won't do it. You don't dare."

Cassie picked up her handbag. "I will, James. I will."

He opened the bottom drawer of his desk and took out a bottle of bourbon. He poured a shot into a silver cup and drank it quickly, then he looked up at her. "Want a drink?"

Cassie was startled. "No. I don't want—"

"Sit down, will you? It makes me nervous to have you wandering around like that."

Cassie sat down, confused.

"You've learned your lessons well, Cassie Taylor."

She smiled suddenly. "I had a good teacher."

He put his big hands flat on his desk. "We seem to have arrived at a stalemate."

"I guess you could call it that."

"Perhaps something can be salvaged."

"Perhaps."

He drummed his fingers on the desk for a few minutes. "I am prepared to offer you a proposition."

She laughed abruptly. "Have you finally run out of hole cards?"

He frowned at her. "I would like to keep this discussion on a businesslike basis."

Cassie felt slightly light-headed. "Oh, of course! We must be businesslike!"

"I want Jimmy in Congress."

"I know what you want. My God, by now I should know!"

"Hear me out," he said abruptly. "If you will drop the idea of divorce and maintain at least a pretense at marriage, I will provide an allowance that will let you live comfortably somewhere out of Ballard, away from Jimmy."

Cassie tried to keep a poker face but her hands were trembling. She had won! She had beaten James Steele! She would be free!

But would she be free?   When the election was over, and when Jimmy Steele was in office, her weapons would lose their cutting edges. She could threaten to cause a scandal, but it would be old news then, already talked to death at the country clubs around the state.   And she had heard enough political discussions that year to know that an incumbent congressman could weather a lot of scandal, even fresh scandal.   James would control the purse strings.   She would live comfortably, he said, but she knew that her comfort would last just so long as she did exactly what James Steele wanted.

She took a deep breath.   "I don't want an allowance from you, James.   I want five thousand dollars cash."

James looked at her for a minute and then leaned back in his desk chair.   He took out a cigar and unwrapped the cellophane.   "That's a tall order.   I guess you're ready to do a little horse trading now, Cassie."

"No.   I have stated my price."

He turned his cigar in the match flame and took a comfortable puff. "Five thousand dollars."   He shook his head.   "That's a hell of a big piece of cash to come up with in a hurry."

"James."   Cassie stood up slowly.   "Don't play the country lawyer with me.   You heard what I said.   Take it or leave it."

He scowled.   "I'll need a couple of days to think it over."

She laughed at him.   "You always say that a banker who can't make a quick decision is a banker who doesn't have a quick mind.   You have a damn quick mind, James.   I want a damn quick decision."

He laid his cigar on the ashtray and stood up.   "All right.   You're a hard woman, Cassie Taylor, but we have ourselves a deal.   Let's shake on it and in a few days we'll get it settled."

Cassie smiled at him sweetly.   "No, James.   I don't want a handshake deal.   I want a cashier's check and I want it before I leave this office today.   Send Whirter downstairs to the bank."

"By God, Cassie, you sound like you don't trust me!"

"By God, James, I don't!"

He laughed unpleasantly.   "You're asking a hell of a price, Cassie Taylor.   What if I refuse to pay it?"

Cassie shrugged.   "I'll drive straight to Tulsa to see Bernard Smithson."

James Steele stared at her for several minutes.

"All right," he said suddenly. "You've got me this time, God damn it!" Steele jabbed the button on his desk and was yelling when Miss Whirter stuck her head in the door. "Bring me my checkbook, the personal one, and get ready to go down to the bank."

Cassie opened an account with the cashier's check and waited to make sure that the money was transferred. She went to the Ballard Hotel and, alone in her room, she made her plans.

Early the next morning she would go to the Steeles' house to pack up her clothes, and then she would leave Ballard forever. Granny would be happy for Cassie. As she had said time and again, "God helps them that helps themselves."

Yes, Granny would be proud. But when Cassie tried to summon up her face and the memory of her voice, Granny was far away, farther away than death.

Cassie walked across to the window. She pulled the curtain back and stared down blankly at the traffic moving along Main Street.

She had won. She had beaten James Steele at his own game. She had every right to feel triumphant, every right in the world. But instead she had the feeling that in the winning she had cast aside something that was terribly important.

She had won. But what had she lost?

Part IV

*I myself have seen the ungodly in great power,
and flourishing like a green bay-tree.*

*I went by, and lo, he was gone:
I sought him, but his place could no where be found.*

*Keep innocency, and take heed unto the thing that is right;
for that shall bring a man peace at the last.*

—Psalm 37,
The Book of Common Prayer

Chapter 25

CASSIE TAYLOR STEELE drove south on U.S. 69 that hot September afternoon of 1945, on a gusty day when red dust rose from the fields along the blacktop highway. South from Ballard, through Eufaula, past the prison at Stringtown, through McAlester and Atoka to the Red River. As she drove, the knots of anguish and hate eased as if the increasing distance weakened James Steele's grip on the strings of his marionette.

She drove across the bridge over the Red River and when she saw the sign she pulled onto the shoulder and let the Oldsmobile roll to a stop.

The sign was large, a cutout in the shape of the state. WELCOME TO TEXAS, it said, and it pictured some of the delights awaiting her. Bluebonnets and cowboys and skyscrapers.

Cassie turned on the leather seat to look back across the river at that other state, at Oklahoma. All of her life was there, on the north side of the river: everyone she had loved, or hated, during the twenty years of her life. Everything was there. Everyone.

The good in her life was back there, but so was the bad. She felt cleansed, as if the old legend had turned out to be true and that by passing over running water she had broken a spell. She had left it behind, the bad and the good, buried like her grandmother in the worn-out red dirt of Eastern Oklahoma.

She had left behind, too, Cassandra Taylor, the country girl who had gone through life trusting people, always trusting, putting her faith in others, in Naomi and Ella Mae and Dale, and Jimmy Steele. Trusting them until, inevitably, they took advantage of that trust.

No more! No more would she wait until they acted against her and she could only react. In her meeting with James, she had made a start on taking control of her own life, and now she, Cassie Taylor Steele, would be in charge.

But first, she had to learn. She had to stop relying on what others told her. She had to know for herself.

Resolutely the new Cassie maneuvered the Oldsmobile back into the line of traffic and drove south into Texas. She drove through Denison and Sherman, negotiating the courthouse square, and she began to see that she had indeed left the red dirt of Oklahoma behind. Here the soil was dark, a rich black loam. Anything could grow in that black dirt, she thought. Anything!

She drove south until the afternoon sun slanted from the west. The Oldsmobile reached the top of a hill and far ahead she saw a red horse turning slowly in the purple haze of the southern horizon. She had read about the Flying Red Horse on top of the Magnolia Building, the tallest building in Dallas, and there it was, a red Pegasus waiting to carry Cassie Taylor Steele up from the earth to the zenith of the deep blue sky.

As she drove into Dallas, however, Cassie's confidence ebbed. Cars zipped past her as if everyone in Dallas had a specific destination and knew exactly how to get there. It took her an hour to find the small brick house in Highland Park.

She rang the doorbell and a tall woman opened the door. "Yes?" she said. "Who's there?"

Cassie looked at the red hair backlit by the lamps in the room.

"Fran?" she said. "Fran, it's me, Cassie."

By the time they went to bed, Fran Jordan had heard most of the story, but Cassie spoke only of a "miscarriage." She had given James her word that she would not tell anyone about the gonorrhea, but more than that she found that she could not reveal her shame even to her old friend.

Fran sat on the side of the bed while Cassie brushed her hair and sneaked an occasional look at her. Living in Dallas had already changed

Fran. Her green eyes were as sharp as ever, but there was a thinner, harder look to her face and when she lit another cigarette her long fingers trembled slightly.

Cassie tied the sash of her seersucker bathrobe. "I love your house, Fran. You've done a beautiful job of decorating it."

"Designing," Fran said absently. "That's the term we're using now. Interior design. Cassie, what are going to do now? How are you going to support yourself?"

Cassie sat down on the dressing-table bench. "Get a job, I guess. I was a good secretary."

Fran snorted. "You'll settle for that? Living in some furnished room, squeezing the pennies? Get up and take off that ugly robe. I want to see how you look now."

Cassie did as she was told, but while Fran looked her over, she did the same to Fran. She had been pretty but now she was striking. Her red hair was tamed and her makeup was subtle and becoming. Fran had the figure for the new postwar flamboyance and the poise to make a mediocre outfit the height of fashion.

Fran shuddered. "My God, the nightgown is worse than the robe! Don't you know that rayon is just plain tacky? Now stand over there by the mirror, and turn around slowly."

As Cassie turned, she caught glimpses of herself in the full-length mirror.

"Big, raw-boned, that healthy country look, ugh. Lift up your hair. Good hair. Yes, really good hair, but we'll have to get it cut properly. Upswept at the sides, I think, to emphasize those high cheekbones. You're thin, Cassie. You must have lost weight during your pregnancy."

"I did."

"Keep turning! Pull up your gown. Higher, for God's sake! I want to see your legs. Oh yes, long legs. Elegant legs. Long narrow feet. Good body, too. You sure don't need a girdle! Okay, that's enough. I can tell you one thing, Cassie Steele: you were made to wear clothes. Adrian! That's it! You have the right body, long lines, broad shoulders. Now stand up straight. No, not like a Marine sergeant. Straight but relaxed. There, that's it."

Cassie stared at herself in the mirror and the Oklahoma girl in the tacky rayon nightgown disappeared. She saw a tall, willowy young woman dressed in the latest styles, broad shoulders, long legs in sleek stockings, long feet in elegant expensive shoes. "Oh," she said softly. "Oh!"

"A model," Fran said. "We could get you a job modeling at Titche's or Neiman's."

"No!" Cassie said, horrified at the thought of parading her body before men, women, anyone who cared to look.

Fran shrugged. "Okay, okay. Whatever you want. I won't fool around with what's inside your head—when it comes to people I stick to exterior design." She looked at Cassie speculatively. "But let me ask you one thing. Is there anything in this Okie morality of yours that would prohibit your making a good salary?"

Cassie whirled around. "Of course I want to make money! The settlement Mr. Steele gave me won't last forever."

Fran hugged her. "Then get some sleep, pal. Tomorrow we're going to dress you to fit the part of a woman who must have a very, very good salary. We'll hit the stores when they open, and we'll have miles to shop before we sleep."

During the next two days, Cassie learned more about clothes than she had ever known, and she learned about Dallas, too. On the first morning Fran took one look at her and grimaced in pain.

"That's what you intend to wear to downtown Dallas, Cassie?"

Cassie looked down at her freshly pressed pale blue linen dress, her straw handbag, and her navy-and-white spectator pumps. "What's wrong with it?"

Fran sighed. "Well, starting at the top and moving down, where's your hat? Never go downtown without a hat and gloves."

"But in Ballard, or even Tulsa—"

"Dallas is not Ballard, thank God, or even an oil town like Tulsa. Dallas is a city, a cosmopolitan city. What's more, it's a dressy city. You do not wear summer clothes in Dallas in September."

"But the heat!" Cassie protested. "I couldn't wear wool when it's this hot."

"You will if you live in Dallas, kid—that is, if you want to be somebody in Dallas. And remember, you must never, never wear white shoes before Memorial Day or after Labor Day."

"Fran, for God's sake! We aren't going to a party! We're only going shopping."

"Only going shopping? My dear, innocent child, we are going to Neiman-Marcus."

Fran took Cassie into the store through the Ervay Street entrance. "If we'd had a chauffeur drop us off, Mr. Stanley Marcus would have been notified and would meet us at the door."

Even without Mr. Stanley, Cassie was awed. The store seemed to have been built around the merchandise, with each department highlighted by the whole and within the department each item of clothing spotlighted for its own worth but, at the same time, included in the opulence that was Neiman-Marcus itself.

The clerks, Cassie thought, had been designed to fit the decor, manufactured from a single mold and shipped direct to Dallas. Their X-ray vision instantly read every label in her clothing and assessed its inferiority.

Fran took them in her stride. "This is what we've got to spend," she said, "and this is what we want." By the time Cassie was installed in a fitting room and stripped to her underwear, the entire store seemed to be involved in her rehabilitation. Clerks fell over each other as they rushed to her with dresses and suits and accessories.

"Honey," one small dark-haired clerk said, "you don't know what a treat it is to dress a good body. These oil wives come in, straight off the farm, and they think a designer suit is going to turn a sack of potatoes into Rita Hayworth!"

On the evening of the second day, Fran announced the end of shopping. Cassie had thought of the two days as an undisciplined orgy of spending, but when they unpacked all the boxes Fran showed her that the items went together like a jigsaw puzzle to make a conservative and elegant wardrobe.

"And this scarf will go with your suit, Cassie, or with the two-piece gray dress for the office. Now do you see what I mean about design? Your list is limited, though. God help us if you spill coffee on two things in the same week." She slumped into an armchair and lit a cigarette. "Listen, Cassie, there's something I have to tell you."

"Sure." Cassie tucked the blue scarf into the neckline of her gray dress. "How does this look?"

"Fine, just fine. Cassie, look, I love having you here, but you'll have to find a place of your own by the end of next week. My . . . my friend is coming back from a business trip."

"Oh, sure, Fran——" Cassie stopped. "You mean a man? He stays here with you?"

Fran looked at her cigarette. "Sometimes. He's . . . well, he's married."

"Oh." Cassie folded the scarf carefully. "I didn't mean to pry."

Fran laughed. "This is not the Dark Ages, you know, it's 1945! Isn't this what our boys fought for!"

Cassie pretended to study the question. "I could be wrong, but I don't remember that being listed in the Atlantic Charter."

Cassie was more worried than she acted. She had spent so much money on clothes. How would she have enough for even a room? What if she did not get a job right away? What would she do? Where would she go?

THE JOB had not been advertised yet, but Fran had heard about it from a client. Cassie Taylor Steele, new from the skin out, stood in front of the man's desk, applying to be personal secretary to a lawyer.

"It says here that you have had experience as a legal secretary, Mrs. Steele." He took off his silver-rimmed glasses and looked up at her. "Where did you work?"

"In Ballard, Oklahoma, Mr. Reilly. For Mr. James Steele."

"And you are Mrs. Steele. Is that a coincidence?"

"No, sir. He was——is my father-in-law, but that was later, after I had worked for him."

" 'Was——is.' Which is it?"

"We——my husband and I are separated."

"Temporarily?"

"Oh, no! I mean, no, sir. It is permanent."

The man seemed to relax, and Cassie relaxed a little, too, and allowed herself to take a good look at him.

Stephen Reilly, attorney-at-law, was about forty, a man with a solid, reliable look, from the set of his body in an expensive-looking dark gray suit, to his clean competent hands, and square jaw. He had a broad forehead and a short nose over a long upper lip and a wide, mobile mouth. His gray eyes were set well apart and one of them was slightly cocked.

He stood up and looked across the desk at her. With the high heels of her new brown kid I. Miller pumps, her eyes were level with his.

His eyes drifted down her body. Cassie blushed, but she could tell that he liked what he saw. "Since you have had no secretarial training beyond high school, I'll want a few skill tests."

"Yes, sir." Cassie had honed her rusty typing skill on Fran's portable, but she was worried about her shorthand.

"Here." He handed her a steno's notebook and a yellow pencil. "Take a letter, if you will."

Cassie sat down in the chair next to his desk. Exterior design, she thought. She crossed her legs, eased her skirt an inch above her knee and looked up. He glanced at her legs and then at her, and grinned.

"To Francis X. Tolman, etc., etc." As he talked he sat down at his desk. "Dear Frank, colon. In the matter of the Baker case, I would suggest that you take a long look at"—he shuffled through the papers on his desk and held one up so that Cassie could see it as he read— "at *Warner v. Nordan & Morris*, 158 s.w.2d 50 (Tex. Civ. App. 1942). It should be helpful in the area of admissible evidence. I don't know where you found Baker, and I must say I don't envy you this client. Paragraph. Hope this cite will help get you out of that corner. Usual closing, sincerely and all that." He looked down at Cassie. "Please read it back to me."

Cassie read it aloud.

"Good," he said. "Now I'll get our office manager to give you a typing test." He took up a paper, dismissing her.

"Mr. Reilly?"

He looked up at her. "Yes?"

Cassie hesitated. What if she made him angry? She would have no job, and within a week, no place to live. But she had to tell him. If she was to work for him, she would have to do a good job from the very first.

"Mr. Reilly, I'm afraid there's something wrong with that letter. A mistake."

"It sounded all right to me."

Her mouth was dry. "That case you mentioned? Mr. Reilly, that case refers to ownership of oil and gas reserves, not to admissible evidence."

"What?" He grabbed a paper from his desk. "What was the cite, *Warner v. Nordan & Morris?*"

"Yes, sir."

"Rob!" he yelled. "Get in here on the double!"

A dark-haired young man skidded through the doorway. "What's wrong, Steve?"

"You gave me the wrong goddamned cite, that's what's wrong!"

The younger man took the paper. "Oh, hell. I sure as hell did. This is for the natural-gas case."

Stephen Reilly's voice was soft but as cold as ice. "I'd have looked like a fool, wouldn't I?"

"It was just a mistake, Steve."

"God damn it, Rob, I don't pay you to make mistakes! Now get your ass back to the law library and this time you double-check, and triple-check if that's what it takes!"

The young man left the office and Reilly sat down and wiped his forehead with a white handkerchief. "Sorry about that, Mrs. Steele. Shouldn't get so angry with the kid."

Cassie smiled tentatively. "The typing test? I'll go out and find—"

"Oh, hell, no," he said. "I don't care if you type ten words a minute. You can think, and thinking is one hell of a lot more important than typing. You are now my personal secretary, Mrs. Steele. You've got yourself a job."

"A JOB WITH Steve Reilly?" Fran said. "Well, what do you know."

"No, Fran." Cassie raised her gin and tonic. "You tell me what you know."

Fran laughed. "Well, what I don't *know*, but what I *suspect* is that you've got yourself in the catbird seat, Cassie. Steve Reilly is a comer. He was a flier, I think, wounded early in the war and discharged. He blew into Dallas about 1942 and three years later he has a growing law practice, a gentleman's ranch down near Cedar Hill and memberships in the best clubs in Dallas."

Cassie was impressed. "He must be a hard worker, and a darn good lawyer."

"Oh, he is! Both of those." Fran snickered. "And a darn good marrier, too. He married Richard Carter's daughter."

Cassie was surprised to feel a little surge of disappointment. "Who is Richard Carter?"

"Oh, my dear little Okie friend, Richard Carter is the man they call 'Mr. Dallas,' and I hear they'll be calling him 'Mr. Texas' before too long. For your information, he is also a lawyer, and is very rich. Old money. Old, old money. And old, old power. He helped start the Dallas Citizens' Council before the war. He's the one they go to."

"Who are 'they'?"

"The doers. The ones who decide if Dallas needs a new hotel or a new stadium—or a new city council. But first they go to Richard Carter to find out what he thinks."

Cassie nodded. "Like James Steele in Ballard."

"No, not like James Steele. Mr. Carter, my dear, is a great big frog in a great big puddle."

"And Steve Reilly married his daughter," Cassie said thoughtfully.

"Yes."

"And his money. And his power."

"I said the man's a comer, Cassie. You're lucky to be hanging on his coattails."

Cassie smiled suddenly. "I am, Fran. I am. It could be an interesting ride."

Fran laughed and finished off her drink. "Why, Cassie, honey, I do believe you're catching on. I think you're catching on at last."

Chapter 26

CASSIE SPENT the first few days in Steve Reilly's law office finding her way around. For a growing practice there was not much of a staff. Rob Penland, the dark-haired young man who had given Mr. Reilly the wrong cite, was a graduate of Harvard Law, but this was his first job. In telling Fran about the office, Cassie could not quite define his function.

"Did you say Penland? Rob Penland?" Fran tapped her fingers on her lower lip. "Oh, sure, I've got it. He must be James Penland's second son. His mother was a Foster. Old Boston money, Cassie, old, old, old money. Reilly probably hired him for his connections, to get a tie-in with eastern money." She looked thoughtful. "Now, I wonder why. Reilly must have ambitions no one suspects. Politics?"

Cassie shook her head sadly. "Wheels within wheels. Fran, how does anyone keep it all straight?"

"Don't worry, you'll pick it up. Just remember to keep your mental scorecard up to date. Can't tell the players without a program, you know."

The office sent its general typing to a secretarial service on the second floor, so the only other employee was a pretty round-faced receptionist named Leta Johnson. Cassie was sure she was not over seventeen.

Rob Penland was Cassie's guide to the office. When he was not white-faced with embarrassment, he was a good-looking man. His black hair wanted to curl, although he kept it controlled to a wave, and his eyes were blue and mischievous. His mother might be a Foster from Boston, but Cassie suspected that black-Irish blood had crept into his family at some point in history.

"Leta's all right," he said. "She's not awfully bright, it's true, but she's conscientious about writing down phone numbers and she's something pleasant for clients to look at while they wait to see Steve."

"Where is she from?"

"Damned if I know. From her grammar, I'd guess West Dallas. She's a nice kid, too, but her heart's a marshmallow. She gets all weepy at the thought of puppies and baby chicks."

From the start Cassie was comfortable in the office. Steve Reilly was as demanding as James Steele had been, but he was quick to commend good work.

Unfortunately, he was also quick to notice it when, on her third morning in the office, Cassie came in twenty minutes late.

"I'm sorry, Mr. Reilly. I got lost."

"Between here and Highland Park?"

"No, sir. In South Dallas."

He waited.

"The landlord would only show the apartment this morning and I guess I took a wrong turn when I left, because I ended up behind the state fair grounds and——"

"I thought you were sharing a house with a friend."

"Only temporarily. I have to be out by the end of next week."

He looked at her for a minute and then pushed the papers on his desk to one side and took out a legal pad and a fountain pen. "How much money do you have, Mrs. Steele?"

Cassie started to tell him it was none of his business, but instead she found herself calculating. "About four thousand dollars."

"And you have a car."

"Yes, sir. A 1941 Oldsmobile convertible."

"I suppose you realize that used cars are at a premium now?"

"Yes, sir."

He jotted some figures on the yellow pad and leaned back in his swivel chair. "I would suggest that instead of renting an apartment, you buy a small house."

"But how could I afford to——"

"It is not a matter of what you can afford to do but of what you cannot afford not to do. Look, as soon as the automobile companies retool for civilian production, your car's value will fall drastically. At the same time, real estate values have already risen but are going to rise even more as more veterans come home. *Q.E.D.*, sell your car for top dollar and invest in real estate."

"But how would I get to work?"

He grinned at her. "You may not have noticed it, Mrs. Steele, but there are bus routes in Dallas, and streetcar lines. Now, take these letters and while you type them I'll make a few phone calls."

Later in the morning Reilly called Cassie into his office and handed her a piece of paper. "Meet this man at this address at noon and when you've finished looking at the house, take you car to this dealer for an appraisal. This once you may stretch your lunch hour for your personal business."

THE REAL ESTATE MAN was small and seedy and so was the house. The location was good, one block from Southern Methodist University and the streetcar line, but the condition was terrible. Grayed wood showed through flaking white paint and one of the posts on the small front porch listed to the left.

Inside, the house was filthy. Stacks of yellowed newspapers half blocked the doorway from the L-shaped living and dining room to the hall. There was some furniture: a couch with a protruding spring, a battered oak sideboard, a rocking chair with frayed caning in the seat and back. The oak dining table looked solid, but the finish was checked where hot dishes had been set.

There were two bedrooms, one large and the other so small that it held a bed, a desk and no more. Both rooms had iron bedsteads thick with yellowed paint and grayed by the dirt caught in every crevice of their fanciful designs. The bathroom was disastrous, with torn linoleum on the floor, a stained claw-foot bathtub and a basin and toilet that would have been appropriate in the rest room of a back-roads gas station.

And then there was the kitchen. Spilled food caked the curling linoleum on the counters and the door of an electric refrigerator with a mildew-spotted coil on top. There were baked-on spills on the old gas stove.

The kitchen door opened onto a porch large enough to hold a paint-dribbled table, two broken chairs and more stacks of newspapers. Through the rusty, torn screen, Cassie saw that the backyard stood knee-high in weeds. Even the leaves of the big maple tree in the center of the yard looked dirty, yellowed not by frost but by lack of watering.

"House needs some cleaning up," the real estate agent said.

"I never saw such a mess in my life! Who on earth could have lived like this?"

"Old man lived here. Real old man. A little . . ." He tapped the side of his head. "Died a couple of months ago—oh, don't worry, he didn't die here. They got him to the hospital." He gave Cassie a quick foxy grin. "Place's got a lot of potential."

Cassie turned away, dejected, and walked back through the house. "It isn't what I'd hoped to—"

"Furniture goes with it," the man said quickly. "Part of an estate, see, and the lawyer figures it ain't worth auctioning off."

Cassie looked at the marred dining table. "I can believe that."

"Here, take this extra key, case you want to bring a friend over to look at it."

"But I won't . . . well, all right."

Cassie's mood improved when she heard how much she could get for the Oldsmobile. She managed to be back at the office by one o'clock. Steve Reilly called her in immediately.

"You saw the house?"

Cassie looked down at the carpet. "Yes. I saw it."

To her surprise, he laughed. "So did I, while you were at the car dealer. It's a dandy investment, that close to the university, and the house is structurally sound. Come on, girl, where's your imagination? Think what some elbow grease and a few buckets of paint would do to it."

She looked up at him, surprised, because suddenly her imagination did take over and she could indeed see the house clean, sparkling with white paint. The furniture was still shabby, but it was usable. And on nice mornings she could have breakfast on the screened porch and look out at the maple tree. Her maple tree. "Yes! Mr. Reilly, if I can afford it, I want to buy it." She hesitated. "The agent didn't tell me what the house would cost. Well, I guess I didn't ask him."

He smiled at her, and she noticed that the smile did not reach his left eye, the slightly cocked one. "Don't worry, my dear, I've put the figures together including repairs and paint, and you can afford it comfortably if you'll sell your car." He glanced at the calendar. "We should be able to close on it and have you move in by the middle of next week."

"But won't I need a bank loan? They won't like it that I've only been working for you for a few days."

He waved away her fears. "It's all arranged, subject to your approval, of course. I do have a little pull in this town, you know."

And what you don't have, she thought in sudden bitterness, your father-in-law does. She felt guilty instantly. Steve Reilly was doing her a favor, a huge favor, and there was no way on God's green earth that she would ever be able to repay it.

The automobile dealer gave her a ride to Fran's house. As soon as she heard the news, Fran bundled Cassie into her car and drove east on Mockingbird Lane.

The place looked no better in the late afternoon light. In fact, Cassie thought the inside looked even worse under the glare of the unshaded ceiling lights. She tried to be enthusiastic as she showed Fran through the house, but her enthusiasm dried up in Fran's silence. Fran poked into closets and cupboards and tugged up the corner of the bathroom linoleum, without making a single comment. She was still silent in the car, driving back to Highland Park.

"You think it's a mistake, don't you?" Cassie said. "You think I was wrong to buy it."

"Hush, I'm thinking."

As directed, Cassie stayed in the living room while Fran puttered around the kitchen. She was as nervous as a cat. Steve Reilly thought the house was a good investment. Great! But he didn't have to live in it. Fran was the expert on houses and she was going to tell Cassie how dumb she had been to buy it. Cassie wanted to cry. All of her good intentions to run her own life, to learn and to make informed decisions, all of them had disappeared the first time a man said, "Do this."

Fran handed Cassie a long-stemmed glass.

"Champagne? What's this for, Fran?"

Fran raised her glass. "To toast the coming of age of Cassie Taylor Steele. And to toast you for getting the best real estate deal in Dallas."

"Wait, now. It was Mr. Reilly who told me to——"

"You made the decision, didn't you?"

"Well, yes, I suppose I——"

"Drink up, then! Besides, I want you all tipsy and agreeable when I try to sell you on my idea."

Cassie grinned. "Listen, one glass of champagne won't make me tipsy, and I'm always agreeable. I go along with whatever anyone tells me to do."

Fran seemed to be measuring her. "You used to, back in Ballard, but now, I'm not so sure."

Fran's proposal was more advantageous for her, Cassie thought, than for Fran. Fran wanted to design the interior in exchange for the right to show it to prospective clients.

"But it's just a little old house," Cassie protested. "People who buy little houses don't hire interior decorators."

"Designers, not decorators! They will, Cassie. The days of good cheap help are over and without servants people are going to want smaller houses. And how about all those veterans in college? They were blue-collar guys, and now they're going to be professional men and their blue-collar wives don't know the first thing about white-collar houses. They'll want help, and to have a place I can take them, a small house of the sort they can afford, would be a big selling point for me. One more thing, too. I want before-and-after pictures. Using the veterans angle, I think I can sell a spread to one of the home magazines."

"Hey, Fran, I think it's time for *me* to toast *you*!" They poured more champagne and Cassie settled back on the sofa. "Will you help me with the cleaning and painting, too?"

Fran threw up her hands in mock dismay. 'What, soil these dainty paws? Never! I advise, dear child, I consult. I do not do windows."

But she did, of course.

Early that Saturday morning Cassie and Fran went to the house equipped with buckets and rags and cleansers and a teen-age boy who was the son of a friend of Fran's.   Later in the morning a furniture refinisher brought his truck to pick up the pieces worth saving and put the others in the alley for trash.   By Sunday night they were exhausted.   Cassie paid off their helper, he went off to catch the last streetcar, and she and Fran stood in the center of the living room.

"Well, it's clean," Fran said.

"But empty," Cassie said.   "Even when your man brings back the furniture, it won't be enough."

"Don't worry, I have sources."

"Fran, I can't afford to buy new furniture, not even cheap things."

"Cheap!"   Fran glared at her.   "Never, never buy cheap furniture. Much better to buy good used furniture than cheap new stuff."

"Even so, I—"

"Wait."   Fran grabbed Cassie's arm to silence her.   She moved her head this way and that as if to hear a soft voice.   "French," she whispered, and then she cried,   "Of course!   Not French provincial, but French rural!"

"Fran, what on earth—"

"Never you mind.   This is my department.   You just do what I tell you to, hear?"

As IT HAPPENED, Fran's friend did not return to Dallas when he was expected.

"He had his wife meet him in New York, the bastard.   They're going to view the autumn foliage in goddamn New England.   For two goddamn weeks."

"I'm sorry, Fran."

"Oh, well, it means you can stay on here till we get your house ready."

"We'll never do it in two weeks."

"The hell we won't."

CASSIE SUSPECTED that Fran was taking out her anger and frustration on people she could see.   She browbeat the seamstress, the refinisher, the house painter, and the yardman, but most of all she browbeat Cassie into working on the house every night.

When the painting was finished, Fran made Cassie give her the house key. "I don't want you going in there again until I say you can."

The next Sunday morning Fran shook her awake. "Pack your stuff in my car. You're going home."

FRAN THREW OPEN the door. The living room was full of sunlight enhanced by crisp white muslin curtains. The armchair looked fresh and snug in a dark blue slipcover with a tiny floral print, and along one wall was a white wicker settee with cushions and covered in the same print. The rocking chair had been stripped and recaned and was the same shade of oak as the bookshelf at the end of the room. The old dining room table and the oak sideboard were the color of brown honey.

The iron beds, stripped and freshly painted, gleamed like white lace over puffy blue-and-while calico spreads. The dresser in the larger bedroom was polished and clean, and in the smaller bedroom, the oak desk was refinished and a comfortable-looking swivel chair was pulled up to it.

Cassie herself had scrubbed down and painted the bathroom and kitchen, but Fran had seen to curtains of the same calico as the bedspreads, and had ordered new floor coverings laid, navy-and-white asphalt tile in a checkerboard pattern.

The back porch had new screens and the table and chairs had been repaired and painted Delft blue. Even the big maple tree looked new, its leaves refreshed by deep-root watering, and instead of weeds, the yard was green with new sprouts of Bermuda grass.

"Fran, oh, Fran!" Cassie whispered. "How can I ever thank you?"

Fran hugged her. "By keeping it clean so I can show it, but also by adding some personal touches to give it life. Something to show that this house is yours."

"Oh, sure. I can—" Cassie stopped. She had never lived in a house of her own. Personal touches? She remembered the calendar in her father's house: the half-naked girl pointing her knee at a tractor tire.   And there was her room at the boarding house in Ballard: the stained ceiling, the faded pink chenille bedspread.   James and Amelia Steele's house: silver-framed photographs, Oriental rugs.   She shook her head slowly.   She had been a sojourner, no more.

But now she owned a house, her very own house.   She could be a person.   "Yes," she said, "personal touches."

Chapter 27

THE FALL RAINS CAME, but Cassie did not mind sloshing home from the streetcar when it was to her own house. She would turn on the floor furnace to take the chill out of the house, cook her own supper in her own kitchen and settle down in her own armchair to listen to the radio and read. She had found a used book-store and her oak shelves were filling. A personal touch.

She found herself selecting books as she had when she worked for James Steele, reading about subjects which had come up during office hours. Steve Reilly specialized in oil and gas law, which she found fascinating. An entire system of law had built up around the oil industry and the system was expanding exponentially.

In the office she listened carefully to Steve Reilly's conversations with his clients and if she did not understand she asked him, later, to explain. He obviously was pleased both with her interest and with her quick grasp of the essentials of a matter.

At least once a week Cassie stayed downtown to catch an early movie. At a foreign-film theater on Main Street she saw Olivier's *Henry V*, and that very week she began to intersperse Shakespeare's plays with her books on oil and gas law.

Some movies, however, made her restless: the love stories. Her house was as pleasant as before, but something was missing, some personal touch.

To Cassie's surprise, Rob Penland, the young associate in the office, asked her to go out with him—in fact, to go to the Christmas dance at the Dallas Country Club.

"Rob." Cassie was embarrassed. "Rob, do you know I'm married?"

He blushed. "Well, yes. But Steve said it was a permanent separation. I thought he meant a divorce action was pending. Listen, that doesn't matter. I just want to take you to a party, that's all."

For once in her life Cassie felt free and young, like any girl excited about going to a big party. She laughed with pleasure. "Rob, I would love to go to the dance with you!"

Cassie borrowed a dress from Fran, a gorgeous dress, dark green crepe with a wide strap over one shoulder and no strap at all over the other. Fran also supplied a stylish mink-dyed squirrel cape.

"And where did you get this cape, Miss Frances Jordan," Cassie said sternly.

"I ain't tellin', Mrs. Cassandra Steele, and you ain't askin' again, not if you want to wear it."

Rob had his father's new Cadillac sedan but he appeared to be as impressed with her house as she was with his car. "Hey, Cassie, it looks like something that came out of *Better Homes and Gardens*!"

"If my friend has her way, it will go *into Better Homes*."

The Dallas Country Club impressed Cassie more than Rob's car. The room was spacious, with big windows overlooking floodlit greens. Inside, the lighting was subdued and romantic, but right enough to illuminate the members' dinner jackets and their wives' expensive gowns, and to glitter on hundreds of diamonds. A five-piece band played just loudly enough to absorb into the music the clink of glasses and the sounds of pleasant laughter.

Rob led Cassie to the dance floor. They danced slowly around the room, pausing now and again while Rob greeted a friend, and then moving on as the music played and the people laughed and talked.

It was after two when Rob kissed Cassie good-night. One kiss. One undemanding kiss and he got into his father's car and drove away. The Cadillac's brake lights blinked red as he slowed at the corner and then drove on.

Cassie closed the door and leaned against it, letting her mind swim in a warm romantic haze.

Rob liked her, she knew, and he liked being seen with her. He liked the open envy in his friends' eyes. He liked their wanting for themselves Rob's beautiful woman.

She let the cape slip from her shoulders and trailed it in one hand as she went to her bedroom. What if Rob came to love her, she thought dreamily. She hung the cape on its padded satin hanger and took off the green dress to hang it up, too. She unhooked her garter belt and sat on the side of her bed to roll down her stockings.

If he loved her, if he wanted to marry her, if she could renegotiate with James and divorce Jimmy. Too many "ifs," she thought, but Rob Penland's wife would be a part of it, of Dallas and the Dallas Country Club and that old, old Boston money, with all the privilege it entailed.

She stretched and saw herself in the full-length mirror on the closet door. Tall and thin, a model's body, Fran had said. Blond hair pulled back into a sleek chignon, blue eyes with heavy dark lashes. High cheekbones, good features. Her lips moved, and the word they shaped surprised her. She said it again, aloud. "No."

The romantic haze dissolved in a cold shower of reality. "I won't do it!" she said to her reflection. "I won't be beholden to any man, not ever again!"

When she had on her flannel nightgown, however, when she was propped against her pillows in the soft light of the bedside lamp, she was less certain. If she did not want a man, what did she want? Her life had to have a center, a focus, but what? For an hour she lay there, thinking about her future, choosing a course of action, rejecting it, choosing another. Suddenly she sat straight up in bed. "Of course!" she cried. "Of course!"

The next morning, Sunday morning, Cassie pulled on jeans and a sweater and settled herself at the desk in the small bedroom. It was late afternoon when she finished checking and rechecking for flaws in her reasoning.

During the next few weeks, Cassie spent every spare minute doing research. Unfortunately, the more information she gathered, the less feasible her plan became.

In January of 1946, universities and graduate schools were discovering that for some years the GI Bill was going to supply them with mature, hardworking, prepaid students. With all of those deserving young men, what use had they for a young woman with little money and an ambiguous marital status, a girl of twenty-one who had never even received a high school diploma? One dean virtually laughed in her face.

"Feel free to fill out an application, Miss . . . ah . . . Mrs. Steele, but . . ."

The "but" told it all.

That night Cassie lay awake, running her fingers along the lacy iron of her bed as if she were tracing a maze.

She did not want to be beholden to any man, but she had to have help. There was no question. She had to get some help.

THE NEXT MORNING Cassie Taylor Steele presented herself in Steve Reilly's office. She knew that she had to say it right away, before her courage failed her.

"Mr. Reilly," she said, and repeated it, trying to filter the shakiness from her voice. "Mr. Reilly."

He sat back and took off his glasses. "Yes, Mrs. Steele? What is it?"

"Mr. Reilly, I have worked for you for only four months but I think you've had time to evaluate my work and to—"

"I have indeed, Mrs. Steele, and I am very much impressed with it. If you are asking for a raise in salary, I think—"

Cassie interrupted him to complete her sentence. "—To get some impression of my character."

He looked puzzled. "Well, yes. I have."

"That's good, because I want to ask your help in a project I have planned." Cassie took a deep breath. "Mr. Reilly, I want to study law. I want to become a lawyer."

Steve Reilly leaned back in his chair. "Well, that's a commendable ambition, but it isn't that easy, is it?" He counted on his fingers the objections Cassie had heard everywhere, even from herself. No college degree, not even a high school diploma. Her need to have a full-time job. Law schools jammed with returning veterans.

"I know," she said. "I just hoped you might . . . well . . . be able to make some suggestions."

He rubbed his square jaw. "Let me think about it. Now, get your book and take a letter to Sid Richardson."

Cassie thought he had forgotten all about their conversation, but three days later he called her into his office and handed her a set of car keys.

"Here, take my car. I want you to go home during your lunch hour and change clothes. Wear that suit you had on the first day you came in here."

"Yes, sir. But why——"

"We have an appointment at two. I want you to meet my father-in-law, Dick Carter, and tell him about your plan."

Richard Carter, Cassie thought. Richard Carter! "Mr. Dallas" himself. She looked down at her nicely cut wool dress. "But isn't this good enough, Mr. Steele?"

He shook his head. "It's fine for the office, but it's not what a woman attorney would wear. Always present yourself as what you intend to become."

Richard Carter was a tall, lanky man with a long, narrow face. His hair was straight and white and his eyes were the pale blue of ice under water. He looked at Cassie as if he were judging the potential of a thoroughbred filly.

"Steve tells me you want to read law, Mrs. Steele, but that you have neither a college nor a high school diploma."

Cassie tried to sound confident. "I can send for my high school diploma, sir. I completed all of the work for it."

"Most beginning law students have undergraduate degrees in history or English, you know. Attorneys are educated men."

"Or women," she said softly.

The blue eyes glittered. "Very few of them are women. What leads you to believe that you could succeed in a man's field?"

Cassie glanced at Steve Reilly, but his face was blank, neither encouraging nor discouraging. "Mr. Carter, I am hardworking and intelligent."

He nodded. "Steve here has vouched for that."

"And I am fairly well read. When I was . . . in Ballard, I had a lot of time to read."

"And what did you read? Novels?"

"Yes, sir. *The Grapes of Wrath*, Dickens, *Middlemarch*. I have read most of Shakespeare's plays, John Donne and quite a lot of history. I have also read about the law."

He took up a paper covered with notes in clear small handwriting. "Your name is Cassandra, I see. A name from mythology?"

"Greek mythology, sir. She was the daughter of Priam, king of Troy, and although her prophecies came true, they were never believed."

"And for yourself you prophesy . . ."

"That I will become an attorney, Mr. Carter," she said firmly. "A successful attorney. If I can get into law school."

He looked at the paper again and then back at her, with more interest. "Is this correct, that you were a sharecropper's daughter in Eastern Oklahoma?"

"Yes, sir."

He looked at her Adrian suit, and Cassie mentally blessed Steve Reilly for insisting that she change clothes. "All I need, sir," she said, "is some help in getting my foot in the door."

"Yes," he said slowly. "I can see that." When he spoke again, his voice was brisk and businesslike. "In Texas an attorney is not required to have a law degree or even an undergraduate one. He—or she—must pass the bar examination and then, under the sponsorship of two reputable members, can be admitted to the bar and licensed to practice. What field interests you?"

Her pulse was beating wildly, but Cassie kept her voice cool and level. "Oil and gas law, sir."

"No," he said, "that won't do. Dallas might accept female attorneys, but it is not ready for female wheeler-dealers. Concentrate on domestic relations."

"Divorce law?" Cassie said. "But I—" She stopped abruptly because Steve Reilly had raised one finger from the arm of his chair in a tiny gesture of warning. "Yes, sir, I will."

"Good. Steve here will oversee your education and I will arrange for you to audit certain law-school courses, particularly during your first year of study. From the start, you must learn to think in an organized way. Twice a year I will interview you and assay your progress."

"Mr. Carter, I don't know how to thank you!"

He smiled at her. "Thank me by passing it on, my dear. Possession, whether of material goods or knowledge, entails a responsibility to encourage ambitious young people."

Cassie smiled at him, too, but her eyes blurred. *"Noblesse oblige,"* she said.

"I suppose so."

As they drove back to the office, Cassie said hesitantly, "Mr. Reilly?"

"Yes?"

"This will be a lot of work for you, I'm afraid. A nuisance."

"Probably." He turned a corner and flashed her a quick grin. "I can take it, though. The question is, Cassie Steele, can you? I intend to work your tail off."

Cassie gripped her handbag until her knuckles were white. "I can take it, Mr. Reilly. I *will* take it!"

DURING THE NEXT four years there were times when Cassie remembered that boast and wanted to cry. She almost forgot what it was to have a full night's sleep. Fran Jordan dropped by frequently, bringing a coffee cake or a bottle of wine or an exceptionally juicy bit of gossip.

"How long do you intend to live this monastic existence, Cassie?"

"Until I'm a lawyer, that's how long."

"I'm sure it's ruining your poor hormones."

"Then to hell with my hormones!"

Once in a while Cassie went to an after-work movie, but no matter what Lauren Bacall was doing on screen, Cassie saw only the stacks of books in her guest room–*cum*–study and worried because she was not at home working. Her semiannual evaluations by Richard Carter seemed to please him, but they left her aware of how little she knew about the law. Torts, contracts, leasehold: there was so much to learn, so much to know, that she despaired of retaining enough of it to pass the bar exam.

When the weather was good, Cassie worked in her garden. Even then she thought about the law, but it was a time when she could let her mind wander through her knowledge to make a whole of the bits and pieces she had acquired.

Toward the end of 1949, there was a subtle shift in responsibilities in Steve Reilly's office. He hired another secretary, Maxine Wells, a highly competent middle-aged war widow. Maxine took care of much of his correspondence and more and more often he called on Cassie to draft simple briefs or to research cases. Studying was less of a grind when she could apply the theory to real cases.

In April of 1950, shortly before Cassie's twenty-fifth birthday, Reilly reluctantly agreed to represent an important client in a divorce action. He turned the case over to Cassie, checking her work from time to time. When the case was settled he called her into his office and handed her a check.

"This is your share of the fee in the divorce case."

She looked at the amount of the check and caught her breath. "But it's—"

"I told the old boy I didn't want to handle a divorce case." Reilly grinned wolfishly. "And I told him that if he had to have my firm, he would pay through the nose. Take it, Mrs. Steele, but I'm going to tell you how to spend it."

"I don't understand."

"Dick Carter wants you to take the bar exam in July."

"I'm not ready!" Cassie felt cold sweat on her forehead. "I can't possibly be ready!"

"You will be by July. You've never taken a vacation, you know, so I'm giving you six weeks of accumulated vacation time, and I want you to use this check to pay for a tutor. Then, by God, then you'll be ready for them!"

Chapter 28

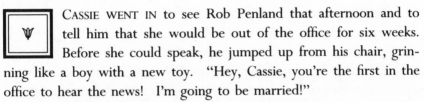 Cassie went in to see Rob Penland that afternoon and to tell him that she would be out of the office for six weeks. Before she could speak, he jumped up from his chair, grinning like a boy with a new toy. "Hey, Cassie, you're the first in the office to hear the news! I'm going to be married!"

"Congratulations, Rob! Do I know her?"

"No, but you're going to love her! She has such a great figure and she has beautiful eyes, and—"

"Does she have a name, too?"

"Oh, sure. She's Linda Lou Bond, Jim Bond's daughter."

Jim Bond, Cassie thought. Old money, too, but old Texas money.

"You'll be getting an invitation, Cassie. I hope you'll come to my wedding!"

"I wouldn't miss it for the world, Rob. Not for the world!"

Instead of being warm and welcoming that night, Cassie's house felt empty. Rob Penland was going to be married. If she had made a different decision the night they danced, if she had chosen a different route into the future, Rob could be marrying Cassie Steele instead of Linda Lou Bond. And Cassie would never have to worry about money or studying for bar exams. She would produce the right number of children and settle into the life of a proper young Dallas matron: taking tennis lessons, doing volunteer work, having her hair done, shopping at Neiman-Marcus. She might even, like Amelia Steele, have a sherry bottle hidden among the hatboxes on her closet shelf.

She wandered back to her study and switched on the desk lamp. Books were stacked on the bed, the floor, everywhere, with piles of scribbled notes that needed to be organized before she started working with the tutor.

She kicked off her shoes and slid onto her desk chair. Just a few minutes, she thought, and then she would fix some supper. She began to read her notes on contracts, underlining a phrase here and there. In ten minutes she had forgotten all about Rob Penland and his Linda Lou.

THE NEXT MORNING Cassie went directly to Steve Reilly's office. She had to know. "Mr. Reilly, when I—if I pass the bar, I will need to find a job."

He was obviously startled. "You'll be an associate here in the firm."

"You mean you'll hire me right away?"

"Of course." He sat down at his desk and grinned. "You don't think I'd train you and let some other office benefit from it, do you? We won't discuss compensation until you pass the bar and begin practice, but I'm sure you will find it more than adequate."

"Yes, sir."

"And you will drop the 'Mr. Reilly, sir' as of now, unless we are in a trial together. In court I want all the deference I can get. It's good for my ego. I am Steve, you are Cassie. Can you handle that?"

Cassie laughed. "Yes, sir. I mean, Yes, Steve."

"Good, Cassie. I'm planning to expand our offices into the suite next door. Rob will have the corner office and you'll have the one next to it, because it has a separate entrance."

"I don't understand."

"In domestic relations law, you will have some clients in highly emotional states. I don't want your women weeping all over my oilmen."

"You think all of my clients will be women?" Cassie said.

"Of course. Women want a woman lawyer to gouge fat settlements out of their errant husbands."

Cassie leaned back in her chair. "Well, we'll see, won't we? You might be surprised."

Steve put on his glasses and looked at her directly. "Will we, indeed? You'll find it hard to teach an old dog new tricks."

IN THE LAST WEEK of June a heat wave hit Dallas. Cassie's house was stifling. She moved her work to the table on the back porch, but even with the electric fan going, she was so sweaty that her notes stuck to her fingers.

In the last week of June, also, North Korean troops crossed the Thirty-eighth Parallel and struck into South Korean territory. At Rob Penland's wedding that weekend, however, war in Korea played second fiddle to the peaceable alliance of two wealthy Dallas families.

The wedding took place in the Texas-Gothic Highland Park Presbyterian Church. It was jammed with wedding guests but the nave was even more crowded, with the minister and his aide, the organist, two soloists, eight bridesmaids, eight groomsmen and the bride and groom. Cassie had seen big weddings in the movies, but she suspected that in real life the behind-the-scenes logistics must have been comparable to those of the invasion of Normandy.

Only one of the gears in the machine showed: a woman who darted around the bridesmaids, adjusting their dresses before they began the trek to the altar, and who made sure that the bride's satin train was properly draped. Fran told Cassie later that the woman was the Neiman-Marcus representative and that she carried a first-aid kit of needles and thread, safety pins and smelling salts: equipment to handle any emergency that might arise at a society wedding.

The reception was held a few blocks away, at the Dallas Country Club. With the green-and-white-striped marquees shading the members of the wedding, the women's long dresses and the men's morning coats, the party had the air of a royal occasion, which, of course, it was. Blood that blue and money that green was royalty in Dallas.

In the reception line Rob introduced Cassie to his bride. Cassie's mental picture was close to the mark, but she had not expected small brown eyes that sharpened to obsidian when the bride found out who Cassie was.

Her voice was soft, but there was a touch of steel in it. "Cassie, honey! Robby's told me about you, and being in that little bitty office—I'm just so relieved to meet you and see what a really nice person you are. It will be so much fun to drop in at the office and see for myself what goes on down there!"

Linda Lou staked out her claim so emphatically that Cassie was glad to escape from the reception line and fade into the crowd. She circulated, watching for incipient divorces as Fran had told her to do, but she left the party with a foreboding that the most likely marriage to break up was the newest, that of Linda Lou and Rob Penland.

CASSIE HANDED in her papers at the end of the bar exam and fled. She had spent two days in that room, two days of marshaling knowledge, outlining and writing. She felt squeezed out, like a sponge dried until it is no more than a hard skeletal creature.

Leta greeted her at the office. "Cassie, was it real tough?"

Maxine Wells stopped typing. "Cassie, you look exhausted!"

Rob Penland burst out of his office. "How was it, Cassie? Did you get a torts question, the way we figured? God, I remember when I took the bar. It almost killed me!"

"What's going on out here?" Steve Reilly stood in the doorway to his office. His necktie was loosened and his shirt sleeves were rolled up. "Ah, Cassie, so it's all over. Rough?"

Cassie was dazed. "Rough? Oh, yes. Rough."

He looked at her more closely. "Okay folks, show's over. You can all get back to work."

Rob protested. "But Cassie is—"

"I'll take care of Cassie. The woman needs a drink. Let me get my coat, Cassie."

He took her to the Dallas Athletic Club, settled her into a comfortable chair and asked Newt Holleman, the black headwaiter, to bring an emergency ration of bourbon and water.

"Okay," Steve said. "Talk about it or not. It's up to you."

Cassie took a sip of her drink and smiled at him gratefully. "I'd rather you did the talking, Steve. I think I've used up all my words."

He laughed. "I know the feeling. Look, don't worry about the results, or at least don't worry too much. You won't get the results for three months. The thing to do is to assume that you passed and get on with your life. Now, I didn't want to tell you till now, but

Dick Carter has a client for you. An acquaintance of his wife's wants to sue for divorce."

Cassie set her glass on the table. "What grounds?"

Steve laughed and settled back in his chair. "I thought that might get your attention. The grounds are adultery, and that is all that I will tell you right now. I want to take my beautiful new associate to dinner and I do not want to talk business, I just want to enjoy the company. Is that understood?"

"Yes, sir, Mr. Reilly." Cassie laughed, too. She was relieved to have the bar exam finished, no matter what the result, but there was more to it than that. It could have been the bourbon or the quiet, pleasant surroundings, or it could have been Steve Reilly's open admiration of her, but she felt more relaxed than she had been for months. She agreed with Steve. She just wanted to enjoy the company.

IN AUGUST Cassie was surprised by a phone call from Ted Abernathy, a Harvard Law classmate of Rob's she had met at the office.

"Why, yes," she said, she would enjoy going dancing with Ted. "To the Plantation? Tex Beneke and the Glenn Miller Band? I would love it!"

Ted had emigrated to Dallas from Connecticut. He was tall and blond and clean-cut, and once Cassie had made it clear that being permanently separated did not equate with being an easy lay, he was a delightful escort. In fact, they laughingly agreed that they were made for each other: he was trying to avoid entanglements until his law practice was built up, and she refused to be committed to a man.

"Actually, Cassie," he said. "It's a relief to be with you. Are you aware that you may be the only twenty-five-year-old woman in Dallas who isn't out to hook herself a husband?"

The results of the bar examination were announced in October: Steele, Cassandra Taylor, was on the list of those who had passed. Steve Reilly took her to dinner to celebrate the good news.

"It's just a matter of paperwork now, Cassie. Dick Carter and I will sponsor you and you'll be admitted to the bar and an attorney licensed to practice in the state of Texas." He raised his glass. "Here's to you, kid. You did it on your own."

Cassie shook her head, smiling. "No, Steve, I did it with a lot of help from my friends.   Most of all, from you."

"Hell, Cassie, don't thank me.   Just get to work and prove I was right!"

Ted Abernathy wanted to celebrate, too.   He invited her to the Texas-Oklahoma football game.   "It's absolutely crazy, a traditional rivalry between the University of Oklahoma and the University of Texas. It's the big wild weekend of the year, the Dallas equivalent of Mardi Gras.   You have to see it to believe it.   Oh, and forget that it's just a football game.   The ladies dress to the teeth!"

No matter that the temperature was ninety-two degrees at kickoff time.   The ladies were indeed dressed to the teeth.   Cassie wore a beige wool skirt, with a champagne-colored velvet jacket, which she soon took off, over a sleeveless silk blouse.   Most of the women were in wool suits, and many carried furs.   Cassie saw one middle-aged woman in a brown satin cocktail dress complete with peplum.

No one paid much attention to the game.   People clambered over spectators to greet friends and exchange flasks and Thermos bottles. Cassie thought that Texans and Oklahomans alike were more interested in the amount of bourbon they could consume than in what was happening on the thirty-yard line.   From the yelling at the end of the game, Cassie thought that the University of Texas had won, but she was never quite sure.

"Now, we have several choices," Ted announced as they left the Cotton Bowl.   "We can go downtown, where the crowd goes.   In fact, the Baker Hotel and the Adolphus have already put their lobby furniture in storage so that it won't be destroyed in the festivities. We'll have to park in a fringe area, though, because traffic comes to a stop when everyone walks down the middle of the street."

"There's a parade?"

"A parade at first, yes, but after that everyone stays in the street because drunks drop paper bags of water from upstairs windows.   Later in the evening, they toss out pillows and phones and furniture and if it gets wild enough, each other."

"My God, Ted!   Let's not go downtown!"

"Well, we could go to the country club, where the drunks are better-behaved but just as noisy.   My suggestion would be that we drop in on a few private parties. They'll be loud, but the crowds won't be as large."

"Or we could go to my house and dance to radio music," Cassie said.

"Not on your life!" He laughed. "We're observers of the social scene tonight, remember? This is one scene that cries out to be observed!"

The party Ted chose was at a rambling stone house in Preston Hollow. It was going full blast when they arrived. An impromptu conga line stumbled around the yard, and the noise from the open front door was like a physical attack. A radio was playing "The Tennessee Waltz" at full volume while a group of Texas supporters tried to drown out an opposing group with "The Eyes of Texas." The Okies had the advantage of louder voices and a better song: "O-K-L-A-H-O-M-A! Oklahoma, OKAY!"

Ted pushed his way to the bar and brought Cassie a drink, but then he was caught up in the conga line and disappeared. Cassie looked for a familiar face. A tall man standing by the window turned, laughing at the conga line, and there was a face so familiar that Cassie's knees almost gave way.

At the same instant the man saw her, and to Cassie it seemed that the other people disappeared like wraiths and she and the man were alone in the room, each seeing only the other.

"Cassie?" She saw his lips shape the word, and then he moved across the room, breaking the conga line, coming directly to her.

"Dix," she whispered. "Dixon Steele."

As he moved toward her, she could see that he had changed. He was more certain in his movements and had an air of confidence, of leadership, that she did not remember.

"Dix, what are you—"

"Cassie, why are you—"

They spoke together and then they laughed, together, and Cassie felt that her laughter had been bottled up inside her, waiting for this instant to come, a time when it could pour out like free-rushing spring water washing away the past.

"Cassie, I'd like to . . ." he said, but the shouts of the conga line drowned his voice. He grimaced and put his hands to his ears.

"Me, too!" Cassie said. He leaned close to her and shook his head, uncomprehending.

He took her hand and she thought that he must feel the electric shock that passed between them, but he only pulled her outside the front door, where it was quieter.

"Cassie, I'd like to talk to you but . . ." He waved his hand toward the door. "I'm staying here, at this house."

"How long will you be here?"

"A few guys chartered a plane, and I came along for the ride. We have to leave early in the morning."

In the morning! Cassie was dismayed. "Can you borrow a car? We can go to my house and talk and then—and then you can come back to the party."

"Well, sure, I can—what about your date? You came with someone, didn't you?"

"Yes. I'll find him and explain. That won't be any problem."

It was no problem. Ted was in pursuit of a University of Texas coed, a buxom girl with enormous blue eyes. Cassie told him that an old friend had turned up and thanked him for the day.

"Sure, Cassie, that's fine. I'll call you . . ." He looked at the girl measuringly. "I'll call you in a few days."

At Cassie's direction, Dix turned from Preston Road onto the Northwest Highway and drove east.

"How is your mother?" Cassie asked politely.

"She's well. Dad is, too, although I keep telling him he works too hard."

"Doesn't Jimmy help him?"

"Sure. When he's not involved in politics. He's running for Congress again, you know."

"I knew he lost the primary in 1946. What are his chances now?"

"It's hard to tell. He's got a tough opponent, a decorated Marine captain from Krebs."

"If he's from Krebs, he must be Italian."

"Right. But the war's over, Cassie, and he won his medals from the American government, not the Italian."

"I didn't mean—and what are you doing, Dix? Are you with the ACLU?"

"No, I hung out my own shingle in Oklahoma City."

"Is your father involved in your practice?"

"Good God, no! We're usually on opposite sides of a case. You should know that. Hey, that's enough about my family. What are you doing? I mean, besides dating handsome young Harvard lawyers?"

Cassie turned quickly, but she could see only his profile against the glow of city lights. "How did you know that?"

"I asked about him when I borrowed my host's car keys."

Was there a thread of irritation in his voice? Surely he could not be jealous, not Dix Steele, but he had taken the trouble to find out who brought her to the party.

For some reason she did not quite understand, Cassie was reluctant to tell Dix anything about her life in Dallas. She was saved by the necessity of giving him directions to her house, and once inside, she busied herself with making drinks while he settled in the armchair.

She went back to the living room, with a glass in each hand, and stopped in the doorway.

He was slumped in the armchair with his long legs stretched straight out in front, but that was not what had stopped her. It was the fact that he looked so right, so at home, as if he belonged in her house.

He stood up immediately, unfolding himself like a Tinker Toy construction. "Here, let me take those." His hand touched hers. He glanced at her and she knew that he had felt the trembling in her fingers. She took her own glass and sat down on the rocking chair while he went back to the armchair.

"This is a delightful house, Cassie. It looks like you."

"Personal touches," she said.

"What?"

"Never mind. Personal joke, too."

"You never did tell me what you're doing with your life."

"I'm in a law office," she said. "Stephen Reilly's office."

"The oil and gas man? He has quite a reputation in Oklahoma, as a hard-driving man, and a smart one. You must be good if you work for him. But then Dad said that you were the best secretary he had ever had."

Cassie set her untouched drink on the table. "I'm not a secretary, Dix. I'm a lawyer."

"Well, I'll be damned!" He jumped up from his chair. "That is really great! Get up, Cassie!"

"Why should I . . ." Cassie said, standing up slowly, but Dix grabbed her in a bear hug.

"Congratulations! I'll want to hear all about it, but first I had to hug you!" He laughed. "I never hugged a lawyer before. Or kissed one."

He kissed her, laughing, but suddenly the laughter was gone from his eyes and he was holding her close and kissing her again.

And Cassie kissed him. She felt light, alive with joy. "Dix," she whispered. "Oh, Dix!"

His arms around her were warm and strong, and within them she felt safe, protected from all the dangers of the world. He kissed her again and she knew that she loved him, only him, and that she would always love him. No matter that she had been married to his brother, that she and Dix had argued, had been apart. They were together now, and she could relax. She could draw on his strength. They were together, drawn to each other across the miles like iron filings brought each to the other by magnetism.

But Dixon Steele pushed her away, gently at first and then more firmly. "I can't do it, damn it. I just can't do it."

"Dix!" She stared up at him, alarmed. "What's wrong?"

"You know. You ought to know. Is it so easy to forget that you're still married to my brother?"

She laughed at the thought of the farcical marriage that had ended five years before.

White-faced, he backed away from her. "What the hell's so funny? Is it so amusing that I honor a moral, not to say a legal, commitment?"

"Oh, Dix. Dix! You're too intelligent for this. I haven't even seen Jimmy since 1945. Do you call that a marriage?"

"The courts consider it one, Cassie. You've never divorced him, you know."

"I can. Dix, I will! I'll divorce him if you and I can—"

"Why now, all of a sudden?" he asked suspiciously. "Why didn't you divorce him when you left Ballard? God knows, you had grounds."

Cassie bit her lip and backed away. "You know? How did you find out?"

"About his infidelity? Hell, Cassie, everyone in Ballard knew."

"Oh, yes. He was unfaithful to me."

"But you never filed suit. Why?"

She shook her head blindly. "I can't tell you."

He peered into her face. "There is something else, isn't there? There's something you aren't telling me."

"I can't! I promised!" It was more than her promise to James Steele, much more. Gonorrhea. How could she say that filthy word to him? The infection was long gone but the memory of it persisted, festering in her mind. She felt as sullied as a medieval leper tolling his warning bell through the streets and crying out, "Unclean, unclean." She turned away.

"Maybe I can guess. Maybe Jimmy had grounds for a countersuit. Maybe you weren't faithful to him, either."

"No! That's not so!"

He glanced around the room. "This house. You own it, don't you? And law school isn't cheap."

"I've been lucky, Dix, and I've worked hard at—"

"But somewhere along the line you got hold of some money. Where did you get it, Cassie?" He smiled unpleasantly. "Did my father give you money?"

"Well, he—I told you, Dix, I made a promise. For God's sake, don't you trust me?"

"Why should I?"

The irony of their squabbling made her want to laugh, or cry. She was begging for his trust when he was the one who had betrayed her. She was sure that he had told James Steele her secret, that Bo was alive and was in California. She did not want to ask him about it. She wanted to forget it, to shove it so far back in her mind that it would never reappear, because it was no longer important. It was only important that the two of them should be together.

"Why should you trust me, Dix? Because I trust you."

"Do you? Do you trust me, Cassie? I wonder."

"Dix . . ." For the first time she said it aloud. "Dix, I love you!"
She said the words, but they worked no magic. He stood there, rigid,
and his eyes were as cold as before. "I love you. Can't you accept
that and accept my word that I have done nothing wrong?"

"Love. Trust. Those are weighty words, Cassie."

"Don't you love me, too? Even a little?"

"Legally, you are my brother's wife. I must honor that."

"Honor." Cassie sank down on the settee. "Of course." She
laughed but stopped quickly, before the laughter became tears. "I
only wish that you could believe in me half as much as you believe in
your fine, sacred honor."

He looked away. "So do I, Cassie. So do I."

She jumped up from the settee. "Then you do love me! You do!"

He grabbed her shoulders and shook her. "God damn it, you drive
me crazy! Of course I love you. I've loved you since the day you
drove me to the lodge, the day we swam in the San Bois creek. But
I have to know! What did you do that was so terrible that my father
paid you to leave Ballard?"

Cassie stared at him, too appalled to answer.

He shook her again. "Can't you see that you must tell me?"

Cassie spoke very slowly, very distinctly. "Take your hands off of
me, Dixon Steele."

He let his hands drop to hang uselessly at his sides. "I'm sorry."

She raised her chin. "I think you should go now, Dix. I think
you should leave."

"Yes. I think so, too."

Cassie locked the door behind him and leaned her forehead against
it. Honor. Their honor was intact. Hooray. But honor didn't keep
your feet warm on a cold night, honor didn't surprise you with quick
laughter. Honor didn't lift your spirit with love.

Honor was an abstract. Honor had sharp edges that could cut deep
into something soft. Into something vulnerable, like the human heart.

Chapter 29

WHEN CASSIE trudged into the office on Wednesday after the Texas-Oklahoma game, her step was as heavy as her heart. It did not help to see Leta Johnson's puffy, tear-washed eyes.

"Leta, what's wrong?"

"Nothing, Cassie."

"Oh, come on! You have the prettiest smile in Dallas and today you look like a little girl who's lost her doll."

Leta tried to smile but instead began crying.

"Leta! Come in my office."

"But the phone—"

"It won't hurt Steve Reilly to answer his own phone for five minutes. Come on!"

In Cassie's office Leta mopped her eyes with a Kleenex. "My sister—oh, Cassie, he did it again! Her husband went on a binge and this time he beat her till she had to go to the hospital!"

Cassie sat down at her desk. "What do you mean, 'this time'? Has this happened before?"

"Oh, yes. Ever since they got married, four years now. He gets mean when he drinks, Vernon does, and he takes it out on Milly."

"And she just puts up with it?"

Leta clasped her hands on her soggy handkerchief. "What can she do, Cassie? She can't leave him, not with them three kids."

"Can you help her financially?"

Leta looked down. "Cassie, I'm the only one in the family that's got a job. Mr. Reilly pays good, but I got to stretch it over my mama and my two little stepsisters and mama's husband that's got a bad back and can't work."

"Leta, where do you live?"

"West Dallas."

Cassie had seen West Dallas only once, a night when Ted Abernathy made a wrong turn. At the time she thought that they had descended into hell instead of the Trinity River bottoms. Unpaved streets, little more than dirt roads, no streetlights. Tumbledown shacks with beaten dirt for front yards. Many of the houses had no electricity and the light of kerosene lamps silhouetted privies in the backyards.

It was West Dallas that had produced the Barrow family, whose boy Clyde had been shot down by Louisiana police along with his neighborhood girl friend Bonnie Parker.

By the time Ted found the highway again that night, Cassie was shivering, not with cold but with memories of just such a shack near San Bois, Oklahoma. But West Dallas lay within two miles of the Republic National Bank and the Baker Hotel and Neiman-Marcus.

She sighed. "Which hospital, Leta?"

"You mean you can help?"

"I can try. I'll want to get a report from the hospital and photographs of your sister's injuries. And I'll need to see her."

"They told her she could get out today if there wasn't no concussion."

"Concussion." Cassie closed her eyes. "Leta, call your sister and have her come here when she leaves the hospital."

When Leta left, Cassie turned her swivel chair to stare out at downtown Dallas. New buildings under construction, traffic lights, new cars everywhere. Everywhere except West Dallas. Slums never changed.

"Oh, God," she whispered. "Dear God in heaven. What kind of a world is this?"

She remembered lines from an Eliot poem.

> *In the room the women come and go*
> *Talking of Michelangelo.*

And drunken men had beaten their wives in the hovels of West Dallas and she had spent the last five years coming and going, talking of contracts and torts, while in the real world human beings were ripped and broken by other human beings.

MILLY JAYSON, Leta's sister, was waiting in the outer office, slumped on the chair as if fatigue and despair had soaked into her very bones. Her clothes were little more than rags, a faded print housedress with a wrinkled scarf at the throat and torn shoes with run-over heels. She might have been a pretty girl once, Cassie thought. There was a hint of Leta's fresh beauty under the bruise that covered the left side of her face from temple to jaw. But Leta, even with her face clouded with worry, was hopeful, and there was no hope left in her sister. There was only misery.

A man was waiting, too, a client of Steve Reilly's. He was tall and well dressed and he looked uncomfortable at being in the company of such a one as Milly Jayson.

"Mrs. Jayson?" Cassie said quickly. "Please come in my office."

The woman eased herself into the chair Cassie indicated, and Cassie sat down at her desk. To avoid looking at the bruise she took up her fountain pen. "It will take a few days to get the hospital reports and the photographs, but maybe you can describe your injuries to me now."

She whispered, "I ain't got no—"

"Mrs. Jayson, please speak up."

The woman shook her head and pulled down the crumpled scarf to show the deep bruises on her throat.

"Oh, my God!" Cassie said. Quickly she moved to the chair next to Milly Jayson. "Just whisper, Milly. I'll make notes."

"Doctor says my voice will clear up in a couple of days. The broke rib's goin' to take a mite longer, but he says I ain't got no concussion."

The husband, a thirty-two-year-old construction laborer, was from the piney woods of East Texas. He was a periodic drunk who went home after each binge and took out his anger and frustration on his wife.

"Not the kids, no'm. He knows he lays one hand on them kids and I'll kill him." She rubbed her throat gently. "Just me. He just beats up on me."

"Well, he's not going to do it again!" Cassie jumped up from her chair. "We'll turn this over to the police, Mrs. Jayson, and we'll put that man in jail where he belongs!"

"No!" Milly clutched her throat. "Don't you go and do a thing like that!"

"Why not? My God, he could kill you next time!"

"You can't take Vernon away, ma'am. I tried and I tried and I can't get no work. You want my little ones to starve? Don't you go puttin' Vernon in no jail, ma'am." She tried to smile. "Besides, he'll be okay for a while. He gets real sorry when he sees me like this. He'll bring little treats to the kids and he'll be real good to me."

Cassie sat down beside her. "Let me get something straight, Milly. Do you want to be with this man? Do you love him?"

Milly made an odd sound, as much a sob as a laugh. "What's love got to do with it? Mrs. Steele, I got another baby comin'. I ain't got much choice."

Much choice, Cassie thought when the woman had gone. No, Milly Jayson was wrong. She had no choice at all. Cassie could get an injunction against him, a peace bond, but if he broke it what good would it do? He would be in jail, and Milly and her children would have nothing.

Milly Jayson had no choice, but what woman did? Cassie thought of her mother and her grandmother, tied to a sharecropper's life by Howard Taylor's shiftlessness. And of herself, infected with venereal disease by her own husband and now infected with distrust by the man she loved. Were all women tethered by men, each to her own specific treadmill, forced to trudge the same pointless path again and again until they fell from exhaustion, or death?

The phone rang and Cassie sat up, pushing at her upswept hair. Her next client was early, and she was not ready. But it was Steve Reilly. "I want you in my office, Cassie. Now."

He put on his glasses and scowled up at her. "What was that . . . who was that person in the lobby?"

"Why, it—she's a client, Steve. Leta's sister. Her lousy husband beat her almost to—"

"I saw her," he said more gently, and then harshly, "and so did my client! Cassie, that man pays me a large retainer, and he made it very clear to me that he does not pay that kind of money to sit around an office with poor white trash. How much will this client of yours pay?"

"Why, nothing, Steve. She doesn't have any money."

"And just what do you call that kind of work?"

Cassie was getting angry. "I call it *pro bono*. I believe I made certain commitments when I joined the bar, and that was one of them." She scowled back at him. "Didn't you make the same commitment?"

He looked uncomfortable. "Of course."

"And where are all your *pro bono* clients, Steve? I've been here for five years now, and I don't remember seeing a one."

"Now, wait just a minute. I'm unpaid counsel for the Boys' Club and the Salvation Army and—"

"So you don't have to look at poor white trash, right? You don't have to let them sit on your chairs."

"Oh, God, what have I got myself into now?" He took off his glasses and wiped his face with a white handkerchief. "Okay, okay! But have her use your private entrance, will you? Please."

"I suppose I can do that."

Cassie stomped back to her own office. "Men!" she said. "Men!"

"I couldn't agree more."

Cassie stopped short. A woman was lounging in the armchair next to Cassie's desk, a well-preserved fifty, probably, beautifully coiffed, wearing a designer silk shantung dress and elegant sandals with three-inch heels. She glistened as if she had been hand-polished with soft, used thousand-dollar bills.

"Mrs. Perkins?" Cassie said.

"Allene, honey. Call me Allene."

"Well." Cassie sat down at her desk and did her best to look intelligent and experienced. This was, after all, the client Richard Carter had sent her. She opened her fountain pen and prepared to make notes. "Would you like to tell me about your problem?"

Allene Perkins took an emery board from her purse and gave one perfect fingernail a whisper of a touch. Satisfied, she put the emery board away and held up her fingers to count off points as she made them.

"The problem, Cassie—it is Cassie, isn't it? The problem is not mine but his. I want a divorce. I want the house, because that's real estate and you always want to get real estate. I want a large—a very large cash settlement, and I want plenty of alimony. *His* problem is that he has gone wild over this woman in New Orleans. I mean, *hog* wild. Just to start with, he's guilty of adultery and miscegenation and bastardy."

Cassie realized that she had dropped her pen and that her mouth was hanging open.

Allene smiled. "Did I go too fast for you, honey?"

"No, I—you obviously know all about divorce actions."

"I ought to. This will be my third."

Cassie recovered her pen and some of her aplomb. "Did you sign a prenuptial financial agreement, Mrs. Perkins?"

"You think I just got off the bus?" She laughed, low in her throat. "I signed one the first time, because I *was* just off the bus from Wichita Falls and I was in lo-o-ove. What a dope! Listen, I was lucky to get out of that one with one measly mink coat. You married, hon? Separated. Well, if you're ever fool enough to get married again, take it from me, don't sign nothing! They're hot for you then, before the wedding, and they ain't going to back out just because you won't sign."

Cassie was intrigued by the bits of West Texas that broke through Allene's Dallas façade. "Well, if we're going to take this to court, we'll need some evidence. Do you have any letters or any reliable testimony—"

"Honey, I've had detectives on Ace-High Perkins for one solid year."

"Did you say his name is—"

"Ace-High, yeah. That's how he got his first well, see. He wasn't anything but an oil-field roustabout till he got that ace-high straight and won himself a drilling rig." She laughed. "He don't know it but he's paid for the detectives himself, under 'exterminators.' Hon, I got eyewitness testimony, I got photographs, a birth certificate for the little bastard, I got—"

"Wait. You said miscegenation?"

"His New Orleans friend's mama is a high-yaller. You know, an octoroon, one-eighth Negro blood."

"Then the woman is only one-sixteenth Negro."

"Well, that's all it takes in Texas, kid, and in Louisiana, too. Don't you worry, though, this won't go to court. You think Ace-High wants the whole world to know what he's growing down there in the Garden District?"

Cassie put down her pen. "Allene. Why do you need a lawyer?"

She laughed. "To fine-print him before his lawyers fine-print me. I'm tired of marrying and divorcing. I just want to get a lot of Ace-High's nice money and settle down on my little old sixteen-bedroom spread in Preston Hollow and have me some fun." Her smile was as fearsome as a shark's. "Might just import about sixteen West Texas cowboys for those bedrooms and have me a permanent party."

Cassie snorted and then she leaned back and laughed, gasping for air. Allene Perkins looked surprised and then she was laughing, too, until her mascara streaked down her face.

Steve Reilly burst in the door. "What the hell's—Allene Perkins! Are you all right? Cassie, what's all this about?"

Cassie tried to control herself. "It's just that—Steve, I've been in a blue funk for days, thinking about what men to do women, how they work them over, and now—now Allene has showed me that it can work both ways!"

Allene hooted. "Cassie, you come on with me now. I'm buying you lunch at the Peacock Room."

"I've had lunch."

"Then we'll just go over to the Athletic Club for a little drinkie-poo."

"But I have to work!"

"Oh, for God's sake, go on," Steve said. "You won't get anything accomplished this afternoon.",

Allene and Cassie left the office laughing so hard that they had to support each other.

"Allene," Cassie gasped, "your mascara is all over your face."

"Who gives a damn, anyway?"

"At least sixteen cowboys will care deeply."

Allene hooted all the way to the street.

Later, after they had dinner together, Allene insisted that University Park was not too far out of her way, so Cassie gave the chauffeur directions to her house.

The black Cadillac limousine rolled to a stop at the house and Allene said, "Cassie! There's a man sitting on your front steps!"

Cassie peered out. It was Jimmy Steele. Her stomach tightened
into a knot.

"It's all right, Allene. It's my husband."

"Ex-husband, you mean."

"I told you, we're just separated."

Allene shook Cassie's shoulder. "For God's sake, why? Dump him,
Cassie. He looks like a drunk."

"I haven't seen him for five years, Allene. I don't want to see him
now."

"Then you dump him, hear? Want me to come in and help you?"

"No! I mean, I'll take care of it."

"Well, fine-print him, Cassie. And if you can't think up enough
fine print, you call me and I'll make up some!"

Cassie walked up to the house. "Jimmy? How did you find me?"

"Dad told me, of course. I called your office but you'd left, so I
came here to wait. Who's in the car?"

"A client. Come out to the car and meet her."

Allene put her window down and took a good look at him, and
Cassie looked, too. In the light from the streetlamp she saw that
Jimmy's face was puffy and that his nose was swollen with small bro-
ken veins. When he turned away from the car, Allene nodded to
Cassie briskly and with her lips formed the words "Dump him."

Inside the house, Jimmy took a good look around the living room.
"Nice place, Cassie. It's little, but then Dad said you'd just started
your practice."

How did James Steele know so much about her? The moment that
she asked the question, she knew the answer. Dixon Steele, the man
of honor, had run right to his daddy to spread the news. After he
had the effrontery to say that she should trust him! So much for
sacred honor.

"Would you like a drink, Jimmy?"

"Sure, I'd—no, I guess not. I'm here to talk business with you."

"With me?" Cassie made herself a light drink and sat down on the
rocking chair. "My goodness, what business would I have with a
future congressman?"

Jimmy flushed. "Damn it, Cassie, you know I lost the election."

"No," she said truthfully, "I didn't know. Who won? The man from Krebs?"

"Yes." Jimmy sat down on the settee and looked at her. "His wife was with him all through the campaign. Sitting on the platform, backing him up."

Cassie set her drink down carefully so that she would not yield to the temptation to throw it at him. "And I was not. Are you implying that your losing was my fault? Or was it difficult for you, Jimmy, when people asked where I was? Did it embarrass you to tell them what a bad sport I was, that after you gave me gonorrhea, I was just no fun anymore?"

"Damn it to hell, Cassie, I didn't come here to talk about that!"

She picked up her glass. "Then why did you come?"

"Cassie, I want a divorce."

She said nothing.

He loosened his necktie. "Aren't you going to say anything?"

"What is there to say?"

"Hell, you've got to say yes. Look, I'm prepared to offer you a settlement."

The thought of sixteen cowboys crossed Cassie's mind and she smiled.

"A good settlement, Cassie," he said desperately. "Dad said—" He stopped.

"And what does 'Dad' think a good settlement would be?"

"Five thousand dollars."

Automatically Cassie said, "No."

"Five thousand dollars is a lot of money, damn it!"

Cassie thought of what the Steele men had done to her family and to her during the years. James Steele's holding her mother and father in semislavery. The poverty her grandmother had suffered. Jimmy's lechery. Gonorrhea. The death of her baby. Dixon Steele's betrayal of her. "No, it isn't," she said. "It isn't much money at all. Tell me, Jimmy, why do you want a divorce, anyway? Why now?"

He looked away. "Dad said you would want to know, but it has nothing to do with you."

" 'Dad said.' My God, Jimmy Steele, there are only two of us in this room, not three. There are only two of us in this travesty of a marriage. You can answer my question honestly or you can leave right now. It's up to you, not your father."

"Oh, God. He said I'd be a fool to tell you. Well, it's because I want to get married. That's why."

"Come on, Jimmy, there's got to be more to it than that. Who is it? Who's the girl?"

"Margaret Wells, from the city."

"From Oklahoma City? Do you mean John Wells' granddaughter?" The family was an Oklahoma legend. Ranching, oil, banking, politics. Power. She whistled softly. "Mercy me, Jimmy, you are flying high, aren't you? Well, now I know just exactly how much a divorce is worth to you."

"Damn it, Cassie—"

"Hush. I want to think." Cassie tried to work logically through the facts, but she was too much tied to the Steeles, too emotional to use her legal training. She had seen her first two clients that day. Milly would continue to suffer beatings in order to feed her children, while Allene was doing the beating herself, with a club made of racial prejudice and money. Which did Cassie want to be? She did not want to be the punished, she knew that. She had worked for five years to get into a position where she could control her life. But neither did she want to be the punisher. She did not want any responsibility for the men of the Steele family, not even that of being their hangman.

What did she want, then? She wanted what was fair, what she had earned, but how could she put a value on the loss of innocence, the loss of trust? On the loss of a baby?

Any figure she named would be arbitrary. She thought of Allene. If it had to be arbitrary, it might just as well be high.

Cassie finished her watery drink and set the glass down with a bang. "All right, Jimmy. I will give you a divorce."

"Hey, Cassie, that's—"

"It will cost your father exactly twenty thousand dollars."

"Twenty thousand? You can't expect him to come up with—"

"Jimmy, call your father. He'll make the decision eventually, so he might as well make it now. Oh, and tell him I want the divorce action in the Oklahoma courts. I will sue you for divorce on the grounds of adultery."

"Wait a minute, now. I can sue you for desertion."

Cassie shrugged. "Fine. I'll subpoena Dr. Mathers and we can have it all out in open court."

"Oh, all right, for Christ's sake. But twenty thousand—"

"When I receive a cashier's check for twenty thousand dollars I will sign the complaint. Call him, Jimmy. The telephone is on the sideboard in the dining room. Oh, yes, and do make it a collect call."

Cassie sat and rocked while Jimmy talked to his father. Just once did he bring her into the conversation.

"Dad says you're forgetting the five thousand dollars he gave you when you left Ballard for Dallas."

"No, Jimmy, I'm not. That was a bribe to keep me from divorcing you. This bribe is to get your divorce."

"I don't like talk about bribes!"

"Call it what you will. And you might explain to your father that I will not negotiate."

Jimmy came back in the living room wiping his sweating face with his handkerchief. "He says he had no choice other than to give in to your blackmail."

"Blackmail? Do you like that term better than 'bribe'?"

To her surprise, Jimmy smiled at her warmly. "I've got to hand it to you, Cassie. Not many people get the best of my father. Say, do you think I could have that drink now?" He moved across the room and put his hand on her shoulder.

Cassie stared at him. "Are you making a pass at me, Jimmy Steele?"

He grinned, a little boy caught in a harmless prank. "Hell, Cassie, why not? I mean, we're still married, aren't we?"

She stood up. "I can't believe this, even of you. Get out of my house, you bastard. Get out!"

"Hey, Cassie, don't be so—"

She crossed the room and held the front door open. "Get out, now! And you remind your father that I'm a lawyer now, too, and that I will check those divorce papers with a fine-tooth comb."

"Now, Cassie—"

Shaking with fury, she slammed the door in his face. As she shot the lock, the telephone rang.

It would be James, she thought. That was all she needed.

"Cassie?" It was Allene Perkins. "You all right, Cassie? Has the drunk left?"

"Yes." Cassie sighed in relief. "The drunk left, permanently. I'm divorcing him."

"Good for you, honey! Wait, are you going to get a good settlement?"

"It's one that's fair by my standards."

"What about real estate? You did get some real estate."

"No real estate, just cash. Not in your league, of course. It wouldn't support even one cowboy."

"Oh, hell, honey, don't you worry about that. I'll give you a couple of mine."

Cassie exploded in laughter. She hung up the phone and laughed and laughed, until she cried.

Chapter 30

CASSIE'S DIVORCE from Jimmy would not go through for months, but she was too busy to give it much thought. She was working on Milly Jayson's case, but two visits to the welfare office had produced little of value. For Milly to receive Aid to Dependent Children, her husband would have to leave the household, and without his pay the welfare allowance would not be enough to support a pregnant woman and three children, even in West Dallas. Milly's attitude was a problem, too. She was afraid to commit herself to a course of action. She could predict her husband's behavior, after all, but she could not predict the changing policies of the welfare office. "Better the devil you know," she told Cassie.

In contrast Allene's divorce, like Allene herself, was as airy as a soufflé. After Cassie met with Ace-High Perkins's lawyer and showed him the evidence Allene's detectives had gathered, it was all over but the shouting. Early in December Ace-High and his lawyer and Allene and Cassie gathered in the judge's chambers to sign the papers that made Allene a free woman and a very rich one. Ace-High glared at Cassie during the meeting as if it had been she who had done the whole thing, but the glares did not bother her at all. She was ready to accept with equanimity the credit for relieving Ace-High of a few of his millions, or the blame, or both.

"How did it go?" Steve asked when she went back to the office.

"Like falling off a log. Allene had done all the work. In fact, I really shouldn't even bill her."

Steve put on his glasses. "Whoa up, there. You want to do *pro bono* work for Allene Perkins?"

Cassie laughed. "Of course not. But I spent so little time on it, Steve. If I bill her by the hour—"

"Cassie, I don't know what they taught in those law classes you audited, but you're in the real world now. What did the settlement come to?"

She giggled. "Sixteen cowboys."

"What?"

"Nothing. Private joke. Counting the house and—I'd say about four million dollars."

Steve nodded and made some rapid calculations on a scratch pad. The fee he named left Cassie speechless.

He grinned at her. "Look, kid, you can't charge too much or your client will think you're stealing from him. But if you don't charge enough, he'll think you aren't much of a lawyer. That Frenchman, the designer Stanley Marcus brought in for Neiman's show last year ago—what was his name?"

"Do you mean Christian Dior?"

"Yes, that's the one. How much do you think he has in one of those ball gowns of his? Not much for material, not with the backs cut that low. If that guy billed his time by the hour, hell, somebody like Allene Perkins wouldn't be caught dead in a dress that cheap. Ergo—"

"Ergo, I see what you mean." She hesitated. "I'm just embarrassed to bill a friend for—"

Steve smacked his flat hand on the desk. "No! Never be embarrassed at billing a client. You think Allene is embarrassed about taking Ace-High Perkins for four million? For that matter, was Ace-High embarrassed at winning that first derrick from a poker buddy?" He paused and looked at her carefully, surveying her from head to toe. "Cassie, you're a big girl, and you're moving into the big leagues. You've got the makings of a damn good lawyer, but you have to believe it yourself before you can convince anyone else."

Cassie looked down at the rug. "Maybe I don't believe it."

Steve laughed softly. "That's all right, Cassie, fake it. Act like you believe it and you'll fool them all. Maybe you'll even fool yourself."

Cassie never quite told Steve Reilly how she spent her share of Allene Perkins's legal fee. Just after Christmas she told him, she told everyone about her first purchase: a brand-new Chevrolet sedan. Only Leta, however, knew about the money Cassie invested in getting a divorce and a good rental house for Milly Jayson. Milly was too pregnant to get a job, but with ADC checks and with the groceries Cassie had Leta sneak to her, she could get by comfortably. Cassie knew that in a roundabout way she was breaking the welfare laws, but to see Milly smiling was worth it. She had a job lined up for Milly, too. When the new baby was old enough, Milly could go to work in a West Dallas grocery store.

While Cassie was between domestic-relations clients, Steve put her to work as his assistant in a complicated oil syndication. She learned more about oil reserve laws in that few months than most law schools could teach. She and Steve fell into a habit of dropping into a private club for an after-work drink. At first they discussed only the case, but they soon found other topics. Steve was well informed, especially about Dallas and Dallas people. He was smooth and witty and most important of all, he did not judge her. He was a reader, too, with tastes even more eclectic than Cassie's. He introduced her to William Faulkner's work and she made it through *The Sound and the Fury* with his help.

"And you see why Faulkner used long complicated sentences, don't you, Cassie? He had long complicated thoughts to express."

Cassie rested her chin on her hand and looked across the table at him. "I wish—I really wish you could have known Naomi Bencher. You two would have so much to talk about."

"Who is Naomi Bencher?"

"Oh, just a friend. Someone I knew once, when I was a child."

In March 1951, another *pro bono* client appeared at Cassie's private entrance. She was a tall woman, thin to the point of emaciation. She was not bruised, however, and she had been divorced for over a year. She needed help only to pry some child-support money out of her ex-husband, a well-paid roustabout in the West Texas oil fields. To garnishee wages was simple compared with what Cassie had needed to do on Milly Jayson's behalf.

Cassie was almost through with her part of the oil reserve research when she came back from lunch one June day and found a client waiting in the lobby. At first glance, Cassie thought that Leta had mistakenly seated a *pro bono* client in the lobby. The woman was older, much older, but she reminded Cassie of Milly Jayson. She had the same air of being defeated by her life. Cassie took another look, however, and saw expensive fashionable shoes, a stylish leather hand-bag and a lightweight suit of Neiman-Marcus quality.

"Mrs. Farley? I have a few moments free now. If you would care to . . ." Cassie gestured toward her office.

The woman perched on the edge of the client's chair. "I want to—he says he—after all these years!" With that, she burst into tears. Cassie ran to bring her a glass of water and sat down at her desk while Mrs. Farley got herself under control.

Finally the woman mopped her eyes and sat up straight. She was of average height and looked frail. Her hands were soft, with mani-cured nails, but Cassie could see that they had done rough work.

"Me and him, we worked hard. Come up from the farm, both of us, but he had him this idea about oil, figured he could make it big." She looked away at something far beyond the books on the shelves. "We lived like pigs out there in the panhandle, me and him, lived in a tent next to his rig. Mud all over, blue northers till you thought tent and drilling rig and you was all going to blow away. We lost our baby to flu, then another one was born dead, and the doctor he said I couldn't have no more. So there was just us two working together, me and him, on that rig. Lived like pigs. Didn't care, though. We was together, and I had faith in that man. I figured he'd make it. And he did, by God. Made it big. Then nothing would do but we got to come down to Dallas. I reckon it was like they told it on us, we come down here with money hanging out of our overalls."

Cassie had heard that said of someone, but she could not remember who it was. Mrs. Farley continued her story.

" 'Myrt,' he says, 'you get yourself down to that there Neiman-Marcus and get you some fancy duds. You and me's going to buy us a house.' And that's what we did. Got a big old house, paid four hundred fifty thousand dollars for that place, and that was seven, eight years ago, worth more now. Hired some young fellow to fix it up and make sure everything matched." Her breath caught in her throat. "Except me. I didn't match. Oh, I got the fancy duds but like the Good Book says, you can't make no silk purse out of a sow's ear."

Cassie cleared her throat. "And now he wants a divorce."

Mrs. Farley glared at her. "Didn't I just tell you? He's found him a silk purse. Pretty little thing. Young, yellow-haired missy. Oh, she'll take him, I don't doubt it. She'll take him for a husband and then she'll take him for every cent she can." She hit the chair arm with her fist, but her eyes were brimming with tears. "But I was the one that worked for that money, wasn't I? I was the one that gave up my babies!"

Cassie caught her breath in sudden sympathy. She knew about giving up a baby, about being forced to give up a baby. Besides that, Fran had told her about other cases like this one, oilmen who struck it rich and wanted everything that went with money: Oxxford suits from Neiman's, Cadillac limousines and mansions. They acquired the proof of their wealth and, later, they acquired young wives as proof of their virility. The old wife did not fit the decor in the new mansion.

"Mrs. Farley," Cassie said firmly, "I will be honored to represent you in the divorce action." She took up her pen. "Now, tell me the whole story, but first let me get down your husband's full name."

The woman looked surprised. "Why, it's Billy Ben, of course. Billy Ben Farley."

Cassie caught her breath. Billy Ben Farley was not an oil king like Clint Murchison and H. L. Hunt and Sid Richardson, but he was at least a prince in the Texas royal line. "What do you want from this, Mrs. Farley? Do you want to stop the divorce or—"

"Hell, I don't care none about that. If he don't want me, I surefire don't want him. I want the money I worked for, that's all."

"Texas is a community-property state, you know, so to get half of the joint assets shouldn't be too—"

"Half? What do you mean, half? Listen, Billy Ben ain't but sixty years old. He can go out and find himself another field and set up a new company. But I'm the same age, and I'm a old woman. I can't do nothing. I'll tell you what I want out of it, honey. I want Farley Oil."

Cassie swallowed. Farley Oil. The woman in front of her was talking about fifty to a hundred million dollars. "You want to control Farley Oil?"

"Damn tooting. Billy Ben thinks he can put me out to pasture but he's got another think coming. I helped build that company and by God I can run it!"

Cassie caught some of her fire. "Well, by God, I'll do everything I can to make sure that you do!" She hesitated. "One question, Mrs. Farley, before we get to work: how did you happen to choose me as your attorney?"

Myrtle Farley smiled and for a second Cassie saw the canny woman who had helped her husband build a multimillion-dollar company. "Well, I'll tell you. Ace-High Perkins was over to the house last month and I heard him bitching to Billy Ben about how Allene and this woman lawyer took him to the cleaners. Soon as Billy Ben come up with this divorce crap, I got Allene to give me your name."

Over drinks that evening, Steve said, "I told you that you were getting into the big leagues! Who's representing Billy Ben?"

"I don't know."

"Well, for God's sake, find out! And check every divorce the lawyer has ever handled. You need to know the opposition's strengths right from the start."

"And their weaknesses?"

"In this league, there won't be many."

Cassie fumbled with her cocktail napkin. "Steve, I'm new, I'm inexperienced. We both know that Allene did most of the work on her case. Do you think I should ask a more seasoned divorce lawyer to work with me on this?"

He rubbed his jaw. "I'm not sure. I think you can handle it, but—I'll tell you what. Check out the opposing attorneys and then we'll evaluate it." He grinned at her. "In the meantime, I'm going to buy you the best dinner in Dallas. How about Benito's?"

"I'd love it!"

IN THE MIRRORED FRONT DOOR of Benito's Cassie saw the two of them coming, the big square-jawed man and the tall blonde in her Jacques Fath suit. They made a good-looking couple, she thought, but then she reminded herself that they were not a couple at all. They were two lawyers, one a married man and a father and the other a woman in the process of getting divorced.

Still, she was uncomfortable when they were seated at a table in the center of the room. Steve Reilly was well known in Dallas. Were people looking at them, people who would misconstrue the situation? Cassie wished she could use one of the metal stands that held Reserved cards to erect an explanatory sign of her own: LAWYERS HAVING DINNER. NO HANKY-PANKY.

Steve obviously had no such qualms. He ordered drinks from his private bottle, the usual device to circumvent Texas liquor laws.

She glanced at her watch. "We'll want to order soon. You have a long drive to the ranch."

"No, I don't. I took an apartment in town last winter, to avoid that drive." He grinned. "Now, don't get in a tizzy about my marriage breaking up or anything silly. Dorothea and I agreed that the daily commute was too much. I go to the ranch every weekend."

Cassie laughed. "That thought did just tiptoe through my mind. Maybe a divorce practice does that to a lawyer. Will I constantly be scouting potential clients?"

"As your boss, I sure as hell hope so."

Over French onion soup, Cassie asked him a question she had wanted to ask for almost six years. "Steve, what's wrong with your left eye?"

"My wandering eye?" He grinned. "Dorothea kids me about that. It's no secret, Cassie. That's my war wound. Didn't you wonder why I got out of the service early in the war?"

"I suppose I did."

"I was in the Army Air Corps, and in December of 1941 I happened to be at Hickam Field, Hawaii."

"Pearl Harbor."

"A Jap bullet smashed my goggles and drove a shred of glass into my eye."

"Oh, Steve, how—"

"And how. They thought I'd lose the eye, but a hotshot young eye doctor risked an operation and it worked. I don't have much vision in it, but the glasses help that and help to keep it from wandering, too." He looked at her steadily. "Most of the time."

She blushed. "I just wondered, Steve."

"And now you know, Cassie."

They talked about the office but tension wound through the innocuous conversation. A crossroads lay ahead, Cassie knew, and she did not know which direction she would choose.

The idle talk died away, leaving only silence. The waiter came with the dessert menu. Without looking up, Steve said, "In a minute," and the man left.

"Shall we have coffee at my apartment?" he said quietly.

Cassie looked down at the big linen napkin in her lap. She folded it once, neatly, unfolded it and then refolded it and held it so tightly that her knuckles whitened. "Yes."

Steve dealt with the check and, without speaking, they left.

In the car Cassie was silent, torn by the decision she was making. Steve was married and so was she, even if only in form. More than that, she knew that she loved another man, hopelessly. What did it matter? she thought angrily. What did it mean if she became what all of the Steeles believed her to be? Sound and fury, signifying nothing.

Steve Reilly's apartment was in the Melrose, an old hotel which had been converted to apartments. His place was not a businessman's weeknight hideaway, but a spacious one-bedroom suite with high ceilings, tall windows and built-in bookshelves, a place for a bookish man who enjoyed his creature comforts.

Cassie followed Steve into the small kitchen.

"I'll make coffee," he said.

"I think I'd rather have a brandy."

"You may have one, but only one," he said as he took a bottle of Rémy Martin from the cabinet. "I want you to make this decision with a clear head."

Suddenly she was almost overwhelmed by gratitude toward Steve Reilly. This was the man who had helped her to become a lawyer, who had guided her on the path toward success. This man wanted her, it was clear, but he wanted her to come to him freely, of her own choice. Unlike the Steeles he respected her not just as a woman, but as a human being.

"Steve," she whispered. "I don't want brandy."

He set the bottle on the drainboard and turned to look at her.

Without speaking, he took her hand and led her through the living room to the bedroom.

She stood motionless in the center of the room while he took off his suitcoat and necktie and hung them over a chair. He came to her, then. "Do you mind the light?"

"No."

He took her face in his hands and looked into her eyes searchingly. "You are sure, Cassie?"

"Yes."

He kissed her once, lightly, and then he pulled the pins from her hair and let it fall to her shoulders. He touched it and then eased her jacket from her shoulders and hung it on the chair with his own things. Slowly he unbuttoned her white silk blouse. He lowered his head and touched his lips to her left breast.

Cassie closed her eyes and stood still, her hands hanging at her side, while he removed her blouse and then her skirt. He moved behind her to unhook her brassiere and her garter belt, and each time his fingers touched her, he bent to kiss the place, gently, his lips soft against her skin, and then more firmly, as if to stake a claim. She felt the kisses and she felt her breasts swelling, rising and falling in the rhythm of her breathing, rising and falling as her breathing quickened.

Slowly he rolled her stockings down, eased off her shoes. He moved away and she heard the bedclothes flap as he pulled them down.

She opened her eyes and went to lie down on the bed. He stood above her, still in his shirt and trousers. He turned away and removed his own clothes more rapidly than he had undressed her, but still with an unhurried, measured rhythm. He slid into bed beside her and smiled at her, his gray eyes glittering, before he switched off the bedside lamp.

In the darkness he ran his hands down her body, touching her everywhere, kissing her everywhere until Cassie moaned at the touch of his lips and, when they left her skin, moaned again until they returned.

"Now you," he said, lying back, and Cassie did for him what he had done for her. She explored his body, learning it with her hands and then with her lips, until he entered her so smoothly that she was aware only of her own body swelling to meet his.

"Now, Steve! Now!"

"Wait," he whispered. He eased out of her, fumbled with something for a moment and then reentered. The rhythm returned with him and Cassie thrust her body up to him, again and once again, until his body and hers were thrusting together, climbing together and exploding, hanging at the top until slowly, easily, their two bodies subsided in a warm glow, contented.

Cassie drew in a breath, a long deep inhalation of warmth and sex and happiness. They dozed together. When Cassie roused they were no longer joined, but even in the dark she knew that Steve was awake. "I love you, Steve," she whispered.

He laughed softly. "I think you do, a little, and I love you, a little. Is that enough, Cassie?"

"Yes." She sighed and was startled to realize that it was with relief.

The bedside lamp clicked on. Cassie shut her eyes against the glare and then opened them to look at Steve, who had raised himself on one elbow and was smiling down at her.

"You are some woman."

Cassie felt alive, wholly alive, for the first time in months, in years. She wanted to sing with joy, to dance. She felt newborn, fresh-hatched: a woman who was free to do anything, say anything. She giggled. "You aren't so bad yourself for an old man."

His eyes widened but he laughed, too. "Hey, kid, you watch it or I'll show you just how old I am."

Cassie made her eyes round and innocent. "Really, Mr. Reilly, I'd love to watch it, but it's so little I can't even see it."

"You—" He grabbed her and cut off her laughter with a long, deep kiss.

Cassie put her hands on his bare back and pulled him down to her. "I still can't see it," she whispered. "I can't see it, but I can feel it and it ain't nowheres as little as I thought."

He snorted a laugh. "You sure know how to take the—the wind out of a man's sails, girl!"

Cassie laughed with him. "Hey, can I have that brandy now?"

Still chuckling Steve pulled on a terry-cloth bathrobe and went to the kitchen. Cassie went in the bathroom and took a quick shower. When she came out, wearing her panties and bra, Steve was sitting on the side of the bed with a brandy snifter in his hand.

"You're going?" he said.

"I think I should. I have an early appointment with Myrtle Farley."

"Yeah. I know." He put his glass on the bedside table and stood up to hug her. "Cassie, you are something else." He stepped back with a sigh. "I'll get dressed and after our brandy, I'll take you downtown to get your car."

In the parking lot Steve stopped his Cadillac next to Cassie's Chevrolet and turned off the engine.

"I'll ask you just once more, Cassie, and then never again. Is a little love enough for you?"

Cassie looked out at the littered parking lot. A night breeze stirred the dirt into a miniature dust devil. "I think so, Steve. Is it enough for you?"

"Yes. No commitments, right? No strings on either of us."

"No strings. Discreet. In the office—"

He laughed. "Now, that will be tough!"

"But you'll stick to the rules?"

"Yes, damn it, I will. Cassie, I wish—"

"No, Steve. No strings and no wishes."

"Okay, have it your way."

As she drove home through the June night, however, Cassie wondered about what he had said. Was she having it her way, or was Steve having it his way?

Was it possible that she was a grown-up at last, free, permitted to have fun without taking on the responsibility for it?

Or was she still just a child wanting a treat?

As she settled into her own pillow she had one last thought: she wished she could tell Fran Jordan. She wanted Fran to know that her hormones were fine, just fine.

Chapter 31

 TWO WEEKS LATER Cassie had to tell Myrtle Farley that private detectives had come up with nothing useful.

"Mrs. Farley, I think there is still a—"

"Myrt. Call me Myrt."

Cassie grinned. "Myrt. If Mr. Farley—if your Billy Ben is . . . well . . ."

"Screwing that girl?"

Cassie blushed. "Well, yes. If he is, he is amazingly discreet about it."

"He would be. Billy Ben, he's pretty damn smart." She seemed to be proud of his ability to hide his affairs from the detectives.

"The problem is, Myrt, that we don't have any leverage. We know we can get half of the assets under community-property law, but your husband's lawyer can probably include the house and cars in your settlement, cutting down on your fifty percent of Farley Oil."

"Well, I ain't settling for no fifty percent anyhow. I want at least sixty. I want control." She leaned forward and laid a work-worn hand on the desk, palm up. "Look at them callouses, girl. Look at them. I got those pulling cable and manhandling drill bits. I worked to build that company! We decided all the big things together, me and him. And now he wants to go it on his own, to decide for himself what he'll do with our company. Well, I ain't having it, that's all. I ain't going to hang out with them others at the Greenhouse and let Neiman-Marcus make me into some high-fashion dodo bird. I want that company, you hear? I want Farley Oil!"

When Myrt left, Cassie turned her chair and stared blankly at the books on her shelves. No matter what Steve had said, she was not ready to play in the major leagues. Twenty-six years of living and six months of law practice had not prepared her to deal with a Billy Ben Farley. She would have to get an expert in on the case. She started to go to Steve's office, but something niggled at her mind. Farley Oil. Something she had read about Farley Oil in a newspaper so long ago that it did not spring to her mind when Myrtle Farley first came to her office.

She tried the old memory trick of reconstructing the setting. She seemed to remember drinking coffee while she read the item. Yes! On her own back porch. She could smell the damp rich odor of freshly turned dirt. She had listened to a mockingbird trying to convince the world that he was a bob-white, and laughed, and looked at the paper and seen the words "Farley Oil . . ." and that was all she could remember. She shook her head in frustration. A spring morning—yes! She jumped up from her chair. It would have been the previous April or May and at breakfast she would have been reading the *Dallas Morning News*.

It took her two hours in the newspaper morgue to find the item on the business page of the *News*. It was in March, as it happened, and she had no idea why a two-line squib in the oil and gas column had stuck in her mind. "Bilbet Company, a subsidiary of Farley Oil, has brought in a new well in the Permian Basin."

Cassie hurried back to the office to call Myrtle Farley. "Myrt? Cassie Steele. What can you tell me about Bilbet Company."

"Spell that, will you? Bilbet. Never heard of it, Cassie."

"That girl Billy Ben wants to marry, do you know her name?"

"Sure. Elizabeth Louise Morgan. He calls her Betty Lou. Say, what's this about, anyhow?"

"I'm just checking something out, Myrt. I'll let you know when I find out what's going on."

Cassie tapped on Steve Reilly's office door. "Are you busy?"

"No, come on in." He motioned to her to close the door. "Cassie. About last night—"

"Not at the office, remember?"

"Tonight? Can we—oh, hell, I've got a Boys' Club dinner."

"And tomorrow is Friday and you'll be going to the ranch, and besides I have a date with Ted Abernathy."

He scowled at her. "Damn it, Cassie, you can cancel a date, and I can skip the ranch for one weekend."

Cassie sat down. "No, we can't do that."

"No strings, right? God, Cassie, I didn't know there were women like you in this world." He grinned at her.

"Neither did I." A black thought slid into her mind. "In fact, I'm not sure what kind of woman I am now."

He put on his glasses and looked at her seriously. "You are a free woman, my dear. Free to do as you like. Free to call this off if you want to, but I hope you won't."

She looked down at her hands and then straight at him. "No, I don't want to call it off."

He started to get up, but instead sat back and smiled at her. "Not in the office, right? How about Monday evening?"

Cassie blushed, but her voice was firm when she answered. "Yes. Monday."

He took up a paper, but Cassie shook her head at him. "Steve, I didn't come in here to talk about us. I want to ask you something."

"Fire away."

Cassie leaned back and stretched luxuriously. "Steve, suppose, just suppose that a joint tenant in a wholly owned corporation siphons assets to another company, one in which he has full ownership, without the knowledge of the other owner of the first corporation. What would you call it?"

"Embezzlement, at the very least."

"Suppose we are talking about millions of dollars?"

Steve put on his glasses. "Grand larceny."

"That's the way I figured it, too."

"Who?"

"Steve, it's only supposition right now. I need figures and dates, access to financial statements and registers of corporation ownership."

"I can get those for you. Who?"

"Billy Ben Farley."

Steve whistled softly. "How did you get a handle on this?"

She told him what Myrt Farley wanted and how Cassie herself had remembered the news item. "And his future wife is named Betty Lou. Billy-Betty, get it? Bilbet."

"Good work, Cassie. Damn good work! Look, I'll get some leg-men on this, both here and in Austin. If this pans out, Myrt can take Billy Ben for everything, and probably send him to jail to boot."

Cassie was startled. "I didn't think about jail. I'm not sure I want to—"

"What you want is not important. It is your duty to bring the information to your client and let her decide."

"But if I don't want to do that?"

"Lawyers, believe it or not, are ethical beings. You'll do it."

Cassie had found a trace of a path, but the Bilbet trail was well camouflaged. In late September, almost three months after Steve had sent his legmen down the path, they still had not found the end. And Cassie was involved in another divorce: her own.

The complaint form and a cashier's check for twenty thousand dollars arrived at the office in the same envelope. When the money was in her account, she signed the form with Rob and Leta as witnesses, and asked Maxine Wells to notarize it.

The envelope was sealed and stamped, but was still in her purse when she let herself into Steve Reilly's apartment that night.

The affair had fallen into a comfortable and comforting pattern. On weekends Steve went to the ranch and Cassie dated Ted Abernathy or another of the young lawyers she had met, but she kept the relationships casual. She suspected that she was getting a reputation as a party girl, but she did not care. It helped to cover the time she spent with Steve. They never appeared together in public, but once or twice a week she parked her car on a residential street a block from the Melrose. The elevator was self-service, and if anyone happened to share it, she got off on a different floor and used the fire stairs. If, from time to time, she felt guilty or besmirched, she did not dwell upon it. She was having fun, that was all. She had earned it.

Steve had a highball waiting for her that night. She sat down in the living room with him.

"You want to talk about your divorce, Cassie?"

She was startled. "How did you—"

"Leta mentioned it. She thought I knew about it."

"I would have told you, Steve. I haven't mailed the papers yet."

"Why not?"

Suddenly Cassie was exhausted. "I don't know."

"I think I do. What does the poet say? 'This is the way the world ends . . . not with a bang but a whimper.'" He finished his drink and stood up. "Come on," he said briskly. "I'm going to take you out to dinner. We'll make the bang!"

Cassie hesitated, looking up at him. "But what if someone sees us and word gets back to your—"

"I will tell my wife. I'll tell her that you filed for divorce and you were sad and I took you out to dinner. The truth."

Cassie laughed. "And will you tell her the whole truth, counselor?"

Steve laughed, too, and pulled her to her feet. "I'm not under oath in this particular hearing."

Cassie mailed the envelope on the way to the restaurant.

DURING THE NEXT FEW DAYS, however, her mood fluctuated. She had cut the last ties with the Steele men, with James and Jimmy and, finally, with Dix. At one moment she felt free and at the next, lonely, because she had cut her ties with Oklahoma, with her past and, somehow, with her grandmother.

She tried to concentrate on the future rather than the past. Steve spent several hours with her, working out an investment plan that would give her good leverage for her money and some relief from income tax. At his suggestion, she used most of the divorce settlement to buy a controlling interest in two down-at-the-heels office buildings in lower downtown.

"Dallas is on the verge of a building explosion, Cassie. If you can hang on to them long enough, you'll make a fortune on these buildings."

Cassie called Allene Perkins that very afternoon. "Allene, you have to be the first to know. My divorce settlement came through and I got some real estate after all."

Allene laughed so loudly that Cassie had to hold the phone away from her ear. "Great, that's just great! Come to dinner tonight so we can celebrate. And hey, Cassie, bring that friend of yours, Fran Jordan. I'll pick her brain for some free hints on interior decoration."

"Design," Cassie said automatically. "How many cowboys are in residence right now, Allene?"

Allene laughed uproariously. "Not even one! I sent them all home to kiss their horses."

Driving out to Preston Hollow, Cassie told Fran about the divorce.

"You got money, real cash money out of James Steele? Cassie, that's blood from a turnip! What do you bet he's all dried up and wizened? Speaking of the Steeles, I talked to my mother last week and she said the Steeles finally have a state senator."

"Jimmy? I thought he——"

"No, the other one. Dixon." Fran smoothed her hair. "You know, I could have gone for him, but nothing ever happened."

"Same here," Cassie said softly.

"You're kidding!"

Cassie caught herself quickly. "Of course I am! Listen, Fran, I should warn you. Allene's going to be picking your brain for free decorating hints."

Fran snorted. "Free? You haven't seen old Frannie in action, have you? I'll bet you a dinner at Benito's that I design her entire house and that she pays for it through the nose."

"Done!" Cassie said. "But you don't know Allene the way I do. I can already taste my free dinner!"

The three of them had a delightful dinner that night at Allene's, well prepared and well served in a dining room imported, paneling and all, from an Italian palazzo.

Allene had drunk more than her share of two bottles of Dom Pérignon and had a distinct list to the south. "So I'll tell you girls just what I'd tell a daughter of my own. Have fun, live it up, but for God's sake don't get tangled up with a married man!"

Cassie glanced at Fran and was surprised to see Fran looking at her and smiling. Cassie felt her face get warm. Fran could not know. She could not possibly know about Steve Reilly.

"Oh, they'll talk divorce," Allene said. " 'I'm going to get me a divorce, lambie pie, and you and me will get married and live happily ever after.' Don't you believe it for a damn minute, girls. A married man, he'll lie to you for the sheer fun of lying."

"Allene," Fran said quickly, "this really is a lovely room, but you might want to buy—"

"What?" The word "buy" acted on Allene like an ice-cold shower. She sat up straight and her eyes instantly cleared and focused on Fran Jordan. "Buy what, Fran dear?"

Fran glanced at Cassie mischievously. "Oh, it's just that *seicento* is not as fashionable as it once was. If anyone should ask me for a hint on interior design right now, I'd say just two words."

Allene leaned forward. "What words, Fran. Tell me."

"I'd say, 'Think contemporary.' "

Allene looked around the magnificent room, obviously displeased with everything she saw. "You mean, like Danish chairs and all?"

"Mercy, no!" Fran laughed merrily. "That's for the suburban housewife, not for a woman of taste and distinction."

Allene looked suspicious. "And money?"

"Of course," Fran said. "If you can afford the best, why shouldn't you have it?"

Allene laughed aloud. "Cassie, I like this girl. I like her! She knows how to handle us rich old bags. Okay, Fran, you're on! I'll spend a hell of a lot of money, and you'll make a hell of a lot for yourself, but by God, you better believe you're going to work for it!"

Fran looked at the painted cherubs on the ceiling, and then at Allene. "This could be the biggest and most profitable job I've ever done. So why do I have this peculiar feeling that I've been had?"

LETA WAS BOUNCING with excitement the next morning. "Cassie, guess what! Milly got another raise and a promotion to supervisor!"

Cassie hugged her. "That's wonderful! And the children?"

"Oh, they're fine, just fine, and with no drunk daddy hanging around they're doing real good in school. Oh, wait, I almost forgot. You had a long-distance call after you left the office yesterday."

Cassie stopped, excited. "From Austin? From Steve's man in Austin?"

"Well, no, it was from Oklahoma. They'll call back."

Cassie was startled. "Put it right through, Leta."

The call did not come until noon, however, and it was not long-distance. "Cassie? I need to talk to you."

Cassie's stomach tightened into a knot. "Dix? What is—where are you?"

"In Dallas. At Love Field. If you can see me, I'll get a cab into town and—"

"No, wait. I'll pick you up. Wait out in front."

Cassie drove to the airport in a daze. Dixon Steele seemed as dazed as she.

He tugged at his necktie. "Cassie, it's a warm day. Can we get out somewhere, walk around?"

"You don't want lunch?"

"Just some fresh air."

Cassie drove north to the park across the lake from the airport and stopped near the picnic shelter. They walked down the path along the lake. The ducks started quacking, but when no day-old bread appeared, they paddled to the next cove.

"Remember the ducks on San Bois Creek, Cassie?" Dix said, not looking at her.

"Of course."

"And the creek itself. Remember when we went swimming, that time when I was home on leave?"

"Yes, I remember."

He stopped and turned to face her. "Cassie, I was in Ballard over the weekend, and I had a long talk with my mother."

She tried to smile. "You flew down from Oklahoma City to tell me that?"

He frowned. "She told me the whole story, Cassie. She told me about the—the disease and the abortion, the whole thing. Cassie, why didn't you tell me?"

She kicked at the clump of dead grass. "I couldn't. I felt so . . . so dirty." She hesitated. "And you didn't trust me, Dix. If I'd told you, you probably would have blamed me for the—"

"For the disease? Cassie, I wouldn't—"

"For the gonorrhea!" she said angrily. "You can't even say the word, can you? Your brother didn't give me 'a disease' like chicken pox or the measles. He gave me a venereal disease. Gonorrhea." Her anger ebbed into sorrow. "And through me, he gave it to the baby, too. And he let them kill it. He killed my baby."

Dix rubbed his long hand across his eyes. "I know. I understand. You must hate them. You must hate all of them."

"Hate?" Cassie examined the word. "I don't think so. No. I don't hate them. It was so long ago. 'And that was in another country and besides, the wench is dead.' "

"The baby? Was it a girl?"

"No! The wench was me. The sharecropper's daughter. The naïve little fool who was so in love, so in love. The girl who thought she was marrying Prince Charming. That wench is dead."

"Let's walk," he said. "Please."

Cassie watched the ducks cut through the gray clouds reflected in the lake. It will probably rain later in the day, she thought. Or during the night.

"Cassie." Dix walked slowly, watching his feet. "If we could start all over again—you told me once that you loved me."

"Yes."

"Do you still? Do you love me, even a little?"

Cassie caught her breath, hearing Steve Reilly say those words as they lay together: "I love you a little, Cassie, and I think you love me a little."

"Cassie?" Dix said.

Even a little love, she thought, deserved a little loyalty. Or did it? She shook her head to clear it. "I don't know. I'm all mixed up."

Dix put her hands on her shoulders and his eyes seemed to peer into her innermost soul. "Cassie, what if we could go back, way back, to the day we first met, when you were thirteen and I was seventeen? You remember that day, don't you? You remember the fun we had? Can we go back, all the way back, and start again?"

Cassie felt her body sagging toward his. "Dix, I wish . . ." But she had heard Steve say those words, too, and she had heard herself say, "No strings, no wishes."

He pulled her to him and held her in his arms. "I love you, Cassie.

I think I have loved you since that day after the war, the day we spent at the farm.   You're free now, Cassie, and so am I.   Can't we be together?"

No strings.   That defined what she and Steve Reilly had together, but it was easier to say the words than to believe in them.   To deny a deeper relationship between them would mean accepting a view of herself that she could not accept.   She had read the books about new freedom for women, but like most women she knew, she still accepted the double standard.   A man who slept around was a real man.   A woman who made love without an emotional commitment was a whore.

"But I'm not free, Dix," she said.   She pushed herself away from him.   "I'm not free."

He stared at her.   "You aren't—is there someone else?"

"Yes.   Someone else."

His black eyes flashed with anger.   "I don't believe you, Cassie! You told me that you loved me."

Cassie was tired, immensely tired.   She ached with fatigue.   She turned away and started walking toward the car.   "You never have believed me, Dix.   You didn't believe me when I said that I was innocent in the breakup of my marriage, did you?   If you didn't believe me then, why should you now?"

Dix stumbled behind her.   "I didn't say that.   I didn't say you were lying."

"You didn't have to, did you?   You left.   That said it all."   She opened the car door.   "I'll take you back to the airport now.   There's a two-fifteen flight to Oklahoma City."

Driving the car was an effort, and shifting gears used all of her strength.   Would she never be free of the Steeles?   The family was like an octopus.   Each time she felt that she was moving ahead freely, on her own, it sent out tentacles to probe into her life, her mind, her soul, to search for weak spots that could be opened into wounds.   She was tired, so tired of fighting the Steeles.

At the airport Dix climbed out of the car, then leaned back in to look at her.   "Cassie," he said, "Cassie."

He looked as sad as she felt.   Am I a fool, she wondered, to let him go like this?   Are we both fools?   Perhaps we are.   Perhaps we could make it work. She shook her head slowly. She was tired, and too much had happened between them. Too much was happening between Cassie and Steve Reilly. It was too late. Too late.

"Cassie," he said once more, but she let her face close against him and as she did she watched his face close, too, like a heavy door that blocked the light.

He closed the car door and she drove away.

NEW YEAR'S DAY of 1952 brought in a sleet storm that broke trees all over Dallas and turned streets and highways into strips of ice. A few days later Steve called Cassie into his office. She took along her latest notes on Billy Ben Farley, but he waved them aside.

He tilted his chair back and looked up at her. "You are very beautiful today, counselor."

Cassie was pleased that he noticed the suit she had bought at Neiman's, with the new shorter skirt length.

She sketched a curtsy. "Thank you, kind sir."

"Just the right outfit for a plane trip to Denver."

"Denver!"

He winked at her. "We have business in Denver, remember? A new client. Not much business, you understand. Just enough to keep me occupied one morning while you get yourself a ski outfit, then we'll forget it all and go to Aspen for six days. How about it, Cassie?"

"But won't people in the office suspect that we're—"

"I'll take care of that."

Cassie had seen pictures of Denver and Aspen in *Life* but she had never expected to go there herself. They spent the first night at the Brown Palace Hotel in Denver, and Cassie could not decide which she liked better, the elegant rotunda or the European-trained hotel staff. There was nothing like it in Dallas.

Hotel Jerome was delightful, a refurbished monument to Aspen's days as a rip-roaring gold-mining town. Their suite had high ceilings, tall narrow windows and, Cassie was certain, the original Victorian furnishings. She luxuriated in her first bath in the immense claw-footed tub, soaking until Steve complained that he deserved a turn, too.

Steve was an experienced skier, but he insisted that Cassie sign up for lessons for her first two days. By the third day she could ski the easier slopes with Steve. She loved the crisp cold air, the sunshine that was hot on her face even though the temperature was below freezing; but most of all she liked the feeling of free flight when she pushed off at the top of the hill and swooped down, practicing her turns. At the end of each run she was exhilarated. Steve waited for her to coast up to him and set her skis parallel to his so that they could kiss, with lips so cold that they tingled.

At night they did the rounds of Aspen—the Copper Kettle, the Crystal Palace and the smoke-filled bars crowded with skiers. Cassie wanted to see every place, every person.

"So these are the beautiful people, Steve!"

"No," he said seriously. "You are the beautiful people, Cassie Steele."

She looked away, uncomfortable, but she could not ignore the fact that something in their relationship was changing from day to day, almost from hour to hour. When they made love Steve was more intense, not physically but emotionally. At the same time, Cassie felt herself holding back, as if to slow a locomotive that was moving too fast, pulling her onward at too great a speed.

On their fourth day in Aspen, Steve stopped in the bar for a drink while Cassie headed gratefully toward their room for a hot soak to ease her overworked muscles.

"Steve?" she called out when she heard him come into their room. "Hasn't this been a fantastic day?"

"Yes," he said shortly.

She heard him moving around, opening the closets, rattling hangers. Curious, she finished her bath and in her robe went out to the bedroom. He had put their suitcases on the bed and was packing his own.

"Steve! What on earth are you doing?"

He turned and sat down on the side of the bed. He looked five years older, and very tired. "We have a problem, Cassie. I ran into Dorothea's cousin Mary Ellen downstairs. She and George have just driven up from Denver to spend four or five days."

Cassie pulled her robe tight and tied the sash as if to protect herself from a peeping Tom. "So we have to leave."

He shrugged. "What else can we do? I told them I had sneaked away from my meetings in Denver and have to drive back down to-night."

She looked out at the clean, snowy streets and the laughing skiers coming home from the slopes.

"What else can we do?" she said.

Chapter 32

STEVE FLEW to Wichita to see a client and Cassie was back in the office two days earlier than he. Rob Penland teased her about the suntan she said she had acquired in Florida, and she was careful to wear long sleeves and dark stockings so that no one would see that her tan went only from forehead to throat.

When Steve returned he called her into his office. "I'm sorry that happened, Cassie. I'm afraid it made you feel—"

"Dirty."

Not looking at her, he tapped a yellow pencil on his desk. "Will you come to my apartment tonight?"

"Steve, I'm not sure I—"

"Please, Cassie. I want to talk to you. It's important."

She felt that she needed time away from him, time to assess her new feelings about their affair, but she agreed reluctantly.

STEVE CAME right to the point. "Cassie, I know that we agreed on no strings, but the situation has changed."

"I don't think there's a—"

"Please. Let me talk." He paced to the kitchen and back before he spoke. "You are very important to me, dear. I hated our having to run away from Aspen."

Cassie folded her hands in her lap. Was he leading toward a breakup?

He stopped pacing and looked her over like a trial lawyer measuring the temperament of a jury. "I am considering getting a divorce."

Cassie looked up, startled. It was the last thing she had expected him to say. She remembered suddenly what Allene Perkins had told her: "A married man, he'll lie to you for the sheer fun of lying." No. Steve Reilly was not that kind of man. But if he meant it, if he really intended to get a divorce, then how would she feel about it? To be— she forced herself to face the word—to be an adultress was bad enough, but to be a homebreaker was worse, far worse. She said it aloud, trying the words. "You would divorce Dorothea?"

He did not look at her. "I thought you should know that I'm thinking about it."

He had not made the decision yet, she thought, and to her surprise she was tremendously relieved.

Steve sat down beside her and took her hand. "I will promise you one thing, Cassie. I will never again put you in a position which could cause you embarrassment. That is beneath you."

"Thank you, Steve."

"For now, shall we just go on as we have been?"

She hesitated a minute too long and then she could only say, "Yes, I suppose so." It was later that she realized she had let pass the one moment when she could have, when she should have, made a statement.

IN APRIL Cassie met Billy Ben Farley for the first time. The interested parties gathered in the office of John Beggs, Farley's attorney. Billy Ben was a big red-faced man who chewed nervously on the stump of a burnt-out cigar. Myrtle Farley looked at her husband once and then concentrated on her big hands, folding and unfolding them in her lap. Billy Ben and Beggs sat on one side of a conference table and on the other side were Myrtle, Cassie and Steve Reilly.

"I know you've kept me up to date on the situation," Steve had told her, "but you don't need my help."

"Just for moral support, Steve. This one is big."

As it turned out, it was big but it was simple. The settlement was the one clear, straightforward fact in a web of interacting companies, of assets transferred, hidden and transferred again. Steve Reilly's leg-men, however, had done their work well, and had guided Cassie along a narrow winding trail through a forest of agreements and company registrations and debentures until she knew it as well as she knew the path from her back door to the alley.

Billy Ben Farley and his lawyer knew the trail, too, and could not deny the fact that it was Billy Ben who had laid it out. With the possibility of criminal charges facing him, he had no choice. In the divorce settlement, he signed over to Myrtle Farley sixty percent of Farley Oil.

When he signed the final paper Cassie thought he looked twenty-five years older than Myrt, but she realized that the man had just signed away years of his life. Her surge of sympathy ended abruptly when he stood up and shouted at Myrtle.

"I'll get you for this, Myrt! You just wait. I'll get Farley Oil away from you in the long run!"

"Mr. Farley," Cassie said briskly, "I hope we do not have to add threatening behavior to a possible list of charges."

He turned on her. "You bitch! You did this!"

Steve pushed his chair back, but Myrtle Farley waved him off.

"You watch your mouth, Billy Benjamin Farley. There's no call for you to yell at Cassie." She smiled at her former husband, almost with love. "Billy Ben, honey, there ain't no use in you getting upset. You just go out and make you a new company, hear? And if you want to fight me for control of Farley Oil, you just do that little thing. I always did like a good fight."

Billy Ben laughed abruptly. "Yeah, Myrt, you surefire did." He sat down and eyed her speculatively. "And I never did see anybody match up to you in a fair fight."

A week later a well-dressed man in his fifties was waiting when Cassie returned from lunch. She went into her office and called Leta. "Are you sure he isn't a client for Steve or Rob?"

"He asked for you."

"Okay, send him in."

She seated the man and he gave her his card. "Joseph T. Bullard, Chairman of the Board, Bullard Drilling, Inc."

Cassie hid her surprise. "How can I help you, Mr. Bullard?"

"My wife's suing me for divorce."

"Yes?"

"It's my second wife, you see. She's a lot younger than me and she wants to take me for a bundle. That's why I came to you."

"I don't understand."

"Oh, your name is getting around in Dallas, young lady. They say you could pry a fat divorce settlement out of Ebenezer Scrooge." He grinned. "I want to get you on retainer before my wife gets a chance at you."

THE NEXT MORNING Steve summoned Cassie to his office. "I've been tied up on the Texas Company deal and haven't congratulated you yet. Good work on the Farley case, Cassie. Excellent work, in fact. You handled the settlement meeting with a good deal of finesse."

"Why, thank you, Steve. And thank you for going to it with me."

"I didn't do a damn thing."

"You were there if I needed you."

"I hope I always will be, Cassie."

To Cassie, there were odd resonances in his statement.

"How many clients do you have now?" he asked, in an abrupt change of subject.

"Well, five."

"How many of those are *pro bono?*"

Cassie blushed. "Two."

"Who are the paying customers?"

"Two women Allene referred to me—"

"They'll be loaded. Good fees there."

"—and a new client who came in this morning. A man."

Steve raised his eyebrows. "I hadn't heard about that. Who?"

"Joe Bullard. Bullard Drilling."

"Well, I'll be damned!" He laughed. "I think you have showed an old dog a new trick. That's great!"

"I hope so. It seems that I'm getting a reputation for wringing husbands dry, and he wants to hire me before his wife can. I'm not very comfortable with that."

"Get comfortable. Believe me, his fee will ease the pain. And look, I want to go over your investment portfolio with you. With the Farley fee coming in, you'll need to make some changes. Tonight?"

"Oh, yes, Steve. I'd appreciate . . ."

He waved off her thanks. "Back to work now."

The next week was hot for April. One still night Cassie and Steve made love and dozed off, but Cassie was awakened later by the sound of rain. A breeze came up and carried in the scent of growing things. She sniffed, but the wisp of scent was overwhelmed by the smell of their bodies, of sweat and stale sex. Cassie pulled away from Steve, who slept on soundly, and sat up in the damp tangled sheets. She put her head on her bare knees, sad because she seemed to have lost something with the loss of that fresh, rainwashed air.

Without waking Steve, Cassie dressed and walked to her car. Driving home she realized that the loss she felt was a memory, no more than that. A memory of something lost years ago: the cool, green smell of spring rain on the farm at San Bois Creek.

JOSEPH BULLARD'S wife was suing him for divorce and his defense would not be an easy one. Joe was right, the woman wanted to take him for a bundle. She had retained a slick lawyer who specialized in society divorces, and Joe, shamefaced, confessed to Cassie that they already had proof of his long-standing adulterous relationship with a department-store buyer.

"Do you intend to marry this woman, Joe?"

"Hell, no! I'm already supporting one ex-wife and it looks like I'll get stuck with another."

Cassie tapped her lower lip with her finger. "You don't seem to know much about your present wife's background, Joe. Would you mind if I put a private detective to work on it?"

"Hell, no! Do anything you can!"

The detective found nothing. Cassie began to think that either Frieda Bullard had been planning the divorce for so long that she had kept her nose clean for two years, or that she was as pure as the driven snow. Her hunch about the woman, however, would not go away. One morning, alerted by the detective, she lurked near the Ervay Street entrance of Neiman-Marcus to watch Mrs. Bullard turn her white Cadillac over to the doorman. Frieda Dorner Bullard was an overblown bleached blonde who looked as if she had known the score since long before the game was played.

Weeks went by, however, and Cassie began to lose confidence. She was twenty-seven and had practiced law for less than two years. Frieda's lawyer was older and much more experienced. At the office Cassie dug through the detective's reports and at home she dug through her memory, trying to think of something, anything that would give her a handle on Frieda Bullard.

She questioned Joe Bullard, doing her best to ignore the hints that he was beginning to worry about his choice of a lawyer. "How long have you known her, Joe, and how did you meet?"

"My first wife hired her as a housekeeper." He was obviously embarrassed. "And within a year, Maryanne and I were divorced and I married Frieda."

"Why was there such a hurry to—no, don't answer that, Joe, you aren't the first man to . . ."

"I guess not. Say, Cassie, I thought of something just as I was going to sleep last night. It seems to me that Frieda worked for the Gregsons, neighbors of ours, before Maryanne hired her."

"Where is Frieda from originally?"

"Kansas City, she said."

In desperation, Cassie called Mrs. Gregson that afternoon. Yes, Frieda Dorner had been her housekeeper for about six months, until Maryanne Bullard had offered her more money.

Cassie remembered the white Cadillac outside Neiman-Marcus. Frieda had plenty of money now, but she had not earned it by housekeeping; she had married it. Idly, she said, "Did Frieda Dorner drive for you, Mrs. Gregson? Did she do errands or—"

"Oh, yes. She was a very good driver."

"And had a driver's license, of course."

"Of course! Our insurance . . ." Mrs. Gregson hesitated. "I don't know that I ever actually *saw* it."

"Do you happen to know where Frieda Dorner came from?"

"Oh, yes." Mrs. Gregson sounded relieved to be on safer ground. "She mentioned it several times. She was from Joplin, Missouri."

Cassie's pulse quickened. She called the detective at once and asked him to check with the driver's license bureaus in both Texas and Missouri.

In the end, the documents revealed a pitiful little story. Frieda cried when Cassie and Joe Bullard confronted her and her lawyer with the proof: the Joplin marriage license and Alfred Dorner's deposition that he had married Frieda and that the marriage had never been dissolved. All she had wanted to do was get away from Alfred, Frieda said, that was all she had wanted. And then when she saw all that money and when Joe Bullard started in—it was just too much for her.

Cassie could understand that feeling of being in a trap. She pulled Joe Bullard out of earshot. "Give her some money anyway, Joe," she said. "At least let her keep the car."

"We ought to throw her in jail! Why give money to a bigamist?"

"I don't know. Maybe just because you have so much and she has so little, so damned little."

"Maybe I will," he said thoughtfully. "Maybe I will." He gave Cassie a fatherly hug. "You did a hell of a job for me, Cassie. You ever want a job with Bullard Drilling, you got it! In the meantime, I'll send you some clients."

"That's fine, Joe. That's just fine."

Cassie called the office and went home. She stood under a hot shower for a long time, but she still did not feel clean.

WHEN THE Bullard fee went through, Cassie deposited her share and went car shopping. She knew precisely what she wanted, and she drove her Chevrolet from dealer to dealer until she found it: a white convertible with red leather seats. Since that first night when Jimmy Steele had driven his car out of the country-club gates, that night when the air was filled with music and she saw the men in light suits and women in linen dresses, since then that car had been to her the symbol of wealth. She could afford it now. The chrome glittered in the sunshine and the fresh white paint gleamed; but most important, when she sat in the car she could smell the leather seats and it was the smell of money.

That night Cassie put the top down on her new car and took a long drive through the countryside. The air was pure and fresh with a hint of sage and there were a million stars in the Texas sky. In the clear night the only cloud was over her own future.

Everyone she loved, even a little, seemed to have clear, unfogged lives. Steve Reilly had once told her that he was a pragmatist. She knew the word, but she had looked up the precise meaning: one who deals with facts and events, a practical man. A man with an important career, a beautiful wife and children, and he still wanted an affair with Cassie Steele. Was she a fact or an event? And there was Dixon Steele, the one man whom she had been able to love. He was an idealist, who dealt not with facts and events as they were but as what he wanted them to be. And there was Granny, who had not had the luxury of choice. Granny had merely survived, but that was valid, too. You had to survive.

And then there was Cassie herself. On one level, a professional level, she was doing much more than surviving. She was succeeding far beyond her dreams. She was driving a white convertible with red leather seats and she had paid for it by her own hard work.

She only wished that the money she had paid over to the dealer had been as pure-white as the car. Digging into people's pasts like an armadillo digging for maggots, searching out the slimy parts of their lives, using their past sins against them: it was a horrible way to live. She had separated Vernon Jayson from his family. She had taken Billy Ben's company away from him. She had sent Frieda Dorner Bullard back to a personal hell called Joplin, Missouri.

To pay for a car. To pay for a way of life. She knew that other lawyers would take the cases if she didn't. A pragmatist could live with that, and dig and cull and spy. But did the fact that someone else would do it anyway justify her doing it?

The choice was hers. She could ignore the reality of life and take only cases in which the participants were noble and generous. An idealist could accept that, but wishing people were noble did not make them so. To reject a plea for help because the pleader was less than perfect could never be justified.

Was there some middle ground between idealism and pragmatism? And if she found that magical place, would she recognize it?

Again and again, as she drove through the cloudless night, she asked one question. How am I to live?

CASSIE ARRANGED to meet Steve the next Tuesday night. He was in the apartment, sitting on the couch, when she arrived.

"Well, hello, Cassie. Want me to fix you a drink?"

She took a deep breath. "Steve, I want to talk to you. I . . . I think we should stop seeing each other."

He leaned forward slowly and braced his hand on the coffee table. "Because I'm married."

Cassie put down her handbag and dropped into a chair. "That and other things, Steve. Your wife, your children—I don't know. It's tangled up with my law practice, too. There is so much dirt in this world, so much cheating."

Steve grinned. "Are you becoming an idealist?"

"No!" More calmly she said, "It's just that I don't feel right about us anymore." She gestured at the room. "It isn't right."

"Is that a valid reason for ending an affair?"

Cassie looked at him steadily. It's as valid as your talk about divorcing your wife."

"I meant that, Cassie Steele!"

"Oh, you did, did you? And what action did you take?"

He looked away. "Well, I meant it when I said it."

Cassie laughed. "Oh, Steve!"

"What's so damn funny?"

"Us! You and me. Hey, you with the trained legal mind, don't you see what we're doing?"

He looked at her suspiciously. "No. I do not see that we are 'doing' anything at all."

"We're trying to assign fault, that's what. It's your tort, not mine! Look, Steve." Cassie went to the couch and sat down next to him. "We both feel guilty as hell. I think we've both been feeling it for quite a while, but we kept trying to convince ourselves that we were too adult, too sophisticated to feel something as old-fashioned as guilt."

"I have never felt guilty!"

"Is that why you had us packed and out of the Hotel Jerome in fifteen minutes flat?"

"I thought that girl would tell Dorothea—"

"Would she have divorced you, or shot you?"

"Of course not."

Cassie laughed. "And I think I had to buy a new car to prove that I didn't feel guilty."

He tried to smile. "Ha! That car cost you more than the trip to Aspen cost me."

"Aspen," Cassie whispered. "Aspen was . . . wonderful, wasn't it, Steve?"

"It was. Maybe if we could just go back—"

"No, love, there's no going back. But we can remember it, can't we?"

"Ah, damn it, Cassie, I don't want to lose you."

"We can't live with it any longer, can we? We can't live with the guilt."

"No. You're right." His face brightened. "You know, I think it's the kids I worry about. They trust me."

"You know they love you, Steve. And so does Dorothea."

"And I love her, damn it." He put his arm around Cassie. "But I loved you, too, a little."

"And I loved you, Steve. A little."

"It will be tough, seeing each other around the office."

"Maybe so, maybe not. We're pretty bright, Steve. We can probably find ways to handle it."

"Oh, what the hell, Cassie Steele. We had a good run for our money, didn't we?"

"That we did, Steve Reilly. That we did."

Chapter 33

DURING THE NEXT TWO YEARS Cassandra Taylor Steele's professional reputation grew rapidly. She was respected not only as a top-notch divorce lawyer, but also as one who managed to stay clean in a business which could become very dirty. Her clientele grew, also, and broadened. Dorothea Reilly sent her a client, a woman in her late forties who was bored with a stodgy, childless marriage to a stodgy, cheerless banker. That case opened the doors of old-money Dallas. Cassie lost a few cases, but she won more. As Steve Reilly put it, somewhat to Cassie's dismay, "You always seem to know where the body is buried."

Cassie began to meet some of the old ranching families, too. In Texas, oil provided the cash but ranching provided the pedigree. Oilman could buy in, but old Texas knew that it took at least one generation of use to put the right kind of patina on new money. Cassie went to weekend parties at grand old houses in West Texas where the furniture was covered with fabric that could live with cowboys' boots and where there was likely to be an executive airplane tied down on a landing strip behind the house.

She was invited to the big parties in Dallas, spectacular affairs like the party at Brook Hollow Country Club, where the walls of the club were draped with twenty-five hundred yards of silver lamé.

She went to parties in Fort Worth, too, where people still quoted Billy Rose's dictum from the 1936 Texas Centennial celebrations: "Go to Dallas to be educated, come to Fort Worth to be entertained."

Her work, however, did not satisfy her, and the parties did not alleviate the problem. She was becoming a well-known lawyer for both her divorce work and her *pro bono* contributions, but she felt restless and without direction. She confessed her unhappiness to Fran one night.

"Too much, too soon," Fran said. "I'll tell you what, let's go out and tie one on. You look like you need it!"

They had some drinks and had dinner, but Cassie did not tie one on. She might not know what she needed, but she did know what she did not need. Her father's life was proof that drinking did not solve problems. She wished that she could find an easy answer. Work was not the answer, because work had to stop sometime, and when it did the skinny black fingers of depression picked away at her mind.

One night she dreamed of the Old-Timers' reunion she had gone to with her grandmother. She saw again the vision of a raft floating down the stream, floating on gray-green water. Granny was on the raft, wearing her blue velvet hat, and her father was there, clear-eyed and happy, and Dixon Steele, tall and lanky and young, with the breeze ruffling his dark hair. And Naomi Bencher, with the Turner School children clutching at her skirt. They were singing an old hymn, and waving good-bye to those left behind on the beach. Cassie was there, too, but she was on the shore, alone, waving and waving and crying, "Wait! Oh, wait for me!"

The dream lingered in her mind for weeks.

Myrtle Farley, who had almost doubled the assets of Farley Oil since she took over the company, invited Cassie to a house party at her ranch north of Amarillo, and Cassie asked Ted Abernathy to go along as her escort.

"That's a hell of a long drive for a party," he said.

"Myrt's sending a plane to pick up some of the Dallas guests. Her new Beechcraft seats eight."

Ted whistled. "Shades of *Giant,*" he said.

Cassie laughed. By July of 1954 everyone with any interest in oil and ranching had read the novel and appeared to be acting it out, either in fun or in real life. "Myrt loves that book, Ted, so you behave yourself. You can dress appropriately, though. Which part do you want to play?"

"Jett Rink, of course! What able-bodied American boy wouldn't want to be a sex fiend like Jett Rink?"

Cassie had learned that the true story of oil and cattle in Texas was far less believable than Edna Ferber's fictional account. From the time Indians found oil seeps and called the spots "sour dirt," the oil business in Texas had been peopled with characters of almost mythic stature. "Dad" Joiner, for instance, was ready to start drilling on a lease north of Beaumont when a woman came running to tell him about her dream the night before. He moved his rig west, to the point the woman had seen in her dream, and in January of 1901 brought in Spindletop, the gusher that spouted oil two hundred feet into the air and opened the great East Texas oil fields. Dad Joiner was a wildcatter, one of the nomadic independent drillers who got by with what equipment they could beg, borrow or steal and found oil by using the science of "creekology": eyeballing streamflow in an area in order to estimate a good drilling site.

There was David Harold Byrd, too, who was known as "Dry-Hole" Byrd, partly because of his initials but mostly because he drilled fifty-six dry holes in a row before he struck oil. And H. L. Hunt of Dallas. In 1948, *Life* had said that he was the richest man in the world, with assets of $260 million and an income of $1 million dollars a week. A conservative banker in Dallas laughed at the figures, however. He said Hunt did not have over a hundred million or so in assets, and that his income wasn't over $1 million dollars a month. "These things," he said soberly, "tend to be exaggerated in the press."

And in the fifties, oilmen bought land and aspired to reach the highest caste in Texas, that of the cattle rancher.

In the ranch house oil had bought for her, Myrtle Farley sashayed among clumps of guests like a bantam hen counting her brood. Myrt was not one to wear the restrained English riding clothes of the East Coast gentry. She wore a white Stetson hat, and a white suede shirt and riding skirt with fringe on every seam and so many brilliants that her outfit resembled a bullfighter's suit of lights. Her custom-made Tony Lama boots were made of ostrich skin dyed fuchsia.

"Oh, my God!" Ted whispered, and Cassie glared at him.

"Don't you say that, Ted Abernathy! Myrtle Farley worked hard for every cent she's got, and if this is the way she wants to enjoy it, then I say more power to her!"

Ted looked down at her coolly. "Funny, isn't it, the way your perceptions change? I can remember when you were eager to learn something about good taste. You think you have enough money now so you can set standards for yourself and everyone else? Think again, kid. You're just a little frog in a big puddle, you know."

Cassie gasped. They had known each other for four years now. At first, he had taken her places, to dinner at the right restaurants, to parties like the one after the TU-OU game, the party where she had seen Dixon Steele. For the last two years, she had taken him to parties such as this, parties where the hosts sent airplanes to pick up their guests, where favors for the ladies might be diamond earrings from Neiman-Marcus. It was nice for her to have him there, ready and willing, when she needed an escort. A woman without a man in her life needed three things: an available escort, a reliable automobile mechanic and a really good jar opener in her kitchen drawer. Jar openers, however, did not talk back. Perhaps it was fair to say that she had used Ted in the beginning, but he had come to use her, too.

"If that's the way you feel, Ted," she said carefully, "I suppose we shouldn't see each other again."

"I've outlived my usefulness?"

Cassie blushed. "Ted, I didn't say——"

"It's all right, I'm a big boy now. And you're a big girl, aren't you? You're getting quite a reputation as one of the comers in Dallas." He hesitated, looking at her oddly. "And quite a reputation as a ball breaker."

"Ted!"

He smiled, a flash of white teeth in the dim room. "My, my, I do believe that's Melinda Burton over there. Rich daddy, very rich daddy, and on top of that, she's a sweet little Southern gal who knows what real men like."

"Real men!" Cassie hissed. "You wouldn't know a real man if you saw him!"

His eyes were wide and innocent. 'Why, I sure would, Cassie, old boy. I can tell a real man when I see her."

Cassie retreated to her room, trying not to cry. It was late when she heard a knock on her door and Myrt's stage whisper.

"Cassie? Cassie, you asleep?"

"I'm awake, Myrt. Come on in."

Cassie had changed into her nightgown and was propped on pillows in the maple-framed double bed. Myrt sat down in the armchair and eased off one fuchsia boot.

"My Lord," she said, rubbing her instep, "all this partying takes it out of you, don't it?"

"Yes. Yes, it does."

"Cassie, listen, I got to talk to you about something. You know, me and Farley Oil are getting along just fine. Old Billy Ben made a big play for the company about a year ago, but I nailed him to the wall and he ain't going to give me no more trouble. I got trouble coming down here from Washington, though. Them bureaucrats up there ain't got no sense when it comes to the oil business. They got these penny-ante regulations and rules—I swear to you, Cassie, they're going to rule-and-regulation me to death!"

Cassie nodded sympathetically. "I know, Myrt. The amount a company has to spend on filling out forms to comply with—"

"Yeah, that's it. Well, Cassie, here's my idea. You done enough divorce work now. You come to work for me, be my in-house counsel or whatever. I'll put you on the board of directors and I'll pay you twice whatever it is you're making now. How about it?"

Cassie sat up straight. "Myrt! Why me?"

Myrtle grinned. "Because you're smart and you're tough. You can take them little government pissants apart limb from tree."

Cassie sank back on her pillows. "Because I'm a ball breaker?"

"You sure as hell are!" Myrt looked puzzled. "Hold on there. That ain't the kind of language you use. What's up?"

"Someone used that term tonight. He called me a ball breaker."

"Who? You tell me who and I'll kick his ass from hell to breakfast!"

"No, Myrt. It doesn't matter. Maybe I needed to learn that about myself."

"Hell, I bet it was that Ted. What happened? You turn him

down, and he had to get back at you? Well, face it, Cassie, you ain't exactly sweetness and light. Most of these yahoos just ain't man enough to handle a woman like you or me."

"Is there any man who can?"

"Hell, yes! Look at Billy Ben! I'll give him credit for that. You just got to find somebody that's as sure about himself as you are about yourself. That's all."

"That's all?" Cassie laughed. "I don't think I'm as self-confident as you think, Myrt."

"Oh yes, you are. You're good, Cassie, damn good, and you know it as well as I do." She pulled on her boot and stood up. "Now, you think about coming to work for me, you hear?"

FOR THE REST of the weekend, Cassie played the field and had more fun than she had had in months. If she was considered too mannish, she might as well have fun as a man. She flirted outrageously but made it clear that she was committed to nothing and to no one.

The party ended, however, and at home in Dallas Cassie found herself sinking back into depression. She worked harder than ever, burning the hours, leaving no time to brood.

One morning she went to Steve Reilly's office. She had long since taken over the running of her own investment portfolio, but she wanted to get his advice on a real estate purchase, development land on the Central Expressway.

Steve glanced over her portfolio and whistled. "Cassie, you're doing extremely well with your investments."

"I've had a good teacher."

He grinned at her. "So you have. Why don't you ever spend any money on yourself? You can afford a bigger house now, you know."

"Why do I need a bigger house? There's only me. But you'll be pleased to hear that I have ordered a new car."

"Ordered it? Why?"

"Because the dealer didn't have what I wanted. Dark green with green leather upholstery."

Steve laughed. "A Cadillac, I assume."

Cassie laughed, too. "Right. I'm not rich enough yet to get away with driving a cheap car. A Cadillac convertible."

"You said, 'yet.' " He leaned back in his chair. "Cassie, I think it's high time you became my partner."

"Steve!" She started to jump up, but instead she sat back. "Before—I think I should tell you something. Myrtle Farley has offered me the job of house counsel for Farley Oil."

Steve frowned. "That's not your field, Cassie."

"At twice what I'm making now."

"I can't match that."

"I know, Steve, and I'm not trying to get you to up the ante. I just thought I should tell you."

He turned his chair and looked out the window. When he turned back, he looked serious. "All right, look. I was going to wait with this, but—Cassie, I want you to take this partnership and use it as a base to move into the political scene."

"I've never even thought about politics!"

"Well, it's time to start thinking. You're getting quite a reputation in Dallas—"

"People keep telling me that," she said bitterly.

"But you need to expand your contacts. Talk to law-school classes, then to civic groups. I've got Dick Carter lined up—"

"And Dorothea?"

"And Dorothea. She's one of your biggest fans."

"I don't know, Steve. I . . ."

"Well, think about it, Cassie. But whether or not you decide on politics, if you decide you want the partnership it goes into effect on the fifteenth of September. Reilly and Steele."

"That's just a few weeks!"

"Oh, mercy me," he said, pretending to be worried. "Is that too soon for you, dear?"

"Not one day too soon!" She jumped up and ran around his desk to hug him. "Thank you, Steve!"

"Oh, hell, kid. You've earned it."

CASSIE DROVE HOME to University Park with her mind whirling. A partnership. Politics! At that moment, politics was more exciting than the partnership. Perhaps it was through politics that she could find a way to live. She could escape pragmatism, dealing with the facts, and idealism, wishing that the facts were different, by using the political system to change those facts.

The minute she was in the house, Cassie called Fran Jordan to tell her the great news, but there was no answer and she remembered that Fran had gone to New York for a week.

She sat down on a dining room chair, her hand still on the telephone. She had to tell someone!

The excitement went out of her like air from a leaky balloon. Slowly she removed her hand from the telephone and laid it flat on the table. There was no one to call. From the packed dirt yard of a sharecropper's shack she had moved to a partner's desk in a successful Dallas law firm. She had reached a major milestone in her life. And there was no one to share it with, not one person who knew the whole story of Cassie Taylor Steele and could see this day in the light of all the days that had gone before it.

She stood up and wandered aimlessly toward the kitchen.

If only Fran were home! There were so few people who had known large parts of her life. Dixon Steele would understand what the partnership meant to her. But she could not, would not call Dix.

Cassie stopped in the middle of the kitchen. There was one other person who knew what the farm was like and what Cassie's life in Whitman had been.

Naomi Bencher would understand a milestone.

Cassie shrugged and took a bottle of milk from the refrigerator. So what? She had not seen Naomi since 1942. Twelve years. She had not seen Naomi since the week before Mrs. Butterfield handed Cassie a letter: gone forever.

Cassie's hand shook and she put the milk bottle on the kitchen counter. Gone forever. Granny. Dix. Naomi. All of the people she had loved were gone from her. Gone forever. Down that beautiful river, on that raft, and she had been left behind.

She went into the dining room and sipped at a glass of milk while she stared at the telephone as if she thought that it would ring and bring her a message, a directive as to how she should proceed.

It did not ring, of course. Why would she expect it to ring? She had worked for everything she had, she thought bitterly. She had worked hard. Why would she expect even small favors at this point in her life? Directives were her own responsibility. She picked up the receiver and dialed Information.

The first long-distance number led to another and that number to yet another, but finally she heard a voice she recognized no matter how crisp and efficient it was, no matter how impersonal.

"Base library, Captain Bencher speaking."

A great displacement occurred within Cassie, like the rumbling shifts of oil before a gusher blows and releases it built-up pressure.

"Naomi? Naomi, it's Cassie Taylor."

ON SATURDAY of Labor Day weekend, Cassie spent the morning preparing the house and trying to prepare her mind for her visitor. As the hours passed she found it more and more difficult to remember the good days at Turner School and in Whitman. She could think only of the things James Steele had told her about Naomi Bencher and the accusations that had been made and then suppressed for the sake of the Women's Army Corps.

She was in the kitchen when she heard a car stop in front of the house. Her eyes darted from cabinet to counter to refrigerator like those of a trapped animal searching for a bolt-hole. She had made a mistake, a dreadful mistake. What on earth had possessed her to call Naomi Bencher? After twelve years, what would they have to say to each other?

A car door slammed. Cassie took a deep breath and went through the house to stand behind the screen door where she could look out without being seen.

A black Plymouth coupe was parked at the curb, a foursquare no-nonsense car, and standing next to it was a woman as foursquare and no-nonsense as the car itself. She was short and stocky, a solid barrel shape in a gray-and-white-striped seersucker dress. Her legs were stocky, too, cylinders ending in plain white pumps with low heels. Her hair was cut short, in an almost masculine style. Her face was indistinct in the glare.

Cassie pushed open the screen and called out, "Naomi?"

The woman raised one hand in an indecisive gesture and Cassie threw open the door and ran out to the street. She stopped at the curb. The woman turned toward her and Cassie saw her face clearly.

Twelve years ago, it had been a thin pale face, but now it was plump and ruddy. The eyes were brown behind thick glasses in clear plastic frames. She smiled and it was Naomi Bencher's smile, sweet and gentle and sad.

"Cassie," she said softly. "I can hardly believe it. Cassie Taylor. I mean, Cassie Steele. You've changed. You've grown up."

"Naomi, I'm twenty-nine years old!"

Naomi laughed uncertainly. "And I'm forty-two. My God." She reached out tentatively, but Cassie became a whirlwind of talk and action.

"Is your overnight bag in the car? Let me get it. And I know you'll want to wash up and change, such a long way from Lawton and on such a miserably hot day. You must be dying of thirst! I'll run right in and make you some iced tea."

Naomi changed into cotton slacks, a loose red shirt and tennis shoes. In spite of the heat, Cassie put down the top of her green Cadillac convertible and drove her all over town, hurrying her from one sight to the next like an overzealous tour guide. She drove past Neiman-Marcus and the Highland Park Village and Southern Methodist University. She showed Naomi Preston Hollow, pointing out the houses where her clients lived. Over dinner, Cassie told her about some of her experiences of the past twelve years, but her account was as well edited as a job application form: 1942–1943, secretary in a law office; 1943–1945, wife to Jimmy Steele, 1945–1954, studying law and practicing her profession.

Naomi reciprocated, telling Cassie about receiving a commission in the WAC in 1942, her rapid promotions as she reorganized the libraries on several expanded wartime army bases and how in 1943 she had been permanently assigned to Fort Sill and, when the war ended, had accepted a lower rank in order to stay in the peacetime army but had been promoted to a captaincy during the "police action" in Korea.

After dinner Cassie kept up her inconsequential chatter while Naomi helped her with the dishes, but when they went out to the back porch in search of a cool place to sit and have their coffee, she ran out of things to say. They sat in uncomfortable silence while the blue sky changed to purple and the lights of Dallas flickered in the night.

A full moon rose in the east, an immense lemon-colored disk pasted on a blue-black sky.

"What is it, Cassie?" Naomi said quietly. "What's wrong?"

"Nothing! I've told you how well my career is going and the——"

"That isn't what I mean, and you know it. Why did you ask me to come here when you can't even stand to look at me?"

Cassie's cup clattered in its saucer. "That's ridiculous, Naomi! I didn't mean to . . ." She leaned back in her chair. She had called Naomi because she needed a friend. A sister. Was there a right way for a sister to be? She herself was not perfect. She was good and bad, like everyone. And so, indeed, was her friend, her sister.

Moonlight crept across the yard and the maple tree was starkly lighted in black and white.

"I know why you left Whitman," Cassie said quietly. "Why you left me. I didn't understand it for a long time, until I found out about the young corporal, the woman."

"So you know." Naomi set her cup on the table carefully, as if a single sound might shatter the pale light. "Then why did you ask me to come here?"

Cassie hesitated, hoping that she had not ruined it. "Because you are my friend."

"And you thought that it wouldn't bother you, but now you find out that it does." She sighed. "All right, I understand. I'll go now." The chair creaked as she pushed herself up.

"No!" Cassie jumped up. "You don't understand at all! That's not it!" She touched Naomi's arm but jerked her hand back as if it had received an electric shock. Slowly, deliberately, she put her hand back on her friend's arm. Naomi's skin was warm and slightly damp with perspiration. "I guess I just don't know how to deal with a . . . with it."

"Say it, Cassie. 'With a lesbian.' The world won't come to an end if you say the word." She waved her hand toward the night. "The moon won't fall out of the sky."

Cassie swallowed. "Lesbian," she whispered, and then she said it again, louder. "Lesbian."

Naomi chuckled. "That's the way. There are other terms for it, quite unpleasant ones, but that one will do. And now that you've said it aloud, Cassie, do I look any different to you?"

"Of course not."

" 'If you prick us, do we not bleed? If you tickle us, do we not laugh?' "

Cassie laughed suddenly. "And if we give you half a chance, do you not quote? I've read Shakespeare, too, you know."

"Well, well. As they said back at Turner School, 'Who'da thunk it?' Cassie Taylor reading Shakespeare." She peered at Cassie in the moonlight. "What have you read?"

Cassie laughed. "You can take the teacher out of Turner School, but you can't take Turner School out of—"

"All right, all right! What Shakespeare have you read?"

"Most of the plays, some of the sonnets."

"I bet you read *Romeo and Juliet* twice."

"How did you know—oh, Naomi!" Cassie threw her arms around her and suddenly the two of them were awash with laughter, as if a dam had broken and released a flood of happiness.

"Wait!" Naomi pushed her away. "I've got a cooler with a bottle of champagne in the trunk of the car. I brought it along just in case."

"Well, 'in case' has happened, Naomi!"

They toasted each other and Cassie's career and the Women's Army Corps, and as the moon crossed the southern sky they sat in the insect-loud darkness and told each other what really had happened since they had last met.

"So the charges weren't suppressed, Cassie, no matter what your father-in-law said about—"

"You don't have to tell me, Naomi. We're friends and that's all that matters."

"No, I want you to know. The charges were dismissed, thrown out of court. The corporal was a mean, vindictive girl who was furious because I would not recommend her for officer candidate school. There was nothing to it."

"Don't you hate her, Naomi? Don't you hate all of them?"

"Hate?" She was silent for a moment. "I suppose I did, at first. But hate doesn't solve anything, does it? And when the truth finally came to light, the army was fair. Believe me, they wouldn't have let me stay in after the war if there were any questions about my moral standards. There was nothing to it, there couldn't have been." She hesitated. "I know what I . . . how I feel, but I've rarely been able to follow through."

"Oh, Naomi, that's sad." Cassie was startled to hear herself say it, but she knew that it was true.

Naomi sighed. "I don't know, Cassie. There are many kinds of love, and few of them are physical."

Cassie looked out at the darkness. "But you've never been attracted to men." She clenched her fists on the table. "Perhaps you're lucky." By the time she had finished telling Naomi about her entanglements with the men of the Steele family, the last of the champagne was flat, and Cassie felt flat, too, with despair.

Naomi did not speak for a long time. Finally she sighed. "I see why you said I was lucky not to be attracted to men. But you, Cassie, are you attracted to men or to their power?"

Cassie laughed bitterly. "Is there any difference?"

Naomi sighed. " 'Aye, there's the rub.' I'm not surprised that you feel that way. You were such an—"

"An innocent, Naomi. That's what you called me back in Whitman. But not now. Not now."

"What about this Steve Reilly, Cassie? What was all that?"

Cassie leaned back in her chair and stared at the night sky. "I don't know. I really don't. But it was important, Naomi. It really was important. And it was good."

"Yes. Yes, I can see that."

BY SUNDAY MORNING they were old friends again. Cassie even showed Naomi the contents of her closet.

"My God," Naomi said in awed respect. "Do you shop anywhere other than Neiman-Marcus, Cassie?"

"Sure, but you can count on Neiman's. Hey, now, don't forget that you're the one who taught me how to dress. 'Neatness and simplicity,' remember?"

"I remember. But I didn't know much about clothes, not really, and I don't know now. I would have never imagined, for instance, that the elegant simplicity of this Dior dress would require such a complicated design."

Cassie glanced at her in delight. "Naomi, oh, Naomi, I love your mind! No wonder I've missed you. That's what life is all about, isn't it?"

"I haven't the foggiest idea what you're talking about."

"Oh, yes, you do. You just said it: how complicated it is to make things simple."

Naomi stared at her for a moment and then nodded slowly. "Yes. I see." She smiled. "And I see that you were right last night. You aren't an innocent now."

Chapter 34

 CAPTAIN NAOMI BENCHER went back to the base library at Fort Sill, Oklahoma, but she left behind a list of books for Cassie to read and one Thoreau quotation to mull over. "Our life is frittered away by detail. . . . Simplify, simplify."

Cassie could not get the words out of her mind. She looked at her office in a new way, and at her life. If she were indeed to go into politics, she had to simplify both her work and her play. She would have to learn to say no.

"I'LL HAVE TO turn down your offer, Myrt," Cassie said over drinks at the Athletic Club. "A partnership in the firm is my best move right now." She did not want to talk about politics yet, not even to Myrtle Farley.

Myrt drank a healthy slug of Wild Turkey. "I can see that, Cassie, but I'm sorry. I wanted to see you give them Washington boys a good going-over. I'd hold the job for you, but I got to get somebody in there pretty quick. Tell you what, though, you do some studying up on oil and gas regulations, and I'll put you on retainer to back up my home team. Will your new partner okay that?"

"A retainer from Farley Oil? Myrt, my new partner will dance in the streets."

Myrt snickered. "Well, I'll be the first to cut in, I'll tell you that. Steve Reilly is one cowboy I could really go for!"

Cassie was delighted to report the entire conversation to Steve the next morning.

He leaned back in his chair. "Myrtle Farley? Hmm. Well, if Dorothea dumps me and my new partner bankrupts the firm to keep up with the Beautiful People in University Park, maybe I'll become a rich woman's plaything. Old Myrt's pretty spry, you know."

"With my retainer from Farley Oil the firm can probably scrape up enough money so I can meet my house payments and not bankrupt Reilly and Steele."

"Oh, I'd say so. Yes, ma'am!" He put on his glasses and picked up his appointment book. "You'll need to clear some time to sit in on my client conferences, Cassie. You have a good grounding in oil and gas law, but we'll want to polish it."

Over the next few months Cassie began a gradual shift from a divorce-oriented practice to oil and gas. She kept up her *pro bono* work, but she began to refer paying clients to Bill Clayman, a new associate in the office.

Her long-distance calls to Naomi made her life outside the office less lonely but still she dreaded the long night hours.

In early March, Cassie suggested to Naomi that since it was almost two hundred miles from Lawton to Dallas they might meet halfway to spend a weekend together. They agreed to meet at Ardmore, where they could enjoy the last weekend of March in the Arbuckle Mountains.

Cassie and Naomi were comfortable together that weekend. Their conversation fluttered like a dragonfly over a stream, resting on the past and then darting off to touch on a book or a movie or Naomi's future with the Women's Army Corps.

For Cassie, as well, there was the treat of being in the countryside in springtime. No sirens, no ringing telephones, no parties in smoky rooms, just the peace of being with an old friend in a comfortable but undemanding environment.

Cassie knew that Naomi would have to leave on Sunday afternoon, but she had warned Steve that she herself would stay in Ardmore that night and not return to the office until Tuesday. She planned to catch up on her reading and to leave Ardmore at noon on Monday for an easy drive home.

Cassie had dinner sent to her room on Sunday night, and while she ate she read the latest oil regulations, making careful notes. At eleven she stretched luxuriously and slipped into bed. She switched off the bedside lamp and with darkness came the darkness in her mind.

Why? she asked silently. She had enjoyed a delightful weekend, she was rested and happy. Why should she suddenly be enfolded in a black cloud of despair? She turned restlessly, seeking as she had done so many times before, searching for an answer or, if not an answer, for some way to live with the unformulated question. Maybe she should get that new drug, Miltown, the one Fran called "the housewife's friend." Or she could sign up for two or three years of psychoanalysis, but she did not want a psychiatrist to help her plunge into the depths of her darkness. She wanted to escape it, instead, to find light.

Finally she slept, and when she woke she knew what she had to do. She had to go back to the source of the darkness, not mentally but physically.

In a flurry of activity she ordered breakfast and packed while she ate. She put her things into her car and lowered the top. At the intersection, however, she did not turn south toward Dallas. Instinctively she drove east into the morning sun, east to pick up U.S. 69 and drive north through McAlester to Ballard and then east again, into the foothills of the Ozarks, east to San Bois and the farm.

BETWEEN BALLARD and San Bois, Cassie had to pull over and raise the top against the rain. As she drove on, the gray drizzle outside and the steady swish of the windshield wipers took her back to the morning of her wedding, when she and Jimmy drove to Ballard to tell his father what they had done. She did not want to think about that.

Instead, she looked at the countryside rolling past. The area was more prosperous than it had been ten years ago, when she drove this road with Dixon Steele. The farmhouses were painted now, and many of the row-crop fields had been reclaimed as pasture for the white-faced cattle grazing in green Bermuda grass. She drove through San Bois, past the clinic and the feedstore.

Cassie eased the Cadillac off of Highway 12 and onto the gravel road. The misty rain obscured the last summer's cornstalks still standing in the fields. She stopped at the place where the old track to the tenant house began. It was chilly and damp when she got out of the heated car, and she took a suede jacket from the backseat and pulled it on. She peered up the hill, into the mist. After a few moments she zipped her jacket and climbed the rocky overgrown track to the top of the hill.

The door of the privy had fallen down since the time she saw it from the road, since that spring day in 1945 when she and Dixon Steele were there together. She kicked at the flat rocks which had been the piers supporting the front porch of the cabin. Where the front room had been, the old iron cookstove, brown with rust, stood drunkenly among mist-soaked weeds. Farther back in the ruins of the house was a twisted iron frame. It took Cassie several minutes to recognize it as the remains of an iron bed frame, of the bed where she and Granny had slept. Tears pricked behind her eyes. The bed where Granny had died. She turned away and, drawn by a vague memory, she walked toward a big old oak tree. With the toe of her shoe, she pushed a rusty object on the ground. It rolled over on the wet red earth and she saw that it was an old saucepan with a few small spots of gray enamel still intact.

Cassie smiled down at the pan. This was her play place, of course. It was the place where she had stirred up pans of red-dirt mush for her babies, for Francine and Mary Priscilla, where she had fussed at her dolls and cuddled them and read aloud to them from the *Bobbs-Merrill Second Reader*. This was the place where she first saw James Steele.

Then she was drawn to look beyond, toward the gray hills where gullies cut down through limestone. Bo's territory. She remembered how silently he had moved through the woods. Not even the blue jays squawked when Bo passed by.

She shivered inside of her jacket and was a child again and the day was hot and dusty and she could hear a voice calling from the porch: "You, Cassie! Fetch me a kettle of water from the spring. Make haste, now!"

Cassie raised her face and let the mist blend with the tears on her cheeks. It was so long ago. It was all so long ago, when her play place was the one part of her limited world that belonged to Cassie Taylor, and to nobody else.

But even that had been only in a child's imagination. Her play place had belonged to James Steele. Like the lodge and the rich bottomlands by the creek, like the hills and the woods, it still belonged to James Steele. She stumbled down the rough track to her car and drove on toward the lodge.

In the gray rain the lodge sat on its foundation of round river rocks looking as if it had grown out of the land, as if it had been there as long as the land itself. The fieldstone chimney was cold and tall vacant windows stared out from beneath the veranda roof. Behind the lodge were the weathered barn and a tool shed.

She thought that she could see people in the misty shadows of the veranda. Her father. Granny, yes. And James Steele. Amelia. Jimmy. And there was Dixon, his high broad shoulders filling out an army tunic. Dixon laughing as he had laughed when they swam together in San Bois Creek. Dixon standing straight-faced and sad at the Dallas airport.

Cassie put her hands over her eyes and her tears flowed. She had been a fool to come back. A fool. What had she hoped to accomplish? To find herself? She was not here. To exorcise ghosts? Your personal ghosts will not stay in one place, submissively awaiting exorcism. They travel with you, wherever you go.

She started the car with a roar and maneuvered a U-turn in the narrow road, almost sliding into the ditch, and then she drove back toward the highway, knowing that she was driving too fast for the rutted, rain-slick clay, knowing, but not caring. Past the overgrown track up the hill, past ditches just starting to green, ditches where in August blackberry canes would be heavy with fruit. Back to the highway.

It was late that night when she pulled up to the curb in front of her house in Dallas. It was late and she was exhausted from wrestling with the steering wheel on wet highways, from wrestling with wishes and regrets. That night, she was tired enough to sleep.

TOWARD THE END OF MARCH, Steve called Cassie on the intercom. "Come to my office at eleven sharp. I want you to talk to our accountant."

"He's already done my 1954 taxes, Steve. I'm right up to date."

"Cassie, it's time to sell your downtown buildings."

"April Fool! I'll bet you thought you got me!"

The intercom speaker emitted an exasperated sigh. "Cassie. I do not joke about money."

"Right," Cassie said soberly. "I'll be there at eleven."

Cassie's thirtieth birthday came a few weeks later. She was still shaken by the size of the profit she had made on the office buildings, even though it had not yet become real money to her. It was Monopoly money, too easily won or lost to qualify as the genuine article.

She had not received any birthday cards and she hoped that she would not. She was all too aware that she had reached the continental divide of her life. On one side the waters ran back to youth, on the other they ran ahead, to old age. And it was beginning to look as though she were going to take that downhill ride all alone. Was she fated to be what Cousin Ella Mae used to call "a maiden lady"? No husband, no children. No one to be there when she needed help, no one to need her.

Allene Perkins called the office late that morning. "Doll, I need your help."

At least someone in the world needed her. "Sure, Allene. What can I do for you?"

"I've got this cowboy overload at the house, and there's a big party at the country club. Will you get all gussied up and meet me there about eight tonight?"

"To go out with one of your cowboys? Allene, I wouldn't even consider—"

"Not with a cowboy, Cassie! With me! You think I want to take a horse kisser to a big party at the country club?"

"Oh, well, in that case—"

"I'll get there early and meet you in the ladies' so we can make a grand entrance."

"Dressed to the teeth, right? Okay!"

After all, it was her birthday, even if no one was celebrating it, least of all the birthday girl. She wore a long dress of white shot silk, a gown that managed to look both virginal and extremely sophisticated. The parking attendant took her Cadillac and she swept into the ladies' room.

"My God, Cassie, you look like Grace Kelly!"

"Oh, Allene! She's gorgeous!"

"So are you, kiddo. And thinner, too."

Cassie walked through the door with Allene at her heel and the room exploded with sound. Champagne corks popped and the orchestra segued into "Happy Birthday." The big party at the Dallas Country Club turned out to be waiting for her, for Cassandra Taylor Steele, the sharecropper's daughter.

Cassie stopped dead in the doorway and Steve Reilly hurried over to take one of her arms while Allene clutched the other. They held a muttered conference.

"Do you think she's going to faint, Steve?"

"No, but she does look sort of pale green, doesn't she?"

Cassie drew herself to her full height. "Let go of me, you idiots! It would be downright tacky to faint at my own birthday party!" She took one step into the room and the party came to her.

The lights, the music, the night whirled around her until she felt that she had entered into fairyland. She began to pick out faces and the party became surreal, though the faces were ones she knew very well indeed. Who had done this for her? Who had organized such a party and had invited such guests? Two federal judges put in brief, dignified appearances and left early. Mr. and Mrs. Dick Carter were there—Mr. Dallas himself—and Dorothea Carter Reilly. Myrt Farley was there, and moreover Billy Ben was there, too, with his new young wife.

Joe Bullard of Bullard Drilling came alone, and Allene was surrounded by three young men who looked slightly bowlegged even in their tuxedos. There were bankers and ranchers and lawyers and oilmen and doctors and real estate developers. Fran showed up with a new man who must have been single, since he dared to face that crowd.

Ted Abernathy claimed a dance, and a kiss, as he said, to prove that they were still friends. Rob Penland wanted a kiss, but had to hurry back to a purse-mouthed and very pregnant Linda Lou. Everyone there, Cassie realized, was someone she knew. It was as if the city of Dallas had come to present her with a testimonial on her thirtieth birthday: "You have arrived now, Cassie Steele. You are one of us."

And there in the end were Cassie's best friends, the ones who had arranged it: Steve Reilly and Fran Jordan, Allene Perkins and Myrtle Farley. She saved the last hugs for them, the best kisses; but when she tried to thank them, they refused to accept her gratitude. "You've done more for us," Myrt said, "than we can ever do for you. Honey, don't you ever forget that you're the one that got me Farley Oil!"

Cassie left the party in a haze of excitement and happiness. Many people had offered to drive her to her house, and several men had offered to take her to their houses, but Cassie Taylor Steele, in the end, drove home alone.

She was too elated to sleep. She made herself a light bourbon highball and slipped on a nightgown and robe. Restlessly, she roamed through the house, picking up something, putting it down, reliving moments of the party. Her mood was tied to the elation she still felt over her profit on the downtown office buildings. She remembered that she had not yet had time to enter the transaction in the account books she kept at home.

What better time to do it? She had been counting the astonishing number of people she knew in Dallas, and now she could count the even more astonishing number of dollars she had made on the buildings. She made another light drink and took it into her study.

By the time she finished her calculations, the ice cubes in her drink had melted and the glass was full of warm watery bourbon. She took one sip and put it aside.

She looked at the figures again, and she didn't need whiskey because she was drunk on numbers. She, Cassie Steele, had a net worth of $261,328.52. She was worth over a quarter of a million dollars.

A quarter of a million dollars. It would not sound like a lot of money to Myrt Farley, who was worth at least fifty million, or to H. L. Hunt, who had a quarter of a billion dollars, but Cassie knew. She knew where she had come from. She knew where she had arrived.

She would buy land, and more land, land in the Central Expressway corridor, well north of the Northwest Highway: a long-term investment.

She made a few notes. She wanted to get this new money invested as soon as possible so that it could go to work for her. Most of it would go into land, but her accountant had an oil deal in mind, too, in which the depletion allowance would give her tax breaks on current income.

She stood up and stretched. Now, she thought, now she would be able to sleep. She washed her face and reached for a towel, but as her fingers touched it she froze. There in the mirror, through some trick of the light reflecting from her wet face, she saw a resemblance to her grandmother's face. She smiled at her reflection and blotted her face with the towel.

How odd, she thought, and how nice. It was as if she had reached back in time, or Granny had reached forward, and for just that one instant they had become one.

Perhaps it was the land, she thought, perhaps it was because she had land ownership so much on her mind.

Own your own land. How often Granny had said that. Cassie wished that Granny could be there, in the house in University Park, that Granny could see those figures with her own eyes. She would be so proud of Cassie. So proud.

Cassie smiled again at her reflection, but the smile faded because she realized that something was not quite right. Own your own land, Granny had said, but what she had meant was to own land that you farmed with your own hands, land that in return would produce living plants to sustain you.

Hanging up the towel, switching off the light, Cassie was uncomfortable. Her land, her development land would be plowed, all right. It would be plowed to break it up and then that good black gumbo soil would be hauled away and discarded. The only things that would grow on Cassie's land were made of steel and brick and glass. Buildings.

For that matter, it would not even be her land at that point, but would long since have been sold to developers. She would never pick up a handful of that soil and let it trickle through her fingers. She would take money from it, yes, but she would never put anything into it other than money.

Maybe Granny would not be proud of her after all.

Cassie got into bed, but she did not turn off the light. She could not stand darkness, not that night. From the bright shimmering lights of the party to the black thoughts of night was too great a distance to travel.

But the room seemed dark to her even with the light on. "Why?" Cassie whispered. "What have I done?" And at that instant she realized that the problem lay not in what she had done but in what she had not done. In her race toward the top, toward success, she had tossed away all of the weights that might impede her progress. She had tossed overboard her grandmother's teachings. She could take, but she had forgotten how to give. She had forgotten how to make a commitment to anything more important, more lasting than a legal brief or a financial statement.

Cassie swung her legs over the side of the bed and stood up, looking around the room as if she would find the answer there in midair, written in fire or at least neon.

She stumbled out to the living room, still looking, and she saw the telephone on the dining room table, and she knew.

She dialed Information and then she dialed the number and waited while it rang and rang and rang. It was almost three in the morning, after all. It rang and a voice answered, a sleepy grunt, and then "Hello?"

"Dix, it's me. It's Cassie."

"Cassie," he said and she knew it could be the distortion of sleep in his voice, but she could hope it was the distortion of waking from sleep that allowed him to say her name that way, with no holding back for once, with no prejudgment of her. "Cassie?" he said again and in that one word she heard all that she had ever wanted from Dixon Steele, warmth and trust and love.

What could she give to him in return? Perhaps nothing more and nothing less than trust.

"Dix," she said, "I want . . . I need . . ." She wanted to tell him what she felt for him, she wanted it desperately, but something held her back. Something would not let her climb out on that fragile limb, not yet. Perhaps, she thought sadly, not ever.

"Cassie? Is that you? What do you want?" That time when he said her name there was the underlying tone she had expected but had not wanted to hear. "Cassie? Are you there?"

"Yes. Yes, Dix, I'm here."

"Well, what do you want?"

"I have to buy something and I can't buy it directly. Can you find someone who would act as a go-between?"

"What the hell is this? Do you have any idea what time it is? What is it you want to buy?"

"You didn't hear me, Dix. I didn't say I want to buy it. I said I have to buy it."

"Okay, okay. God! What is it you have to buy?"

"Your father's farm at San Bois, Dix. I have to buy that farm."

"Oh, my God. At three o'clock in the morning? Look, I'll call you back tomorrow."

IT WAS NO EASIER to explain to Dixon Steele at ten o'clock in the morning than it had been at three. Cassie was not even able to explain it to herself.

"All I can tell you is that I want that farm, Dix. I have to have it!"

His irritation was obvious. "And that's why you called me in the middle of the night? You called me just to tell me that you wanted to buy that farm?"

"No, I wanted to . . ." What had she wanted to do? What had she really wanted? Was it to buy the farm or was it just to hear his voice, to hear him say "Cassie?" in just the tone he had first used: trusting, unguarded, almost loving. She could not say that to him. "I can't explain it, Dix. I just had to—listen, will you do it? Will you arrange for a go-between? You know your father would never sell the place to me directly."

"And now you want me to go behind my father's back."

She hesitated. "I suppose I do. Is that asking too much, Dix?"

There was a long silence. "I don't know. I just don't know."

"But you'll do it, anyway?"

"Oh, God, I guess so."

Cassie replaced the receiver carefully. She was glad she had not told him. She was glad she had not gone out on the limb.

Chapter 35

 CASSIE MADE IT to the office on time the next morning and grimaced when Leta said a new client was waiting inside.

"Another *pro bono*. Are her clothes terrible?"

"No," Leta said, "her clothes are okay. It's just that . . . well, you'll see."

The woman was young and her clothes were worn but good—a well-pressed seersucker suit, a wicker handbag. Cassie introduced herself and saw immediately why Leta had thought it necessary to have the new client wait in the office. It was the anguish in her face that was the problem. Looking into her eyes was like staring into an open wound.

"Mrs. Brown? May I note down some information before we discuss your problem?"

Mrs. Margaret Brown was twenty-eight. She lived with her husband and five-year-old daughter in Oak Cliff, near the hospital where her husband was a resident in obstetrics and gynecology. Since Dr. Kenneth Brown's salary was little more than an honorium, Mrs. Brown had worked as a waitress for the dinner shift at a restaurant until recently, when she had been fired after a third episode of uncontrollable weeping.

"How can I help you, Mrs. Brown? Do you want a divorce?"

"No! I mean, yes, of course! Oh, Mrs. Steele . . . I don't know! I just want to make him leave her alone!"

Cassie sighed. Adultery again. As a divorce lawyer she had begun to think that the song "The Music Goes 'Round and 'Round" should be changed to "Adultery Goes 'Round and 'Round." It made her uncomfortable to remember that at one time she herself had been the other woman in a relationship. "Who is the woman? A nurse at the hospital? That seems to be a——"

Margaret Brown looked startled. "I guess I thought you knew, that everyone knew. It's not a nurse. It's Peggy."

"Peggy?"

"My——our daughter." Her face crumpled into weeping. "Our five-year-old daughter. My husband's been using her . . . sexually."

Cassie jerked back as if she had been struck. Her hand shook as she forced herself to get up and take a box of Kleenex to Margaret Brown. She went back to her chair slowly, trying to hold on to reality.

Incest. Cassie had come all too close to it herself, on the night the tenant house burned. She had run across cases in her West Dallas practice and had even arranged a safe abortion for a thirteen-year-old girl made pregnant by her father. But that was among poor and ignorant people who barely clung to the bottom rung of the ladder.

Margaret Brown was obviously intelligent and well educated, and presumably her doctor-husband was the same. And the child was five years old. And Bo, Cassie's own brother, was in a California prison for——no! She would have to turn this case over to an associate. She could not deal with it.

"What do the police say, Margaret?"

"I couldn't——I can't tell them. Ken said he would lose his residency if I told and wouldn't be able to get another. We don't have any savings, you see, and I don't know what we would do if——"

"He's not still living at home!"

"Oh, no! I insisted——he's living at the hospital. He said I should just forget about it, that it won't happen again, but——" She gripped the arms of her chair. "I can't do that! I can't just——I came to you because I thought a woman might be better able to understand. Don't you see? I just don't know what to do!"

Cassie looked at her closely. The woman was hanging on by a thread, but she did not need sympathy or even outrage. She needed a plan, something concrete that would impose order on the chaos of her life. "I'm afraid there are several things you must do whether you want to or not. First, this man must be removed from society immediately, for Peggy's protection and for yours. He could turn on you, you know. Second, we must get your little girl to a sensitive psychiatrist, someone who can help her. Margaret, how did you find out about this?"

"Peggy told me."

"She just came out with it?"

"Oh, no! I knew that something was worrying her and I kept asking until finally she broke down and—" She grabbed a tissue. "He—it started last Christmas night, when she was only four."

"That was four months ago! Why didn't the child tell you earlier?"

"Ken told her he would hurt me if she told."

"Oh, God," Cassie said. "Where is Peggy now?"

"An old friend in East Dallas took us in. She's keeping Peggy today."

"Does your husband know about your friend?"

"No, he doesn't."

Cassie sat back, trying to maintain detachment. She had heard one side of a story based on the report of a five-year-old. A child could imagine something, or could misconstrue an adult's actions.

She put her hand over her eyes. She could not turn it over to an associate. She had been involved before Margaret Brown came into her office, since that night of fire in the tenant shack. She might not be able to help Peggy Brown, but she had to try. The blackness in Dr. Brown sought out the blackness in her own heart, the darkness she had fought for years. She had to stop the man. She had to do it. At least the child was safe for the time being. "Look, Mrs. Brown, I need to consult my partner about this. I'll have Leta bring you some iced tea. Just relax, hear?"

Steve Reilly's face was red with anger by the time Cassie finished her report on the Brown case.

"That guy ought to be castrated."

"If the story is true, Steve. We have to be sure."

He slowly tapped his pencil on his desk. "Of course. We'll have to take it to the district attorney's office." He grunted. "Not that they'll have an easy time getting a conviction."

"The court won't hear a child's testimony, will it?"

"It depends on the child. The mother's testimony is only hearsay evidence."

Cassie stood up. "I'll take Mrs. Brown out to East Dallas and see if the little girl will talk to me. If it looks like the story is true, I'll take her down to sign the complaint, and I'll ask the D.A.'s office to get a doctor and a child psychiatrist." She paused in the doorway. "Steve, if this is true, if that—that bastard even touched her—we have to get him. We must!"

"Do it, Cassie. I'm with you all the way."

PEGGY BROWN was playing in the yard with the children of Margaret's college friend. She ran to her mother, but stopped when she saw Cassie.

Peggy was a thin girl with long blond hair. There was a distinct resemblance to her mother in her facial structure, and more, in the haunted look of her blue eyes. Cassie listened to the child talking to her mother. Her enunciation was precise and clear.

"And Mama, Aunt Barbara said, tell you that the neighbor lady, the one in the white house with green shutters, is watching me and Bobby and Linda while Aunt Barbara's at the store. And she didn't have much to buy, some spaghetti and two cans of tomatoes for her sauce and some cat food for Tiger and gas for her car."

"Fine, Peggy," her mother said, distracted. "Thank you for telling me." Peggy ran back to her friends.

"Margaret?" Cassie said. "Does Peggy always deliver messages as precisely as that?"

Margaret's laugh was shaky, but it was genuine. "Oh, yes. I'm afraid I almost use her like a note pad sometimes. Her Sunday school teacher is a retired primary teacher and she says that it is probably an early sign of a photographic memory, but that since she is just learning to read, her mind photographs visual details and actions instead of words."

"May I ask her a few questions, Margaret?"

The woman hesitated. "You mean, about what he did to her?"

Cassie hesitated. "No, I'll leave that for the district attorney's office. I might touch the edges of it, but I want to find out if she is willing to talk to me."

Margaret called Peggy and settled her with Cassie at the picnic table. "Peggy, Cassie is a friend of ours—a good friend. You can talk to her. I'm going inside to make lemonade for everyone."

Peggy perched on the bench like a little bird that would explode into flight at the first hint of danger.

"Well, Peggy," Cassie said. "Do you like animals?"

"Yes'm. I like Tiger because he thinks he's tough. He goes stomping around like he's ready to fight, but if you give him a lap to sit on, he cuddles up and purrs."

"Is Tiger your cat, or your friends'?"

"Tiger is *my* cat! He lives at my house where I—where I used to live?" In the question were a normal five-year-old's confusions about adult decisions and, Cassie thought, a hint of fear.

"Does Tiger like Christmas?" she said hastily.

"Yes'm!" Peggy beamed. "Tiger just *loves* Christmas! Me, too!"

Cassie gave her a quick, light hug. "When did Santa Claus come to your house last Christmas? I'll bet you were sound asleep."

Peggy considered the matter carefully. "I think I was asleep, but I *think* I heard some bells, little tinkly bells, like reindeer bells."

"I guess that was on Christmas Eve."

"Yes,'m, it was, because when I waked up on Christmas, Santa Claus had left all my presents on the floor right under the Christmas tree! There was a doll with yellow hair and a picture book and—" She giggled. "And my best present of all."

"What was that, Peggy?"

She jumped off the bench and whirled around. "Tiger! It was Tiger!"

When she sat down, Cassie said, "Did your mother and father give you presents, too?"

"Mama gave me a black-haired dolly, and Daddy gave me a pink fuzzy nightie."

"I bet you don't remember how they were wrapped!"

"I do so!" Peggy said indignantly. "The dolly was in a green box with a red ribbon, and the nightie was in a white box with a big blue bow."

"Who wants lemonade?" Margaret Brown said.

Cassie could check on the gift wrappings with Margaret, she thought, but it was obvious that this child had almost total recall.

Casually, she said, "Did you wear your new nightie on Christmas night, Peggy?"

"Yes'm, until Daddy told me to——" She stopped abruptly and looked at her mother.

"It's all right, honey," Margaret said softly. "You can tell Cassie."

Peggy hesitated, but then she turned to Cassie. "Daddy said take off my nightie so we could play doctor so I did. And he listened to my tummy with his ear thing, his stettysope, and then he put his finger in a little hole in me to take my tempature and that hurt, but he didn't stop and he said——"

"That's enough, honey," Cassie said as calmly as she could. "I may ask you to tell this to a friend of mine tomorrow. Can you do that?"

Peggy looked from her mother to Cassie. "No. Only Mama and you."

Cassie hugged Peggy and sent her to play with the other children. "Margaret, I think Peggy has built up some rules of her own around this, but I don't know. I don't want to push her before we see a psychiatrist. It may be a defense that she needs."

Margaret twisted her hands in her lap. "Cassie. I can't—you do know that I can't pay for all this, don't you?"

Cassie patted her shoulder. "Don't worry about money. Let's concentrate on helping Peggy."

As they walked to Cassie's car Margaret still looked terribly worried, but Cassie thought there was a glimmer of hope in her eyes.

ARNOLD WILSON, the assistant district attorney, welcomed Cassie and Margaret Brown into his office. He was a tall young man with deep-set black eyes. Cassie spoke with him alone first, in the hall outside his office.

"I don't know, Cassie, kids make things up sometimes——"

"Not this kid," she said firmly. "I talked to her. I'm sure."

He rubbed his jaw. "Well, if you say so. . . ."

"Let me tell you how she describes things, Arnie." She gave him a quick report on her conversation with Peggy and on what Mrs. Brown had told her that morning.

Arnie Wilson and Cassie joined Margaret Brown in his office.

"Cassie has told me the bare bones of the case, Mrs. Brown. It will be painful, I know, but please tell me the whole story."

Margaret Brown told the story, and it seemed to Cassie that she was more relaxed, perhaps because she was no longer alone with her problem.

Arnie's dark eyes were angry when Margaret finished. "Believe me, I will put everything we've got into this one, Mrs. Brown. There's no excuse for such behavior, but for a doctor, a man who knows what this can do to a child physically and mentally—we'll get him! I will get him!"

He asked Cassie to wait for a minute, and with her he was less sanguine about getting a conviction. "Our only witness is Peggy, and she's—"

"Five years old." Cassie sighed. "Will you set up appointments with the M.D. and the psychiatrist for tomorrow, Arnie?"

"Sure. But we can't do it all with expert testimony."

DIXON STEEL called at nine that night. "I tried to get you earlier."

"I worked late. I have a case that—"

"With your boss, I suppose. With that Reilly guy."

"With my partner, Steve Reilly, yes."

"Well, I've got a go-between for you."

"Dix, that's great!"

"It's an outfit called Farmco, a holding company that buys farms and leases them out. The owner is a client of mine, so he'll buy the farm and sell it to you for ten percent profit."

"What will it—I wonder if I can afford it."

"Believe me, you can. Farmco has checked it out and learned that Dad is selling out in Clifton County and buying up wheat land west of Ballard, land better-suited to large-scale farming practices. Farmco thinks the whole thing will set you back about twenty thousand dollars. Can you finance that in Dallas or—"

"I'll take care of it, Dix. You just tell me when to show up with the cash."

He chuckled. "I suspect Farmco would rather have a cashier's check than cash. Now, I still want to know why you want the farm so damn bad."

"I'm still not sure myself. When I figure it out, I'll——"

"Sure you will. Sure." The amusement had left his voice. "God, why do I let myself get involved in this, anyway."

"Because you are my friend?"

"Am I, Cassie? We'll see." He hung up.

Yes, Cassie thought. We'll see.

ARNIE WILSON called Cassie at the office early the next morning. "Cassie, I told the D.A. what you said about Peggy's talking only to her mother or you, and he says will you accept a temporary assignment as an assistant D.A., just for this one case?"

"I'd have to clear it with Steve Reilly."

"It's cleared. I caught Steve just as he was leaving the office last night. Cassie, we really need you on this one."

"Then you've got me."

The temporary credentials helped Cassie with Dr. Slater, the child psychiatrist. They agreed that when Margaret brought Peggy to the office, Cassie should be the one to question her, with Margaret in the room to provide reassurance. Dr. Slater would observe the interview through a one-way window, and further, it would be recorded on sound film for Dr. Slater's study and in the hope that a judge might accept the film in evidence.

Cassie tried to make the ordeal as easy as possible for Peggy. They broke off frequently for snacks and trips to the water fountain down the hall. Cassie noticed that each time they resumed the interview, Peggy returned to her story at the precise point where she had left it.

When it was finished, the receptionist took Peggy out for an ice cream cone.

Dr. Slater looked at his notes and then across the desk at Margaret Brown and Cassie. His face was white with anger. "I am supposed to be impartial, but I find it almost impossible to keep my feelings under control in this case." He sat back in his chair, holding the sheaf of notes. "There appear to have been eleven incidents." He took a deep breath. "Peggy is an amazing child, with a memory for detail that is startling in a child of five."

Margaret leaned foward. "Will she—will the experience mark her for life?"

"I don't think so. The detached way in which she described the events seems to indicate that she is already filing them away, as it were, to deal with as needed. She appears to be a very resilient child, with a strong sense of self. While this was a traumatic experience, I believe that she will weather it. Her memory is uncanny. Tell me, Mrs. Brown, have you heard her relate other incidents with so much detail?"

"Oh, yes. Last night, for instance, she told my school friend about our last visit to my parents in Arizona. She described her grandfather's taking out his false teeth with so much detail that it was all we could do not to laugh out loud. If my father suspected for one minute that we know the color of his denture cleaner and the fact that he uses warm, not cold, water in the pink glass he stores them in over-night—yes, Dr. Slater, Peggy has quite a memory for detail."

Cassie glanced at her watch. "We must take her for a physical examination now, Dr. Slater, but I'd like to talk with you late this afternoon."

"Are you in such a hurry?"

"Yes, I am. We have to build a case for the arraignment that will justify denial of bail."

Dr. Slater scowled. "I am at your service, Mrs. Steele. Call me anytime you like."

Cassie waited in the pediatrician's private office while he examined Peggy in her mother's presence.

Again there was a red-faced angry man looking across a desk at the two women, while the child played in another room.

"This child has been brutally injured. The scar tissue proves that he—where were you, Mrs. Brown. My God, woman, how could you not know what was going on?"

Cassie raised her hand. "Now, wait a minute—"

Margaret interrupted, in a low bitter voice. "Do you think I haven't asked myself that question, Dr. Jones? Do you think I haven't blamed myself every waking minute? I was working, that's where I was. I was earning money to support my family. And don't forget that my— that the man who did this was a doctor. He knew how to treat wounds and how to cover them up."

Dr. Jones looked uncomfortable. "Yes. I see. Did you notice any physical changes, when you bathed her for instance?"

"He bathed her. Remember, I worked nights. Or the baby-sitter bathed her, and she never mentioned anything. Once, though . . ."

"Yes?"

"Peggy seemed to be overtired, Dr. Jones. She wasn't eating well. It wasn't anything I could put my finger on, but she seemed . . . well, just not quite right. So I took her to a pediatrician at the hospital. Professional courtesy, you know. He wouldn't bill me."

"And he examined her? Do you know if he examined her vagina?"

She shook her head. "No. I was there. He did not."

Dr. Jones scowled. "Medical schools don't teach us enough about sexual mistreatment of children. What did he tell you?"

Margaret Brown looked him straight in the eye. "Vitamins. He prescribed vitamins, Dr. Jones."

"Vitamins." Dr. Jones sighed. "Yes. Well, I'll tell you something that will make you feel somewhat better, Mrs. Brown. It appears to me that Peggy will be all right physically. We'll want to keep a close watch, especially at puberty, but I believe that you won't have that worry, at least." He smiled at her warmly, but then he turned to Cassie and scowled. "Now, Mrs. Steele, what can I do to help you put this monster in prison?"

"I'll call you, Dr. Jones," she said. "And thank you."

ARNIE WILSON had said that they could not get a conviction on expert testimony alone, but it proved to be enough for the arraignment. Dr. Kenneth Brown was refused bail and was remanded for trial in June. Margaret Brown and Peggy were able to move back to their apartment and Margaret went back to work, switching to a daytime waitress job, at the psychiatrist's suggestion, so that she could be home at night. She placed Peggy in the supervised kindergarten he recommended.

She told Cassie that she definitely wanted to divorce Kenneth Brown. "I'll save up until I have enough to pay for it."

"Don't worry about that, Margaret. If we convict him, you'll have your divorce. A felony conviction is automatic grounds for divorce in Texas. He won't be able to contest the suit."

Cassie tried to catch up on her other work, but she spent hours conferring with Arnie and Dr. Slater. They still hoped that the court would accept the filmed interview in evidence, but they had to be ready, too, for an in-court interview in case the judge would accept a five-year-old witness.

ONE HOT EVENING at the end of May, Cassie was in her study, where she had installed an air-conditioning window unit. She had read and reread the transcript of her interview with Peggy and was trying to think of questions that would elicit the answers she wanted in any future interview.

She was startled when the phone rang and even more startled to hear Dixon Steele's voice. Her mind had been so full of the Brown case that she had hardly thought of the farm, of Farmco, or even of Dix himself.

"Cassie, you've got yourself a farm. Can you get up here Wednesday for the closing?"

"This Wednesday? Dix, I just can't! I'm involved in a case and besides, I have a new client coming in Wednesday afternoon and he has to leave that night for Mexico."

Dix laughed. "Got yourself a fly-by-night client, have you?"

"The man has oil holdings in Mexico," Cassie said stiffly.

"Hey, can't you take a joke? Look, I can act for you at the closing. Send me a power of attorney, though. Air mail, special delivery. If you can get it off tomorrow——"

"I will! Thank you, Dix!"

"Shall I mail the file to you afterwards?"

"That would be——wait." Cassie mentally rearranged her calendar. The Brown trial was set for June 14, and she needed to do more preparation for that, but she had to see the farm. She had to set her foot on the land, on her land. "Dix, listen. I think I'll drive up to the farm Friday and stay through Monday. If you could——if it wouldn't be too much trouble to——Dix, will you bring the papers there, to the farm?" The telephone was silent. "I'll promise you some good bourbon and steaks from the German butcher in Deep Elm. Aged, heavy beef—"

"Whoa!" He laughed. "I wasn't hesitating so you'd up the ante. I was just thinking about . . . Cassie, I'll do it. But you don't have to bring steaks. I'd just like to see you."

Cassie's breath caught in her throat. "I'd like to see you, too, Dix. Till Friday then?"

"Yes. Till Friday."

THE NEXT FEW DAYS were hectic, but to Cassie they seemed to creep. Dix called on Wednesday, but Cassie was tied up with her new client and Leta took the message: the closing had gone through, the keys to the lodge were hidden under the second step of the veranda and Dix would bring the papers to the farm about dinnertime on Friday night.

Cassie rose very early on Friday and was well north of Dallas at first light. There had been rain in the night and the sun rose on a sparkling world. Each blade of grass, each weed, each strand of barbed wire glistened like a diamond. Cassie stopped to lower the convertible top. Later she would have to raise it against the heat of the June sun and would need to turn on the air-conditioning, but for a few hours she could enjoy the wind of her passage through the fresh-washed fields of North Texas.

The Cadillac's speed kept increasing, as if the car were rushing to a rendezvous. Cassie slowed down but soon the car was speeding again, and it became more and more difficult for her to hold it back.

She was at the farm by lunchtime. She did not hesitate at the rough track to the ruins on the hill, but drove straight on to the lodge.

In the noon sun, the house looked surprised, its tall, narrow windows like startled, disapproving eyes. Cassie stopped the Cadillac by the split-rail fence, and it took her a few minutes to work up the courage to open the car door. Finally she climbed out and walked through the weeds of the front yard. She knelt down to find the keys and then tiptoed up the front steps and across the veranda as if she were afraid that she would disturb the rightful owner, as if James Steele would open that door at any second and glare at her, the interloper.

Halfway across the porch she stopped to straighten her back, reminding herself aloud, "I am the rightful owner!" She stomped up to the front door, making as much noise as she could. She turned around, her back to the door, and looked out across the fields.

"These are my fields," she said aloud, "not James Steele's. This is my farm!" She tossed the key in her hand, caught it and turned to the door. "And this is my house!"

She unlocked the door, but her rightful ownership did not quite give her the courage to stomp into the hall. Instead she pushed the door open tentatively and eased her way into her house.

Chapter 36

CASSIE TIPTOED into the living room to open the curtains. The room was smaller than she remembered and the furniture was shabby, but it was her house and her furniture. It would say so in the deed Dix was going to bring: "The house and outbuildings including all furnishings and equipment and appurtenances."

She touched a dusty end table. "This is my end table," she whispered, and then she laughed aloud. "My table!" She ran through the rooms laughing with pleasure, touching each thing, making it hers. "My bookcase! My cookstove!" She stopped abruptly in front of that one locked door and tried every key, but none of them fit the padlock, so she hurried out to the tool shed and found a pry bar.

One good heave was enough to pull the hasp away from the doorframe. She turned the knob and opened the door gently.

The yellowed sheets tacked over the windows made the sunlight dim and wavery, like light under water, but the room had not changed since she peeked into the window and thought she saw a dead baby on the floor. The pink canopy on the mahogany four-poster bed hung down in tatters over a narrow mattress splotched with mildew. Against the wall next to the window, where Cassie had not been able to see it from outside, was a low shelf with toys lined up like children on a bench at school: a dusty pink rabbit with floppy ears, a nutcracker soldier, a doll with stringy black hair and surprised black eyes and a worn faded teddy bear that was more like a memory of a teddy bear than the thing itself.

"Julia Steele," Cassie whispered. "Little Julia."

Cassie ripped the sheets from the windows. Light poured into the room and the toys were only toys again, not memories.

She inspected the other rooms, but the silent house seemed to be listening to her steps and marking her as an intruder. She turned on the old arch-shaped Zenith radio in the living room and organ music filled the room. Cassie sang with it the half remembered words of "Juanita."

The music faded away and in a sepulchral tone, a man's voice said, "And now . . . *The Romance of Helen Trent*. When we left them yesterday, Helen feared that Gil would . . ."

She was instantly back in the Hodges' house in Whitman. In a minute, surely, she would hear Ella Mae's querulous voice: "Cassie? Bring me a glass of that buttermilk, hear?"

Cassie snorted and then laughed until she had to brace herself against the kitchen door. When she wiped the tears from her eyes she glanced at the kitchen table, and the laughter disappeared because there seemed to be someone huddled on the kitchen chair: Granny on that hot day when she and Cassie had come to clean the lodge for Mr. Steele, Granny gray-faced and gasping for breath.

"No," Cassie whispered. "Please. No more memories."

She hurried into the living room and spun the dial on the Zenith until she found a concert of German band music that was sure to drive out the most persistent memory. She carried in the boxes she had brought from Dallas: cleaning supplies, linens, all bought new for this house, for the farm. Her last load was a box of food, enough for the weekend, and a picnic cooler with milk and butter and two filet mignons from the German butcher in Deep Elm.

Cassie oom-pah-pahed through the house, throwing open every window to let in sunshine and fresh June air. Then she went to work on her house like a dog pawing at a blanket to make a nest before he settles down to sleep. Dusting and vacuuming and washing, polishing and moving the furniture, she arranged at least part of her house to fit her body rather than the bodies of those people who had been in

it before her. She closed off three of the bedrooms, including Julia's.
She could deal with them another day.

As she worked, however, she thought more and more of the meeting, or confrontation, that would come with the night. Dix was on
his way to her. One moment she felt as light as sunshine and the
next as heavy as a sack of old rags, sodden from the rain. Would
they quarrel again, and part, or could they just this once rekindle their
special fire? She turned the radio louder, but she could not drown
her fears. Would they break it off? Would he? Would she? She
knew only that she wanted to see him, to be with him, more than she
had ever wanted anything in her life.

It was late afternoon when Cassie had her house in order. She
took a shower and changed to a fresh cotton dress. He was coming.
Dix was coming. But when, she wondered, when?

She went out to sit on the wicker rocking chair on the veranda,
and as she rocked the peace of the country evening seeped into her
soul: the buzz of insects in the fields, the low cry of a whippoorwill,
the smell of fresh-plowed dirt, the glitter of the late sun on San Bois
Creek at the bottom of the hill. She rocked slowly, savoring the
evening and the knowledge that she was on her own veranda, on her
own land. Yes, she thought, yes. Now Granny would be proud of
her. Within her, a core of blackness dissolved, melting and disappearing like dry ice changing to vapor and drifting away.

It was then that she heard the car.

The headlights appeared first, two disks of light in the gathering
darkness beneath cedar branches that were black jagged masses against
the darkening blue of the sky. The car stopped behind her Cadillac,
next to the split-rail fence.

Cassie went to the edge of the veranda to watch him unfold himself
from the car. "Dix?" she called softly.

"Yes, Cassie." He walked through the weeds to stand at the bottom of the steps. His face looking up at her became as much a part
of the peaceful dusk as the night breeze rustling in the woods, as
appropriate and, to her, as necessary. His face: the heavy black eyebrows, the dark questioning eyes, the wide mouth, half smiling, brought
the world into focus.

He cleared his throat. "It's strange to see you standing there."

"It's strange to be here. I felt like an intruder at first."

He held up a manila envelope. "You aren't an intruder. You own the place, lock, stock and barrel."

They hesitated, and then broke the silence simultaneously.

"Dix, come up on the—"

"Cassie, may I—"

They laughed together, and the next few minutes were filled with bustle. Dix climbed the steps and handed Cassie the envelope, she offered him a drink, he followed her into the kitchen and helped with the ice. "Have you been cleaning house all afternoon?" he said.

"Well, yes. It was pretty grim. I could only do part of it."

He shook his head. "I'll bet! I don't think any of the family has been here for two years."

"Aha! That's why those spiders were able to build webs as strong as the Red River bridge!"

With a drink in his hand, Dix said, "May I look around?"

"Of course! Let me put the potatoes in to bake and I'll come with you. And I did stop off at the German butcher's, but if you don't want steak . . ."

"Are you insane, woman? Say, there used to be a charcoal cooker in the shed. I'll take a look."

An easiness developed as they moved through the house occupying their thoughts and actions with objects, but when they sat down at the dining table, across from each other, tension began to build. They talked about the food, they joked a little, but their eyes did not quite meet. Their words crossed the space between them in a minuet of approach, withdrawal, approach.

"I heard that you were elected to the state senate, Dix."

"Yes. It's interesting, and just as frustrating. I suppose I wanted to change things for the better, but it's difficult."

Cassie did not mention her own political ambitions. "Are your parents well? And Jimmy?"

He looked at her and then away. "They're fine, my folks. And from all I hear, Jimmy and his new wife are happy. I don't know why. All they do is hang around the country club and drink."

Cassie grinned. "Hog heaven for Jimmy Steele!"

"How about you, Cassie? And your law practice? You concentrate on domestic relations, don't you?"

The thought of little Peggy Brown made Cassie miss a step in the dance. "Domestic relations. I suppose you could say that. But I'm spending more time on oil and gas cases."

His eyes glinted wickedly. "Your fly-by-night client?"

Cassie laughed, but that one look of his had broken the progress of the minuet. That one direct look had pricked her bubble of self-control. It was no longer enough to engage in a word dance with Dixon Steele. She needed to feel his touch, to have his hands on her flesh, his body against hers. She forced herself to get up from the table. "Coffee, Dix? It won't take a minute."

He looked up at her. "Yes. Please." The tone of his answer was more serious than the question warranted. Cassie hurried to the kitchen, hurried away from what might have been no more than good manners.

They took their coffee out to the veranda and sat together in white-painted wicker chairs, listening to the night. The croaking of frogs came from the creek, a continuous low bubbling interrupted occasionally by the deep-voiced chirrump of a bullfrog. Insects buzzed in the night with a hard metallic trilling like the faraway sound of a telephone ringing and ringing with no one to answer it. A whippoorwill cried again and again until another bird called an answer from the dark hills behind the lodge.

"I miss it," Dix said suddenly. "The hills. The woods. There's no place quite like Eastern Oklahoma, is there?"

"No," Cassie said. Dallas was very far away.

They sat in silence but it was a tense silence, not the quiet that comes over old friends who do not speak because there is no need for talk. Cassie felt the moment ebbing away. There was too much that needed to be said and too little that could be said.

The wicker chair creaked, and Dix stood up. "It's getting late, Cassie. I'd better be on my way."

Cassie stood up, too, bewildered by a sudden rush of sorrow. "Dix?"

There was one moment of absolute stillness, as if time had been interrupted by that one tremulous word, as if the very night were waiting.

Dix held out his hand, pale in the darkness, and Cassie reached out to touch it.   As if that brief contact completed a circuit, the night began again.   The chorus of cicadas built and a night bird cried, and Dix folded her hand within his and drew her to him.   She put her right hand flat on his chest and through his thin cotton shirt she could feel his muscular chest and the steady beat of his heart.   She slid her left hand up his arm, to his shoulder, around to the back of his neck, where the clipped hair prickled on her fingertips.   Warmth suffused her body and she remembered vaguely a man's face from long ago, and his words: "A man has needs."   She knew then what he had meant. After Jimmy, after Steve, she knew what it was all about.

Trusting herself, trusting him, she whispered, "I need you, Dix." He pulled her head back and leaned over her, kissing her gently, and then they were kissing each other, kissing voraciously, as if each could absorb the other.

One of them moved toward the door and they were in the house, he pulling her with him, she guiding him until they stumbled into the dimly lit bedroom and still locked in that interminable kiss fell onto the bed.

Abruptly he shoved her away.   "Dix!"   Before she could cry out again, he had pulled off his clothes and was with her.

In the dim light she could see his face above hers.   His eyes were moist.   "Cassie," he whispered.   "My Cassie."

Slowly, as if there were no such thing as time, slowly he unbuttoned her cotton dress and eased her out of it.   He kissed her gently while his hands slipped under her back and fumbled at her bra.   The fastening gave way and he slipped the straps down her arms as gently as if he were handling a china figurine.   He leaned his head down over her small breasts and Cassie arched her back to push them up to him.   He kissed her nipples, one and then the other, and then her stomach.

"Darling," he whispered.   "My darling."   He used both hands to roll her panties down her body, stroking her hips, her legs, her ankles.

To Cassie it seemed that each place his hands touched burned with an icy fire that etched through her skin like acid and penetrated the very center of her body.

"Dix!" she cried, reaching out to him.   "Dix, please!"

He looked down at her and his eyes were no longer moist but were hard and glittering and then he was in her arms and she was in his.

He entered her and her body opened to him as if it had waited all through time for this one moment when their two bodies could be joined together and become one body, one being that was greater than the sum of the two. For an electric moment they lay sealed together and then he thrust himself deeper into her, once and then again, and she rose to meet him, to move with him, and every fiber of her body burned with the frenzy of it.

"Cassie!" he shouted and drove into her once more, and she no longer had a body but was pure feeling, whirling and spinning through space like a wild comet burning itself out as it flew through the black universe again and again and again.

Then it was over, as suddenly as it had begun, and she was back on earth, back on her own bed, in Dix's arms. Her body throbbed with joy and she was floating on a gray-green river of love, in a gentle current of peace she had never known before, never in all of her life.

Dix kissed her softly. "My darling. My Cassie."

She put a shaky hand to his cheek. "I love you."

He turned his head to kiss the palm of her hand. "And I love you, Cassie. I love you."

He moved and his still-firm penis moved within her. She jerked as if from an electric shock. Dix laughed. "Sorry!"

"Oh, no," she said, and she laughed, too, and suddenly they were both laughing with relief and happiness. They laughed until they cried, they laughed until they rolled over and over on the bed, until they stopped laughing in simultaneous awareness that it was happening again.

It was slower the second time, slower and more tender. Their first encounter was an explosion, but their second was an exploration. They investigated each other, exchanging touches, exchanging information with soft, loving whispers.

"Here, Cassie?"

"Oh, yes. There."

Cassie ran her fingertips down his side and he jerked away from her. "Hey, stop that!"

"Dix Steele, you're ticklish!"

"Mmm. I'm not ticklish there, love, not ticklish at all."

He cupped her breast with one hand and with the other pressed her buttocks, sealing her to him.

"Oh, love," she whispered. "Oh, my love."

She traced the hollow below his collarbone, trailed her fingers across the back of his neck, and with sudden urgency pulled his head down, pulled his mouth to hers.

They melted together, they floated through time, and when they found release it was with sighs that eased into sleepy whispers.

"I love you, Dix."

"Will you marry me?"

"Of course."

Of course. There was no other answer then because in that soft peaceful night there were no other people in the world and no problems and no responsibilities. There were only the two of them, the two of them wrapped in each other's arms in a world that was theirs alone.

IN THE EARLY MORNING a pair of phoebes perched in the cedar tree outside the bedroom window and woke Cassie with their noisy cries. She came up from sleep slowly, as if waking from a lovely, peaceful dream. When she realized where she was and what had happened in the night, she knew that the dream was reality and more beautiful than any sleeping fantasy. Dix was there, in bed next to her. That was the way it should always have been, the way it should be forever: Dix and Cassie together, with their very nakedness creating an innocence.

She raised herself on her elbow to look at him. The sheet covered his legs and hips but above it his long spine, sunken between the hard muscles of his back, led up to his shaved neck and to his thick black hair. The back of his neck was touchingly thin, like a boy's, and vulnerable. She put her fingertip on it and he stirred and turned his head on the pillow to face her. His eyes were closed, but he smiled as if he too were waking into a long-imagined dream.

She sighed happily and lay back on her pillow. Dix opened one eye and looked at her and then past her. She turned her head to look out of the open window with him. Through a gap in the cedars she could see the bottomlands hazed with green and beyond them the dancing sparkles of sunlight on San Bois Creek.

"It's beautiful," Dix whispered.

Cassie turned her head back to look at him. "You're beautiful," she said.

He laughed and his dark eyes sparkled like the light on the rippling creek. "Hey, I'm the one who is supposed to say that!"

"So say it."

He grinned. "Not till I'm sure of my facts." He sat up and reached out a long arm to pull away the sheet that covered her, slowly, as if he were unveiling a work of art. She pushed herself up on her elbow and her eyes joined his in a slow tracing of the lines of her body.

She had seen that body a thousand times before, but it seemed to have changed during the long night. Her breasts were more rounded and her nipples were hard and erect. Her stomach was flat above the pale blond patch of hair, and her long muscular legs were soft and yielding.

Dix laid his hand on her stomach. "You are beautiful, Cassie."

Cassie smiled at him. She pulled at the sheet that had covered him to his waist and together they looked down his long body. Broad bony shoulders with hollows beneath the collarbone, strong chest with a mat of black hair which narrowed into a streak that traveled down a hard flat stomach to the black bush from which his penis stood erect. Long, hard-muscled legs. On his left leg the scar stretched from his groin almost to his knee. It was less angry-looking, but still purple and deeply indented. It made Cassie want to cry. She looked back to his face, to his dark eyes. They were serious now, and still. She leaned toward him and kissed him gently.

Dix folded her in his arms and again they made love. That time, the third time, was different from the others. In the early light, in the warmth of a June morning, there was a religious solemnity to their lovemaking. There was a commitment.

Afterward, they dozed in each other's arms. Cassie woke to the feeling of something touching her face, something as light as a butterfly. It was Dix's finger, tracing the contours of her high cheekbones, of her jaw, of her lips.

"Cassie, I'm starving."

"How romantic!" She stretched and let the happiness flow through her body. "And I'm ravenous! You take a shower while I fry us up some bacon and eggs."

"No, ma'am!" He kissed her lightly and swung his legs around to sit up on the side of the bed. "You take the first shower and I'll do the cooking."

"You can cook?"

"Lady, I've batched since I first left home. Hell, yes, I can cook!"

Over the sound of the shower she could hear him singing in an Oklahoma twang as discordant as the jangle of a mistuned banjo.

> *"Oh, do you remember sweet Betsy from Pike?*
> *She crossed the wide prairies with her lover Ike,*
> *With two yoke of oxen and one yaller dawg,*
> *A tall Shanghai rooster and one spotted hawg."*

Cassie laughed with delight and turned her face up to the shower to let the spray of water wash her face.

Chapter 37

AFTER BREAKFAST, Dix wanted to see the farm. Hand in hand they tramped through the woods and over the fields, talking as they went. He told her about his law firm in Oklahoma City. "We seem to be getting a reputation as the local liberals. We get all the segregation cases, the union problems, that sort of thing." He glanced at her wickedly. "None of your high-fee men with 'oil holdings in Mexico.' "

"Golly, Dix," Cassie said with feigned awe, "at my law school they taught us that every American deserves legal representation, no matter how poor, or how rich he is."

"At mine they taught us how to add up fees, but I think I missed class that day."

"What does your father think about your practice?"

"I think he has convinced himself that it doesn't exist. When I go home to Ballard, he never even mentions it."

"Isn't he proud of your being a state senator?"

Dix laughed bitterly. "You still don't understand my father, do you, Cassie? I am not *his* state senator."

In the cornfield near the ruins of the tenant house, Cassie knelt down to poke at the soil. "This would make good irrigated pasture."

Dix stood watching her, with his hands stuck into the hip pockets of his chino pants. "You mean that you plan to farm the place?"

Cassie straightened and dusted the red dirt from her hands. "Well, sure. What did you think?"

"Maybe that you wanted to be a gentleman farmer."

Cassie laughed. "Sir, I am not a gentleman."

"I noticed that last night."

"Were you surprised?"

"Delighted," he said, grinning. "Where would you get the water for your irrigated pasture? Isn't it too far from the creek?"

"I really haven't made any plans yet, but there's a good spring in the woods over there."

"There will be plenty of time to plan. We'll keep the farm, of course, when we're married." He hugged her. "Hey, you look surprised! Remember last night? I proposed to you, and you accepted."

"Oh," she said, "that's right. Of course."

"What spring are you talking about, Cassie? I don't remember a spring up here."

Cassie grabbed his hand. "Come on, I'll show you!"

It was cool in the slate-floored grotto. The spring had a good flow but the old split log that carried the water had become more moss than wood. "I'd have to drive a pipe in there," Cassie said, "and maybe sink an oil drum here for a catch basin."

Dix raised his hands in mock amazement. "Lordy, you farmers know how to do just about everything, don't you?"

"Why, sure. And if there's something we don't know, I reckon you politicians can show us how." She grinned at him, daring him.

He grabbed her and kissed her. "That the sort of thing you mean, farmer?"

"Yes," she said breathlessly. "Yes!"

Dix was breathless, too, when the kissing finished. "Ah, where were we? Oh, I meant to ask you something. I know Dad has a contract farmer working the place—it came up at the closing. "Do you intend to keep him on?"

"I don't know. I guess I'll have to, until I have time to get some things organized."

"How the hell are you going to run a law practice in Dallas and a farm in Oklahoma?"

She blushed, embarrassed by her obvious lack of planning. "I guess that's the first thing I have to figure out. Let's go down and take a look at the bottomland by the creek."

She hurried ahead of him, but the June sun was hot and by the time they had walked through the pastures Cassie was sweating.

"Hey, counselor!" she called. "How about a swim in the creek to cool off?"

He grinned at her. "Didn't bring any swimming trunks."

She stopped and turned to face him. "Who needs swimming suits? You're an officer and a gentleman, remember? You won't peek."

He raised his eyebrows. "I know I won't peek. It's you I'm worried about. Will you promise, cross your heart, not to sneak a look?"

She snorted with laughter. "Come on, you! Last one in is a crybaby!"

Cassie ran toward the creek, but after a dozen yards she looked back and saw that Dix had fallen behind and was limping slightly. She stopped and waited for him. "I'm sorry, Dix. I didn't know that your leg still bothered you."

He looked away. "Only after a lot of walking."

Cassie forced herself to laugh lightly. "Well, I'm glad to know that my virtue is safe! I can always outrun you."

He laughed, too, and the pain left his eyes. "What virtue was that?" He grabbed for her, but she skipped out of his reach and ran ahead to the creek.

On the rocky bank, however, she hesitated, suddenly shy of taking off her clothes in front of Dix under the immense blue sky. She turned and waited for him, but he stopped on the upstream side of the bridge.

"It's not that I don't trust you, lady, but I'm going down behind the bridge to undress."

"Dix, you idiot!"

He ducked down behind the bridge and Cassie quickly took off her clothes and piled them on the bank. She waded into the creek, into water deep enough so that only her head was showing.

Peek or not, she watched Dix coming down the bank from the bridge. He was like a god, she thought: tall and strong and lithe. She giggled then, because what god would grimace and lurch with exaggerated pain every time his bare foot hit the sharp rocks of the bank? "You should have kept your shoes on!" she called.

"It would have spoiled the pastoral scene." He splashed into the water beside her. "Stick your foot out of the water. Just as I suspected. My God, the vision of a water nymph in dirty blue tennis shoes. Woman, have you no sense of the esthetic?" He lowered himself into the creek. "That water's cold!" He put his arms around her and kissed her. "Mmm. That's better."

They lay back in the water and kissed again while the current lightly pushed them to and fro. Cassie closed her eyes and it seemed to her that they were floating together, floating and clinging to each other, with the water at once lifting them and sealing their naked bodies together in a clean, pure baptism of love.

Dix grabbed his foot. "Hell! Next time, esthetics be damned, I'm going to keep my sneakers on!"

Cassie slipped away to deeper water and let her arms float near the surface of the water. A tiny silver minnow came up to nudge at her wrist.

"Next time," she said thoughtfully. "Next time." Cassie was on the verge, she thought, of understanding something important, but Dix splashed her.

"Next time?" He grinned. "Come back here, woman!"

"In a minute," Cassie said.

Dix lay back in the water and stretched. Cassie bobbed on her haunches in the cool water. Next time, she thought, all the next times. When they were married, as they had agreed last night. When they were married. She picked up a handful of gravel from the creek bottom and let it trickle between her fingers to splash in the creek like the cornbread crumbs she had dropped when she stopped on her way to school to feed the wild ducks.

It was what she wanted, after all. It was what she had wanted from the day Dix came back from war. To be married to Dixon Steele. It had been so simple, so straightforward all those years. Perhaps, she thought, it had not been simple but simplistic instead, because now that the moment had come, now that her fantasy was to become reality, it was not simple at all. When she was a secretary in Steve Reilly's firm, even when she was a fledgling lawyer, it would have been simple. But she had responsibilities now, to the firm, to oilmen with holdings in Mexico and beaten women and to Peggy Brown. And there were her political ambitions, too.

Angrily she tossed a handful of rocks into the creek. Her rocks? Her creek? There were too many responsibilities, too many claims made on her. Granny reaching from beyond the grave: "Buy the land, Cassie. The land." Steve waving the taunting red cape of power in front of her: "A law career, Cassie. Politics." Naomi touting responsibility, Fran advertising the high life and now, Dix: "Marry me, Cassie."

"Dix?" she said.

He half opened his eyes and then closed them again. "Mmm?"

"If we get married, where will we live?"

He grimaced as he raised himself on an elbow planted in the rocks of the creek bottom. "No *if* about it, darling. *When* we are married. . . . Why, Oklahoma City, of course. My law practice is there, and the state legislature." He grinned. "And we will come down here for weekends, right?"

Cassie turned a stone in her hand, watching the light glitter on the wet surface. "What about my law practice?"

"Oh, you'll pass the Oklahoma bar with no trouble. And believe me, there are lots of divorce clients in the city. Hey, how does Steele and Steele sound for a law firm?"

"I'm phasing out divorce work to concentrate on oil and gas law. Steve said I'll be the first female wheeler-dealer in Dallas."

He laughed lazily. "Great! Be the first in Oklahoma City instead."

"Oklahoma City isn't . . . it's not the same thing."

He was telling her what to do, she thought, just as his father had done before him. He would make her decisions for her.

"Dix?" She hesitated. "Why don't you move to Dallas instead?"

Dix stood up in the water and looked down at her, blank-faced. "I'm going to get dressed now."

He limped toward the bridge, but this time Cassie did not laugh at his careful progress on the sharp rocks. She got out of the water and, after drying herself with her blouse, put on her damp clothes.

She was sitting on a wide flat rock when Dix came back, but he did not join her. He took a handful of rocks and as he spoke he threw them into the water, one by one. "All my life, Cassie, as long as I can remember, my father has been trying to run my life. 'Trust me, Dixon,' he said. 'Trust me, I know what's best for you.' Whether it was taking a commission and riding out the war on a desk chair or running for office, representing his people, the rich and the powerful. 'Trust me, Dixon. Do as I say.' "

Cassie looked down at the rocky ground. "Steve wants me to— I've been thinking about going into politics myself."

Dix whirled around. "And what is your constituency, Cassie? Oilmen with holdings in Mexico?"

"That's not fair! You aren't the only person in the world who is honorable, you know. I do a lot of *pro bono* work!"

"I'm sure you do." He laughed. "Enough to satisfy the bar association, anyway."

Cassie jumped up from the log. "No! I—" She stopped abruptly. She was proud of what she did. She did not have to defend it to anyone, not even to Dixon Steele. She turned and walked quickly up the hill to the lodge.

When Dix came into the kitchen, Cassie was washing the breakfast dishes. It was not easy with her vision blurred by anger, and by sorrow.

"Cassie?" he said tentatively. "I'm sorry. It wasn't fair to compare you to my father."

"Oh, Dix!" She dropped the dishcloth into the water and turned to him.

Ignoring her soapy hands he pulled her close and put his arms around her. "God damn it, Cassie, why do we do this to each other? Why do we fight like this?"

She buried her face in his chest. "I don't know. What's wrong with us? Why can't we trust each other?"

Suddenly he was very still. "Trust. Yes, that's it."

Cassie stepped back. "What do you mean?"

"Maybe I just never learned to trust anyone. My mother loved me, but she was . . . she wasn't always there, after Julia's death. And my father . . ."

"Yes?"

Dix seemed to be far away. "I was the good boy, you know."

"I remember. I remember that Thanksgiving, when Granny brought me here to the lodge, and you were so polite to her. You had nice manners, even then."

"Nice manners." He laughed shortly. "Oh, yes. And straight A's in school. I never got into trouble, but that wasn't enough, I guess, for my father. Jimmy—Jimmy was the one. I tried, oh, boy, did I try. When Jimmy finally let him down he turned to me, but it was too late. I'd had to get by on my own and it was too late for me to become the pawn he wanted. And it was far too late for him to become what I had always wanted—a wise, loving father."

"So you didn't trust him."

"No, I didn't. I don't."

"Is there anyone you do trust, Dix?"

He did not speak for a moment. "I don't know."

"Do you trust me?"

He looked at her, pleading. "Can I?"

Cassie took a deep breath. "I'm not your father, you know. I'm not anything like your father."

He looked at her strangely. "Are you sure?" Before Cassie could answer, he said, "Do you trust him?"

"After what he did to me? After he killed my baby? How could I trust that man?"

"And Jimmy. You don't trust Jimmy either." He moved away and leaned against the kitchen doorjamb.

Cassie could not look at him. His next question, obviously, would be, "Do you trust me?" How would she answer? He had betrayed her at least once, when he told his father that Bo was alive and in California. She was angry now, hurt by his casual dismissal of her career, and it would be easy to lash out at him and remind him that she had given her love, herself, to a man who had told her secret.

Dix might have suspected that she knew about it, she thought, because he did not ask the question she had expected.

Instead, he said, "Maybe you don't trust anyone named Steele."

"I didn't say that." Cassie looked at him and then away. "You forget. My name is Steele, too."

"Do you trust yourself?"

"Yes!" she said, but she looked at him standing by the kitchen door and she could see him taking one more step and going out of that door and out of her life, forever. Her distrust of him disappeared in an overwhelming sense of loss. "Dix! Oh, Dix, do we have to keep talking about it? You love me and I love you. Isn't that enough?"

In one long stride he was with her and his arms were around her.

In the urgency of their need for reassurance, they went to the bedroom and made love once more. There was a wariness, however, that was not there before: wariness and a strained attempt by each to please the other. Afterward they lay back on the pillows, not touching.

Cassie felt that they were leaving each other even as they lay together. Not again, she thought. Not again. "Dix," she whispered. "We need to trust each other. We must have faith."

"I know." He turned his head on the pillow and she saw that his eyes were sad. "I know, Cassie." He sat up in bed and took her hand. "We can't . . . we can't afford to lose each other."

"Oh, no!"

"Then let's try it, Cassie. Let's try trusting each other. Let's just get married and work from there."

Cassie sat up slowly and pulled the sheet over her breasts. "But there's so much, Dix, so many things to work out."

"Do you love me?"

"Of course."

"Cassie Steele." He smiled and his eyes twinkled. "Will you marry me?"

"Oh, Dix!" She reached out to him, letting the sheet fall. "I love—"

The telephone rang.

"Don't answer that, Cassie. It's undoubtedly a wrong number."

She laughed. "Right now, darling, any number is wrong, but I have to answer it." She took her silk robe from the foot of the bed and ran to the living room.

"Cassie, it's Steve."

Cassie pulled on the robe. "Steve! Is something wrong?"

"It sure as hell is! The Brown case is falling apart on us. Arnie Wilson just called from the D.A.'s office, and the judge won't accept the movie of Peggy Brown in evidence."

"Oh, God, I thought it was all set. What can we do, Steve? We know the court probably won't let her testify."

"We have to try, damn it, or let that bastard go scot-free. Look, Cassie, you've got to get down here. Arnie has set up a hearing to qualify Peggy as a witness, but you're the only attorney the child will talk to. You have to convince the judge that her testimony is reliable."

"I see. Steve," she said nervously, "when is the hearing?"

"Tomorrow at two P.M."

"Tomorrow! But that means I'll have to leave here today!"

"Yeah. Right away. We need to get together with Arnie."

"Okay, okay. Steve, I'll call when I get to Dallas."

Cassie went back to the bedroom, already so deep into the problem that she was almost startled to see Dix propped against the pillows.

"Dix, I have to get back to Dallas."

"I heard."

She put her suitcase on the foot of the bed, but he did not move. "My case, Dix, this case I've been working on is falling apart, and they need me to—"

"I heard. That oilman, I suppose."

Cassie looked up from the suitcase in surprise. "What makes you think—" His blank face stopped her.

Silently he got up and dressed. He smoothed his hair at the mirror and turned to look at her. "Counselor," he said quietly, "I am not sure that you heard the question. Please listen carefully, because I will repeat it only once."

"Dix, I—"

He waved her to silence. "Cassie Steele, will you marry me?"

"Oh, Dix, I can't make plans now! This case is too—"

"Yes. The case. Your oilman with holdings in Mexico. God forbid that the man shouldn't have his highly paid divorce lawyer at his side for the hearing."

"Dix, it isn't that case at all! It's—"

She stopped suddenly, because his face, like his mind, was closed against her. His eyes were angry, as if once again his suspicions had been confirmed.

No, she thought, I will not apologize, I will not crawl to Dixon Steele, to any Steele. She shook her head.

He looked at her for a moment and she thought he was going to say something, but without a word he left the room. She heard the front door slam. She heard an engine start and roar. And then she heard nothing.

Slowly Cassie dressed, slowly she packed, but as she locked the windows and doors she began to hurry.

When she was in the car she hesitated with her hand on the key, ready to start the engine of her Cadillac. She looked up at the old lodge standing in the noonday heat.

It did not look like Dick and Jane's house, she thought. It never had looked one thing like Dick and Jane's house.

Chapter 38

JUDGE PICKENS agreed to the experiment Cassie suggested, but only because Arnold Wilson and Cassie had done their homework. For every objection Dr. Kenneth Brown's attorney made, they could cite a high-court ruling. They lost on two points, however. They had asked that Peggy Brown be allowed to testify in chambers and that her father be excluded from the proceedings.

At one o'clock everyone gathered in the judge's chambers for the preliminaries to the hearing: Dr. Brown and his lawyer, Arnie Wilson and Cassie and the court reporter. It was Cassie's first look at Kenneth Brown and she did not like what she saw. He was tall and blond, but something about him reminded her of Bo. It was concealed by a veneer of civilization, but she knew it was there, at the back of those wide-open, innocent blue eyes. When Peggy came in and saw her father she gripped her mother's hand.

The judge cleared his throat. "Let the record show that the interested parties have agreed that this informal, if unusual, proceeding shall be made a part of the case of *The People* vs. *Kenneth Brown*. Mrs. Steele, you may begin."

Cassie sat down next to Peggy and took her hand. "Peggy, are you all right?"

"Yes'm, Cassie."

"Fine. Now, we grown-ups are going to talk for a while, but you don't have to pay any attention to us."

"Yes'm."

"Arnold," Cassie said, "what do you think of the baseball season so far?"

"Well, I'm a Cardinals fan myself, but I think the Cubs have a good chance at the pennant. Do you follow baseball, your honor?"

Judge Pickens played his part, laughing comfortably. "My boy, I was a shortstop in the minors. Never made it to the majors, though."

"You have now, sir."

"Well, I suppose you could say—" He was interrupted by a knock on the door. "Come in. Ah, Ida May, you're just in time. This is thirsty work."

A black waitress from the courthouse café offered a tray of cold drinks around the room. As she left, the uniformed bailiff came into the room.

"What is it, Will?" the judge asked.

"You about ready, your honor?"

Judge Pickens looked at Cassie and she nodded.

"We'll just finish our drinks, Will."

After a few minutes of desultory chatting, everyone except the judge left the room and went down the hall. Peggy and her mother stopped in the rest room and then joined Arnie and Cassie at the prosecutors' table. Cassie saw Peggy look once at her father, at the defense table, and take a tighter grip on her mother's hand.

The judge ordered the court cleared of all but the interested parties.

"Counsel will approach the bench."

The judge looked at Brown's attorney. "You still agree with the arrangements as made."

"Yes, your honor. My client accepts them because of his desire to keep the pressures on his daughter to an absolute minimum."

The judge nodded.

As they went back to the prosecutors' table, Arnie whispered, "Cassie, I hope to hell we're doing the right thing."

"It's the only chance we have."

"But for a kid to talk about a tea party and then have to tell about her father's—"

He stopped when Peggy Brown looked up at him.

Cassie stepped toward the bench. "Your honor, the State requests that the following evidence be entered into the record of the arraignment so that it may be considered in the matter of bail."

Dr. Brown's attorney half rose from his chair. "Defense concurs."

"So be it. Mrs. Steele?"

"I call as witness Miss Peggy Brown, minor child."

Cassie squeezed Peggy's hand as they walked to the witness stand.

Peggy was sworn in, and Cassie said, "Peggy, do you understand what you just said?"

"Yes'm, Cassie. You told me about it this morning, remember? I promised I wouldn't tell a lie."

"And why did you put your hand on the Bible?"

"That's God's book and I promised God not to lie, too."

Cassie looked at the judge.

"Peggy," he said, "do you understand that if you tell a lie you will be punished?"

The child looked up at him. "You mean, like a spanking?"

He looked at her severely. "I mean, put in jail. Do you know what a jail is?"

"Oh, yes. It has bars on the door and you don't get to play outside." She looked frightened, but then she smiled up at him. "Cassie said you were a nice man, though, and if I don't tell a lie everything will be okay."

The judge covered his mouth with his hand and nodded to Cassie. "You may proceed."

"Now, Peggy," Cassie said, "will you tell us what happened just before we came in here?"

"Mama took me to the bathroom so I could peepee."

"No, honey, before that."

"I was in a room, not as big as this, with that man . . ." She pointed at the judge. "And with you and Mama and . . . and Daddy." She listed everyone who had been in the judge's chambers. "And all the grown-ups talked and that man is a cardalsfan and—"

"A what?"

"He said, 'I'm a cardalsfan, myself. . . .' "

"A Cardinals fan?"

"That's it. And the man in the dress was a minor stopshort—"

The bailiff snorted and the judge scowled at him.

Peggy continued her recital, including the waitress's name and the cold drink each person had requested.

"And the man in the dress asked for a Grapette——"

"Wait," the judge said. "I drank Dr Pepper. Helen, check that against your notes, please."

The stenotypist looked back through her tape. "That's right, your honor, you drank a Dr Pepper because——"

"Aha!" the judge said.

"Because Ida May didn't have the Grapette you asked for."

Peggy finished a few minutes later. "And Mama and me went to the bathroom and I——"

"That's enough, honey," Cassie said hastily.

The judge nodded. "Helen, will you compare this record with the one you made in my chambers?"

The reporter laid two tapes side by side and went through them, occasionally marking the second one with a red check. Cassie glanced at Arnie nervously. Too many red checks, she thought.

Finally the woman finished and shook her head. "You honor, except for a few minor points such as 'stopshort' for 'shortstop' and a few mispronunciations, that child's verbal record was as complete as mine. I've never seen anything like it!"

The judge frowned. "Strike your personal comment——no, on second thought, let it stand. And let the record so show. Let it also show that this witness has fulfilled the requirements for acceptance of the testimony of a minor. Mrs. Steele, you may proceed with your questioning."

Cassie nodded. "Thank you, your honor. Peggy, are you tired? Do you want to rest for a while?"

"No'm."

"Do you remember that you swore——that you promised to tell the truth, all of the truth?"

"Yes'm, Cassie."

"Then please tell the court——that means the judge up there——the truth about the things your father did to you."

Peggy looked at her mother, who nodded reassuringly, and then she took Cassie at her word. She got up on her knees and looked directly at the judge. "I had on my new pink nightie because it was Christmas night and Daddy said take it off so we can play doctor and I did. And he listened to my tummy with his stettysope and then he put his finger in a little . . ."

Judge Pickens listened, his face changing in progressive stages of red, and the stenotypist's fingers flew, but Cassie watched Dr. Kenneth Brown. He sank back in his chair, white-faced, and as the small, high voice went on, inexorably on, he leaned forward over the defense table and covered his face with his hands.

Peggy told the judge how her father had threatened to hurt her mother if Peggy reported his actions. "And then there was this big thing on him that was part of him and he put it—"

"No!" Brown jumped to his feet. "No! I can't stand any more!"

The judge banged his gavel and Brown's lawyer pulled at his client's arm, but the doctor shook free.

"Don't make me listen to any more! I'm guilty, God knows. I'm guilty! I'll sign—anything. Just don't make me listen to—"

He sank onto his chair, sobbing.

"Five minutes," the judge barked. "A five-minute recess. And you, counselor, you get your client under control, you hear?"

Court reopened, but it was all over. Brown pleaded guilty and the judge set a date for sentencing. Cassie helped Peggy down from the witness chair and hugged her, but the child pulled away and looked up at the judge.

"Mr. Court? Daddy said don't tell and I told. Is he going to hurt my mama?"

Judge Pickens's face was red, but he smiled down at her. "He won't hurt your mama, Peggy, and he won't hurt you. I won't let that man hurt anyone at all."

Three weeks later Cassie settled the divorce case for her client with oil holdings in Mexico. Her fee was large, but it was a tiny percentage of the amount his third wife had tried to take from him.

"Are you planning to remarry, Tom?" Cassie said.

"Aw, hell, Cassie, I probably will. I reckon I'm just the marrying kind."

"Well, you come see me before the wedding next time, instead of after it. It will save me some time and it will save you a hell of a lot of money."

He laughed and gave her a pat on the back that almost knocked her down. "Hey, kid, you available yourself?"

"No, Tom, I'd be too expensive. I write a mean prenuptial contract."

Cassie called Naomi a week later.

"Cassie! I've been meaning to write—how are you?"

"Tired. It's been miserably hot down here."

"Oh, God, Oklahoma's been hot, too. It's not even August yet, but they're already saying this is going to be a record breaker. Cassie? You sound sort of . . . well, sort of down. Is anything wrong?"

"I'm just not feeling too good. The heat, and I guess I'm all worn out. That incest case, you know. We won, but it took a lot out of me."

"Well, I want to hear all about it. Why don't we meet someplace? How about the farm, your brand-new farm? I'm dying to see that place."

"No!" Cassie said quickly. "Not the farm. It would be too—it's too hot there."

The phone was silent for a moment. "Okay. Not the farm. You know, you really do sound at the end of your—hey, I've got a great idea! A friend of mine has a cabin in Colorado and he's said I can use it anytime at all. I've got some leave coming. Why don't we go there? It will be cool—we'll probably need a fire in the fireplace most nights."

Cassie's spirits lifted as though she was already breathing the thin, cool mountain air. "That sounds like heaven! Can we lie around and read a lot, and talk about books?"

"If you'll turn me loose now and then to go fly-fishing."

"Just let me talk to my boss—I mean, my partner. I'll call you tomorrow night!"

"Steve," Cassie said, "what do you say I take a week off? This heat is getting me down."

"Why the hell don't you move? You need a better house, with some decent air-conditioning."

"I need a vacation, that's what I need. I want to go to someplace cool."

"That farm of yours won't be cool."

"I know. I wasn't planning to go there."

A new client, an important one, came in that afternoon, and Cassie was not able to take a week off. She called Naomi that night, and they agreed to make it later in the summer when a break from the heat would be even more welcome.

Cassie waited until it was foolish to wait any longer. She took one day off then, in the first week of August, but where she went was to her doctor's office.

She kept trying to convince the doctor and trying to convince herself that she was coming down with something. He smiled at her and he ran the tests and he called her a few days later to tell her what she had known all along and did not want to know.

"You're coming down with something, all right. It's called pregnancy. Congratulations are in order, my dear. You're going to have a baby."

Chapter 39

"NAOMI?" Cassie said. "Can you come to Dallas this weekend? I need you."

The telephone crackled and Naomi said, "What's wrong? Are you in some kind of trouble?"

Cassie choked back a hysterical laugh. "I guess you could say that, yes."

Naomi did not hesitate. "I'll drive down Friday night, Cassie."

"No! Fly, Naomi! I'll pay your fare."

Cassie met Naomi at Love Field but they only chatted while they drove to University Park.

"Oh," Naomi said. "Your house is so cool!"

"Yes," Cassie said absently. "I had two new air-conditioning window units put in this week. I'll need them, what with—"

Naomi looked at her shrewdly. "What with being pregnant."

"How did you know!"

"You forget that I've been a WAC officer for years. I can spot a pregnant private at two hundred paces."

Cassie tried to laugh. "Or a pregnant lawyer."

"Dix? At the farm?"

"Yes."

"You've left it too late to . . . to get rid of the baby, haven't you? Why?"

Cassie had never told her about the therapeutic abortion. "Because I want to have it," she said. "I want my baby."

"Have you told Dix?"

"No! This is *my* baby!"

Naomi looked at her steadily for a moment. "He has the right to know, Cassie." Cassie said nothing, and finally Naomi said, "Whatever you decide, I'm with you." She laughed. "Hey, let's get a bottle of champagne! This calls for a toast!"

Cassie laughed in relief. "Naomi, thank you! That's just what I needed to hear!"

IT WAS NOT as easy for Cassie to tell Steve Reilly about her pregnancy, but it was not fair to the firm to delay.

Steve's first question was: "Who, Cassie? Who's the father?"

"I'm not going to tell you, or anyone else. This is my baby, Steve."

He tapped his pencil on his desk. "You know what this is going to do to your career, I suppose."

"Of course." She took a deep breath. "I'll resign from the firm as soon as you like."

"It isn't only your law practice I'm talking about, Cassie. It's your future in politics, too."

She looked down at her hands. "I guess I'm resigning from that, too, before it has even started."

Steve banged his fist on his desk. "God damn it, Cassie, you know about birth control! We were always careful."

Cassie blushed. "I know, Steve, I know. But you and I loved each other, a little. This was more . . ."

"Sure, sure. You loved each other more than life itself and all that crap. If he loves you so damn much, why won't he marry you?"

"He doesn't know about the baby and I'm not going to tell him. It was love, Steve, but it isn't love now. Look, I thought I'd work till early October so I can finish up my present cases. Then I'll resign and go to Oklahoma to have the baby. I have enough to live on and get the farm producing again."

He nodded. "You'll be four months along then? You won't be showing much, with your height." He took off his glasses and rubbed his eyes. "Cassie, give yourself an out. Don't resign, take a leave of absence, instead."

"What good would that do?"

"It would give you time to come to your senses! You told me your net worth is right at a quarter-million, right? You're just getting to the point where your money will start making money for you. If you come back to your practice, you'll probably be a millionaire within ten years. How does that grab you?"

A millionaire, Cassie thought. A millionaire! She laughed. "It grabs me, all right. But who would want an unwed mother for a lawyer?"

"Why would people have to know about the baby?" He put on his glasses and leaned forward. "Look, use your maiden name and buy a little house in Oak Cliff or someplace out of the way. Hire some woman to care for the kid. You can spend a lot of your free time there without anyone knowing about it, and when the kid is old enough, you can put it in boarding school."

"Steve, I don't think I'd want to—I think the farm would be better for a child."

"For the kid, maybe. You would lose your marbles. No wheeler-dealers, no hotshot friends, no big cars and parties. No making money. Don't kid me, Cassie Steele, and don't kid yourself. You can't go back to being a starry-eyed little farmer's daughter."

Cassie corrected him. "Sharecropper's daughter." Maybe he was right, she thought, maybe she would be bored. She shook her head briskly. "Steve, I can't do that. I can't send my baby off to be raised by someone else in secret. But I will take a leave of absence, because it will mean fewer explanations. I'll say my doctor wants me to get a long rest."

"I've got a better idea. We'll tell people you're going to write a book on governmental regulation of the oil and gas industry. That's just boring enough to keep anyone from asking about it."

As IT HAPPENED, it was the third of November when Cassie left the office. She had been careful in her choice of outfits for a month, and her pregnancy had not become obvious.

She had rented her house, furnished, to a law student and his wife who were delighted to escape from married students' housing. Cassie was equally delighted to have someone reliable in her house, even at the low rent she charged them.

Fran Jordan invited her to have dinner and spend the night before she left Dallas. Cassie was reluctant, afraid that Fran might discover the real reason behind her move to the farm, but she need not have worried. Steve's plan succeeded, even with Fran. Cassie's vague remarks about the proposed book were more than Fran wanted to hear. Instead, she told Cassie a great deal about the new man in her life. He was not married and, to Cassie's surprise, he sounded very stodgy. He apparently had other virtues to recommend him, however, including a number of producing oil wells in the Permian Basin.

Early Friday morning Cassie left Fran's and drove north, her car packed full of clothes and books and household goods.

As she drove through the black-dirt region of North Texas, she felt strong and triumphant, a victor returning home not on a white steed but in a green Cadillac convertible. She had attacked Dallas and she was carrying home the spoils: her fashionable clothes, which included a good selection of maternity clothes from the new Page Boy shop, and the stable income engendered by her investments.

She had left the farm at San Bois a penniless orphan committed to work for her cousins. She was returning a successful attorney with an education and friends and plenty of money. She had left as a sharecropper's daughter and she would return as a landowner.

Her green steed carried her across the long bridge over the Red River and onto Oklahoma soil, and Cassie's mood changed.

She was carrying a baby home, too, a baby who would be born illegitimate because its mother could not or would not find a way to live with its father. Whether the failure lay in Dix or in Cassie herself had become irrelevant. It was enough that the failure existed and that in a few months there would be another human being whose life would be ordered by that failure.

As Cassie drove through Ballard, she could see Ballard Heights from the highway. What would James Steele think if he knew that his unborn grandchild was traveling through his town, past his house, in the body of a woman James hated? She tried to laugh at the irony, but she could not.

The closer she came to San Bois and the farm, the unhappier she was. Why had she come to Oklahoma? She should have stayed in Dallas, in her own house, among her friends. She should have fought it out, faced down her detractors, but instead she had exiled herself to this woebegone countryside and a dry, windy November when red dust rose from the fields and hazed the air.

She turned onto the gravel road to the farm, going slower and slower, not to ease the car over the ruts, but to put off the time when she would arrive at the empty, ghost-crowded jail to which she had committed herself.

The car rolled slowly around the last clump of woods, and there in front of Cassie was the lodge.   There also, however, was a black Plymouth, Naomi Bencher's foursquare car.   And on a wicker chair on the veranda was Naomi Bencher's foursquare self, waiting.

She slammed on the brakes and jumped out of the car.   "Naomi! You came!"

Naomi waved and ran down the steps.   "I hope you don't mind."

"Mind!" Cassie threw her arms around her friend.   "How did you know I would need you?   I didn't even know it myself!"

Naomi grinned at her.   "Never mind that.   Let's get started unpacking that battleship of yours.   We've got work to do!"

An hour later the car was unloaded and Cassie and Naomi were standing in the center of the living room, dismayed.   They had just begun to realize how much work there was to be done.

Naomi shook her head helplessly.   "You're going to have to hire someone, Cassie.   You need to get a room painted for the baby, and wood hauled in for the fireplace, and there's the outside work.   You can't be scything weeds now."

"Look, I'm healthy as a horse, Naomi. There's no reason I can't—"

"I can think of one right fast.   Considering the size of the parents involved, I think you're going to be big as a house by the time this baby is due."   She looked at her watch.   "Listen, we have to go to town for groceries before the general store closes.   Let's ask around about help."

Will Wilson at the store was all ears when Cassie told him her name was Steele.   "Well, now, I heard that Mr. James Steele sold that farm."   He rested his belly on the counter and looked at her with flat blue eyes.

"He did, Mr. Wilson," Cassie said.   "I own it now, and I'll be living there."

His eyes skimmed lower, to her stomach. "You and Mr. Steele? Which Mr. Steele is that, Miz Steele?"

"Sir?" Naomi called from the back of the store. "Can you help me? I can't reach that jar of mustard."

He went to the back of the store and Cassie heard Naomi talking to him in a low, hurried voice. When he came back to the counter his eyes were warm and sympathetic.

"Now, Miz Steele, you just give me that there list. I'll make up the order and put the boxes in your car for you. No, don't try to pay me. I'll just put it on account for you. And I'll pass the word that you're looking for a hired man."

When they left the store, Cassie said, "My God, Naomi, what did you tell that man?"

Naomi's eyes twinkled. "I said your pregnancy was secret, because of a tragedy in your life."

"You didn't! It will be all over town in an hour."

"I'd estimate ten minutes. You forget that I was a teacher here when you were a mere infant. I know San Bois. A beautiful young woman, pregnant, with no visible husband? Put it that way and you'll be thrown out of town. Hint at a mysterious tragedy and you'll be a soap-opera heroine. Everyone in town will have a theory."

"Naomi, they'll all be talking about me!"

"Of course. But they would be anyway, and this way they'll be on your side. Now, let's go to the drugstore soda fountain while the story spreads and your groceries get packed into the car."

Naomi snored lightly in one of the spare bedrooms that night, but Cassie could not sleep in the bed she had shared with Dixon Steele that one night in June, the bed she shared now with only his unborn child. The bed had been small in the spring, and cozy, but in November it was as big and empty as the Sahara.

It was nine the next morning when Cassie was awakened by the sound of Naomi's voice outside. She hurriedly slipped on her clothes and went out to the veranda.

Naomi was talking to a grizzled man standing next to a battered pre-war pickup truck.

"Oh, Cassie," Naomi said with relief, "this gentleman wants to talk to you about a job. I'll get back to making coffee."

The man looked Cassie over as frankly as she did him. His face was tanned to leather and as wrinkled as an overripe persimmon. His hair was black, flecked with white, and his small eyes were a clear pale brown. A straw dangled from the corner of his mouth.

"Fellow said you was lookin' for help out here," he said.

"And you want a job?"

"Might be. Might not. Depends."

"Depends on what?" Cassie said.

He smiled, showing yellow crooked teeth, but he did not answer.

"Do you live around here?" she said.

"Farmed near San Bois for thirty years on and off."

"I'm Cassie Steele," she said. She went over to the fence and held out her hand.

"Henry Starr," he said, shaking her hand carefully, as if it might break.

Cassie laughed. "Was the outlaw Belle Starr a relative of yours?"

"Might be. Might not. Depends."

"Well, Mr. Starr, I need someone to do the heavy work around the place, cleaning, painting, cutting firewood, getting the yard in shape and putting in a garden, come spring. I'm . . . well, I'm expecting a baby." She tried to appear mysterious and vaguely tragic, but it made her want to giggle. There was an honesty about the man that made subterfuge ridiculous. She looked directly at him. "Do you want the job?"

Henry Starr took the straw out of his mouth and turned slowly, surveying the place. He nodded once. "Wages paid Saturday mornin's, weekends off and lodgin'."

"But I don't have a tenant house, Mr. Starr, and since I live alone you really couldn't stay in the——"

"That there shed," he said quickly, his tanned face reddening. "I can bunk down in that shed."

"That's fine, then. You get yourself set up and come in the house later. We'll have supper and make some plans."

He stuck the straw back in his mouth and looked past her, at the shed. "Might. Might not. Depends."

The hammering in the shed began while Cassie was still in the kitchen telling Naomi about the man.

During the next few weeks Cassie began to wonder who was working for whom. Henry Starr set the ground rules. He would not eat a meal in her house, and came into the kitchen only when it was time for them to plan the work. He collected his pay on Saturday mornings and disappeared until Sunday dusk. He was so clean that Cassie suspected that he bathed and washed his clothes in the creek, November or not. Even though they rarely had a conversation, Cassie liked having him on the place.

Henry did the outside work and Cassie spent the gray November days working at the desk by the fireplace. Steve Reilly's suggestion of writing a book on federal regulation of the oil and gas industry had undergone a sea change from a subterfuge to a workable plan. She ordered the books she needed from a store in Dallas, and the more she read, the more interesting she found the subject.

Thanksgiving slipped by but when Naomi came for Christmas, Cassie was ready for company and hungry for good talk. She also got a good talking-to. Naomi was appalled that Cassie had not yet been to see the doctor in San Bois.

Two days after Christmas, Cassie dutifully presented herself to Dr. Hill at his small clinic in San Bois. With his thin gray hair, bushy white eyebrows, rosy cheeks and rimless glasses, the doctor looked as if he had stepped out of a Norman Rockwell painting.

"Cassie, you're fit as a fiddle." He leaned back in his oak swivel chair. "You know, I haven't seen any of the Steeles for a long time, but there's good blood there, like there was in your mama's family. Reckon you'll have a fine baby. Now, which one of the boys are you married to?"

Cassie had expected the question. The town would know, finally, the sordid truth that lay behind Naomi's hints at a mysterious tragedy. She looked directly at him. "I'm not married, Dr. Hill. And I'm sorry but I can't tell you the father's name."

He looked at her carefully, measuring her. "All right," he said finally. "All right. I admired your grandmother, Cassie Taylor, and I expect she taught you right from wrong. I'll keep your secret, and don't you worry, it won't be the first secret I've kept from San Bois.

Who's going to look after you when your time comes?"

"Henry Starr is living on the place, and Naomi Bencher is going to come over from Lawton when I need her."

He raised his eyebrows. "The Naomi Bencher that used to teach at Turner School? Well, you're in excellent hands there, girl." He smiled at her. "And Henry doesn't talk much, but he's a good man. I won't have to worry about you." He turned the pages of his desk calendar. "Looks like you're due about March tenth, Cassie, but I'll want to see you before that." He stood up, smiling at Cassie, but she made no move to get up.

"There's one more thing, Dr. Hill," she said softly. "Do you remember when James Steele's daughter Julia was killed?"

He sat down and the pink left his cheeks. "Yes. I was there."

"She died of a skull fracture, didn't she?"

He moved some papers on his cluttered desk. "If they had called me in earlier, maybe I could have . . ."

"Was there anything else? Were there any marks on her face?"

He looked at her with narrowed eyes. "What's this all about, Cassie? Why are you asking me now?"

She quickly covered her own eyes with her hand. "It preys on me, doctor, living out there and all."

"You can't dwell on something like that, girl. Yes," he said suddenly. "There was . . . a mark. A bruise on her left cheek."

Cassie looked up at him, but he seemed to be far away. Carefully, she said, "Did it look as if someone had hit her?"

He did not speak for a moment. "She told you, didn't she? Your grandmother told you that James Steele did it. Leona—your mother and I were the only ones to know and we decided we wouldn't let it get out, but I guess she had to tell her own mama."

Cassie sank back in her chair. She knew now that what she had always suspected was the truth. She knew, and she wished that she did not. "But why?" she whispered. "Why?"

"Why did he hit her?" The doctor shrugged. "That confounded temper of his. He told Leona after little Julia died, how she wouldn't come when he called, how he lost his temper and slapped her." He seemed to look back in time. "Leona said he was crying. James Steele was crying. He said he hit her harder than he meant to. Said she fell off the swing and hit her head on a root of that big old maple tree. Hard as rock, a maple root."

"But why didn't my mother—why didn't you call the police?"

He turned his swivel chair and looked out the window. "Leona and I, we talked it over. Amelia Steele broke down, you know, and we were scared that the truth would push her right over the edge." He turned back to her. "She needed him, Cassie. He was the only one she could hold on to. You can see that, can't you?"

"I suppose so, but—"

"We made a decision, and maybe we were wrong. I don't know."

Cassie rubbed her eyes. "I don't know either."

He sighed and then stood up slowly. "Well, I do know one thing, girl. I know it won't do you any good to brood over this. You've got to let it go. What's past is past, girl, and I want you thinking happy thoughts while you're carrying this baby." He ushered her out of the office before she could say another word. "I'll see you in three weeks!"

By THE MIDDLE of February of 1956, Cassie was so big that Henry muttered about twins. He would not let her do any of the heavy work around the house: mopping and vacuuming and keeping the fire built up in the fieldstone fireplace. Cassie worked on her research, but gradually she sank into a pleasant torpor, reading for hours by the fire, putting her book down only to waddle into the kitchen and make herself a cup of cocoa.

Naomi began to come every other weekend, bringing a stack of new library books and some out-of-season fruit. She and Henry Starr had become friends and often while Cassie sat by the fire with her feet up and a book balanced on her enormous belly, she could hear them talking in the kitchen, and laughing.

At the end of February, Henry got out the tractor and plowed up a patch for a vegetable garden. "How come you want such a big garden, Cassie? Ain't but the two of us to eat garden truck."

"I'm going to buy a deep freeze, Henry, and fill it up so we can have fresh vegetables all winter long."

"Us and who else, that's what I want to know. Us and the whole Russian army?"

Cassie turned around in surprise. Henry Starr had made a joke! He seemed to be as startled as she. He walked away, making a sound like the wheezing of a broken pump. It might have been laughter.

There were no jokes, however, when it came to planting the garden. Henry almost wore out his *Farmer's Almanac* checking astrological signs and the stages of the moon.

"Got to plant them beans when the sign ain't in the arms, like Virgo. You plant them in Virgo, you're goin' to have big plants and lots of bloom, but they ain't goin' to make good beans. Now, you take your corn, you want to plant that in the dark of the moon, when the hickory buds is about the size of squirrels' ears. There's them that says you wait till you hear the first dove coo or till the martins come back, but I don't hold with none of that."

Cassie was lost in a welter of new moons and olden moons, of arms signs and feet signs, the superstitions with which Henry Starr tried to impose some order on his world. Maybe it worked for him, she thought, just as well as shouting "Praise God!" or following the service in the *Book of Common Prayer*.

On the fifth of March, Cassie decided that gray skies or not, she had to wash the windows. She had finished the living room and started on the dining room when she felt the first twinge low in her back. After a half hour or so, however, she realized that the twinges were coming at regular five-minute intervals.

"Henry!" she yelled from the back door. "Henry, I need you!"

He came out of the barn wiping his hands on a greasy rag. "Sure, Cassie, what you want me to do?"

"Drive me to the clinic, that's what! The baby's coming!"

"But it ain't due for five more days!" Henry looked from one side to the other desperately, as if he expected the Seventh Cavalry to show up in the nick of time.

"Now, Henry, now! Get the car started while I grab a bag!"

Cassie called the doctor and, pausing occasionally to grab at a chair or the dresser for support, she closed up her suitcase and got her coat.

Henry was in the driver's seat of the Cadillac, clutching the steering wheel.

"Why haven't you started the car?"

"Don't know how. Ain't never drove no automatic transmission."

Cassie braced herself against the dashboard as another pain hit, one that started in her back and moved around to the front. "For God's sake, Henry!"

She had to coach him all the way into town, concentrating so hard on his driving that she scarcely had time to think about her contractions.

Dr. Hill and his nurse met her at the door with a wheelchair. Annabelle helped her get undressed and into a hospital gown and the doctor gave her a quick examination. "By God, girl, you just made it! Get back in that wheelchair!"

The nurse opened the door and jumped back. Henry Starr was in the hall, brandishing an ax.

"Oh, for God's sake, Henry," Dr. Hill said, but he gave the nurse a push. "Go on, Annabelle, you know what it's for. Put it on the floor under the delivery table."

"It's good and sharp, Doc," Henry said.

When she was on the table a new kind of contraction hit, and Cassie felt as if her body were being ripped apart.

"That was a real good one, Cassie," he said calmly. "A delivery contraction. No point giving you any dope now, the baby will be here before it would take effect."

"Doctor!" Cassie cried as another long, deep pain tore through her body.

"You can take one more, can't you? A big strong girl like you— here she comes!"

Another contraction ripped through her body and Cassie tried to raise her head to see. "Is it a girl? What is it?"

"Hell, Cassie, that part hasn't come out yet!"

One more, smaller pain, and then miraculously it was over and Cassie felt only a smooth sliding sensation as something soft and small left her body.

"A boy, Cassie! You got yourself a fine big boy. Annabelle, let her hold him for a minute before I cut the cord."

The nurse laid the baby on Cassie's stomach. He was covered with white mucus and blood and the umbilical cord trailed from his navel, and he had a shock of wet black hair. His face contorted into a red wad and he let out a lusty yell; he was the most beautiful thing Cassie had ever seen in her life.

"My son," she whispered, "my son."

Chapter 40

Dr. Hill marched into Cassie's hospital room. "Well, my dear, I've checked your boy from head to toe."

Cassie pushed herself up on one elbow. "Is he all right?"

"Very much so. A fine healthy specimen of *Homo sapiens.* He weighed in at eight pounds, six ounces, and he's twenty-one inches long. Now, I want to give you something so you can get a good rest, but I reckon you'll want to phone somebody first."

Cassie hesitated. "Just Naomi Bencher."

Dr. Hill raised his white eyebrows. "No one else?"

"No."

"All right. I'll call her for you, if you like. She'll be glad to hear it was such an easy birth."

"An easy birth!" she said indignantly.

A voice came from the doorway. "Sure!" Henry Starr was grinning from ear to ear. "That's on account of the ax. Had it all sharpened up and ready to go. You want your ax sharp, see, so it will cut the pain of birthin'." He turned his old felt hat in his hands. "Hear tell you got you a fine boy, Cassie. Anything you want me to do down at the place?"

The doctor said, "There's something I want you to do, Henry Starr, and that's to pick up your ax and get out of here so Cassie can get some rest."

To Cassie's delight, Naomi was there to drive her and the baby home from the hospital. "I'm taking three weeks of leave, Cassie. No, don't you argue with me! I want to see you two off to a good start. I don't know the first thing about taking care of babies, but I can take care of the house for you."

"Naomi, what on earth would I do without you!"

CASSIE'S SON thrived from the first. She nursed him when he was hungry, changed him when he was wet and loved him all of the time.

"Who wouldn't thrive?" Naomi said. "I do think you should give the child a name. You can't go on calling him 'sweetie' forever."

Cassie laughed. "I could choose one of the names I've heard you call him. 'Dumpling' or 'Naomi's baby-boo.'"

Naomi sniffed. "Don't eavesdrop on private conversations. So I'm dotty about the child. What's wrong with that?"

"If you're so dotty about him, you can change the next messy diaper."

Naomi sat up straight, every inch an officer. "I will! You'll see, I really will!"

Steve Reilly called Cassie two days later. "Well?"

"I was going to call you, Steve. It's a boy, and he's healthy and strong, and—"

"And how is the mother? Are you bored yet?"

Cassie laughed. "Steve, with a two-week-old baby you don't have time to be bored!"

"When you are going to get back to work on your book?"

"Soon, I promise!"

Fran Jordan called a week later. "What's this I hear about you? You told me you were going to create a book, not a baby!"

"My God, Fran, is the word around Dallas already?"

"Not 'around Dallas,' Cassie. I happened to call Allene, and she had talked to Steve Reilly and—"

"Oh, no! Everyone will know!"

"Only your best friends, silly, and we're green with envy. Who's the father?"

"I'm not going to tell you."

"You don't have to, smarty. This is old Fran, remember? I can add up to nine months, and I know who you saw at the farm."

"Fran, you won't tell anyone in Dallas!"

"Of course not. Now, when are you coming home?"

"Home?" Cassie had to think for a minute. "Fran, I am home."

"I'll just bet!" Fran laughed. "I've been through San Bois, love, I've seen all the theaters and big houses and parties. You'll be back when the peace and quiet starts driving you bananas."

When the conversation ended, Cassie was restless until she firmly reminded herself that she was contented and that she would stay contented with her choice.

She wandered out to the veranda, where Naomi was industriously changing the baby's diaper. "See! You didn't think I would do it!" She cuddled the baby and smoothed his fine black hair. "Let's see, how would this sound: 'Baby-boo Steele was elected governor of Oklahoma today. Asked for his reaction, Governor Baby-boo said——' "

"All right, Naomi, all right! I'm going to name him Taylor."

"No middle name? Just Taylor Steele?"

"Maybe a middle name later. Dr. Hill said he would misplace the birth certificate on his desk until I was ready."

"Well, let's see what the gentleman himself thinks of it." Carefully supporting his head, Naomi lifted the baby. "Hi, Taylor. Do you like that name?"

The baby's blue eyes opened wide and he smiled.

Cassie laughed softly. "That wasn't really a smile, only a gas pain."

"Nonsense," Naomi said. "It was clearly a smile of approval. Taylor has chosen his name."

Henry Starr ambled around the corner of the house and sat down on the steps, fanning himself with his hat. "This hot in March, this summer's going to be a booger. A wet one, too, lots of rain."

"Why do you say that?" Naomi asked.

"We got us a dry March, ain't we? That means plenty of rain and good crops later on. Like they say, 'A bushel of dust in March is worth a bushel of silver in September.' "

"Now, Henry," Naomi said, "don't tell me you believe——"

Cassie frowned, but Henry did not seem to have heard.

"There's sign, too," he said dreamily. "Lots of sign. Like the kingfishers, they're building their nests up high, clean away from the stream. That always means a wet summer. And the oaks budded out before the ash trees did."

Naomi looked as if she were beginning to believe it. "And what does that mean, Henry?"

"Car's comin'."

"The oak buds mean there's a car coming?"

Henry stood up and looked down the road. "I hear it comin'."

They all saw it at once, a long black Cadillac dusted with red from the dirt road. It stopped across the road from the lodge and after a minute or two the door opened and an old man climbed out of the car. Cassie shaded her eyes.

"Who is it?" Naomi said.

Cassie stood up slowly. "James Steele."

The old man walked slowly across the road and into the yard. Cassie watched him, wondering how he could have aged so in those few years. But it had been eleven years since she had seen him.

He had been almost sixty then, so he must be seventy or close to it. And the James Steele of her mind was the man who had come to the tenant house when she was a child, the powerful man who had loomed over her family and ruled their lives. A quarter of a century later, she was an adult at her physical peak, and he was old. How much energy had she wasted in trying to beat James Steele? In the end there was only one winner: time.

He stopped at the bottom of the steps and looked up at her. "Cassie Taylor."

"James Steele." She nodded toward the others on the porch. "These are my friends, Naomi Bencher and Henry Starr."

He nodded distantly. "Your friends. And this is my . . . is this the baby?"

"How did you know about him?"

He laughed disdainfully. "You've never understood, have you? This is my state."

"Give me Taylor, Naomi," Cassie said quietly. She held him up for the old man to see. "This is my baby, James."

He nodded. "I hear he is Dixon's child."

Cassie's breath caught in her throat. "Does Dix know? Did you tell him?"

"No. I wanted to see for myself what kind of trick you were trying to play." James Steele grinned and with that cold smile seemed to regain his old power over her. He climbed the steps and looked down at the baby. "He's a Steele, all right. My grandson!"

Cassie stepped back holding the baby close. "No! He's not yours. He is my son!"

Henry Starr came forward. "Want me to run him off the place?"

"I'll call the sheriff!" Naomi said.

"No," Cassie said, watching James Steele. "I can handle it. Why don't you two wait inside?"

Reluctantly they went into the house and Cassie heard their voices in the kitchen.

"James?" a voice called. Cassie looked past him at the car. A woman was standing by the open door on the passenger's side.

"Amelia?" Cassie said uncertainly.

"Yes. May I—is it all right for me to see the baby?"

Cassie nodded and watched Amelia pick her way across the yard. Her hair was pure white in the sunshine and her step was unsteady on the rough ground.

James went down the steps and took Amelia's arm to help her to the veranda. In that simple, wordless courtesy Cassie saw all that the two of them had lost and all that they had won. Each had only the other but they had, in the end, each other.

With a tentative finger Amelia touched the baby's clenched fist.

"Would you like to hold him?" Cassie said softly.

"Oh, yes!" Amelia sat down on a wicker armchair and Cassie put the baby in her arms. Amelia looked at him closely. "He's like Dixon," she said. "He is very much like Dixon."

"You know I am not married to Dixon," Cassie said. "Can you accept this baby?"

Amelia looked up and her eyes flashed with more spirit than Cassie thought she had. "He is my grandson! It is not his fault that his parents are fools!"

James laughed unpleasantly. "I hope you have access to a damn good lawyer, Cassie Taylor. You're going to need one."

Cassie whirled around. "I *am* a damn good lawyer, James Steele, and you don't frighten me!"

The baby fussed and Amelia said, "You two! You've waked him!"

"He's just hungry," Cassie said. "I'll need to nurse him soon."

Amelia reluctantly surrendered him. "You aren't . . ." She lowered her voice. "Surely you aren't breastfeeding the poor little mite."

"Of course I am! And the little mite is thriving on it. My mother nursed me and I turned out to be a big strapping girl."

"Oh yes, dear." Amelia wiped her hands on a lacy handkerchief. "But it's just not done. I mean, people of our kind—"

"Our kind!" Cassie was so surprised that she burst out laughing. "Oh, Amelia! You can accept a bastard grandson but you can't accept a breast-fed one? Doesn't that prove that he's my baby, that he has nothing to do with you? Taylor isn't your kind, at all. He's my kind!"

"Amelia, come with me," James Steele said. "I won't have you insulted like this."

"No, James, wait. Cassie . . ." Amelia looked at the baby in Cassie's arms. "May I come back now and then?"

"Of course," Cassie said. She would never bar Amelia from her grandson. "I would like that, Amelia. I want Taylor to know his grandmother."

"I—I'm afraid I'm a very foolish woman."

"No," Cassie said, "you aren't foolish, Amelia. It's just that you've always done as you were told."

"Cassie," James said angrily, "I'll fight you!"

"You don't need to, James, because I won't fight you. You are Taylor's grandfather. You are welcome, too."

James Steele was startled. "You won't fight me? What has changed your mind?"

Cassie sighed. "We were wrong. We both were wrong, all the way. It isn't the winning that counts. It isn't even having all the chips. Rich isn't enough, James. Even land isn't enough. Loving is all that counts. Loving and being loved."

James watched her closely. "And what about his father? What rights does he have?"

"I don't want to discuss it."

"Yes. I can understand that." James nodded slowly, as if he were considering a weighty decision. "I said once that I would never do another favor for you, Cassie Steele, but I have changed my mind. I will do this one thing. I will not tell Dixon about the baby. How to handle the situation will be your decision, and yours alone."

Cassie was startled. "James, I appreciate your—"

"I don't want your thanks, Cassie. Come, Amelia. We'll go home now, but we'll come again soon."

He helped Amelia into the car, hesitated, and walked back to the fence to look up at the big sugar maple tree in front of the house.

Cassie stepped down from the veranda. "That's where it happened, isn't it, James?"

"What?" He jerked his head toward her. "What did you say?"

"It's where you . . . it's where Julia died, isn't it?"

"You have not used it against me."

"No, I guess I haven't."

"For Amelia's sake, I suppose." James Steele straightened his shoulders. "But perhaps for mine, too. Thank you, Cassie."

She stood on the edge of the veranda, holding her son. "You are welcome, James."

Naomi Bencher could hardly believe that Cassie had made peace of a sort with James Steele.

"He's old, Naomi. I don't want to fight him anymore."

"Motherhood has worked wonders, I must say. Now, when are you going to make peace with their son?"

Cassie looked away. "I don't know."

"You'd better figure it out!" More gently, Naomi said, "Cassie, Taylor is Dixon's son, too. You owe it to him to—"

"I don't owe anything to Dixon Steele! Not a damn thing!"

"Then perhaps you owe it to his son, to your son. Taylor has the right to a legitimate name, and the right to a father, too. Think about it, Cassie. That's all I ask."

Cassie did think about it. After Naomi had returned to Fort Sill, she thought about it through the lonely evenings when Henry Starr had gone to the shed and Taylor was asleep in his crib. When all else failed, she resorted to breaking the question down into its component parts.

She could do as Steve Reilly suggested. She could be a pragmatist and turn the baby over to a housekeeper while she pursued her million dollars. Or she could be a realist. She had enough money to make improvements at the farm and change it over to a cattle operation. It would be a good life for a boy and for that boy's mother. There was one other choice. She could be as idealistic as Dix, as her son's father, and risk all for love.

As a lawyer she tried to consider all the ramifications, but she kept coming up against one insurmountable hurdle. She loved Dixon Steele. Whatever happened, however it came out, in the long run she had but one choice.

The decision was made, but it was less simple to act upon it. One morning she would awake full of confidence. The next day, she was immobilized by fear.

On her thirty-first birthday Cassie called Dixon Steele in the morning, before her courage could ebb.

"Dix?"

"Cassie? Where are you?"

"At the farm."

"Oh, that's right, Dad said you were spending some time there."

"What else did he say?"

"That's all, I guess. No, he said your old friend Naomi Bencher was there, too."

"Did he tell you that I live on the farm now?"

"No, he didn't—what the hell is this, Cassie? When do we get to the sixty-four-thousand-dollar question?"

Cassie laughed nervously. "Now, I guess. Right now. Did your father tell you I have a baby?"

The phone was silent and then Dix said suspiciously, "Is this supposed to be a joke?"

"No. It's not a joke."

"Whose baby is it?"

"Mine, of course!"

"Who are you, the Virgin Mary? Who the hell is the father?"

"Who the hell do you think, Dixon Steele?" Cassie said angrily. "He was born on March fifth and human beings have a gestation period of nine months. You figure it out."

"My God. Cassie? Cassie, are you still there?"

"I'm still here."

"Look, I'll cancel all my appointments. I'll be there in a few hours. Wait for me!"

"I wasn't planning to go anywhere, Dix. Dix?"

He had hung up on her.

WHEN DIX'S CAR skidded to a stop in a plume of red dust, Cassie was on the veranda holding her sleeping baby.

Dix ran across the yard but stopped at the foot of the steps. "Is it all right—can I come up there?"

"Of course."

He climbed the steps and looked down at the sleeping baby. "Why didn't you tell me?" he whispered.

"You don't have to whisper. Taylor's a sound sleeper."

"Taylor? May I . . ." He stroked the baby's soft black hair with one long finger. "I like the name."

Cassie stood up. "Would you like to hold him?"

Dix looked startled. "I don't know how."

"Sit down."

He sat in the wicker rocking chair and Cassie put the baby against his shoulder. "Hold your hand here, to support his head."

"Yes, I see." Taylor snuggled into his shoulder. "He seems to be all right."

"He is, Dix. He's a fine, healthy baby."

"Cassie, for God's sake, why didn't you tell me?"

She sat down in the armchair. "I didn't think you would believe he was yours."

"Look at him! But I couldn't have seen him before he was born, could I? Or been sure of the dates."

"No, you couldn't."

Dix closed his eyes. When he looked at her again his eyes were soft. "Cassie, I was a real bastard."

"So was I."

"No, women aren't bastards."

"Only babies are bastards."

"Not my son! He'll have my name!"

"Taylor is my son, Dix. Don't you forget that."

"Ours."

"You want to share him."

"If you will let me share him, Cassie. I promise I won't try to take him away from you."

The baby cried out and Cassie took him and patted him to sleep. "You swear you wouldn't try to take him from me?"

Dix spread his hands. "How could I? He's yours."

Cassie looked out at the woods. "Your mother was here. She said she was foolish, but she isn't. It's just that she has always believed everything that the Steeles told her."

"You don't trust me, is that it?"

"You're a Steele, aren't you?"

He looked at her closely. "Once you told me that you are a Steele, too."

"Like your mother, Dix, I've had to learn the hard way."

"Then you won't believe me when I say I love you."

There was a flutter in her chest, but she tried to ignore it. "I want to believe you, Dix. Oh, God, how I want to believe you."

"Why?"

It was time, she knew, time to take the risk. Time to be a crazy idealist. Time, possibly, to have her hopes dashed to earth again. She put the baby against her shoulder and stood up. Bracing the baby with one hand, she reached out to Dixon Steele with the other.

"Because I love you, Dix. No matter what you say or do now, no matter even whether you can trust me and believe in me, I have to tell you the truth. I love you, Dixon Steele, and I will always love you." She turned away, afraid to look into his eyes and see disbelief, afraid to see rejection.

His wicker chair creaked, but she looked only at the hills, at the green hills rising to the blue Ozarks.

His hands touched her shoulders and he turned her gently toward him. She looked into his eyes and saw love, and then, the same immense delight that was expanding inside of her.

"Cassie, my God! Cassie!" He wrapped his arms around her. "I love you, too, I've loved you since that day we swam in the creek. There's never been anyone but you! But my stupid suspicions have kept me away from you!"

He kissed her and she kissed him and they held each other so tightly that the baby yelled in protest.

Dix laughed aloud. "Hey, boy! You trying to come between your mother and me?"

"He's hungry," she said. "Will it . . . bother you, if I nurse him?"

"Hell, no!"

She sat down with the baby and pulled up her blouse. The little mouth searched frantically until it found the nipple. He sucked so noisily that Dix laughed.

"Hungry little devil, isn't he?" He pulled another chair close and took her hand. "We'll want to get married in a hurry."

Cassie laughed. "It's still a little late, isn't it?"

"We'll make sure the next one is strictly legit."

"The next one? Already? Now, Dix . . ."

" 'Now, Cassie . . .' " he mimicked. "I'm not worried about the next one yet. I just want to sleep with the mother of this one."

"In honorable matrimony?"

"Yes. With the woman I love." He looked at her seriously. "And thereto I plight thee my troth."

" 'Troth.' What a lovely word. And I will plight mine, too, darling: my sacred honor."

"Oh, Cassie!" Dix jumped up and paced back and forth on the veranda. "We have so much to do, so many plans to make. Your law career, mine, politics—look, what do you say we work out some sort of partnership with your Steve Reilly, and have offices in both Dallas and Oklahoma City?"

"No, I'll take the Oklahoma bar when Taylor is old enough. Don't forget, the name Steele means more politically in Oklahoma than in Texas. Mmm. I can see it now: DIXON STEELE FOR GOVERNOR."

He stopped pacing and looked down at her. "You mean that? You'd chose Oklahoma City over Dallas?"

"I'd choose the Upper Amazon, Dix, if it meant being with you."

He grinned. "Then how about CASSIE STEELE FOR U.S. SENATE?"

She lifted the baby into the air. "Taylor? How would you and your siblings like to live in Washington?"

" 'Siblings' plural, Cassie?"

"Why not?"

He pulled her up and hugged her. "Why not, indeed?"

"Dix, we'll keep the farm, right?"

He put his arm around her and Taylor. "Always, Cassie. No matter what we do or where we go, we'll have the farm to come home to—for us and for our children."

"Let me put the baby down for his nap."

"And I'll get on the phone and make arrangements for a wedding, Cassie."

"Here?"

"Sure. Is tomorrow too soon?"

"How can you manage that, with the license and—"

"Hey, don't forget, my father has some pull in this county!"

Cassie hesitated. "Dix, if he helps us . . ." She laughed. "What can he do to us now? Call him! Call anyone you like."

"Right!" He put his arm around her and drew her close. "I love you, Cassie."

CASSIE TUCKED the baby in his crib and whispered, "You're going to have both a father and a mother, you lucky kid."

The commotion would begin when she and Dix told Naomi and Henry Starr their plans, and she wanted to be alone for a few minutes first. She went through the living room and whispered to Dix, who was already on the telephone, that the baby was asleep and that she was going outside. He smiled at her and nodded.

Cassie walked down the hill to the creek and the pond where the mallards wintered. The pond was still and the water a sheet of gold in the light of the setting sun. She kicked at the rocky bank and a scatter of gravel splashed on the water like crumbs of dry cornbread and splintered the reflections into ripples of yellow light.

She watched the water flow and eddy, and pictures washed through her mind. The tenant house, Granny's hands, the Old-Timers' reunion and the raft floating down the beautiful river with all its smiling passengers: Cassie and Dix and little Taylor, Granny, Naomi, even Henry Starr, even Amelia and James Steele, drifting down the endless river of time. In a sharp, sweet mix of pain and joy, the memories drifted past her as the waters of San Bois Creek washed gray-green against rocky banks that sparkled like gold in the slanting light. She was humming, she realized, humming the old song that flowed with the memories.

Cassie Taylor Steele stood on the bank of the creek, alone but not lonely, in the green pastures of her farm. The windows of the lodge lighted one by one and the woods behind the house changed from green to black as the surrounding hills darkened to purple and blended into the deep blue of the eastern sky.

The first cries of the night birds filled the valley and Cassie sang to herself, for herself. Her voice rose high and clear over the night sounds floating on the evening air.

> *"Yes, we will gather at the river,*
> *The beautiful, the beautiful river.*
> *Yes, we will gather at the river*
> *That flows past the throne of God."*